KNOCK OUT
FIGHTING FOR LOVE
BOOK FOUR

JIFFY KATE

WWW.SMARTYPANTSROMANCE.COM

COPYRIGHT

Print Edition
ISBN: 978-1-959097-21-1

CHAPTER 1

OZZI

"*I*, Leif Cage Erickson, take you, Tempest June Cassidy, to be my lawfully wedded wife."

My badass big brother chokes on those last two words and for a second, I think he's going to start bawling like a baby. Thankfully, he pulls it together and completes his vows, but as I look across the meadow, there aren't many dry eyes.

Even Baby Freya is making a fuss.

From my spot between Gunnar and Vali, I tilt my head over until I'm in her line of sight and I wiggle my fingers, trying to get her attention.

Tempest's mom is holding her and she looks so damn cute in a pink dress with a matching bow that's bigger than her perfectly round, still nearly-bald head.

Who would've thought one little baby could turn an entire family, like the Ericksons, into a group of bumbling idiots? But here we are. It's not just Cage who's a goner—the rest of us are right there with him, wrapped around her finger.

When she starts to coo, I can't help but smile and it's all I can do to keep from getting out of my spot and snatching her up. She always smells so good. Well, most of the time. And just holding her squishy little body is the best stress reliever known to man.

"I now pronounce you husband and wife," the minister says, bringing my attention back to the makeshift altar that's positioned under a cluster of birch trees. "Cage, you may kiss your bride."

Everyone hoots and hollers as my brother dips Tempest back and kisses her passionately, as if there weren't a field full of witnesses.

Vali elbows me in my side as he turns to me with a wide grin, clapping for the newlyweds. And I don't miss how Gunnar is looking at Frankie across the way, where she's standing in front of Maggie.

"Get a room," Viggo calls out, making Cage finally come up for air.

Looking out, I see our dad with his arms around our mom.

I have to admit, all the love in the air is making me a little nauseous. Not that I'm anti-love, but I have no plans of getting hitched any time soon. I enjoy my freedom and being able to take myself where the wind blows.

Being one of the two last brothers standing, I'm holding onto my bachelor status with a tight grip.

Cage and Tempest take their first walk as husband and wife, the minister announcing them as "Mr. and Mrs. Erickson," and our families cheer.

Not going to lie, it does make my heart feel good. I like seeing my family happy, especially Cage. After his career-ending injury, he was in a bad place. Then, he moved to the backwoods of Tennessee, met a girl, started his own gym, and now he's the happiest guy I know.

But getting a sister and niece is the best part.

I have a feeling Gunnar and Vali will be taking the same leap soon, and more power to them. Frankie and Maggie are great. I already consider them members of the family. But it still doesn't make me want to jump on that train any time soon.

"Oh, I'm just so happy," my mother gushes as she embraces Tempest and Cage. "Sorry I'm such a mess, but I promise these are happy tears."

Everyone congregates toward the back of the meadow, congratulating the newlyweds, until someone announces over the chatter that dinner will be served at Viking MMA in half an hour.

That's the cue for Viggo and me to jump in my Jeep and try to get a head start on everyone else. We promised Cage we'd make sure everything is set and ready to go for the reception. Plus, the sooner we get there, the sooner we can eat.

When I left Dallas, I decided to pack all my shit in my Jeep and just drive, so I'd have my options wide open. The drive was actually relaxing and gave me a chance to clear my head. And once I reached Tennessee, I knew I was where I needed to be. Since I don't have a house to go back to plus some money in the bank, I plan on hanging around here until I know what I want to do with my life.

"Well, that's done," Viggo says, gingerly stretching his long legs out in front of him as he loosens his tie.

I chuckle. "Don't get too comfortable. We're supposed to take a few photos at the gym."

He groans but doesn't respond.

Out of all of us, Viggo can definitely be the most cantankerous, especially since the gym sold. He was in favor of it, we all were, but I think it set some things in motion he wasn't ready to deal with—like what *he* wants to do with the rest of his life.

I'm basically in the same boat, but things like that don't bother me.

I figure, if the Universe wants me somewhere, it'll put me there, and I'll work the rest of the shit out as I go.

As we walk inside Viking MMA, I can hardly believe my eyes.

When I say the place has been transformed, I mean in every sense of the word. Fabric was draped from the ceiling to the floor and a flower shop basically threw up in here.

"Shit," Viggo mutters, eyes roaming the space. "This is what they meant by a small affair?"

Laughing, I slap him on the back. "Guess so."

All I know is that it smells amazing and I'm starving. But Viggo's question is valid. When they first started planning this shindig after Freya was born, it was going to be "small" and I guess in terms of guests, it was small. The guest list included the Ericksons, the Cassidys, and a few townsfolk, like Tempest's boss from the bakery and some of the clients from Viking MMA.

Half an hour later, everyone is seated at the long family-style tables and dinner is being served. Conversation flows easily, just like the bottles of wine.

"Can Freya have some mashed potatoes?" Vali asks with a spoon already in the air.

Tempest whips around. "Uh, I guess… a tiny bite," she says, watching like a hawk while Vali delivers the creamy goodness. At first, Freya doesn't know what to think, it's obviously very different from the peas and carrots baby food she's been eating, but then she seems to catch on and opens her mouth like a baby bird for more.

Of course, everyone laughs and coos, like this is the most entertaining thing we've ever seen.

"You're so precious," my mother says from beside me. "Yes, you are."

"Thanks, Mom," I tease, earning me a swat to the arm.

My dad laughs. "I hate to break it to y'all, but she never oohed and ahhed over any of you like she does this baby. What they say, about grandkids being your reward for making it through parenthood, is right."

"Amen, to that," Tempest's mom says from down the table.

"If we'd known how good they'd be, we would've had them first. Isn't that right?" Tempest's dad, Butch, chimes in, and everyone laughs, while still making goo-goo eyes at Freya.

My dad laughs and I'm surprised he doesn't reach across the table and high five the man.

It's like they've formed some sort of Grandparents Club.

"This is what happens when you live in sin," I whisper-yell to Vali, pointing to Freya.

I expect him to sling some potatoes at me, or at least a dirty look, but all he does is smirk.

I'm momentarily distracted by Gunnar who's taking bets at the end of the table on how long after Cage and Tempest's honeymoon until the next golden child is born.

"Twenty bucks says we have a new niece or nephew arriving by Christmas," he says with a grin.

"I wouldn't be opposed," our mother singsongs, reaching across to wipe at Freya's pouty little mouth that now has mashed potatoes smeared all over it.

She's still the cutest thing in the room.

"The wedding was beautiful," Tempest's mom says, also getting in on the baby canoodling, as she walks around and frees Freya from her highchair. "I loved everything about it."

"It was perfect," Mom agrees.

Glancing across the table, I watch as Maggie slips an arm through Vali's and snuggles close.

"Not as perfect as ours," she whispers, low enough that no one else besides me can hear. Everyone else is either complimenting the wedding or still hung up on the adorable baby… or the possibility of more.

But I heard every word she said.

"Did I hear that correctly?" I ask, drawing the attention of some of our family. "Do we have another wedding being planned?"

Maggie's cheeks grow pinker than her dress as she pulls away from Vali, giving him a sideways glance. "No," she says, shaking her head and clearing her throat. "I, uh—I said *this* was a perfect wedding."

"No," I counter, liking the way I can get a rise out of her. "You said, *not as perfect as ours*."

The table grows quiet and for a second I think Maggie's going to bolt, but instead, she and Vali share another look before she squares her shoulders.

"Guess this is as good a time as any," she mutters, placing her napkin on the table beside her plate. When she looks up and meets my eyes, I see a thin layer of annoyance, but it's overshadowed by sheer resolve. "We wanted to wait until today was over, for obvious reasons."

Her eyes narrow on me and I sink back into my chair a little.

These women my brothers have attached themselves to are fierce.

And a little scary, if I'm being honest.

"But it seems as though we're doing this now," she continues, giving Tempest an apologetic half-smile. "Vali and I haven't been *living in sin* for the past few months."

I love her a little more for throwing my words back at me.

"We've actually been married."

"Since Vegas," Vali adds, holding up their joined hands.

Sure enough, on the fourth finger of her left hand is a wedding ring. How had I not noticed until now?

"We wanted to tell everyone," Maggie says, her eyes pleading with her own mother who's seated beside her. "But after we got back, it was kind of fun keeping the secret and then we were all in full wedding-planning mode... and the longer we waited—"

"I'd just like to say that even though we eloped, I did ask her father first," Vali says, looking over at Maggie's father, Mr. O'Neal, who's sitting there with an odd expression on his face. "And we were in Vegas... and God, I love her so much, I just didn't want to wait."

"Neither did I," Maggie says, grinning from ear to ear with tears shining in her eyes. "So we got married."

It's then I hear Mrs. O'Neal sniff and I look over to see her dabbing at the corner of her eyes with her napkin.

The entire table is quiet for a moment.

As a matter of fact, the entire gym seems to grow quiet, while we all wait.

For what, I'm not sure.

Mrs. O'Neal finally breaks the trance we're all in, when she gushes, "My baby is married!"

6

Then, Tempest gets out of her seat by Cage and goes to hug Maggie, congratulating her while also scolding her for keeping the secret, which seems to be everyone's reaction.

"How dare you keep this from us," mixed with, "I'm so happy for y'all!"

What could've been quite the ordeal turns out to be a dual celebration, but I overhear Mrs. O'Neal and Mom talking about how they can make this right. Plans for some sort of celebration are already taking place, while we're still in the midst of a wedding.

Between marriages and babies, I have a feeling there will be a lot of this going on for the foreseeable future.

CHAPTER 2

WILLOW

"*Y*ou need to stop working so efficiently. You're gonna make the rest of us look bad."

Glancing up, I see my co-worker, Krista, watching me with her hands on her hips.

"Sorry," I grunt out as I stand. The stool I was sitting on while restocking cans on the lower shelves is smaller than my ass and about as comfortable as a concrete slab, but it's better than sitting on the hard floor.

"I'm just messing with you," Krista says with a wave of her hand. "You've been showing us up since you started working here. It won't be long until it's noticed and you're given a promotion, I bet."

Internally, I cringe at the thought. Not that there's anything wrong with working your way up the ranks at the Piggly Wiggly; it's just not where I saw myself at the ripe age of twenty-two.

The extra money would be nice, though.

"What about you?" I ask. "Don't you want to move up and have more responsibilities here?"

"Heck, no! In fact, I doubt I'll be here much longer. I'm gonna audition for a job at The Pink Pony."

Moving to another shelf full of soup, I absentmindedly ask, "What is that, a party place for little girls?"

Krista's laugh is so loud, it echoes across the entire store. "You're hilarious!" When she sees I'm not laughing, she corrects herself. "Oh, you really don't know! I forget you're new here. The Pink Pony is the local strip club. But it's, like, classy and shit. Hank takes good care of his girls. My cousin used to work there and she made a crap ton of money."

Before I can fully process what she's said, my manager, Tony, calls out from the end of aisle six, where I'm now stocking the beanie weenies. "Willow, you got a phone call."

I look around, wondering if there's another Willow here I don't know about, because why in the heck would anyone call me? And *who* would call me? Literally, everyone I know is at this store.

"Are you sure someone is calling for *me*?" I ask.

"The lady specifically asked for *Willow Bernard* and that's your name so, yeah, the call is for you," Tony states dryly.

Turning back to the shelf to hide my eye roll, I place two cans in their spots before standing up and following Tony to the office in the back of the store. When he hands me the phone, I mutter, "This better not be about extending my car warranty."

Tony shakes his head at my sarcasm as he leaves the room, giving me some privacy to answer the call.

"Hello," I say into the receiver, my greeting sounding more like a question.

"Is this Willow Marie Bernard?"

The use of my full name catches me off guard. "Yes, this is Willow. Who is this?"

"Could you verify your date of birth?"

Her cold tone makes the hairs on my arms stand up. "Who is this?"

"My name is Sue Harrison. I'm with the Johnson County Sheriff's Department."

I feel the blood drain from my face and then my extremities. My hand shakes as I grip the telephone. "If this is about my mother… if she's in some sort of trouble or something, I have no connection with her. And I'd appreciate it if you—"

Forget you found me. Lose my number. Whatever you do, don't give it to her.

All of those thoughts flood my mind when she cuts me off.

"Willow, can you please verify your date of birth?" This time her request is absolute. And something about her tone makes me acquiesce.

"July twenty-fifth nineteen-ninety-eight."

There's a long, drawn-out sigh before she speaks again. "I regret to inform you that your mother was found deceased in her home on February twentieth. You are her next of kin and we've been trying to track you down for the past two weeks."

"How?" I don't know why that's the first question out of my mouth. Maybe it's just human nature—the need to know the cause of death. I think it goes back to self-preservation. If we know how someone else died, maybe we can prevent it from happening to us.

But I don't need to know how my mother died. I already know that.

"According to the coroner's report, it was a drug overdose."

There's another long pause and I try to feel something besides the resounding numbness I've associated with my mother for the past fifteen years.

"I know this probably comes as a shock," she begins again, but she couldn't be further from the truth. I'm only shocked it took this long. "But your mother was also cremated two days ago. We tried to find you, but without a point of contact, it took a little longer than we hoped."

Cremated.

I swallow, my mind conjuring up images of a beautiful woman I once knew and loved. Every memory of my mother isn't bad. There were happy times, before my dad died.

But then, she became someone I didn't recognize. And that woman didn't love me. If she did, she would've tried harder. She would've put my needs in front of her own. She would've loved me more than the drugs.

11

"I'm sorry to unload all of this on you at once, but I also need to let you know you have a sibling."

That piece of information snaps me from my thoughts. My eyes flicker from a bulletin board littered with messages to the open door and I blink several times. "What?" I ask, certain I didn't hear her correctly.

"A sibling. Your mother had recently regained custody of her after she was removed from the home two years ago."

"She?" I ask, still unable to form complete sentences.

"Yes."

A sister?

I have a sister?

My mother had another child and I didn't know about her?

So many questions are flooding my brain that I'm frozen, unable to communicate.

"She's currently in temporary state custody. In situations like this, we like to give a family member the opportunity to step up. Unfortunately, her father was never identified and has never come forward. Without any other blood relatives, that really only leaves you."

Me?

A guardian?

"H—How old is she?" I ask, swallowing down a lump in my throat.

My mother's death made me numb, but knowing I have a sister who's now in state custody makes me feel everything—sadness, urgency, knowing.

I've been in her place.

Fifteen years ago, I was her.

She is me.

And all I can think about are the horrible things I went through.

All of my placements weren't horrible, but they weren't great either.

As a matter of fact, they were never great, just occasionally tolerable.

When I was thirteen, I was placed with the Holderman's and my life became gray—not white and not black, just gray. It's the only way I can describe it. They weren't mean, necessarily. But they weren't nice either. I was fed three meals a day, made to do normal chores, and expected to keep up my grades. We barely exchanged words, unless I was being reprimanded.

But I survived.

Now I know there is more to life than surviving and I would never wish that existence on anyone, especially *my sister*.

"According to the file, she just turned nine."

Nine.

I've had a sister for nine years and not known. The thought kills me and I absent-mindedly rub at my chest to ease the ache.

Which means she went to foster care at the same age I did. My father was killed in a car wreck when I was five and my mother started using drugs around the same time. When I was seven, she was arrested and sent to prison and I went into the system.

There weren't any sisters to take me in. No aunts or uncles or grandparents.

No one wanted me.

My mom was paroled when I was ten, but she relinquished her rights because she still wasn't able—or just didn't want—to care for me.

And then, three years later, she had another baby, I think to myself as I try to put the pieces of my life together.

"What's her name?" I ask, needing a name to put with the faceless image I'm beginning to create in my mind, in a new space marked *sister*. I might've just found out about her, but the one thing I've always wanted above anything else was a family—people to call my own. Or a person.

"Hazel."

Hazel.

Somehow, that name already fits her and I don't even know what she looks like.

I wonder if she looks at all like me—dark hair, dark eyes, olive skin? I got so much of that from my father, so that's unlikely. Very little about me is my mother, except for the shape of my nose. Every time I look in the mirror, my gaze is drawn to it. At one point, I even thought about getting a nose job.

But that costs money and I haven't had much of that.

"Where is she right now?" I ask, realizing there is so much I don't know. I've been living in this little bubble ever since I got to Green Valley. I work every day at the Piggly Wiggly, taking any shift they'll give me, which means I'm here from morning to night. When I'm not here, I'm at the RV park on the outskirts of town.

It's really meant for people vacationing in the mountains, but the old man who runs it doesn't mind me being a more permanent fixture. I have a small travel trailer I bought when I still lived in Merryville. It was cheap and, honestly, a piece of shit. But it has a bed and a small kitchen, all I need to survive.

However, it won't be good enough for Hazel.

The state will never grant guardianship to a twenty-two-year-old living in a travel trailer.

"She's here in Mountain City," Sue says. "A family agreed to take her in temporarily, but they don't plan on keeping her long."

Mountain City. I haven't thought of that place in so long. My first placement was with a family who lived in a town about thirty minutes from there. After that, I was placed with a family who relocated to Merryville. I've bounced around to a lot of places, but never back to Mountain City.

"And then what?" I ask, feeling the urgency.

"I guess that depends on you," she says, her words making my heart stutter. "I know I've dropped a lot on you, so I'll give you some time to think about it. Either a social worker or I will be back in touch in a week or so."

From the moment she told me I have a sister, I knew I wanted her.

I want her.

But it's not that easy. I can only imagine the hoops I'll have to jump through for that to happen—applications and home visits. What if they deem me unfit? I'm not exactly living in the optimal environment for a nine-year-old. Plus there's the fact I've never taken care of another human being besides myself. What if I'm not good at it?

There's a lot to think about and not much I can do in a week, but at least she's giving me a few days before I have to make the decision. And in the meantime, I can try to come up with a plan.

"Is there another phone number I can reach you at?" she asks, drawing me out of my thoughts and back to the present.

Damn it. "No, I—I don't have a phone."

She sighs. "Okay, I'll call you back at this number. Are you there most days?"

"Yes, practically every day."

"Good. We'll talk more soon."

We end the call and I fall back down into the swivel chair, my head reeling.

My mother's dead.

I have a sister.

Which means, I need to find a place to live with at least enough room for two beds, among other things, like a phone. All things that require money. Fortunately, I have a little in savings, but not enough.

When I walk back out into the store, I find Krista still standing in the canned goods aisle, slowly stocking the shelf I'd been working on.

"Tell me more about this Pink Pony," I demand, taking the cans from her and fixing everything she messed up while I was gone. "How much money are you talking about?"

CHAPTER 3

OZZI

"Family meeting," Cage announces as he strolls through the gym. It's Sunday and the gym is closed to the public, but Gunnar has been getting in some practice rounds with Cage and Viggo in the ring, while Vali and I have been sparring on the mats.

It feels like old times when we were back in Dallas at Erickson MMA, but yet not.

The vibe is different here—more laid back and less competitive. That's all thanks to Cage and the way he's approached the business. In the beginning, he was basically only offering self-defense classes, which were a good foundation. He built a clientele quickly, with the local law enforcement and first responders making up the bulk of his students.

But then Gunnar moved to town and Cage amped up the mixed martial arts training, along with kickboxing. Now, he's offering everything we used to at Erickson, plus some.

"Are we waiting for the girls?" Vali asks, taking a seat across from Gunnar.

Cage takes a towel and wipes it down his face and then loops it around his neck. He's not quite as huge as he used to be, but he's still in amazing shape. Between training Gunnar and a few other local fighters, he gets his fair share of ring time.

"No," Cage says, turning a chair around and throwing a leg over the seat, resting his elbows on the back. "They're shopping in Merryville today, something to do with the wedding reception."

Vali chuckles, shaking his head. "This isn't going to be a small event, is it?"

"Not even close," Cage deadpans.

When Maggie and Vali dropped the bomb that they've been married since Vegas, it came as a shock to everyone, but no one was upset about it. Her mom was probably the most emotional, rightly so, but they're making it up to everyone by planning a big reception and there's even talk of a vow renewal or something like that.

"Just like your wedding wasn't a small event," I add. "I mean, maybe in head-count, but y'all made up for it in the amount of food and booze that was served."

Cage smirks. "None of that mattered to me, as long as at the end of the day Tempest was officially my wife."

I see the glint of recognition in Vali's eyes as he nods in agreement.

Damn, the two of them are whipped.

"What's this meeting about?" Viggo asks, bringing everyone's attention down the table to where he's sitting.

Cage runs a hand down his beard. "I guess I just need to know what everyone's plans are. Now that Mom and Dad have officially become residents of Tennessee, Gunnar and Vali are already here, and the two of you sold your place in Dallas," he says, pointing at me and Viggo. "Who's planning on sticking around and working at the gym?"

"I'm leaving in two days to head back to Dallas," Viggo says gruffly.

That's been his attitude ever since the gym sold. I can't say I blame him. That gym was his life. The day Dad retired, Viggo took over, and between him and Vali, they ran the business side of things for a long time.

But when the offer came in, since we all had a share in the business, we all got a vote, and it was a majority rules type vote.

Viggo was the only one who didn't want to sell.

I was on the fence, but after much consideration, I realized it was a good move financially for all of us. In hindsight, I know it was the right move. It gave Vali the freedom to move out here. It gave Cage the extra money to install the ring. And it gave Mom and Dad the cash flow to enjoy their retirement and live wherever they want.

It was best for my family, Viggo included.

Because whether he wants to admit it or not, he needed a fresh start as much as anyone else.

And while he's searching right now, he'll figure his shit out.

He just needs time.

"And what about you?" Cage asks, pulling me out of my thoughts. "Are you headed back to Dallas or sticking around for a while?"

I shrug, leaning forward to rest my elbows on the table. "Well, I don't have a job or an apartment to go back to," I start. "Brought my Jeep out with me and sold everything that didn't fit in the back, so I think you're stuck with me for a while."

Cage nods. "Alright then," he says, eyeing Viggo warily, and then turning his attention back to me. "I'm going to put you to work."

"Make me your bitch," I say, arms outstretched. "You know I hate sitting around with nothing to do."

"I've got plenty of shit for you to do too," Cage says to Viggo. "If you change your mind, you've always got a place here."

Viggo stares at the table, but nods. "Thanks, appreciate it."

We haven't talked a lot since we left Dallas. Even though he rode here with me, most of the trip was spent with the top rolled back and the radio up. I could tell he wasn't in the mood for conversation and I didn't push.

It's always been like that between us.

If he wants to talk, he knows I'll listen.

But if I try to force him to, that always ends in a knock-down-drag-out.

You could say Viggo and I have a love-hate relationship, but deep down, he knows I've got his back, no matter what he chooses to do.

"Also," Cage says from his spot at the head of the table. "As you all know, Tempest and I will be leaving on our honeymoon a week from today and Freya will be in all of your care." His eyebrows lift and then he exhales a deep breath.

"Don't worry about Freya," Vali says, slapping a hand on Cage's shoulder.

"Yeah, bro," Gunnar chimes in. "We've got her covered."

Cage runs a hand down his beard again, and then up through his hair, making his blond strands stand on end. Probably looking like he's feeling—on edge. "I don't know who's more nervous, me or Tempest."

"Freya's going to be fine," I assure him. "None of us would ever let anything happen to her. You know that."

"I know," he says, nodding. "But babies are—"

"A lot of work. We know," Vali says. "Plus, it won't just be us. Tempest's mom and dad will have her most nights and you know Mom and Dad will be here all the time. Besides all of the doting grandparents, you've got Maggie and Frankie, who's practically a doctor."

Cage lifts his hands in surrender. "I know. She's going to be fine."

"And you and Tempest deserve some time away," Gunnar adds.

At that, Cage's expression shifts. "I am looking forward to that."

"Don't knock her up while you're gone," I warn. "Or do...whatever floats your boat." Because, damn it if I don't really love this uncle gig.

Cage laughs, shaking his head. "One is enough... for now."

From the look on this face, I know it won't be long before Freya is a big sister.

"But I'll also need you all to step up while we're gone," he says, shifting back to boss mode. "Frankie is going to take over Tempest's all-women's self-defense classes. I think she's going to get Maggie to help her with that. Gunnar, you're in charge of your own training, and I expect you to follow the plan. We've got a big fight coming up in a few months. You're also going to handle all of our first responder classes. Vali, you'll handle all the day-to-day business. And, Ozzi, since you'll be sticking around, I'm putting you in charge of all other training sessions."

Bracing his hands on the chair, he stands, looking around the table. "Any questions?"

Gunnar, Vali, and I look at each other and then back to Cage.

"Sounds like a plan," Vali says, then turns his attention down to Viggo. "You sure you don't want to stick around for all this fun?"

Viggo sighs, leaning back in his chair. "No, I've gotta figure out what the fuck I'm gonna do with the rest of my life."

I feel his pain. Even though it's not my own, I can empathize with him. We're basically in the same boat, but I just handle this sort of shit better than him. Where Viggo needs a plan and structure, I can generally go with the flow and see where the Universe puts me.

He's not like that. So, I understand that all this change has been hard on him.

"Where are you going?" Gunnar asks.

Viggo shakes his head. "No clue… back to Texas, for now, I guess. But I don't really want to stay in Dallas. I'm actually thinking about renting a car instead of flying back, just to give myself time to think."

"That doesn't sound half bad," Cage says. "Just promise you'll keep us in the loop. Don't make us put out an APB on your ass."

CHAPTER 4

WILLOW

*a*s I walk into the Pink Pony, I swallow the anxiety clogging my throat. New places freak me out. Especially one like this; a strip club. I've barely been inside a bar, let alone a place where scantily dressed women dance on poles.

And here I am, walking in, looking for a job.

The taste of bile on my tongue makes me cringe, along with the onslaught of pink. The interior of the club fits the name perfectly. Everything is pink, from the carpet to the walls, like someone doused the place in Pepto Bismol.

I could use a hit of that about now, actually.

Locking eyes with a man behind the bar, he gives me a welcoming grin and it eases my nerves a little. Walking over to where he's pouring drinks, I decide ordering one for myself might not be a bad idea. "What can I get for you?" he asks as he continues pouring shots and mixing drinks.

The way he does it all without looking at a recipe card or even blinking is mesmerizing. Maybe if I don't qualify as a dancer I could learn to mix drinks.

"I'm looking for Hank," I finally say, my eyes still on the glasses of amber liquid.

"He's usually pretty busy. Can I help you with something or maybe get a message to him for you?" he asks, eyeing me with a little suspicion.

"Right," I say, nodding as I chew on the corner of my lip. "Of course." I should've thought about that, but Krista had made everything sound so easy. "I was wondering if I could maybe get an application or an... audition?"

I can't believe I'm doing this. Sure, I need cash and I need it fast, but never in a million years did I think I'd entertain the thought of working at a place like this. Not that there's anything wrong with it. If stripping and dancing are how you make your living, I respect that.

But this isn't my scene. I'm not an extrovert. I don't mingle with people. So, what makes me think I can land a job at a place like this?

I blame all of this on Krista. She made it sound so appealing I couldn't pass up the opportunity without at least considering it. According to her, one of her cousins used to work here and would often take home a few hundred dollars a night in tips alone.

That's the kind of cash I need.

He pauses for a moment, giving me an inquisitive stare. It's not creepy or lingering, just curious. "I'm Floyd," he says, reaching out across the bar to shake my hand. "Bartender and whatever else needs done around here."

Some of my earlier nerves subside a tiny bit with the gesture. "Willow," I reply, giving him a firm shake. "And I really have no clue what I'm doing here."

There's something that flashes across his face, maybe recognition, not in me as a person, but the desperation in my eyes, perhaps.

"Let me finish up these orders and I'll get your name and number," Floyd says. "Can I get you a drink while you wait?"

I shake my head and give him a hesitant smile. "No, thank you."

When Floyd moves down to the other end of the bar, a man in a sleeveless flannel shirt slides onto the bar stool beside me. I try to inconspicuously slide over, putting some space between us, but he turns toward me and invades my space.

Floyd walks back over and places a piece of paper and pen in front of me. "Just put down your information and I'll make sure Hank gets it. If he's looking for someone, he'll call."

My information, like a phone number?

Shit, I didn't think about that. Quickly, I jot down the phone number for the Piggly Wiggly. Way to go, Willow. There's nothing like listing your current employer's number on a piece of paper of a potential new employer. And that new potential employer being a strip club. But it's not like I'm going to quit my job at The Pig. I need both.

Right now, I need everything I can get.

However, buying a cell phone is the next order of business on my long list of things I need to do before I could be considered a viable candidate to get Hazel.

"So you're trying to get a job here?" the man beside me says, still infiltrating my personal space.

Trying not to look at him or even acknowledge his existence, I block the piece of paper and write my name below the telephone number, trying to think if I should add anything else.

"You could audition for me," he says suggestively, leaning over even closer. The smell of beer and body odor make my stomach turn. If I was feeling nauseous when I walked in, I'm downright ill now.

"Don't touch me," I warn in my most menacing tone. Typically, when I turn on the ice, people give me a wide birth, but my cold demeanor seems to only make this guy more eager.

He laughs, slapping a hand on the bar. "Little mama has some fight in her. I like that. How about you get up on this bar and show me what you got. Maybe even take some of these clothes off while you're at it."

The second his fingers graze the neckline of my t-shirt, I lose it.

No longer am I in control of my actions. People always describe their vision turning red when they're so angry they inflict bodily harm, but not me. It's just a blur. My heart rate spikes and everything happens at once.

One second, I'm standing and so is he. The next thing I know, my knee is in his groin and I'm swiping his feet out from under him. Once he's facedown on the ground, I twist his arm behind his back and lean in with my knee in his spine. "Don't you *ever* touch me again," I seethe.

When a rough hand touches my shoulder, I whirl around, ready to fight anyone else who wants to put their hands where they don't belong, but then I see it's Floyd.

He steps back, hands up as he gives me some space. "Whoa, it's just me. How about you let us take it from here, yeah?"

Another guy with arms the size of tree trunks is standing beside Floyd with a pissed off expression and when I finally release the man beneath me, Floyd lifts him and pushes him toward the exit.

"Toss him," Floyd instructs as I stand to my feet. We watch while the unruly customer is forcefully escorted out the door and then Floyd turns back to me. "You okay?"

I nod, taking a deep breath as the adrenaline slowly starts to fade.

"Where'd you learn to do that?" Floyd asks, eyes on me.

I feel the weight of his stare and everyone else's around me. Grabbing my bag from where it fell to the floor beside the bar stool, I clear my throat. "What do you mean?" I ask, trying to deflect so I can get the hell out of here.

This obviously was a bad mistake.

I could never fit in here.

"Those moves," he says with a laugh, shaking his head. "I blinked and you had that guy eating concrete. Those are some serious skills. You some sort of ninja or take that Tae Kwon Do shit?"

"No," I say, shaking my head. "Just instinct, I guess."

Floyd shakes his head again and I can't miss the smile on his face. "Ever heard of Viking MMA?" he asks, cocking his head. "My friend owns the gym and I think you'd be a good fit down there."

Now I'm the one laughing. "I don't have time for extracurricular activities. So, unless they need someone to clean the gym, I doubt they have a use for me."

Reaching back across the counter, he takes the piece of paper and flips it over, writing something on the back.

"Do me a favor and at least go check out the gym. I'll call ahead and tell the owner you're coming. He'll let you do one class for free. If you like it, maybe y'all can work something out. If you don't, maybe you can ask him if he needs any help around the gym."

Walking out of the Pink Pony, I check both directions just to make sure the guy from the bar isn't waiting on me. But the coast is clear and everything seems quiet out here. So, I stuff my hands into the pockets of my jeans and quickly walk to my truck.

I'm not sure if I'll take Floyd up on his suggestion, but maybe I will. If I'm desperate enough to come to The Pink Pony, then why wouldn't I give something like Viking MMA a shot? Like Floyd said, if nothing else, maybe they could use some extra help.

As I drive out of the parking lot, I feel too anxious to go home just yet so I decide to take the long way and circle through Green Valley. Floyd's words still playing through my mind.

He thinks I have skills.

No one has ever told me that before.

What he witnessed tonight was years of having to be on guard and ready to defend myself at a moment's notice. It was pure instinct and the result of living through the foster care system and being the target for bullies at school.

I've never had anyone show me how to do anything when it comes to fighting. I don't even like it, really. But I've also never backed down from a confrontation. I learned early on that if I cowered, it made me an even bigger target. So, even before I grew into my full five-foot-eight height, I faked the bravado.

With the streetlamps lighting the sidewalks of downtown Green Valley, I drive slowly as I pass by Donner Bakery and the old hardware store, then come to a complete stop in front of Viking MMA.

I've driven past here a few times since I came to town, but never gave it a second glance.

Like I told Floyd, extracurricular activities aren't part of my routine. I get my exercise by working my ass off at the Piggly Wiggly and going for a run on my days off.

Letting my old truck idle by the curb, I take in what I can see of the gym—walls of mirrors, bags hanging from the ceiling in the back, and mats covering a lot of the floor.

Thanks to an old newspaper clipping that's hanging on the bulletin board at the Piggly Wiggly, I know about their big ring where the owner has held a couple fights, like the ones you see on television.

At night, with a few dim lights illuminating the space, it looks like something out of a movie. Maybe that's just my imagination, but it feels bigger than this space or this town, and that makes it intimidating.

But according to Floyd, the guy that owns it is his friend and the people who work here are nice, which intrigues me.

Maybe I'll do it.

It kind of feels like one of those *what-do-I-have-to-lose* moments.

I'm twenty-two years old and I've never truly done anything for myself.

For my entire life, I've been in survivor mode. And now, all of my efforts have turned toward Hazel—finding her, meeting her, and hopefully, bringing her to live with me… if that's what she wants. But a small voice inside is telling me it's okay to do one thing just for me.

As I make the quiet drive back to the outskirts of town and to my tiny trailer, I contemplate the last few hours.

Me going to the Pink Pony.

Actually auditioning.

The guy putting his hands on me.

Because, let's face it, that was bound to happen at some point and it was better for it to happen tonight, before I got in over my head. Maybe it was a higher power redirecting my path, because now that I take a step back, even though I could've made some fast cash, it probably wasn't the best idea.

My head is still reeling as I make myself a cup of hot tea and try to decompress from all the adrenaline and anxiousness.

When I crawl into bed and close my eyes, all I can think about is Viking MMA, because the one thing that definitely felt good tonight was putting that guy on his ass.

I said it was a blur and that part is true, but it was like everything around me slowed to a crawl and I just handled the situation, never thinking twice about the whys or hows.

I just did it.

* * *

TWO DAYS LATER, after much internal debating, I'm standing inside Viking MMA, the gym I've only seen from the road. A place I never would've imagined myself walking into a few days ago.

But here I am.

Sweaty palms.

Nervous stomach.

Unsure of what I'm really doing, but unable to turn back now.

It smells like cleaning supplies, mixed with sweat and something I can't quite put my finger on—Ambition? Drive?

Things that aren't foreign to me, but I also haven't ever been completely immersed in them, like I am now.

As I'm taking in every exposed beam and industrial element of the space, a female voice greets me and I jump. Placing a hand on my chest, right over my racing heart, I turn to face her.

With an apologetic expression, she smiles. "Sorry, didn't mean to startle you."

"It's fine," I tell her, shaking my head. "I'm, uh, I think I'm here for a class?"

She glances down at a computer screen. "Did you call ahead?"

"No." My palms get even more sweaty as my nerves kick into high gear. "Floyd, the bartender from the Pink Pony, sent me."

As the words come out of my mouth, I think about how crazy they sound, but she doesn't bat a lash.

"Willow, right?" a hulk of a man says as he walks up to the desk. "Floyd called me a couple days ago and said you might be by."

"Uh, yeah, that's me."

Stretching his muscular arm out, he offers me his hand in a friendly gesture. "I'm Cage Erickson and this is my wife, Tempest."

The beautiful redhead smiles even wider and leans into his side.

Accepting his outstretched hand, I hope he doesn't feel the sweat and smell my fear. "I'm Willow, but you already knew that."

With an awkward chuckle, I pull my hand back and drop my arms to my side, trying to quell my anxiety. "Sorry, I guess I'm a little nervous. This is totally out of my comfort zone."

"According to Floyd, you've got some natural talent."

My cheeks warm and I look away with a shrug. "I don't know about that."

I've been conditioned to keep people's expectations of me low, then they can't be disappointed if I fail. And if I succeed, it's a pleasant surprise for everyone.

"Since I'm the professional"—he steps back toward the mats—"why don't you let me be the judge of that."

"Okay," I agree with a slight nod.

Waving me over, he calls out, "Let's start over here."

Thankfully, I went ahead and wore some sweatpants and a sports bra. I wasn't sure if this would actually happen today, but unlike when I went to the Pink Pony, I wanted to at least be semi-prepared if it did.

Surprisingly, under all of the nerves, I feel a sense of ease.

There's a small class being conducted to one side of the gym and as we walk toward the back where some bags are hanging, I can see a couple guys sparring in the big ring.

It's so cool.

The entire place is, actually. And I almost run right into the back of Cage because I'm gawking instead of paying attention to where I'm going.

"Sorry," I say, giving him an apologetic smile.

His ice blue eyes squint. "Nervous?"

"Just a little," I admit.

He nods, walking over to grab a pair of gloves and some tape. "That's normal, especially if you've never done anything like this before. No classes or training, right?"

"Right," I say, sticking out my hands when he approaches.

"This is a freebie. I like to give all my newcomers a chance to just check the place out before they sign-up. It's definitely not for everyone, but in my humble opinion, everyone could benefit from something we teach here."

I like the quiet confidence he has. It has a calming effect on me and as he tapes up my hands, instead of growing more nervous, my heart eases into an even, steady rhythm.

"Floyd mentioned you've got quite the roundhouse," he says with a smirk, glancing up at me.

"I have no clue what that is."

This time, he actually laughs, rubbing a hand down his beard. "How about you just show me what you did at the Pink Pony the other night and we'll go from there?"

For a moment, I just stare at the bag and then back at him. "It was really just... I don't know—"

"A knee-jerk reaction? Instinct?" he asks, standing on the other side of the bag.

Nodding, I shake out my arms, feeling the weight of the gloves. "Basically."

31

"Go back there," he instructs. "Think about how you felt and then just react."

Closing my eyes, I think back to being at the bar—all the nerves, edginess, vulnerability. Then I think about the guy who was invading my space, and finally the feel of his unwelcomed touch.

The same clarity washes over me as I whirl around, my foot making contact with the heavy bag.

Jabbing my right arm out, I feel a jolt—welcome it—as I follow through with my fists. First my right, and then my left, letting that instinct take over.

Once I've worked up a sheen of sweat across my brow, Cage steps in and holds the bag, stilling it as he stares at me. "How would you like to take a few classes?"

Taking a deep cleansing breath, I brace my gloved hands on my knees. "I don't have money for classes," I say, letting my head drop between my shoulders. "The reason I was at The Pink Pony was because I was looking for a job." I don't look up for a few seconds, just letting my lungs fill with air as I try to catch my breath.

When he doesn't respond right away, I look up at him. I'm not sure what I expect, but the knowing glint in his eye isn't it.

"What if I told you you don't need any?"

Standing to my full height, I lock eyes with Cage. "I'd tell you I don't need or want charity."

"It's not charity, it's business."

CHAPTER 5

OZZI

"Oz, come spar with me."

I stop folding the clean towels we have on hand for clients and look at Gunnar as though he just sprouted a third eye. "Are you out of your mind?"

"No, I'm bored and need to burn off some energy. Get your ass in the ring and fight me."

"I don't really feel like getting my ass kicked today but thanks for asking." I fold the last towel and carry the stack to a nearby shelf.

This doesn't mean I can't handle myself in a fight because I sure as fuck can, but when it comes to getting into a ring with the current Light Heavyweight UFC title holder, I'll only do it when I have to. Besides, I let him pound on me a couple days ago and I'm still sore.

"Aww, come on," Gunnar says, following me. "I'll go easy on you. Throw on some pads and let's go a few rounds."

"Why don't you go for a run or something?"

"I already did. It didn't help."

"Why are you so worked up anyway?"

Gunnar is always running full throttle, but he's usually really good at managing all of his energy. So for him to be this worked up and needing a distraction, something's definitely going on.

He lets out a sigh before grabbing a jump rope and putting it to use. "Frankie has an interview at Doc Thurstan's office. He's hiring a PA and she'd really love to be in town every day. I guess I'm just nervous for her."

Frankie has been a great addition to the gym. When she's not working at the hospital in Merryville, she's here. Sometimes, she just hangs out with Gunnar, but she also pitches in with Tempest's self-defense classes and tends to minor bumps and bruises.

It used to be kind of weird seeing my baby brother so goo-goo eyed over a girl but even I can admit he and Frankie are pretty cute together. Sickeningly sweet, if I'm being honest, but they're growing on me. Not enough to make me want to follow in their footsteps any time soon, but even I can recognize what they have is pretty special.

"I'm sure she'll rock it, man. Stop worrying."

"Get in that ring and stop me yourself."

I'm about to tell Gunnar to go screw himself when Cage stalks over and calls my name.

"What's up?"

"I need you to do something for me," he says, his expression serious, which isn't unusual. He's definitely more surly than the rest of us. Well, except for Viggo.

I guess the two of them have that in common.

"Sure. Whatcha need?" I ask.

"So, you'll help him but not me? Thanks a lot," Gunnar scoffs. Cage is about to respond when Gunnar takes out his phone and smiles after reading the screen. "Never mind, bitches. I'm going to go see my woman." He turns and walks off, not giving us another look.

I'm assuming Frankie has good news to share.

"Anyway," Cage continues, completely ignoring Gunnar. "I have a new fighter I want you to train."

"You mean, while you and Tempest are on your honeymoon?" I ask, a little confused because I've already agreed to taking on whatever he needs me to do while they're gone.

"No, I mean, I want you to train her, period."

I've helped train fighters at Erickson, but my brothers all have more experience than I do. I can't help but wonder what the catch is if Cage is specifically asking me to train someone.

Wait.

Did he say "her"?

"Did you say *her*?"

"I did." He crosses his massive arms over his even bigger chest and gives me his best big-brother-slash-boss look, daring me to question him again. "Is that going to be a problem?"

"No, I'm just trying to figure out why you want me to do something you could obviously do better." I figure I might as well shoot straight. There's no need to beat around the bush. Cage and I have always been pretty open with each other.

He shrugs. "Call it intuition, but I feel like you'll be a good fit. Besides, my schedule is pretty stacked and we just got a new client, it's as simple as that."

I have a strong desire to call bullshit, but I'll keep that to myself for now and see how this all plays out. I really have no reason to be so suspicious and what does it matter anyway? If I'm going to stay here and help out, I'll have to do what Cage says.

Putting my hands on my hips and facing him straight on, I respond. "So, tell me about this new client."

Cage eyes me for a moment, like he's gauging my sincerity. When he seems satisfied, he starts laying it all out on the line. "Her name is Willow Bernard. It's kind of a long story, but Floyd, a friend of mine from The Pink Pony, sent her over. She's young—like, really young. And I'm not gonna lie, she's completely green, never had a class or a lick of instruction. Shit, I bet her first time on a mat was when she stopped by the gym, but she's full of natural talent."

He pauses for a second, rubbing at his beard. "Don't think I'm just pawning her off on you, either. I meant what I said. I've seen you with newbies and you're always patient with them. You've got a good eye for talent and you're a solid trainer. Plus, I really think she has something special and could go far, if she sticks with it. In fact, there's a tournament in Nashville in a few months. If you can get her ready to compete by then, I'll pay the entry fees and all the travel expenses."

Again, I can't help but wonder what's so special about this girl and why Cage has assigned her to me but I'm ready to find out. She must be something for Cage to already be thinking about her competing. But, regardless, I now have a job to do and I'm always up for any challenge that comes my way.

"When do I get to meet her?" I ask.

"How does right now sound?" Cage replies.

Not expecting that answer, I chuckle. "Let's do this."

Following Cage through the maze of various exercise equipment, mats, and punching bags, we come to a stop in the small reception area at the front of the gym.

Tempest is talking to a girl—Willow, I presume—and writing down whatever information Willow is giving her. While they chat, I focus my attention on Willow's body since I can't see her face at the moment.

It's not a pervy perusal, but rather an evaluation of her fitness. If I'm going to be training her, I need to know what I'm working with.

At first glance, I can't help but notice her firm thighs and tight ass.

Professionally speaking, of course.

She has a slight hourglass shape that will serve her well as she trains and competes, keeping her balance solid. Her arms are on the smaller side but I think they'll be pretty easy to bulk up, giving them more shape as well as strength.

I'm still checking her out when I hear Cage clear his throat then say my name. When I look up at him, I can't help but notice his unamused expression. Doing a quick glance around our space, it dawns on me I've just been busted ogling the new client.

Shit.

"Yeah, what's up?" is what I manage to blurt out, continuing to embarrass myself even further and earning a fiery glance from Cage. When I give him an apologetic shrug, trying to convey that it wasn't what it looked like, he rolls his eyes, and I can practically see the regret of his decision all over his face.

"This is Willow, your new client."

Knowing I need to smooth things over, I attempt to hit her with the Erickson charm and offer her a wide smile. But when she turns to fully face me, I nearly choke on my tongue.

Willow is absolutely gorgeous.

Not cute, like a puppy. Not pretty, like a flower.

Stunning.

A fucking knockout.

Like I could stare at her all day and still find new details to obsess over.

Unfortunately for me, I only get this one shot—this split second. Because as of this moment, she's my client and that makes her officially off-limits. It's not a rule or anything. My brothers have hooked up with plenty of people from the gym over the years, but not me. It just feels too complicated, and I don't do complicated.

I also don't do relationships, and one-night stands with people you're going to see on a regular basis never work out in your favor.

After a few seconds of awkward silence, Cage nudges me, giving me another stern look that breaks me out of my stupor.

"I'm Ozzi," I finally manage, sticking out my hand.

Her grip doesn't disappoint, but her expression sure does. With her full lips pressed in a straight line, she gives me an icy stare, making my balls shrivel.

Squeezing a little harder, she clears her throat. "It's nice to meet you."

But it's obvious that statement couldn't be further from the truth.

When she lets go of my hand, I give it a little shake before clearing my throat. "It's great to meet you too. I'm looking forward to training you."

Fuck, does everything have to sound so creepy now?

"I mean, um, have you decided when you'd like to start training?"

"Soon, if possible. My job at the Piggly Wiggly is pretty flexible." Her gaze is still cool, but when she looks back to Cage and Tempest, it seems to warm. "I can call once my schedule is posted for the week."

"Sounds good," Cage says with a nod, glancing at me. "Ozzi's schedule is wide open, so whatever times work for you will work for him."

Nodding, I smile, still trying to smooth things over. She doesn't have to like me, but my job will be much harder if she hates me. Besides, I'm not used to people not liking me and if I'm being honest, it eats at me when I think I've gotten on someone's bad side.

When she walks out, my shoulders relax and I exhale loudly. Scrubbing my hands down my face, I don't even look at Cage. I won't be able to take the disappointment, but I hear his rumbling chuckle as I walk off.

I don't even know what just happened. I'm never that awkward around people, especially women. It was as though all my swagger had left the building, leaving me barely able to have a conversation.

This is going to be so fun.

CHAPTER 6

WILLOW

"So I heard your audition didn't go so well," Krista says as we walk out of the breakroom to start our shift. It's hard to believe that less than a week ago she was telling me about The Pink Pony. Soon after, I got the call from the sheriff's department and everything became a blur for a few days.

It was like I was back in the system and scrambling to find my footing.

I hate that feeling.

Between finding out my mom is dead and that I have a sister I didn't know about, it was a bit much and a lot to process. It's all still slowly sinking in, especially the part about my mom. Even though it wasn't a shock, it's made me feel off-kilter.

"That's putting it mildly," I mutter as we pass an older lady in the produce section.

Krista chuckles. "Word around the dressing room is you're now the town badass."

"Great," I deadpan. "That's exactly what I was going for."

"It fits your vibe," she points out.

"What's that supposed to mean?"

When we get to the checkout register, she pauses, shrugging. "I don't know. Ever since the first time I met you, I've always thought, *damn, she could kick my ass.* I knew that first day I would much rather you be my friend than my enemy."

Fighting back a smile, I shake my head. "I'm not that bad."

I've always known I come off as someone who's not very personable, but it's not intentional. After years of having my guard up, it's damn near impossible to let it down. Everyone I meet is a suspect until proven innocent and trustworthy.

"It's not a bad thing," Krista clarifies. "I admire you for it, actually. I wish I had an ounce of your badassery."

"My badassery?"

She laughs, adjusting her blonde hair that's up in a high ponytail. "I said what I said."

"Well, my badassery got me tossed out of The Pink Pony along with my chance to make some much-needed extra money."

There aren't any customers checking out at the moment. It's a slow time of day; there's probably only a handful of shoppers in the entire store. But I need to go stock the cereal and check the inventory on the cleaning supplies.

I know I go above and beyond my role here at the Piggly Wiggly, but I also know my hard work pays off in extra hours. And hopefully, one of these days, when a management position becomes available, I'll be first in line for a promotion.

It's not a grand ambition, but it's something, and until a better opportunity comes along, I'm going to appreciate what I have.

"Do you know of anywhere else hiring?" I ask. "Are there any restaurants that are open late… or bars?"

Krista's eyes grow wide. "The only other bar I know of is a biker bar, but you don't want to work there."

Groaning, I straighten some magazines by the register Krista is opening. "Well, I've got to figure out something."

"I'll keep my ears open for you."

"Thanks."

Walking toward the stockroom, I think back to that phone call with Officer Harrison—my mother's death, the revelation I have a sister, and the need to get to her. I haven't told anyone about that. But every night, when I lay down to go to sleep, it's all I think about.

I've known about my mother's death for six days.

And I still don't know how I feel about it.

Numb.

Resigned.

Angry.

Sad.

Sue said she was cremated, which feels so final. Not that death isn't, but there's no chance of me ever seeing her again, whether I wanted to or not.

If I don't claim her remains, she'll be placed in a community grave.

That makes me sad.

Not for her, but the idea that anyone wouldn't be claimed at the end of their life. We all deserve to be wanted. And regardless of how badass Krista thinks I am, I do have a heart. And despite its cracks and holes held loosely together with lingering hopes and forgotten wishes, it still beats and feels.

Barely.

Throwing myself into work to keep from thinking about my dead mother, I forget to take a lunch break and the next thing I know, Krista is calling my name from the end of the aisle.

"What?" I ask, looking up from the clipboard of inventory sheets I'm holding. Whoa, nearly every aisle is marked off.

"I'm leaving and you're supposed to take over my register."

"Oh, right. Sorry," I tell her. "I'll be right there."

Finishing up a few line items, I clip my pen to my shirt and head to the front.

After a few more hours on the register, my shift ends and I head to the break-room to grab my bag and head to my truck. I'm supposed to go to Viking MMA tonight for my first class or session or whatever you call it, but I'm still on the fence about it, to be honest.

As much as I enjoyed myself last week, I don't know what kicking a bag is going to do for me.

Cage Erickson seems to think I have natural talent, whatever that means.

And then there's his brother, Ozzi.

When I caught him checking me out, my hackles went up. Knowing he's going to be my instructor is another reason I don't know if I want to entertain this friv-olous idea.

I need to spend my time making money and figuring out a way to help my sister, not in a gym with beefy, tattooed Vikings.

But somehow, after going back to my trailer and taking a shower in my bathroom that's the size of a Cracker Jack box, I end up changed and ready for the gym. With my damp hair in a tight bun and my favorite pair of sweats paired with a sports bra and tank, I head back to my truck, questions still racing through my mind.

What the hell am I doing?

Why am I so drawn to this place?

And why did my brief class last week feel so good?

That last question is enough to keep me driving. I've never been one to do some-thing just for myself. My entire life has been a documentary on survival. But for once, I feel a pull to do something just for me. Which seems crazy since my life is in another state of upheaval, but I can't stop thinking about how good it felt to lose myself and let a dormant—and what felt like a dominant—part of me take over.

When I was pounding that bag, letting instinct carry me, I felt more like myself than I ever have in all my twenty-two years.

Five minutes later, I'm crawling to a stop in front of the gym and after letting my truck idle for a minute, I decide to turn the engine off and just get it over with.

The faster you get in there and prove to yourself and everyone else that this is a waste of time, the faster you can get on with your life.

It's with that same attitude, I walk through the doors of Viking MMA.

Walls up.

Guarded.

Ready to put an end to this farce.

But then the familiar smell from the other day hits me—sweat and determination, mixed with the leather bags and concrete walls... wood and metal. That description might make it sound cold and unwelcoming, but it's just the opposite.

"Hello," a friendly voice greets from behind the desk. It's not Tempest, who I met last week, but she seems just as nice and has a bright smile. "Are you here for our self-defense class?"

"Uh, no," I say, searching the space for Ozzi, but when I don't see him, I almost turn to leave. Maybe I got the day or time wrong. Or maybe he decided I'm not worth his time.

"Oh, you must be Willow," she says, flipping through the pages of what looks like a schedule book. "Sorry, I'm not usually the one working the desk. Tempest and Cage left for their honeymoon. So, we're all filling in."

The way she talks to me like we're already acquainted startles me a little. I should be used to it by now, I've been in Green Valley for a little over six months and everyone here is so nice and friendly. But it still catches me off guard sometimes.

"I'm Maggie," she introduces herself. "Ozzi should be down any time. Want me to show you around?"

"I'm good," I tell her. "I'll just wait for him."

She smiles. "Okay, let me know if you need anything."

"Thanks."

Walking toward where the bags are hanging from heavy-duty chains, I place my bag and water bottle by the wall and then begin stretching out my muscles.

I didn't lie that I've never been in a class or had any formal training, but when I was about ten, I was placed with a family who owned a gymnastics studio. It was a short-term placement, but I loved it there. The man and woman were nice. My room was clean. The food was good. And when I wasn't at school, I got to spend time at the gym—jumping on trampolines and learning how to do cartwheels and backflips.

It was the most fun I ever had as a child, or ever.

The smell here reminds me of there.

Maybe that's why I like it so much.

That and I like the way I feel when I'm here.

I like how it feels when I unleash on the bag, all of my bottled-up emotions fueling each punch and kick.

"Hey," Ozzi's familiar voice comes from behind me. I don't turn immediately, schooling my features and composing myself as I let go of the memories and bring myself back to the present.

Pulling my knees into my chest, I push myself off the mat and stand to face him.

"Hi," I say, crossing my arms over my chest and locking eyes with him.

He gives me a crooked smile and I suppose if I wasn't me, if I was any other warm-blooded female, I might think it was attractive or endearing. But I'm me, and I don't succumb to things like crooked smiles and penetrating blue eyes.

That's for girls who are weak.

I'm not weak.

"Let's get started, shall we?" he finally asks after a few moments of the two of us sizing each other up. I think he was waiting for me to say something, but I don't have anything to say. I'm here and that's about all I can offer at the moment.

Thankfully, he doesn't try to force conversation out of me. Instead, he guides me through a lot of basic calisthenics. For about fifteen minutes, it's like I'm back in junior high PE class.

After a series of squats and lunges, he stands and grabs the same gloves Cage had me wear the first night I was here. "I know some of this might seem trivial, but I need to see where you're at physically."

Ozzi's tone and instruction are all-business and I haven't caught him checking me out once, which is a relief. I'd already decided that if he came onto me, I'd walk out.

I don't have time for that.

Unlike when Cage just let me loose, Ozzi instructs me on proper form and technique.

"This is a speed bag," he says, walking over to a small teardrop-shaped bag hanging from a lower part of the ceiling. "You're going to strike the bag with the back of your hand in a circular motion." He demonstrates as he speaks. "This helps with hand-eye coordination and speed, of course, hence the name."

Stepping back, he nods toward the bag. "Give it a shot."

As I begin to slowly hit the bag like he showed me, I slip into a rhythm.

"That's it," Ozzi encourages, walking behind me and then to the other side. "Listen to the bag, don't depend on eyesight alone. Hear it, feel it."

I do as he says and before long, the bag is a blur of movement and sweat beads on my forehead.

"That's good, great actually," he says, sounding impressed and I hate to admit that his praise makes me feel good. "Take a short break, get a drink of water, and then we'll go to the heavy bag."

For the next hour, Ozzi leads me around the studio, instructing and demonstrating and then letting me try each skill. And every time, he seems satisfied with what I'm capable of.

With each drill he puts me through, I feel a spark of something growing inside me.

"I think that's enough for one night," he finally says, tossing me a towel.

Spent and completely exhausted, I lower myself to the mat and catch my breath as I wipe the sweat from my forehead.

"What do you think?" he asks, sitting across from me.

Still catching my breath, I glance over at him, trying hard not to notice things about him. Not just his blue eyes or his crooked smile, but the impressive tattoos on his forearms, the sharp edge of his jaw, and the way his features are so symmetrical and pleasing to the eye.

But I'm not here for that.

I'm here for me, which is a foreign concept, but I'm trying to embrace it.

"I like it."

He laughs and the sound echoes off the concrete walls. It's then I realize we're the only two people left in the gym. Any other time, that would make me feel guarded and on edge, but I don't feel either of those things.

I just feel spent and... good.

My head is clear.

Tension in my shoulders has released.

And my burdens feel lighter.

"I think it's safe to say Cage was right. You're a natural. For someone who's never had any training or taken classes, you're an anomaly. Seriously leaps and bounds above any beginner I've ever seen. We always say there's one thing you can't teach and that's God-given talent."

Pausing, he shakes his head. "And you've got that in spades."

"What does that mean?"

He stands and the fluid movement uncommon in a guy his size. I try not to stare, but it's hard.

"It means with some training you could do something with all that talent."

Pushing myself up, I feel every muscle that was put to use tonight. Some that hadn't been used in a while, or possibly ever. "Like what?" I ask, unsure of what he's getting at.

"Like competing."

"Cage didn't say anything about that," I counter, trying to wrap my mind around the idea of fighting someone. That's what he means, right? The last time I was here, I saw a couple guys fighting in the ring that's on the other side of the gym, but I don't think I could do that.

Just because I have the moves doesn't mean I want to use them.

"He might not have said anything to you, but he did to me. He saw the same thing I saw tonight, and he knows you could make a name for yourself."

"I don't think I can." Admitting that catches me off guard. Normally, I wouldn't say anything. I'd just bolt. When it's fight or flight, I typically choose flight. But something about exerting myself like I just did, batters my defensive walls and makes me want to be more open.

I can't decide if that scares me or makes me feel free.

Maybe a little of both.

"Oh, I think you can," Ozzi counters. "You just have to believe it, because you definitely have what it takes."

Chewing on my bottom lip, I think about what he said—*believe in myself.* I'm not sure I've ever really done that.

Push myself?

Yes.

Save myself?

More than once.

But believe in myself?

"I don't know."

"You don't have to decide tonight," Ozzi says with that crooked smile. "Give it at least a few more sessions. If you want to give this a go, we'll kick it into high gear and talk about what's next. If you just want to come in from time to time and pound the bags, we can work that out too."

Nodding, I meet his eyes again. "Okay."

CHAPTER 7

OZZI

I'm dreaming about eating ice cream when a loud, shrill scream rudely wakes me, nearly making me shit my pants and fall off the couch at the same time.

"What's happening? Who's dying?" I ask, still groggy, as I stumble into Cage and Tempest's kitchen.

Vali turns to face me, panic written all over his face, and that's when I see he's holding Freya and she is *not* happy. I don't think I've ever seen her this upset and to be perfectly honest, it scares the hell out of me.

Her face is red and tear-streaked, and it breaks my heart, but I swear, if her head starts spinning while she projectile-vomits pea soup, I'm out of here.

"She won't stop crying, man, and I don't know what to do. You gotta help me out here," my big brother pleads.

"Will she let me hold her or will that piss her off even more?" I ask, tentatively stepping closer.

"Take her and let's find out. It can't get worse than it already is, right?"

"Shit, man, I don't know but I don't want to tempt fate."

I gently rub the tip of my finger over the top of her hand and begin speaking in what I hope is a soothing voice. "Hey, Freya. Can Uncle Ozzi hold you?"

She watches me for a few seconds, crocodile tears still streaming down her face. But then she hiccups and leans forward, signaling her agreement to my request. As I remove her from Vali's arms and settle her into mine, I hold my breath and hope for the best. She's somewhat calmer than she was a few minutes ago but she's still crying in spurts.

Looking back at Vali, I ask, "Has she eaten?"

"Yeah, she had a bottle and I changed her diaper. She's even napped twice today. What more could she want?"

I know what I want. My dream about ice cream is still floating around my brain and I almost suggest we get some but I know we need to focus on Freya right now, and she can't have ice cream. Tempest would kick my ass if I gave her junk food.

I shrug my shoulders. "I don't know. Naps and food are what make me happy, so I have no idea why she's upset. She didn't get hurt or anything, did she?"

"She's been with Maggie most of the day and when she passed her off to me, she didn't mention anything being wrong." Vali peers down at her, his brows pulled tight. "What if she just doesn't like me?"

If I wasn't worried about Freya, I'd use this opportunity to tease Vali for getting his feelings hurt by a little baby. But even I know now's not the time for that.

"I'm sure that's not it but we need to figure out what's going on. We can't just let her cry like this. If Mom shows up and she's crying, we'll never hear the end of it." I move Freya from my hip, holding her out in front of me so I can talk to her. "What's wrong, sweetheart? Tell Uncle Oz what's bothering you."

Her face is in full pout mode but she's not crying... until I hold her up in the air, trying to see if there's an injury Vali and I have missed. Her body goes rigid and she's back to being pissed off and screaming.

"Sorry, sorry, sorry," I tell her, quickly bringing her body back to mine. "She definitely doesn't like that. Maybe she's missing her parents," I suggest.

Vali's face lights up as he takes his cell phone out of his back pocket. I'm getting ready to tell him we're not calling Cage and Tempest, when he says, "Frankie!"

I'm confused for a second until he clarifies. "Frankie's a nurse, she'll know what to do."

"Oh, yeah, that's true. Great idea, bro." My body sags in relief, knowing we have someone in the family who can give us some answers.

Vali dials Frankie's number then puts the call on speaker and holds it between us.

"Hey, Vali, what's up?" Frankie asks, sounding busy. But when she hears Freya's whimpering she tells someone she'll be right back and then the background noise grows quiet. "What's wrong with the baby?"

Frankie's tone is clipped and I'm worried we caught her at a bad time.

"She's been crying for a while," Vali says, running a hand through his hair as he makes eye contact with me and then focuses back on Freya. "It's just me and Ozzi. Mom and Dad went to Knoxville to pick up some supplies for their remodel, and Mr. and Mrs. Cassidy drove to Merryville for a doctor's appointment. Maggie left about an hour ago to go work at the feed store."

She must hear the desperation in his voice because she sighs and then softens her tone. "Okay, well, don't get too worked up. Babies cry... a lot. She might be teething. Does she feel hot?"

"Not really, unless she's crying," he answers.

"It's hard for me to guess exactly what's going on without actually examining her. Unfortunately, I don't get off work for couple of hours but I promise I'll come to check her out as soon as I can. In the meantime, why don't you or Ozzi go to the grocery store and get some of those baby popsicles that are really just frozen electrolyte drinks? Eating something cold will soothe her gums if she's teething and the electrolytes will keep her hydrated. Plus, it may be a fun treat that will distract her from whatever's bothering her."

I *knew* ice cream was the answer. Ice cream solves all problems.

"I'll go!" I quickly volunteer, handing Freya back to Vali and grabbing my keys off the kitchen counter. He doesn't look too happy to be stranded with the baby but I'm out the door before he can protest.

Once I'm in the Piggly Wiggly, I head straight for the frozen foods section, specifically, the ice cream section, searching for my favorite flavor of Blue Bell.

51

If you're from Texas, it's really the only choice, and I'm not even sure if it's sold in Tennessee. But honestly, I'll take just about anything at this point.

When I locate the familiar tub with its beautiful golden lid, I nearly weep with joy.

They even have Chocolate Chip Cookie Dough.

This small ass town really isn't so bad.

Of course, thanks to this discovery, I'll have to work out double time tomorrow between clients, but it's fucking worth it.

Unfortunately, I don't see any kind of frozen treats for babies, and I definitely can't find anything with the word "electrolytes" on the box, so I'm at a loss at what to do.

When I glance around the aisle, I don't see anyone I can ask, which means I've got to find someone.

Vali will murder me without a second thought if I come back with only a tub of ice cream.

Checking my watch, I realize I've already been gone for almost twenty minutes. And if Freya's still crying like she was when I left, I'm quickly running out of time.

I'm practically jogging from aisle to aisle, searching for an employee. The stares I'm getting aren't surprising. Not only am I running around carrying three gallons of ice cream, but when you're as tall as I am, you get used to people staring.

It never fails that someone will inevitably ask me how tall I am and then usually need my assistance reaching something on a top shelf. I've been tempted to find a short person and ask them to get something off the bottom shelf for me, just to see their reaction.

Finally, I spot a woman in a red Piggly Wiggly vest and call out to her. "Hey, ma'am! I need some help."

When the woman turns, I realize it's Willow and I nearly drop my precious frozen cargo.

She seems to be as surprised as I am but handles it better. Her smile is polite, but not warm. She's professional, but not very welcoming, definitely giving off an *I'll help you because I have to but don't fuck with me* vibe.

I dig it.

Before I can explain what I need, she turns and grabs a shopping cart and pushes it toward me. "Why don't you put your items in here for safe keeping."

"Good idea, thanks." I tell her, as I place the cartons in the basket.

When I turn to look at her, she's staring at me with her brows furrowed, like she's still trying to figure me out or something. And the feeling is mutual.

"So, you need help with something?" she asks, holding my gaze.

"Yeah, do y'all have frozen electrolytes for babies?"

Now she's looking at me as though I've lost my mind and I almost start thinking the same but remember Frankie, an actual medical professional, told me what to get and she can't be wrong.

I decide to try again. "You know, those little popsicles that have electrolytes for babies that won't stop crying?"

Willow is clearly confused but I don't know any other way to describe what I'm looking for.

"You have a baby?" Her question catches me off guard and I wonder why that would be so weird or surprising to her.

"Well, she's not my baby, she's my niece, Cage's daughter. The whole family is taking care of her while he and Tempest are on their honeymoon. Vali and I are in charge right now and we can't get her to stop crying. We called Frankie, our brother Gunnar's girlfriend who's a physician's assistant, and she said to give Freya some frozen thing that has electrolytes until she can come and check her out."

I'm pretty sure that's the most I've said to Willow since meeting her and I'm feeling a little winded, but I'm going to blame that on the urgency of this situation.

Willow's eyes brighten before she replies, "I think I know what you're talking about. Follow me."

And so I do.

I also make sure to focus on my ice cream as I walk behind her and not her fine ass, even though it's just as tempting.

Ice cream, I can have.

Willow, I cannot.

When she stops walking, I see we're in the baby aisle. Literally across the store from the frozen section.

"Here you go." She hands me a box of plastic tubes filled with electrolytes like I asked for but these tubes are definitely not cold.

"They don't come already frozen? Freya needs them now. How long will it take for them to freeze?"

Willow shrugs. "Probably a couple of hours. What, exactly, are her symptoms?"

"She just won't stop crying but she's not running a fever or anything."

She pauses for a moment—her brows knitting tightly back together. "Is her stomach tight?"

I think back to when I was holding her and remember her tensing when I held her up in front of me. "Yeah, her whole little body felt tense, but I just figured it was from her crying and being upset."

Willow scans the shelves until she finds what she's looking for and hands me another box. "Try this while you wait for the fluids to freeze."

"What is it?"

"It's for gas relief in babies. It's pretty magical."

"How do you know so much about babies?" I can't help but ask.

Not looking at my eyes, she answers, "I was around quite a few babies while growing up. I picked up some tips along the way."

The way she answers me is kind of odd. She could've said she had a younger brother or sister or cousin, even, but she doesn't go into specifics.

It's easy to see Willow is a mystery—keeping her cards close to her chest—but it's also easy to see she prefers it that way.

54

And that just makes me want to know her more.

"Well, you obviously have more experience than I do, so thanks for your help."

"I can ring you up if you're ready." She points to a cash register and starts walking toward it.

Just like earlier, I follow her without a word.

Willow is quiet as she rings up my few items. As I'm paying for the ice cream and baby stuff, without thinking it through, I blurt out, "Wanna come home with me?"

"Excuse me?" Her eyes are narrowed as she places her hands on her hips and two thoughts fly through my head. One, damn, she's pretty. And two, that glare will definitely help her win bouts.

But, then I realize what I asked and how it came across and I feel like such a douche nozzle.

"I didn't mean it like that," I say, holding up a hand in surrender. "I swear. I just thought, if you were about to get off work, you could come over and meet Freya. Maybe make sure I give her the gas drops correctly? I'll even share my ice cream with you."

I give her the most innocent-looking expression I can and pray it works.

Cage will kill me if I fuck this up.

Willow thinks on it for a second, chewing her bottom lip in the process. She surprises us both when she says "okay". I can tell by the way she blinks her dark lashes and pulls her head back, like she can't believe what just came out of her mouth.

I want to laugh at her reaction to her response, but I don't want to push my luck, so I tamp down my amusement and grab my grocery bags. To my credit, I even hold back a wink and instead, just give her a nod of my head.

"We're in the apartment above the gym. Feel free to come on up when you get there."

CHAPTER 8

WILLOW

This entire scenario feels familiar.

I'm sitting in my truck outside of Viking MMA, questioning my life choices.

Why did I say I would come here?

What is it about this place?

And the men? Or Vikings, rather.

At first, I thought it was just a clever name for a gym, but quickly realized it was an accurate description of the men who run it. So far, I've met Cage, and he's a hulking man with cut muscles, chiseled features, and a full blond beard.

And then there's Ozzi. He's… well, he's not as big as Cage, but still muscular. And his blue eyes are what get me. Every time I try not to look at him, they draw me in.

Even today in the Piggly Wiggly I tried to ignore the pull. I tried to just help him find what he was looking for and go back to doing my job. But I couldn't. One second I was busying myself with organizing the shelves, waiting for customers, and the next I was ensnared in Ozzi Erickson.

Fully engaged in his woes about his niece.

I'm also a sucker for babies.

When he asked me how I knew so much about them, it was on the tip of my tongue to spill the details, which is totally unlike me. I never tell too much, only enough to get by. Even my relationship with Krista, who's my closest friend, is very superficial. She barely knows my full name, let alone anything about my past.

And there I was, standing in the baby aisle, getting ready to tell my life story to a virtual stranger.

Now, I'm sitting outside the gym, trying to talk myself out of going in there and inserting myself even further into this setting... these people's lives.

What no one knows about me, something I barely admit to myself, is I want connections.

I long for a deep friendship.

I want a family.

That thought makes me think of Hazel, but I can't let myself go there right now.

The harsh reality of my life is that every person I've ever been attached to has either betrayed me or left me. Or both. And after so many years of being abandoned and pushed aside, it's hard for me to let my guard down.

So, why am I here?

The truth is I don't know the answer to that question, but instead of letting that scare me off, I decide to ignore the indecision and fear and get out of the truck.

Walking into the gym, I notice it's unusually quiet. But it is early afternoon and I've only been here in the evening, when the gym is buzzing with activity.

"Hello?" I call out, looking around the space.

There are a couple guys sparring in the ring, but other than that, I don't see anyone. One guy is Cage and Ozzi's brother. I've seen him once before. He's another larger-than-life Viking, looking a lot like Cage and Ozzi, with longer hair, but the same piercing blue eyes.

Neither of the men hear me come in, so I watch them for a minute.

His movements are so fluid.

His fists are fast.

And his kicks are swift, taking out the other guy.

I feel myself tense, waiting for something—retaliation, anger, pain. But all I hear is laughter as Gunnar leans over the guy and sticks out his gloved hand, helping him off his ass.

"Fuck," the guy groans, still laughing. "I think I'm done for the day."

"No way, sucker," Gunnar says, jumping around the ring on the balls of his feet. "We still need three more rounds. You know Cage probably has cameras set up, making sure we check off everything on his training checklist."

The guy puts his hands on his knees as he pants, and after a few moments, he pops back up. "Okay, let's go."

When they start sparring again, I look around, wondering what I'm supposed to do. But then I remember what Ozzi had said—*we're in the apartment above the gym.* Eyeing the stairs, I walk over to them and glance up, seeing the apartment Ozzi alluded to, but no sign of him.

"Hello?" I call out again and I'm met with a baby's cry.

Yep, definitely in the right place.

"Up here," Ozzi says, appearing at the top of the step with a baby strapped to his chest.

Tentatively, I make my way up the stairs, still asking myself what the hell I'm doing here.

"Did the gas drops work?" I ask, heading to the top and coming to a stop in front of Ozzi and the baby.

Ozzi peers down at the baby. "Yeah, I think they did. She's still a little fussy, but nothing like earlier."

"Can I see her?" I ask instinctively, reaching out to brush the top of her head.

He looks up at me, eyeing me cautiously for a second. But then he must see something that puts him at ease, because he nods and lifts her from the carrier, handing her over to me.

"Hey, baby," I coo, bringing her to my chest and taking a deep inhale of her little head. It smells like baby shampoo and lavender. "Are you having a rough day?"

With a slight bounce in my step, I walk over to the large, plush couch that's against one wall and lay her down on her back. One time, I was placed in a foster home temporarily and the man and woman had just had twin boys six months prior. They were so cute and I loved being there. It was one of the times I wished my foster family would adopt me.

But I remember one night when one of the twins was super fussy and it woke me up. I walked into the nursery to find Gwen, the mother, doing funny little exercises with his legs. She said it helped move the gas out of his belly. Sure enough, a few minutes later, he let out the loudest fart I'd ever heard from a baby, and the next thing we knew, he was sound asleep.

When I start to bicycle her legs, Ozzi walks over and sits down on the other side of her. "What are you doing?"

"Helping work some gas out of her tummy," I tell him, focusing on the baby. But when I feel the tension rolling off him, I look up to see his troubled expression. "Don't worry, I'm not going to hurt her."

"I know," he says, his brows furrowing. "I just… I hate that I don't know what to do for her."

The sincerity in his tone is evident and it's obvious how much he loves his niece.

"Well, watch what I'm doing so you'll know for next time."

Ozzi lets out a humorless laugh. "Let's hope there won't be a next time."

I shake my head. "Babies are kind of like little walking time bombs. You just never know when they're going to erupt."

About that time, Freya lets out a continuous stream of little toots.

Ozzi laughs again, and this time it's full of amusement. "Freya," he says, leaning over the baby. "That's my girl. Put it here." He takes her little fist and bumps it to his.

When Freya coos, I feel a sense of peace wash over me. There's something about soothing a baby that soothes me.

"Is she feeling better?" a male voice asks from the doorway that I'm assuming goes to a bedroom. When I glance up, I see another guy I recognize from the gym. He's definitely another brother, but he has ash blonde hair and darker blue eyes.

"Oh, hey," he says when he sees me. "You must be Willow."

"Uh… yeah, I just came to see if I could help with the baby," I tell him, running my palms down my thighs.

"This is my brother Vali," Ozzi says, picking Freya up.

Vali walks forward, smiling down at his niece. "You obviously worked some magic. She hasn't been this happy or content all day."

"Dude," Ozzi says. "You should've heard her. Willow did these exercises with her legs and she let out some wicked gas."

Releasing out a chuckle, I glance back to the stairs, thinking I should probably go now.

"Is that all that was wrong with you?" Vali asks in a high-pitched tone as he takes the baby from Ozzi and holds her up in front of him. "You little stinker. If we would've known all you needed to do was fart, we wouldn't have worried so damn much."

Just as I'm thinking about making an excuse to leave, I hear footsteps on the stairs.

"Okay, where's the baby?" a female voice says, sounding winded like she'd run the whole way here. "I tried to break away earlier but just couldn't make it happen. And then, as I was leaving Merryville, I—"

Her montage breaks off abruptly when she reaches the stairs and I turn to see a familiar face.

"Frankie?" I squeak, my heart speeding up to racehorse fast.

"Willow?"

"Wait, you two know each other?" Ozzi asks.

I swallow as my eyes meet hers, but there's a flash of knowing and I feel myself relax. Frankie would never betray me. Our history is brief, but in a short week, she proved trustworthy. And she helped me when I had no one else to turn to and nowhere else to go.

"We met in Merryville," Frankie says, leaving it at that. "But we haven't seen each other in… what? Two years?"

Yeah, it had been almost two years since I'd showed up at the women's shelter, seeking refuge.

Forcing a smile, I nod. "Yeah, it's been a while."

"Well, it's good to see you." The way she looks at me and then looks away, I know she means that in a deeper sense than what it comes across. She's glad to see me healthy, safe, and alive.

One thing I remember about Frankie is that from the moment we met, I saw something in her I identified with. It was like she understood me on a level only someone who had been through tough shit would understand. She never pried for information and she gave me a safe place to land, helping me get back on my feet.

I'll always be grateful.

She could give me the Spanish Inquisition, asking a million questions, but she doesn't.

I'm grateful for that as well.

However, I would like to know what her connection is to Ozzi and Vali. Is she dating one of them? Related? But I don't ask.

"Looks like y'all figured it out," she says, walking over to inspect Freya. "She seems totally content now."

"That's all Willow," Ozzi says, moving next to them. "She's a miracle worker."

"It was just gas," I say, waving off Ozzi's inflated assessment of the situation. "And I should probably get going. I need to—"

"Stay," Vali says, glancing over at me. "We rescheduled all the classes for today and Maggie is bringing a lasagna her mom made over for dinner."

I have no clue who Maggie is, but I do love lasagna. And the rescheduling of classes explains why the gym is so quiet.

Also, I can't remember the last time I had a meal with other people, especially a meal made by a mom. My mouth is already watering at the prospect, but a *no* is still on the tip of my tongue.

"You'll hurt our feelings if you bail," Vali adds. "We're going to get the impression you only like the baby."

That makes me laugh and I see Frankie crack a small smile.

"Well, I am kind of partial to babies," I hedge, even surprising myself with the teasing tone that comes out of my mouth.

"Great, go set an extra plate," Vali says, turning to Ozzi. "And I'll call Maggie and ask her to pick up a bottle of wine. I think we could all use a drink."

Frankie gives me a covert wink. "I'm going down to tell Gunnar that we're eating as soon as Maggie gets here."

Gunnar.

So, that's the connection.

She's with Gunnar, the other brother and beast of a fighter I saw in the ring earlier.

I can tell by the way she says his name there's admiration and familiarity there. Are they dating? Engaged? Married? And what about the rest of these guys? I'm assuming Maggie is someone special to Vali. Does Ozzi have a girlfriend as well?

Not that it's any of my business.

Or that I care.

He's only my trainer, if I can even call him that, since I haven't decided if I'm going to continue doing this MMA thing.

"Need some help?" I ask Ozzi as he starts setting a long table that sits out in the middle of the room. From downstairs, you'd never guess that this amazing apartment is up here.

It's so open and inviting.

Much more so than my tiny trailer.

"Could you grab some glasses from that cabinet?" he asks, pointing above the sink.

Doing as he asks, I glance back to see there are six plates, so I pull out six glasses. The two of us work in tandem, setting the table. It's not fancy, but it feels like a dream. I've always wanted to be a part of a big family like this.

Not that I'm part of this family, but I let myself pretend for a moment.

"I'm here," a chipper voice calls up the stairs. "Where's Freya? Is she feeling better?"

When I glance up, I see Maggie, looking regal and beautiful, a bag thrown over her shoulder and a large pan in her hands.

"Let me help," I say, going to her and taking the still-warm dish from her.

It smells amazing.

"Hi Willow," she says with a bright smile and a bit out of breath as she hands off the dish. "I see you've met the crowd. I'm Vali's wife." The way she beams over at him where he's sitting on the couch playing with the baby floods my chest with warmth. "I really love that I get to say that now... out loud."

I'm lost for a second before Ozzi jumps in. "Well, that's what happens when you elope to Vegas and keep secrets from your family."

I take her proffered hand. "Ah, I get the connection now. And, for what it's worth, I think eloping is romantic."

Maggie turns her smile back to me. "I knew I'd like you."

Warmth creeps up my cheeks and I hope it's not noticeable. Normally, I don't blush...like ever. But there's something about this freaking family that makes my walls come down and for the dozenth time since I walked up those stairs, I'm positive I should leave.

I don't belong here.

I don't belong anywhere.

But I especially don't belong here—in the middle of this big, seemingly loving, family. This isn't me. I don't do dinners with strangers. Shit, I don't do dinners with friends. Krista and I have only eaten at the same time in the breakroom, and even that has only happened a handful of times in the six months I've been working at the Piggly Wiggly.

"And look at you," Maggie says, moving from in front of me to Vali, holding out her arms as she silently demands the baby. Vali doesn't hesitate to give her up and Maggie immediately cuddles her to her chest. "I heard you had a bad day, but you look as perfect as ever."

It's obvious this baby is seriously loved. And doted on. Exactly how a baby should be.

"Willow saved the day." Vali's words intensify the heat in my cheeks.

Maggie turns to look at me, giving me another warm smile, just as Frankie and Gunnar come up the stairs. He's still sweaty from his time in the gym, but he's now wearing a shirt.

"Something smells good," he says, clapping his hands and rubbing them together.

"Lasagna," Maggie announces. "Oh, and I brought a salad and bread, but they're still in the bag."

"What about the wine?" Vali calls out as she goes to the kitchen to finish preparing the food.

Maggie smiles, bringing Freya away from her chest so she can see her face. "Yes, Uncle Vali, I remembered the wine."

Everyone starts claiming seats at the table and I feel frozen in place, until Ozzi catches my attention and motions to a seat to the right of him. Still feeling like I'm on the verge of fight or flight, I take the seat.

Once the food starts being passed, I'm relieved that the conversation is random and no one seems to even acknowledge that a stranger is sitting at the table.

Mostly, they focus on Freya, who's in a highchair at the head of the table.

With Maggie on one side and Vali on the other, they cut up tiny pieces of the lasagna noodles and let her pick them up off the tray with her chubby little hands.

As I take my first bite, I force back a moan of approval. "Oh, gosh, this is good," I mutter.

"Mrs. O'Neal is a good cook," Ozzi says before taking a large bite of salad.

"She's the best," Vali chimes in.

Glancing down the table, I see Frankie watching me out of the corner of her eye. I'm sure she has questions, but I'm relieved she hasn't asked them. Surprisingly, no one does and I make it through the entire meal without anyone putting me on the spot.

They include me in their conversations.

I listen and laugh at their banter.

Sitting back, I watch them interact, noticing their closeness and similarities, but also their differences.

Gunnar is sweet, especially with Frankie, and I really like that for her.

Vali is a little more serious, but I can also see he has a fun side.

Ozzi is kind of a smart-ass, but he's also charming.

At first glance, I would've guessed he's younger than Gunnar, but through the course of dinner, I find out he's older, by two years. Vali is the middle child and someone named Viggo is the oldest, with Cage falling right under him.

"Do you have a big family?" Gunnar asks.

His question is innocent and I know he's not prying for information, but it doesn't make it easier to answer. "No," I say, fidgeting with the napkin that's clutched in my hand. "When I was little, it was just me and my mom."

I leave it at that, because that's the truth, but it's all I'll be sharing. Anything else would be too complicated and messy and I'm just not ready for that.

Thankfully, Freya's babbling saves me from any further questions and all the attention is directed back to her.

When I'm ready to leave, Ozzi walks me downstairs and waits for me to get into my truck before locking the front door of the gym behind him. It's a sweet gesture, and like everything else tonight, something I'm not used to.

Before I put my truck into drive, I sit for a moment, letting my mind wander over the past few hours. From Ozzi showing up at the Piggly Wiggly to having dinner with the Ericksons—it was all so unexpected.

I don't have much of that in my life these days, but I can honestly say I enjoyed it.

And that scares me, because it's easier for me to pretend like my life is fine the way it is when I don't know what I'm missing out on.

CHAPTER 9

OZZI

*W*hen I walk across the gym to the heavy bags, I see the long dark, sleek hair I've come to associate with Willow Bernard. She's pulling it up off her neck and tying it into a high ponytail, making my fingers tingle.

Would the strands be as soft as they look?

Clearing my throat, I get her attention in the mirror and give her a nod. "Ready to kick some ass?"

Her eyes stay on mine for a long moment and I swear there's something that passes between us. And not for the first time, I wonder if she's thought about me as much as I've thought about her over the past few days.

Shit, last night when I walked her downstairs, I'd fought the instinct to ask her to call me when she got home so I'd know she made it safely. Which, again, is ridiculous.

"Can I ask you something?" she says, turning around to face me, her expression unreadable.

Nodding again, I grab a set of gloves and some tape and walk toward her. "You can ask me anything." I mean it. Unlike her, I'd give her any information she wants.

I'm a goddamn open book.

I just wish I could say the same for her, but even her off-handed comments give me whiplash.

First, she told me yesterday at the Piggly Wiggly that she was around a lot of kids growing up. So, I assumed she's part of a large family, like ours.

But then yesterday evening, when Gunnar asked about her family, she said it was just her and her mom, which made it sound like she's an only child.

The mystery surrounding Willow Bernard keeps building.

"Do you really think I'm any good at this?"

Picking my head up, I realize how close we are—so close I can see that her brown eyes are flecked with green—and also how serious she is.

And she has really long, dark lashes.

"You're really fucking good," I mutter as I begin to wrap tape around her wrists.

I can see the skepticism written all over her face. "You don't believe me."

Shaking her head slightly, she meets my gaze again. "I've never been good at anything."

The thick veil that's always shrouding Willow lifts momentarily and I see past the hard façade. Under her hard-as-nails exterior is a girl who's unsure of herself and looking for approval, whether she wants to admit it or not.

As a trainer, it's my job to see those types of things and look deeper than surface level, seeking out my clients' strengths and weaknesses.

Willow's strengths are obvious. Her natural talent and drive are hard to miss. Shit, anyone could see it. Even if they didn't know what they were looking for, they'd see her and think, *this girl's got something special.*

Her weaknesses, however, are buried deep. But the more I'm around her and the more she lets down her guard, I can see those just as clearly. She lacks confidence, whether that stems from her childhood or inexperience, I don't know yet, but I plan to find out. She also doesn't see herself clearly, which adds to the skepticism.

If she'd only step outside of herself, get out of her head, she'd see what I see—someone who is strong, capable, and a force to be reckoned with.

"I beg to differ," I say, stepping around her and going to the bag. "I've never seen raw talent like yours. Cage saw it too. You can deny it if you want, but that would really suck because I think you could do something great with it. However, no one is forcing you to do this. If you're done, then just say you're done and walk away. No harm, no foul."

This is my version of tough love, and I don't really mean it. If she tries to walk out the door right now, I'm not above begging her to give it one more try. The thought is crazy, because I've never begged anyone to do anything. But that's how much I believe in her.

"What's in it for me?" she asks, sounding defensive or like she's looking for an argument.

I chuckle, shaking my head.

Fuck if I don't want to rile her up and give her what she's asking for. I bet a pissed off Willow Bernard is a sight to see, but honestly, it's counterproductive for me at the moment.

I need her to get on the same page and if I know her like I think I do, it's going to have to be her idea. No one is going to force her to do anything by arguing their point or otherwise.

"There might not be anything in it for you," I say, being as honest as I can be. "But, on the other hand, there might be a lot."

"Like what?"

She steps around and positions her fists in front of her face, readying herself to attack the bag. When I don't say anything, she strikes.

For a few minutes, she pounds the heavy leather relentlessly and I see a spark from her I haven't before. It's brighter and burns hotter. Her eyes find mine and she holds my gaze as she punches… over and over and over.

"The competition you mentioned," she says, taking a step back from the bag to catch her breath. "Would it be for money?"

I nod, wondering where she's going with this.

I'd love for her to be all in, but like I said, I need it to be her idea—her want, her desire.

"Do you think I have a chance to win?"

Nodding again, I step around the bag until I'm practically toe-to-toe with her. Placing my hands on my knees, I look her straight in her gorgeous brown eyes. "I think you'd kick ass."

"And if I don't?"

Shrugging, I shake my head. "We'll cross that bridge when we get there."

"Would I have to pay back money for these sessions?"

That's one thing I've definitely figured out about Willow, money is a stumbling block. She was hung up about it during our first session. And after talking to Cage, I know she made her way here via Hank. She auditioned for a spot on his stage, and he knew she wasn't an ideal candidate for the job, so he sent her our way.

Thank fuck for that.

"No, you won't owe us anything."

"But if I do win, then what?"

Shrugging again, I tilt my head, thinking before I speak. "We'll take a small percentage, nothing too crazy."

She breathes deeply, filling her chest and then exhaling before dropping her head.

"I can't believe I'm saying this," she mutters, almost to herself, before continuing. "I really need to make some money. The logical part of my brain is telling me to find another job, but something inside me," she says, pointing to her chest as she brings her eyes back up to meet mine. "Something in here is telling me to do this."

That veil is down and it's like I can see into her soul. If I'm being honest, it scares the shit out of me, because it makes me feel things I haven't felt in a long time, if ever.

A connection.

Attraction.

Investment in someone else's life.

"I need—" she begins before stopping herself from saying more.

There's a plea on the tip of my tongue and I have to bite down on the inside of my cheek to keep it from spilling out. *Tell me what you need, Willow.*

"I'm going to keep my options open," she finally says. "If a second job opportunity comes up, I can't promise that I won't take it and that it won't interfere with our sessions. But if nothing comes up, I'll be here."

My family has always told me I'm afraid of commitment—never wanting to be tied down anywhere, always willing to go where the four winds take me. But I might've met my match with Willow.

She could possibly have me beat.

In more ways than one.

"Why do you need money?" I ask the question before thinking better of it and a shadow passes over Willow's face, taking all expression with it.

"I don't want to talk about it," she says, turning her back to me and facing the bag.

That's fine.

I don't need to know all of her secrets to turn her into a kick-ass fighter.

CHAPTER 10

WILLOW

*A*s I'm making a PB&J for breakfast a glob of strawberry jelly falls down the front of my work shirt. Grabbing a washcloth from my tiny bathroom, I go to work on the spot. Thankfully, my shirt is black so at least I don't need to change because it's already been a morning.

First, I spilled what little bit of milk I had left.

Then, I realized I forgot to wash and dry my favorite pair of jeans before I went to bed last night.

Now, I'm making a mess all over my shirt and I need to leave for work in five minutes.

But in all honesty, I've been in quite the mood these last couple of days.

My mind has been so consumed with thoughts of Hazel and my mother that I can't sleep at night. I lie there, staring at the ceiling while I toss and turn. I've tried everything—reading my book from the library, a late-night snack, hot tea—and nothing helps.

Last night's session with Ozzi was particularly disarming. There's something about being there, in that gym with him, that hammers at my walls. The more I lose myself in the physicality of it all, the more I find myself coming undone.

I was on the verge of walking out last night.

The more I opened up to Ozzi, the more I wanted to keep doing it.

And that scared me.

It's been seven days since I got the call from the Johnson County Sheriff's Office. Sue, the deputy who called, said she'd be in touch. But I haven't heard back from her. I thought about calling her yesterday from work, but I couldn't bring myself to do it.

Yesterday evening, after I left the Piggly Wiggly and before I went to Viking MMA, I stopped by the library before it closed. I needed to return the book I'd been reading and check out a new one, but I also wanted to use their computer to do some research.

A quick Google search brought me to my mother's brief obituary and something about seeing it in black and white made it feel more real.

Final.

Now that I've had some time to let it sink in, I have felt something besides numbness. There's an echo of sadness for a life lost. The person that brought me into this world, regardless of how horrible she was at being a mother, is gone.

I would've liked to have been able to see her one last time. I'm not sure what I would've said, but having that opportunity stolen from me feels sadly poetic and on par with the rest of my life.

But more than anything, the news has made me feel untethered.

There was something about the idea of her being out in the world that gave me a sense of belonging, knowing where I came from.

And then there's Hazel. The sister I didn't even know existed, who's also left without a mother or anyone else to call family. When I truly let myself think about it, my heart breaks for her. The only real tears I've shed since Sue's phone call have been for Hazel's loss.

Is she scared?

Feeling alone?

Abandoned?

I know how all of that feels and I want to talk to her and let her know she's not alone.

And then there's that nagging voice in the back of my brain telling me she probably doesn't want to know me. Who am I? A stranger who's going to swoop in and try to save the day?

Snorting to myself as I wrap my sandwich in a paper towel and grab my bag, I shake my head at that thought.

I'm no one's savior.

But I know I won't be able to rest until I've at least tried to do something to help her.

Once I'm at work, I take over at one of the registers and lose myself in the mundane tasks of scanning groceries, making small talk with customers, and trying not to think about the upheaval of my life.

That is until Tony walks over and informs me I have another phone call.

Turning out the light on my register and placing a closed sign on the conveyor belt, I hurry to the office. When I get there, I take a deep breath before picking up the receiver.

"Hello?"

"Willow?" Sue's now familiar voice is both welcomed and not. On one hand, I've been waiting on this call with bated breath, and on the other, I've been dreading it.

"Yeah, hello."

Slowly lowering myself into the desk chair, I try to calm my racing heart.

"This is Sue Harrison again with the Johnson County Sheriff's Department," she says, like I would've forgotten between last week and now.

I almost laugh, because I can promise her I will never forget her name. It's burnt into my memory, along with finding out my mother is dead and that I have a sister.

"How is Hazel?" I blurt out, needing this piece of information like I need my next breath. "Have you seen her or heard from the family who has her?"

"I have," Sue says evenly. "She's doing as well as can be expected."

"What does that mean?" I ask, gripping the coiled cord of the phone.

Sue sighs. "It means exactly what you think it means. She has a bed to sleep in and a roof over her head. They take her to school every day and make sure she's picked up in the afternoon. Food is provided for her, but it doesn't necessarily get eaten."

She pauses for a moment and I digest her words and let out a small sigh of my own.

"Her basic needs are being met, but I think you know what she's going through and it's not easy."

That statement catches me a little off guard and I draw back.

"Willow," Sue continues, "I glanced over your file. I know you've been through a lot and if you're not willing or able to take guardianship of Hazel, that's understandable."

Sitting up straight, I square my shoulders. "I want her. I know I might not be the most qualified or ideal person for her to go to, but I'm the only family she's got... and she's all I've got."

Those words aren't easy for me to say out loud, but I do it.

I do it for Hazel.

And I do it for myself.

This might be a long shot, but I want to take it.

"Alrighty," Sue says and I can hear some papers shuffling in the background. "Do you have an email address? I have the paperwork you'll have to fill out to petition the court. That will be our first step."

The court.

Right.

As I clear my throat, I try to calm my racing heart. "Yeah, I have an old email account. I haven't used it in a while, but I should still be able to get to it."

I opened the email account after I aged out of the system, and let my social worker know, just in case my mother ever wanted to get in touch with me. But after months of faithfully checking it, without ever hearing from her, I lost hope.

"You'll need to bring the completed paperwork to the Johnson County Courthouse, along with the filing fee. If you can't afford to pay the fee, I can get you a waiver, but that will take a little more time."

"I can pay it," I assure her, without even asking how much.

But it doesn't matter, because I realize at this moment, I'll do whatever it takes to get Hazel.

After I give her my email address, she tells me a little more information about Hazel's placement. She's with a family that lives just outside of Mountain City. They've been fostering children for the past ten years and have a good track record, which puts my mind at ease a little.

"I'm going to keep a good eye on her until we can get this handled," Sue assures me. "In the meantime, I'm going to contact the caseworker. I think it's time the two of you meet."

* * *

"GOOD AFTERNOON," a friendly voice says as I walk through the doors of the Green Valley Library.

Smiling at the familiar face, I give her a nod before heading straight to the bank of computers. When I check the time on my watch, I see I only have about thirty minutes before they close, but that should be plenty of time to pull up my email and print out the papers Sue sent over.

Before we ended our call earlier, I took down her direct number and promised I'd be in touch.

That is, after I drive to Merryville tomorrow and buy a phone.

My trip to the library this afternoon is multipurpose. I need these forms to fill out, but I also know they have a community board where people list things for rent and sale, so I'm hoping to check that out and see if I can find a different place to live that's in my meager budget.

Also, I want to check out a couple books on adoption and parenting.

Ever since I was little, even before I went into foster care, I've had a love affair with books. I firmly believe knowledge is power, so I'm hoping to gain a little before I have to face a court or a nine-year-old who just lost her mother.

Thankfully, I remember the password to my email account and I'm able to access the files Sue sent over. After sending them to print, I go up to the desk to check out.

"It will be one dollar and fifteen cents," the lady behind the desk tells me.

Pulling out my wallet I pay for the printing. "I know you're getting ready to close, but could you direct me to any books you might have on adoption and parenting."

She eyes me curiously for a moment, but without question, she walks around the desk and nods toward her left. "Over here."

Quickly, she pulls out two books from one shelf and then turns to another. "These are my recommendations," she says confidently. "But my best piece of advice is to go into it with an open mind and heart."

Accepting the books, I give her a grateful smile. "Thanks."

When she pats my hand, it's a gesture that makes my eyes well up with unshed tears. Or maybe it's the occasional crash with reality that does it. Whatever it is, I clear my throat and take a deep breath through my nose.

When we get back to the front, she goes about checking the books out to me while I check out the bulletin board.

There are a few listings—a couple houses for sale and a garage apartment for rent.

"Do you know Faye Alberty?" I ask, reading the information on the strip of paper.

She smiles, her eyes still trained on the books. "Oh, yes. Everyone knows Miss Faye."

From the way she says her name, it sounds like she thinks fondly of the person in question. There's not a lot of information listed, but it does say there are two bedrooms, which is my biggest requirement.

When she hands me my stack of books, I place the forms on top and tuck the strip of paper into my pocket. "Thanks so much for your help."

"Any time," she says. "And good luck."

Taking a deep breath, I nod. "Thank you."

I'm going to need it.

After the library, I go home to change clothes before heading to Viking MMA.

Ever since my conversation with Sue this afternoon, I've felt like I'm on autopilot.

Get the forms printed.

Come up with a game plan.

Execute game plan.

Showing up for a training session with Ozzi feels like another automatic response, even though it has nothing to do with my current issues. I know he said I could compete and possibly make money at it, which could help me in the long run, but it does nothing for my current situation.

So, again, why am I here?

Unlike the previous time I've questioned myself about it, I don't dwell on it tonight. Instead, I throw myself into training—pouring everything I'm feeling into the bag and sparring with Ozzi. I soak in every piece of instruction, clearing my brain of anything that's not right in front of me.

It's cathartic.

And exactly what I need.

But it also makes me feel exposed, like my skin has been peeled back and everything inside me is on display.

Panting, I brace my gloved hands on my knees and breathe deeply, trying to keep a sudden rush of emotions from flooding to the surface.

"Are you good?" Ozzi asks, his words come out choppy as he catches his breath too.

No.

I want to tell him. I want to spill my guts on this mat and unload all of it—the hurt, the confusion, the worry, the fear. And that makes me even more emotional because I've never wanted to tell anyone, never wanted to allow anyone to see beneath my hard exterior.

When my eyes flood with unshed tears, I turn and try to furiously blink them away, wiping at my face with my forearm.

"Can you take these off?" I choke out, holding my hands out to Ozzi. "Please."

He doesn't say anything or ask any questions, just quietly goes about unlacing the gloves, then unwrapping the tape around my wrists and freeing my hands. The second my hands are free, I walk over to my bag and pull out a towel, burying my face in the familiar scent of my laundry soap.

Taking a few deep breaths, I don't surface until I'm sure I won't break down right here in the middle of the gym.

"I won't be here tomorrow." My words come out almost robotically.

A part of me wants to say I won't be back ever, because I'm scared of the way this place makes me feel, but I know that's a lie.

I'll be back.

"Did you find a job?" Ozzi asks with a tentativeness in his voice that makes me turn to look at him.

His brows are furrowed, and a muscle twitches in his sharp jaw.

"No," I say, averting my gaze because the intensity of his blue eyes is too much. "I have to go to Merryville tomorrow to get a phone."

And depending on what my next phone call with Sue is like, there's a chance I'll be making a trip to Mountain City soon, or at least the Johnson County Court-house to file the papers.

But I don't tell him that part.

I still have boundaries and I'm definitely not ready to tell Ozzi about my dead mother or my newfound sister.

"Did you break yours?"

It takes me a second to register his question. As I put my towel back in my bag and collect my water bottle, I shake my head. "No, I don't have one and I need one."

There's a brief moment of silence and I feel like bolting out the door, but Ozzi stops me with his words.

"You don't have a phone?"

"No."

"That's not safe. You need a phone."

His tone isn't filled with judgment, but something that resembles care and it's such a foreign concept that I don't know what to do with it.

So, in true Willow Bernard fashion, I lash out.

"Don't be such a caveman," I retort, smoothing back my ponytail and squaring my shoulders. "Just because I don't have a dick doesn't mean I can't take care of myself. And I don't need a phone to do that."

Unlike Ozzi's comment, there's a bite to my words and I feel the moment they make contact. His brows go up in a moment of surprise before his expression shifts into concern.

"Willow," he says, holding a hand to his chest. "I didn't mean it like that."

Our eyes meet and I know he's sincere. I knew it before I said what I said. But I'm not used to someone caring about my well-being. It's unnerving, but also feels good and that scares me.

Without a goodbye, I turn and walk out of the gym.

I need some space.

I need to breathe.

I need a reality check and a chance to remember why I don't trust people, especially with my heart, before it's too late.

CHAPTER 11

OZZI

esides ice cream, pizza is the next best food. It's delicious, it's versatile—breakfast pizza for the win—and it's relatively cheap. Takeout pizza is great and homemade is even better. But sometimes you live in a small-ass town, don't feel like cooking, and need a fix, so frozen pizza it is.

Make that *two* frozen pizzas, because leftover pizza is also amazing, regardless of where it comes from.

And that's why I'm at the Piggly Wiggly… to buy frozen pizza.

Not to look for a certain person who I haven't heard from in three days.

I know Willow doesn't need to check in with me and we don't have a schedule that's set in stone, but I assumed she would show up a couple nights ago and she didn't.

Cage and Tempest got back from their honeymoon and the first thing he wanted to know was how things were going with Willow. I told him everything is going great, because when it comes to the girl's skills and training, I couldn't be happier. She's killing it. Every new skill I throw her way she makes it her bitch.

I'm convinced she was Muhammad Ali in another life.

Or an Erickson.

Because the only people I've ever witnessed with this much natural talent are my brothers and my father.

But over the past couple days, I haven't seen her. She hasn't called the gym or left a message at the front desk. I'm hoping she did what she said and got that damn phone. To say I haven't thought about that over the past few days would be a lie. I've replayed our last conversation over and over in my head. Part of me wishes I would've kept my trap shut and not said anything. I feel like Willow and I were on the verge of some sort of breakthrough. But the second I said she needed a phone and that it's not safe for her to be without one, she shut me out again.

I should've seen that coming, but my reaction was simple instinct. In a short period of time, I've come to care for her. I can't help it. She's like a magnet and I'm drawn to her.

And I'm... I don't know, worried, I guess? She's so quiet and secretive and that's all well and good, but not hearing from her makes me automatically think something's wrong. And if something is wrong, does she even have anyone to go to for help?

She was supposed to get a cell phone the other day, so I make a mental note to give her my phone number the next time I see her, which hopefully will be soon. I've already looked for her down three aisles on my way to the frozen food section and I only have a few more to go.

When I glance down aisle number four, I do a double take because just when I was about to give up, there she is.

For a second, I watch as she methodically checks the inventory of coffee pods in front of her, and I can't help but notice she's just as focused on her work here as she is when she's at the gym.

I like that. A lot.

It shows great character and only solidifies my instincts about her—she's a good person and a hard worker and someone I'd like to know more than just in the confines of a gym.

Although, she doesn't seem to get worked up here like she does at the gym. It's pretty common for a workout to bring out strong emotions in people. But I was still caught off guard when it happened with Willow the other night. I think the

86

difference between her and others I've witnessed that happen to is, those people let their emotions out. They welcomed the release. Willow seemed to fight as hard hiding her feelings as she did the punching bag. I'm no shrink but I know she has some things to work out and I'd like to be the one she trusts with those things, if she'd let me.

"Counting k-cups, eh?" I ask a few feet away, not wanting to startle her.

Willow's pencil stops mid-air but she doesn't turn to look at me. "Just another glamorous night at the Pig."

Chuckling, I step closer, eyeing her carefully. "How have you been?"

She blows out a breath before finally facing me. "Did you come here to check on me? Pressure me back into the gym?"

"Whoa." I hold up my hands and narrow my eyes at her. "What's this about pressuring you? Willow, that was never my intent. I thought you were enjoying the sessions but maybe I was wrong. You haven't been at the gym in a few days, so I thought I'd check in with you since I was already here shopping."

I can tell by the tightness in her jaw and the way she draws her full lips into a straight line that she wants me to leave her alone. I've witnessed this display enough now that I'm starting to read her body language. But I want her to know she doesn't scare me. I can take her cold shoulder and her tough exterior.

Growing up in a gym that catered to boxers and fighters with four brothers who never cut me a break, I learned how to handle every situation that was thrown at me.

And I'm no stranger to fighting for what I want, whether that's freedom to forge my own path or the last carton of Blue Bell. It might come as a surprise to most, but I've got just as much Erickson in me as any of my brothers and even though I don't put it all out there in a ring in front of hundreds and thousands of people, I *can* scrap with the best of them.

I've never wanted to fight for a girl before, but Willow is bringing things out in me that I never knew existed. And as with anything else in my life, I'm just rolling with it.

So before giving her the space she's silently asking for, I give it one more try.

"I'm not trying to push your boundaries, Willow. I get that you've got some shit going on in your life that you're not ready to talk about, but when you're ready, I'll be here. I'd like to be your friend, if you'll let me. If you don't want me to be, that's cool too, but don't let that keep you from the gym. I'll even forfeit the privilege of being your trainer, if need be. But I think the sport needs a fresh breath of air like Willow Bernard and I think you need it too."

Willow hangs her head with her eyes closed and I just stand there, watching her, waiting for her to dismiss me.

"I'm sorry." She clears her throat before looking at me again. "I'm really stressed right now and I took it out on you when you have nothing to do with it."

Fuck, why do I have the sudden urge to hold her? My arms are vibrating with the need to wrap around her and pull her to me. But I know she doesn't want that and I shouldn't either, so I try to push the thoughts as far back in my brain as I can.

"Sounds like you could use some pizza and a workout," I offer. "Scratch that. How about a workout then some pizza instead? No one needs to puke tonight."

She gives me a small smile and I consider that a win. I mean, it's practically a KO where Willow is concerned.

"Yeah, okay," she finally says, shaking her head slightly as if she's as much in disbelief as I am that she's agreeing to this spur-of-the-moment invite. "I get off in an hour. Is that too late to stop by the gym?"

"Absolutely not. Come by whenever you're ready." I give her a wink to let her know all is forgiven then head for the frozen food section.

Instead of two, I buy three pizzas.

* * *

A LITTLE OVER AN HOUR LATER, I'm trying not to watch the clock as I organize the equipment when I hear the bell on the front door chime. It's late enough that everyone else is gone. Gunnar isn't even here. He and Frankie left about thirty minutes ago with Vali and Maggie. They went to Genie's to grab a beer. And Cage and Tempest are upstairs in their apartment with Freya.

So, I know it's Willow, but even if fifty people were in the gym, I think I'd still know it's her. The air in the gym shifts the moment she walks through the doors.

"Ozzi?"

"Right here," I answer, as I jog toward the front. "Go ahead and get warmed up. I'm going to lock the door so we're not disturbed." Technically, we're closed but I don't want anyone thinking they can come in just because the lights are on.

I flip the sign on the door to "closed" and turn the lock before grabbing a few towels and meeting Willow by the treadmills. She's already running at a decent pace, so I hop on the machine next to hers and start jogging.

"How do you feel your stamina is doing? Can you tell if it's increasing?" I ask.

Willow thinks for a moment then nods. "Yeah, I can. I'm not nearly as tired and winded as I was when I first started."

"That's great. Stamina is crucial for MMA. We should start working on your flexibility, too. I can show you some yoga moves you can do at home until you feel ready to take a class."

She glances at me quickly so she doesn't lose her balance and asks, "You do yoga?"

I can't help but laugh at her question because it's a common surprise for people who aren't familiar with MMA fighting or training. "Yeah, some. I like staying loose but Gunnar does it every day. He swears it helps with everything: stamina, flexibility, strength, balance, and the mental side of fighting."

"Tell me more about that. The mental stuff."

I'm elated that my little trick worked. I was hoping our conversation would lead to this because I need her to know what she's getting herself into. I also want her to know, even if she never steps foot inside a ring professionally, this will help her if she's open to it.

"Well, you have to be mentally strong as well as physically strong and what that means is, you have to be committed and focused. You know, have your mind set on your goal and not let anyone or anything get in your way. You also have to have the courage it takes to protect yourself while harming someone else. It sounds easy but I promise it's not."

Willow starts slowing down her treadmill until it's at a cool down pace. "I've been meaning to ask about that."

"What's that?"

"Will I really have to hurt someone?"

Before I can answer, she continues. "I know that must sound stupid but I haven't really thought about that side of things until now."

"It's not stupid but it is something you need to think about. And yes, if you choose to fight, you will have to hit, kick, knee, and wrestle your opponent and if you're doing it right, it's gonna hurt them. It may even hurt you, too. That's why I'm bringing it up now. I want you to be prepared."

"What if I don't want to or can't hurt another person?"

At this, I bring my machine to a stop and grab a towel, tossing one to her as well. "That's something you have to figure out for yourself. Just know, it's nothing personal, at least at first. Sometimes opponents will hold a grudge if you kick their ass too hard and want to retaliate the next time you fight. But, if you get in that ring, you must know the person you're facing is going to attack you and you can either lay there and take it or protect yourself and fight back."

"I've never hit anyone before. Even when... well, I've just never thought of myself as a fighter... in any way." She doesn't make eye contact when she says this and I'm dying to know more but I don't pry.

"Only you can change that and only if you want to. Like I've said before, I think you have amazing talent but I'll never force you to do something you don't want to do. You're the boss of your destiny, Willow. I'm just here to help."

She seems to be pondering my words pretty deeply so I try to add some reassurances. "Besides, we'd never send you to a bout without a lot of sparring practice beforehand."

"Will I only spar with you?"

"At first, then we'd find a female fighter to make it a fairer fight."

When she doesn't say anything for a minute or two, I wonder if this is all too much and if I've taken this much-needed conversation a little too far for one night. "You okay?"

"Yeah, I'm just trying to wrap my head around all this. Never did I think I'd be willing to fight and possibly hurt someone for money."

Leaning my back against the treadmill, I cross my arms over my chest and try to help her make sense of all this. "Everyone has their own reasons for doing the things they do. Don't judge yourself so harshly but stay true to yourself. No one is asking you to be anyone other than who you are."

"Wow," she deadpans. "Who knew Viking fighters could be so deep?" The side of her mouth quirks up as though she's trying not to laugh, and I swear I can see a faint blush covering her cheeks.

"Did you just crack a joke?" I ask incredulously.

"You were getting pretty serious there. I had to do something," she explains. Her soft giggle is making my shorts tighten against my crotch and I need to shut that shit down immediately.

Do not get aroused by your client, dickhead.

Willow and I take a quick water break before I start showing her some basic wrestling drills. She's already picked up the fundamental skills for throwing punches, jabs, kicks, and knees and these new skills tonight are no exception.

She's a fucking natural for sure.

An hour later, I can tell that Willow is exhausted, not just in body, but in her mind. The levity from our conversation earlier started to wane about half an hour ago and in its place is heaviness and the stress she mentioned earlier. I can see it in the lines around her eyes and the way she presses her lips together.

When we started sparring, there were a few times I pulled back because I thought she was struggling. But it wasn't physical, it was like she was fighting another mental battle, similar to the other night. But this time, she didn't break.

"How about I go check on those pizzas?"

Willow gives me a thumbs up while she drinks from her water bottle, so I jog over to the stairs and head for the apartment on the opposite side of the gym. Vali was living here before he and Maggie found their own place. So thankfully, I have the entire apartment to myself.

I've heard the horror stories from Gunnar about when he first moved to Green Valley.

His bedroom shared a wall with Tempest and Cage. Every night, when I close my eyes, I thank my lucky stars that I don't have to endure that kind of torture.

While Willow was wrapping up her session earlier, I had come up and popped two pizzas in the oven, so they should be perfect by now. When I open the oven, the sweet aroma of pepperoni and cheese fills the air. My mouth waters as I pull them out and slice them up, putting three pieces each on mine and Willow's plates. If she's as hungry as I am, she'll have no problem eating these. And if she wants more, I'll happily come back for more.

I'd thought about inviting Willow up here to eat but didn't want to make it weird.

Or push my own boundaries.

I mean, come on. There's only so much temptation a man can take and as much as I've tried to fight it, I'm attracted to Willow. And having her up in the apartment, while it's just the two of us, feels too intimate right now.

Grabbing a handful of paper towels, I head back down to the gym. The pizzas smell amazing and I can't freaking wait to dig into them. It'll be a struggle to not embarrass myself while I eat in front of Willow. I'm already moaning and I haven't even had a bite.

When I approach the mats, I don't see Willow and assume she's in the bathroom. So I go about setting up our makeshift pizza picnic, until I hear a sound coming from the corner behind me.

A few feet away, Willow is on her hands and knees, breathing sporadically and shaking.

Not wanting to do more damage than good, I calmly but quickly move to her side and sit on the floor next to her. After scanning her and the area around her, I can see she's not injured so I assume she's having a panic attack. I've never had one before but I've seen other people have them, even Viggo once, so I'm somewhat familiar.

"Hey, Willow, I'm right here," I say, hoping whatever triggered this didn't have anything to do with me. "Is it okay if I touch your back? I promise I'm not going to hurt you."

She doesn't look at me but she nods her head as she lets out a quiet sob, so I gently but firmly place my palm on the middle of her back and begin rubbing circles.

"I need you to breathe for me, okay?" I say, keeping my voice low and even. "Try to take in a long, deep breath then let it out." I follow my own instructions, exaggerating them a bit, to show her what I'm wanting her to do. She eventually brings her head up and watches me for a bit then starts inhaling deeply just like I asked.

A couple of minutes pass, both of us still breathing and looking at each other, until she finally sits back on her heels and wipes at her face, letting out a long exhale.

Her normal olive complexion seems pale, but at least her breathing is back to normal.

That instinct from earlier to wrap her in my arms is back and so strong I have to stand to keep from doing it. Walking over to her bag, I grab her water bottle and hand it to her. She greedily accepts it and begins chugging.

After she empties it, she wipes her mouth with the back of her hand and stands up.

"I should go," she mutters.

"Please don't," I say, my voice soft, yet raw, sounding like I swallowed a handful of gravel.

But it's just this girl and what she's doing to me.

She's the one who just suffered a panic attack but watching her go through that was no picnic. When I look up at her, I can see her eyes are filled with tears and I'm hit yet again with the urge to hold her... soothe her... do whatever I can to make her not hurt so fucking much.

"Ozzi—"

"Willow, stay." I almost plead with her, but I try to remain calm in hopes she'll do the same. I don't want to make a big deal out of what happened because I don't want to make her feel bad about it. She's free to feel however she wants, but I'd also like to keep her around long enough to make sure she's okay. "You don't have to talk about anything you don't want to. But, you do have to help me eat all this pizza. There's no way I can eat two all by myself."

She smiles while rolling her eyes. I can tell by the way her shoulders ease that I've got her, but I go in for a little more to seal the deal. Patting my flat stomach, I inhale deeply. "You wouldn't want me to ruin my figure, would you?" I ask with a wink. "Do you know how much running I'd have to do to work off another whole ass pizza?"

This time, she full on laughs and it's music to my ears. When she sits back down next to me, the relief I feel is indescribable. But I play it off while I get up and grab our food, bringing it back to our spot on the floor.

CHAPTER 12

WILLOW

*O*zzi and I eat in relative silence for a few minutes. I say relative because he groans after each bite of pizza and each time, I have to bite the inside of my cheek to keep from laughing.

I also have to force myself not to think about the sexy sounds and wondering what else could elicit those noises from him.

He's my trainer.

That's it.

And possibly a pseudo-friend.

But nothing else.

Absolutely nothing sexual, which is where my mind goes—straight into the gutter—remembering the couple times I've caught a glimpse of his abs and the smattering of hair that disappears below the waistband of his pants.

His pants that don't necessarily hide everything they should.

When he clears his throat, my face heats because it feels like I've been caught with my hand in the proverbial cookie jar. But then, he says, "Wanna tell me what happened earlier?"

No. That's my knee-jerk reaction. But oddly enough the thought of telling Ozzi about what's going on in my life and what I was experiencing when I felt like I couldn't breathe, doesn't completely freak me out.

"My mom died."

I don't know why I started with that, but it's out of my mouth before I can take it back and I guess it's as good of a place to start as any. It's the catalyst for everything else I'm dealing with right now and I'm still struggling with the reality of it. After days of poor sleep and not being able to shut my brain off, I think I just snapped.

Ozzi is quiet for a moment, but I don't look up at him. I don't want pity if that's all he has to offer. I don't know what I want from him, but pity is definitely not it.

"I'm sorry," he says tentatively. "Was it… was she sick?"

For a minute, I think about his question. She didn't have cancer or anything like that, but she was sick. She had to be. Healthy people don't abuse drugs and choose them over their children. I could take the out and just say yes, but instead, I lean into the truth.

"She died of an overdose… almost two weeks ago."

Ozzi exhales and, out of my periphery, I see him run a hand through his hair. "Shit, Willow. That sucks."

"What sucks even more, is I haven't seen her in fifteen years." The confessions just keep coming. "She could've passed me on the street and not even recognized me. She didn't give a shit about me, but ever since I found out she died, all I can think about is that I didn't get a chance to talk to her. As much as I hate her, I can't help but feel an overwhelming sadness when I think about the fact she's gone."

We're quiet for a moment and I should probably stop there, but I don't.

"They cremated her because they couldn't find me."

My throat is tight, but it doesn't close in like earlier. I can still breathe and I have to wonder if that's because Ozzi is sitting next to me, lending me some of his calmness.

"And now they want me to pick up her remains." I got a call from Sue on my new phone. The first call I received and it was to inform me that what was left of my mother and her possessions were ready to be picked up. "What am I supposed to do?"

The question comes out in a whisper and I'm not really asking Ozzi for his advice, just voicing the reality plaguing my mind for the past couple weeks.

What am I supposed to do?

That goes further than what I should do with my mother's remains. It extends to Hazel and everything I'm getting ready to face when it comes to trying to be her guardian, but I don't have it in me to tackle that one tonight.

"I'm not even going to pretend like I know the answer to that," Ozzi says. "So I'm just going to go with my gut on this one and tell you that you need to do what's right for you. If you feel like you could get some closure, then it might be a good thing. But if all it would bring is more grief, don't do it."

I really like that Ozzi always gives me a choice. He doesn't even know what he's doing when he says things like that. He doesn't know that, for the majority of my life, I never had a choice about anything.

And I realize how much I need that—to feel like I have a choice in my own life.

"Closure might be good," I finally say, giving it some thought. "As much as I don't want to do it, I think I'll regret it if I don't."

Another thing I didn't realize until now is how much I needed to get that off my chest.

My head feels so much clearer and my shoulders feel lighter than they have in two weeks.

Maybe I'll finally be able to get some sleep tonight.

"That day at the Piggly Wiggly, you said you grew up around a lot of kids," Ozzi says, his tone changing to something more conversational. "But then you told Gunnar that it was just you and your mom growing up. I'm not trying to pry, just curious."

Finishing off a bite of pizza, I wipe my hands on my towel. Usually, when people ask about my family, I deflect. Kind of like I did the night in question.

But after opening up to Ozzi about my mom's death, it feels easier to talk about my past.

"Both are true," I say, picking up my water bottle and taking a drink, still feeling thirsty from my training session and the panic attack that followed. "My dad died in a car accident when I was five, so for a couple years, it was just me and my mom. But when I was seven, I went into foster care and I lived with a lot of different families."

When I look over at Ozzi, he's eyeing me with an expression I can't quite put my finger on. It's not pity, thank goodness, but it's more than just pure curiosity. There's something else there and I wonder for a split second what it would've been like to meet Ozzi outside of this scenario.

Would I have talked to him?

Would he have talked to me?

I'm not sure what the answer to either of those questions would be, but I can say I'm glad I met him, regardless of the hows and whys. He's the first person in a long time, maybe ever, I've felt like talking to.

"I'm sure it was nothing like growing up with four rowdy brothers," I say with a chuckle, trying to lighten the mood.

Ozzi grins, shaking his head and making his hair fall in his face. There's something about the action that's so boyish it makes warmth spread through my chest.

"It was a little crazy and not always fun, especially being one of the youngest. Gunnar and I took a lot of shit for being the babies of the family. But he got away with way more than I did and don't ever let him tell you differently."

"Y'all aren't from Tennessee, right?"

Ozzi shakes his head, finishing off his last bite of pizza. "No, Dallas."

"How did you end up here?" I ask, feeling just as curious about Ozzi as he is about me.

"It's kind of a long story, but Cage came here first. He was fighting professionally and messed up his shoulder. When he realized he wouldn't ever fight again, at least not at the level he had been, he came here while he was trying to figure out what he wanted to do with his life. And then the fucker went and fell in love."

He laughs and I can't help but watch the way his blue eyes crinkle at the edges.

"What about the rest of you?" I ask, enjoying this conversation way more than I probably should.

Ozzi shrugs, leaning back and stretching his legs out in front of him. "Gunnar wanted to train with Cage after he graduated from college, so he was next. Then Vali needed to get out of Dallas for a while and that fucker fell in love too."

He pauses for a second, shaking his head. "Shit, Viggo and I are the only two left standing."

"And Viggo is the oldest, right?" I ask, remembering hearing about him last week when we all had dinner.

"Yeah, he's off wandering, living the nomad life."

"What happened to the gym in Dallas?"

Ozzi exhales, pushing himself onto his feet and gathering our plates. "Sold it."

There are so many more questions on the tip of my tongue, but they all feel invasive and I know how it feels to be interrogated, so I hold back.

"More pizza?" Ozzie asks, nodding toward the stairs that lead to the apartment.

"No, I'm good."

I'm just getting ready to tell him I should get going when there's some commotion at the front door. Ozzi and I both turn to look just as Gunnar and Frankie walk inside.

"Frankie left her backpack," Gunnar announces, then sees me. "Oh, hey, Willow. How was the training session?"

"Good," I say, standing to my feet and brushing my hands down the front of my sweatpants, suddenly feeling like I shouldn't be here.

It's late, and our training session was over a long time ago.

And a lot has transpired between then and now.

But Gunnar and Frankie walking in kind of bursts the bubble we've been in, bringing me back to the present and giving me a swift reality check.

"I'm going to run these plates upstairs," Ozzi says, continuing toward the stairs. "Y'all want some pizza?"

"None for me," Gunnar says, rubbing his taut stomach. "Too close to fight night."

"Too late for me," Frankie says with a half-smile. "Eating pizza late at night gives me weird dreams."

Ozzi's footsteps retreat up the stairs and I feel like this is my chance to bail, so I grab my bag and stuff my towel and water bottle inside. "I should get going."

Frankie and Gunnar share a quiet conversation before she turns back to me. "I'll walk you out."

I'm getting ready to tell her she doesn't have to, but I see the unwavering look on her face, and I know the two of us are overdue for a chat.

"Great," I say, forcing a smile. "Could you tell Ozzi thank you for the pizza... and everything?"

Gunnar gives me a nod. "No problem. See ya later."

"See ya."

Frankie and I walk outside into the cool night air and for a moment the only sound is our feet shuffling on the concrete sidewalk. A few of the businesses have signs that are lit and there are quaint streetlamps lined up giving the town a warm glow, but no cars or people.

The second we're away from the door, Frankie wraps her arms around my neck and I hug her back. Neither of us is the super affectionate type, and I don't know about her, but I'm guessing Frankie probably thought she'd never see me again.

I know I thought I'd never see her again.

"I'm so glad to know you're safe," Frankie says, pulling away. "It's good to see you."

"You too," I tell her, giving her a brief smile.

"So," Frankie drawls, crossing her arms over her chest to keep out the late-night chill. "How have you been?"

I open the passenger side door of my truck and toss my bag inside and then shut the door, leaning against the cold metal. "I've been good."

The last couple of weeks have been a mind fuck, but everything leading up to that was good.

"What brought you to Green Valley?"

Inhaling the fresh air, I turn my gaze down the street. "When I left Merryville, I needed a change of scenery, so I bounced around a little, but didn't have much money. When I visited here about six months ago, I liked what I saw, so I found a place to park my trailer and got a job at the Piggly Wiggly—"

"Wait. You work at the Piggly Wiggly?" Frankie asks, abruptly cutting me off. "How have I not seen you there?"

"Not sure, I'm there almost every day."

Frankie shakes her head in disbelief. "I go there every Tuesday night to grocery shop."

"Tuesday is the only day I get off early."

She chuckles, shaking her head. "Well, that explains it."

"What about you?" I ask. "How have you been? How did you end up here?"

"I've been good... great, actually," she says, smiling as she rubs her hands together to warm them up. "I've lived here for a while. I just commute to Merryville every day."

I nod. "How's the shelter?"

Frankie's knowing eyes meet mine. "Good."

There.

I broke the ice.

Made the acknowledgment.

Maybe there's an unspoken rule that you can't bring up the shelter to another person unless they do it first.

"And Helen?" I ask, not because I'm still trying to break the ice, but because I'm genuinely interested. She was really nice to me when I was there, and I've thought a lot about her and Frankie since I'd left the shelter.

Without them, who knows where I would be or how things would've ended up.

"She's good too. We're getting ready to expand the shelter. Thanks to some generous recent donations, we're building a new facility behind the church."

"That's really great."

"Helen was happy to know I saw you," Frankie adds, surprising me with that piece of information. "She said to tell you hello."

For some reason, the fact Helen and Frankie even remember me makes me feel good, like maybe I'm not so easily forgotten.

"I really appreciate what you both did for me," I tell her, eyeing the gym and feeling a twinge of guilt for leaving without telling Ozzi bye and thanking him for tonight. He did a lot for me too. If it hadn't been for him, I would've possibly been passed out on the gym floor when Gunnar and Frankie walked in.

Frankie gives me another small smile. "That's what we're there for."

"I know, but I also know you don't get paid big bucks for doing what you do and I think you should know that you make a difference."

"Thanks for that," she says. "And how crazy is it that we meet again, here of all places?"

We both chuckle. "If you would've told me two years ago that I'd be training at an MMA gym, I would've said you were crazy."

"Word on the street is that you're really good," Frankie muses. "Gunnar and Vali were talking about you tonight."

I feel my face heat. "I'm not sure about that... I just." Pausing, I try to put it into words. "I just fit. This place fits. Strangely enough, I feel like I belong here."

Frankie's expression grows serious and she nods in understanding. "I think that's really great, Willow. I'm happy for you."

"But I'm still not exactly sure what I'm doing," I admit. "Ozzi seems to think I could compete, but I don't know if I'm cut out for that, you know?"

She nods again. "I do. I totally get it. When I first met Gunnar, I had my own reservations. But, speaking from experience...give it a chance. Those guys in there," she says, motioning behind her toward the gym, "they're good people. If you can trust anyone, you can trust them."

Exhaling, I kick off the truck and walk around the front, making my way to the driver's side. "That's easier said than done," I tell her, opening the door.

"You're right. It is."

"I should go. It's getting late."

Frankie takes a couple steps back toward the gym, but stops. "Come have donuts and coffee with me, Maggie, and Tempest. We meet up on Sunday mornings at Daisy's Nut House."

An all too familiar anxiety creeps in that makes me immediately shut down the possibility of interacting with people I don't really know that well. "I work on Sunday."

"We meet at six-thirty," she says, her tone leaving no room for argument. "I know The Pig doesn't open until eight. You can meet us for at least thirty minutes."

CHAPTER 13

OZZI

"So how are things going with Willow?" Cage asks as he keeps pace to my right. Vali and Gunnar are running ahead of us as we make our way back into town.

We started our run before daylight and the sun is now breaking the horizon, peeping out over the tall trees.

"Good," I say, choosing short answers because, unlike my freak brothers, I'm not a conversationalist while running my ass off.

Cage grunts and I know he wants more information than that, but honestly, I don't know what else to say. There are times when I think Willow's head is in it and we can definitely be ready for the exhibition fight Cage has mentioned signing her up for in a couple months. But then there are times when I think Willow's mental game is far from ready.

Physically, she's a beast.

Mentally, she has a lot to work through.

And competing in this sport is seventy-five percent mental. If your head isn't in it, your opponent will wipe the floor with you.

I could never let that happen to Willow.

"Even though we've only been at this a few weeks, she's well-conditioned," I say, my words coming out choppy as I try to control my breathing. "Good form. Tight moves. She's sparring well, but I'd like to get her in the ring."

"She should come with us to Knoxville next week," Cage says, eyes trained on the road ahead. "It would be good for her to see a live fight. There are a few female bouts in the prelims."

I nod. "That's a good idea. I'll ask her."

Willow has a lot of other shit going on right now, but I think coming to the gym and training is good for her, even if nothing comes of it. But a sure-fire way to see if she's ready for a real fight is to take her to one, let her size up the competition, and be able to visualize herself in the ring.

"Everyone will be there," Cage adds. "She seems to be comfortable around the girls, so let her know Tempest, Maggie, and Frankie will be going too."

"I still want to know how she and Frankie know each other," I mutter, more to myself than Cage. I asked Frankie, but all she said is they know each other from Merryville. When I asked if they were friends, she gave me a non-committal answer, saying they were acquaintances.

I've thought a lot about it and came up with a couple scenarios.

One, she was a patient in the emergency room and Frankie treated her.

Or two, she stayed at the women's shelter.

Either option makes sense why Frankie won't talk, but it doesn't lessen my curiosity.

I'm drawn to Willow, there's no getting around that. For now, I'm trying to be her friend, but that doesn't mean I'm not attracted to her. It's like my mind and body are wired to respond to her.

From the first moment we met at the gym, I knew she was someone I'd never forget.

It's not just her gorgeous face or long, dark hair.

It's everything—her natural talent, drive, tenacity. Not to mention, she's a constant mystery, one that I could spend the rest of my life trying to solve. But

I've recently started putting some pieces of the Willow puzzle together and I know her childhood plays a big part in making her who she is.

"Are y'all training today?" Cage asks, pulling me out of my thoughts. "I'd like to sit in on a session."

"She has some personal stuff to do today," I tell him. Even though I could elaborate, I don't. The more Willow lets me in and shows me her vulnerable side, the more I want to protect her and keep her from harm.

Not that I have to worry about my family when it comes to Willow, but I know how private she is and I don't want to betray her trust by running my big mouth.

"The hot muffins sign is on," Vali calls out, pointing ahead to Donner Bakery like it's a beacon in the night.

Cage grunts again, but this time, I can hear a faint chuckle behind it. He wants muffins more than the rest of us, but of course, he kind of has an in with the baker.

Tempest—used to be Cassidy, now Erickson—is well known around this small town for her creative concoctions. And even though she could quit and stay home with Freya, she doesn't want to. According to her, muffins are her therapy, and if she wasn't baking, she'd go crazy.

I don't know how she does it, though. Baking most mornings at Donner Bakery. Helping run the business side of things at the gym. Teaching a very popular self-defense class. Not to mention, being an awesome mom to my favorite niece.

She even takes Freya to the bakery with her in the mornings.

If she keeps that up, Freya will be baking before she walks.

When the guy working the front counter sees all four of us walking into the small bakery, his eyes grow wide. In his defense, we're probably an intimidating crew.

"Mikey," Cage says in greeting, reaching a fist across the counter for him to bump.

The kid knocks knuckles with Cage and then clears his throat. "What can I get for you?"

"Are my girls still back there?" Cage asks, leaning against the counter as he motions toward the kitchen area.

"Yeah, want me to get Tempest for you?"

"Just tell her I'm here."

He gives a small smile and nods before turning on his heels.

"What are you getting?" I ask Vali.

"I'm hoping my favorite sister-in-law stashed me a Folsom Prison Blues."

"Islands in the Stream," Cage grumbles. "That's where it's at."

Gunnar walks between the two of them, throwing his arms over their shoulders. "Do we need to have a taste test? Seeing as how I've been deprived of most of Tempest's creations due to the grueling meal plan set by my asshole trainer, I'm the perfect candidate."

"You've had your fair share," Cage retorts. "She babies the shit out of you after every fight by baking your favorites."

"But I haven't had them since," Gunnar says, practically whining like a baby.

Speaking of babies, Tempest walks toward the front carrying my favorite baby in the whole wide world.

All four of us throw elbows in an effort to be the one who gets dibs on Freya, but unfortunately, her behemoth of a father wins out.

"Well, well, well," Tempest says cheerfully. "To what do I owe the pleasure?"

"Morning run," Vali says, patting his flat stomach. "I'm hoping for a Folsom Prison Blues for my recovery meal."

I roll my eyes. "It's not like you ran a marathon, jackass."

"Language," Tempest says with a sugary sweet smile.

Sometimes, I wonder if she feels like she has five children, instead of one.

"Sorry," I say, leaning over to kiss Freya's cheek.

Tempest pulls a box from under the counter and hands it over. "Two Folsom Prison Blues, Two Islands in the Stream, Two Rings of Fire, and one Livin' on Love."

Tilting her head apologetically, she looks over at Gunnar. "It might not be the most decadent muffin, but it's definitely made with love and Cage-approved." She gives my older brother a wink and the way he looks at her in return should be illegal in all fifty states.

"Want me to take Freya?" he asks.

"I think someone's ready for a nap," Tempest coos, reaching across the counter to smooth Freya's soft baby hair. "If you want to take her home and put her down, I should be there before she wakes up."

"If not, I'll watch her until you get home," I chime in. "She needs some Uncle Ozzi time. Isn't that right, Freya."

Vali and Gunnar both start trying to argue that they're her favorite, but they're both full of shit.

She loves me more.

As the four of us walk out of the bakery with muffins and a baby in hand, an elderly lady is stepping out of a sleek Cadillac.

"My goodness," she says with a smile. "What a greeting committee. The four of you and this sweet baby."

"Miss Faye," my brothers say in unison.

"I don't believe we've met yet," she says, walking up to me and reaching out her hand. "I'm Faye Alberty. You must be related to these striking gentlemen. The family resemblance is as strong as the four of you."

For some reason, I feel my face heat up as I nod and shake her hand. "I'm Ozzi Erickson, ma'am. It's nice to meet you."

She winks, then turns her attention to Vali. "I haven't seen you at the salon recently."

"I just made an appointment for later this week."

"Maybe I'll see you there," she says with a wink.

If I didn't know better, I'd think this woman is flirting with my brother.

Just as I'm getting ready to give him shit about it, my phone buzzes in my pocket.

Unknown: Hi, this is Willow.

Unknown: I wanted to remind you that I won't be at the gym for training tonight.

Unknown: And this is my new number.

Smiling down at my phone, I quickly save her contact information and then text her back.

Me: Thanks for texting me.

Me: Good luck today. You're stronger than you give yourself credit for.

CHAPTER 14

WILLOW

*T*oday is a mixed feelings kind of day. It's a day I've been dreading, causing my stomach to tense up every time I think about it, but also a day I'm ready to tackle and get over with.

At least I *think* I'm ready.

Whether I am or not doesn't really matter anymore since I'm already two hours into my three-hour drive to Mountain City, because today is the day I file for guardianship of Hazel.

It's also the day I pick up my mother's remains.

But I'm trying not to think about that right now. It's still something I can't wrap my brain around or figure out what I'm supposed to do with. What does one do with their dead mother's remains? I'm sure for people who are close to that parent, they thoughtfully display them or spread their ashes somewhere meaningful. I don't have that connection. Trying to process it has consumed many hours of my life, but today, I'm choosing to focus on doing what I need to do for Hazel first.

The rest will have to wait until later, when I'm forced to face it head on.

Eventually, I pull into the lot adjacent to the Johnson County courthouse and park. The enormity of this moment is hitting me hard right now and I haven't even stepped out of my car.

After today, I could possibly—hopefully—be responsible for a sister I've never met and that's a big fucking deal. It'd be crazy to not be freaked out right now but I know deep down in my gut I have to do this.

I *need* to do this.

For a moment, I just sit in my truck and try to breathe, repeating to myself what Ozzi texted me earlier—*You're stronger than you give yourself credit for.*

Once I've collected myself and feel more confident, I get out of my truck and walk into the building. After I make my way through the metal detector, I find the directory on the wall. Locating the office I need isn't hard and after taking a flight of stairs, I come to a door that has instructions to take a number and be seated.

Doing as instructed, I glance down the long hall and find an empty seat.

While I wait, my thoughts turn back to Ozzi, something that's been happening more often than I'd like to admit. I think about texting him again, if only to distract myself, but instead I read over our brief exchange from earlier, amazed how that simple connection makes me feel.

How he makes me feel—strong, capable... enough.

He barely knows me and yet his confidence in me is unwavering. I don't understand that. If I spoke to a therapist about it, I'm sure they'd tell me it goes back to my abandonment and trust issues. Lord knows I've got plenty of those. And I guess Ozzi's faith in me could be an act—a strategy trainers use to motivate their clients—but he seems so genuine.

I want to take Frankie's advice and trust him. But it's hard. I don't have the best track record and my judgment of character has been questionable in the past. But Ozzi makes it feel so easy.

My attraction to him scares me.

"Miss Bernard?"

I startle at my name being called but quickly put my phone back in my purse and walk to the open door where an older man is waiting for me.

"I'm Miss Bernard... Willow Bernard."

"I'm Arnold Cooper. How may I help you today?"

Clearing my throat, I try to make my voice sound strong and confident. "I'd like to file for guardianship of my sister."

Mr. Cooper smiles as he takes a seat at his desk, motioning across for me to sit. "You've come to the right place. First thing you'll need to do is fill out some forms."

"Yes, I printed them out at the library and filled them out," I say, pulling them out of my purse and nervously smoothing out the wrinkles. "But I have a few questions."

"I'm here to help," he says, his kind face and direct gaze easing my anxiety a little.

How much time do you have, Mr. Cooper? I grimly think to myself.

"Well, my situation is... complicated," I say, trying to think of a good place to start. "I, uh, recently found out my mother passed away and that I have a younger sister I was unaware of. She's nine and currently in foster care. We don't have any other family, so I'd like to be her guardian."

I pause for a second, all the nerves roar back in full force.

"Can I do that?" With that question, my voice wavers but I'm able to maintain eye contact and I see how Mr. Cooper's gaze softens.

He smiles and it's comforting, not judgmental, so I relax my shoulders a bit and wait for his response. "It's always preferable for guardianship to be given to a family member, if at all possible."

"Even if we don't know each other?"

"Well, the judge may require you to have supervised visits at first. After that, you might have a home visit from one of our social workers, and then later, unsupervised visits, until you're both comfortable with each other."

When he explains it like that, it doesn't sound so hard or scary, but I'm not used to anything in life being easy. So, I feel the doubt creeping in. "What are my odds, Mr. Cooper? Honestly. Is there a chance the judge will rule in favor of the system over me?"

He sighs, dipping his head in understanding. "The judge will make his or her decision based on the child's best interests and like I said before, it's almost always best for a child to be with a blood relative. But I guess there is a chance they might decide foster care is the better option for the child."

"What's my next step?" I ask, suddenly feeling more determined than ever. Even though I don't know Hazel and she doesn't know me, I'm her best bet.

That's sad, given the situation.

But if I was ever given the chance to be with family over foster care, I would've chosen family any day. Plus, even though I might not be the most financially stable or have a big fancy house, I can give her something no one else can.

A sister.

Unconditional love.

Because even though we've never met, I already love her.

Which is crazy, because I've never even said that word to another human being before. However, deep in my soul, I'm already tied to Hazel and the love I harbor for her is the most natural feeling I've ever had.

"You'll need to pay the processing fee and we'll get these papers filed," he says with his elbows on the desk as he leans closer. "After that, someone will be in touch to set up some visitation times and schedule a home visit."

After I hand over my paperwork, he looks over everything, confirming the forms are all filled out correctly, and then I pay the fee.

"Not that it matters, but I think this is an honorable thing you're doing for your sister."

"It matters to me," I tell him, wishing I could give him a hug for being so kind. "Thank you."

He stands and holds out a business card. "You should hear something in seven to ten days. If you haven't received a call within two weeks, give me a call and I'll see what the holdup is."

"Thanks again," I tell him, taking the card and putting it in my purse for safe-keeping. "I appreciate it."

"Good luck, Willow."

With that major item checked off my to-do list, I walk out of the office feeling lighter, like a huge weight has been lifted off my shoulders. I know it's not over. Quite the opposite, it's just beginning, but I made the first step and it feels good.

But with that being said, I'm now forced to face the thing I've been dreading for the past few weeks.

As I drive the few blocks to the police station, I'm hit with the realization that, even though I'm back in the town I grew up in, this place doesn't feel like home to me. I don't know if it ever did but it certainly doesn't now. Not much has changed as far as how the area looks and the businesses that are still here, but I've changed a lot and I can say honestly say, I'm glad I don't live here anymore.

I've always been afraid I'd end up like my mother, a deadbeat drug addict who couldn't take care of herself much less her child or *children*, I should say. And, I guess, I assumed if I stayed in Mountain City or anywhere near here, my fate would be sealed, so I made sure to get out and go far away as soon as I could.

It was one of the best decisions I've ever made.

Finding a parking spot close to the front door, I ease my truck next to the curb and turn off the engine.

You're stronger than you give yourself credit for.

Reluctantly, I get out of my truck and walk into the station.

"I'm Willow Bernard," I tell the lady behind the plexiglass window. "I'm here to see Sue Harrison. She's expecting me."

After I got my phone the other day, my first call was to Sue. I passed on my new number and we made plans to meet today.

A few minutes later, I heard a buzz and then a door at the end of the hall opened. A tall lady with silvery white hair stood there. "Willow?"

"Yes." Gripping my purse tighter, I take a tentative step toward her.

"I'm Sue," she says, offering her hand for me to shake.

Taking it, I notice her firm grip.

"It's nice to finally meet you in person. Follow me."

She might be older, but she's definitely not frail. From the moment we first spoke, I could tell she was a no-nonsense kind of woman. But seeing her in person lets me know her appearance backs that up.

"Let's have a seat in here," she says, stopping in front of what looks like an interrogation room.

Taking a deep breath, I nod and give her a tight smile as I walk past her and into the grey room. Everything from the concrete room to its monochromatic contents makes me cold inside.

When I sit down at the metal table and see the box, I shiver.

"Coffee?" Sue asks before she sits.

"No, I'm okay."

She nods, taking a seat across from me and opening a folder. "Since your mother was merely a tenant, most of her possessions were left on the premises. A few items the lessor felt were of worth and sentiment are in this box. Since you are now being noted as her next of kin, any communication will come directly to you."

Glancing over the forms, they seem very straight forward so I begin to fill them out while she continues to talk.

"Her remains are at Mountain City Funeral Home on the outskirts of town. I called Harold the other day and told him you'd be by, so he's expecting you," she says, taking the first completed form from me and placing it back in the folder. "He should have a few copies of her death certificate for you, just in case you need it for any bill collectors who might come calling."

"Will I have to pay her debts?" I ask, a feeling of dread creeping in. I hadn't thought about that.

Sue shakes her head. "No, anything she owed will be written off, but you might need to provide a death certificate if they contact you."

"Not that I want her money, but did she have a bank account or anything?"

She takes the final form from me and puts it with the other before closing the file. "If she did, we don't know about it. As far as we know, she didn't have a checking account or any type of insurance policies."

"What about the funeral home?" I ask, feeling so ignorant when it comes to this stuff. "Do I need to pay them?"

"No," Sue says. "Since we weren't able to locate you right away, we treated it as unclaimed."

She slides the box over to me. "Any other questions?"

"When can I see Hazel?" I ask, standing when Sue does.

"Her social worker should be contacting you soon to make the initial arrangements. You filed the paperwork this morning?"

I nod. "Yes, before I came here."

"Good. You should hear from them in a week or so."

As I pick up the box, I notice how light it is, which means there can't be much inside.

How poetic. As empty as my mother's life.

"I would say I hope to see you around," Sue says, opening the door and holding it for me. "But given the circumstances, I really hope I don't."

Giving her a brief smile, I chuckle. "Thank you, for everything."

"Just doing my job."

But that's not true, just like Mr. Cooper at the courthouse, Sue doesn't have to be so nice. But she is and I appreciate it. People like her and Mr. Cooper make it easier to deal with difficult situations.

"I appreciate you finding me," I say as she walks me back to the front of the station. "I'm sure it would've been easier to stop looking, because quite frankly, I didn't want to be found, especially by anyone from Mountain City. When I left this place, I never planned on coming back. But I'm glad you kept searching, if for no other reason than giving me the chance to meet my sister, even if that doesn't work out."

Sue smiles, making her face look ten years younger. "You've got a good head on your shoulders and your priorities are right. I think the judge will see that. I know I'll be putting in a good word for you."

Ten minutes later, I'm pulling into the funeral home parking lot, a place I've seen so many times I can't even count. It's the last place you see before leaving Mountain City, but a place I'd always hoped I wouldn't have to visit.

A large man with a bald head steps out of the side door and waves.

He must be Harold.

"Hello," I call out, stepping out of my truck.

"Willow?"

"Yes."

Waving me inside, he walks in ahead of me. The second I cross the threshold, I feel the need to hold my breath. Nothing against Harold or his funeral home, but it smells old and musty.

"Sue told me you'd be by."

I just grimace and nod.

He goes into a closet and comes out with a cardboard box, half the size of the one from the police station. "This is what you came for and I'll just need you to sign this paper."

Placing the paper on top of the box, he hands me a pen.

I sign my name for what feels like the hundredth time for the day and pass the pen back.

"I'm sorry about your mother," Harold says, sounding remorseful, but I doubt he's truly sorry. Anyone who really knew her, knew she was a drug addict who slept with men for money and cared more about her addiction than she did her children.

"Thank you," I reply.

KNOCK OUT

He lets me know that the death certificates are inside the box and if I need any more to call him.

Five minutes later, I'm back in my truck with two cardboard boxes sitting beside me, making my way back home. If it weren't for Hazel, I'd say I hope I never have to come back to this town again. Unfortunately, I'll have to.

But for now, I can't wait to get back to Green Valley.

As I drive down the highway, I crack my window and let the cool mountain air do its thing while I play a little game I always played when I was in foster care. Any time I was having an exceptionally hard day, I'd start listing anything that made me happy. It could be as simple as a yellow wildflower in the yard or an interesting cloud in the sky.

There were times I would have to get really creative, like listing the fact I had something to eat that day, even if it was a piece of stale toast.

As hard as today was, it's still better than my best day in foster care. Not only do I have air in my lungs and a bag of my favorite chips in the seat next to me. I also have so many other things to be grateful for.

The tiny trailer I call home.

The Piggly Wiggly.

Checking out books at the library.

Everything about Viking MMA.

Including Ozzi.

Peanut butter and jelly sandwiches, even though I eat them practically every day.

Pizza.

Pizza with Ozzi.

Okay, I need a new focus, because these thoughts of Ozzi are getting harder to ignore. Readjusting myself in my seat, I lean closer to the steering wheel and concentrate on the road as I steer my truck around a tight curve.

This drive *is* beautiful.

The trees are tall and green and when the horizon opens up, there's nothing but clear skies. It's still early spring, so our days are getting warmer, but the evenings and nights are still cool. I heard a rumor the other day in the Piggly Wiggly that there's snow in the forecast for next week.

Gotta love living in the mountains.

As I come to one of the openings, something like a vista is on display in front of me and the sky is a dusky pink that fades into blue. Another hour or so and the sun will set completely.

Which makes my mind drift to a time long ago, one I'd pushed so far back into my memories the edges are fuzzy. But it's there.

Me.

My mom.

A warm blanket.

And a gorgeous sunset.

Glancing over at the cardboard box, a lump forms in my throat. It's crazy. I shouldn't have a tear left to shed for the woman whose life has been condensed into two boxes. But she was the only mom I ever had. And that's just sad.

No matter how you look at it.

I let the tears fall for a few miles, one hand on the wheel and the other resting on the lid of the box. Coming around another bend, I catch the glimpse of the sun breaking in the western sky. It's just coming out from a line of clouds and it's gorgeous.

For a brief moment, I hold my breath, not wanting to miss a second of it as I try to keep my eyes on the road and the sky at the same time.

When I pass a road sign that says Green Valley is only ten miles away, an idea starts to form.

Normally, I want to do things on my own, but for some reason, tonight, I don't.

Picking up my phone, I tap one of the only contacts I have stored.

CHAPTER 15

OZZI

"*H*ello?"

"Hey."

I know it's Willow, but she sounds a little distant and there's something off about her tone.

"Willow?"

"Yeah, hi," she says and that's when I hear the background noise and realize she's driving in her truck. "Is this a bad time?"

I finish wiping down the heavy bag, the last thing that needed cleaned before I can call it a day, and toss the rag in the laundry basket. "No, it's a great time. What's up?"

It's on the tip of my tongue to tell her it's never a bad time for her, but I refrain. I also refrain from asking her what's wrong, because I can tell she's either crying or has been crying. I only know this because I witnessed her panic attack and I know now what that sounds like.

The vision of her bent over, struggling for breath and falling apart on the gym floor, has haunted me for the past few days.

"I'm on the outskirts of Green Valley and I, uh... I need your help with something."

Willow asking for help is out of character, but the fact she called me makes me happier than I care to admit. "Anything," I blurt out before she even has a chance to tell me what it is.

"Do you know where Bandit Lake is?"

No.

"Sure."

"Can you meet me there in about half an hour?"

I glance down at my watch and see it's just now a little after six. "Yeah, I can be there."

"I just have something I need to do," she continues. "And I don't want to do it alone."

That last confession is so quiet I almost miss it and I'm not sure she meant for me to hear, but I did and I'm glad. "I'll be there."

After we hang up, I walk over to the stairs that lead to Tempest and Cage's apartment and call out. "Where is Bandit Lake?"

A few minutes later, I'm headed out of town. On my way out the door, I grabbed a thermos and filled it up with a few cups of coffee from the Keurig and snagged a box of muffins Tempest had brought home with her from the bakery.

Since I like to fly by the seat of my pants, my Jeep is pretty well equipped—bottled water, blankets, emergency stash of food. I even have a pop-up tent, because you just never know where life will take you and I always like to be prepared.

Following Tempest's instructions, I easily find my turn off. As I approach the lake, I see Willow's truck and pull up beside it.

It's cooling off, so I grab the blanket and coffee and head down to where she's standing beside the water. The sun is setting and the sky is painted in pinks and orange and blue.

Willow's silhouette, paired with the impending sunset, rivals any piece of art hanging in the most prestigious art gallery. Some moments jump out at you, forcing you to remember them.

This is one of them.

And when she glances over her shoulder, I forget to breathe for a second.

"Thanks for coming," she says, the rawness in her voice pulling me forward and reminding me why I'm here.

Willow needs me.

She doesn't want to be alone.

"No need to thank me," I tell her as I walk up beside her and take in the lake and sunset. "This sure is pretty. I lied when I said I knew where this place was. I've never been here."

That makes her chuckle, and the sound eases the tightness I've had in my chest ever since she called.

"I've only been here once," she murmurs, eyes back on the sky. "I was driving home and thinking…"

She drifts off and I'm unsure if I should push, ask her why she called, or just wait it out.

Then she begins again. "My mom used to watch the sunset. It's such a vague memory, but it's like it started creeping back into my mind as I drove."

When she pauses this time, I hear a quiet sniffle, but keep my eyes trained ahead. I should've known when she called and didn't sound like herself that it had to do with her mother, just like her panic attack.

"I have her ashes, and at first, I didn't know what to do with them. Taking them home just didn't feel right, but I couldn't just leave her at the funeral home. And even though I often felt like she threw me away, I couldn't do that either. So," she says, inhaling deeply. "Here we are."

The sunset.

The lake.

Her mother's ashes.

It all makes sense now.

Without another word, she turns and walks to her truck, opening the passenger door. When she comes back, she's carrying a small cardboard box. Stepping closer to the shoreline, she opens it and takes out what looks like a plastic container.

For a second, I think she's just going to toss the ashes in and get it over with, like ripping off a bandage, but then she stops. Her breath starts coming in choppy huffs, kind of like when she had the panic attack and I step up beside her, placing my hand on her back.

"Breathe," I whisper, rubbing slow, soothing circles.

I don't know what else to say.

I've never been in her shoes. I haven't lost a parent. The closest thing I can relate to is losing my grandparents, which sucked. But I had my whole family for support.

Willow has no one.

"I'm right here." I don't know if my presence is enough to calm her, or give her some peace, but she did call me and ask me to come out here with her. That has to mean something.

After a minute or two, she exhales loudly. "I don't know how to do this."

"Maybe we could say a few words?" I ask, reaching back for the blanket I'd brought and spreading it out on the ground behind us. Guiding Willow back, I take a seat and pull her down beside me. "Just take your time and do whatever feels right."

The sun is barely hanging on the horizon as Willow picks up the container, holding her mother's ashes, and begins to speak. "I want to say you were a horrible mother, but the older I get, the more I wonder if it was your addiction that was horrible. Because moments, like today, when a brief glimpse of a memory reappears and I remember something good, I wonder if that was more of who you were. I know there was a you before Dad died and I think that person was good. But then, you just gave up..."

Her voice trails off and she dips her head. I can't tell if she's crying again or not, but my heart breaks for her all the same.

In the same way I can't relate to losing a parent, I also can't relate to having a parent give up on me. Being one of five brothers, I was never alone. Our mom and dad were always around. We did everything together.

Sitting quietly beside Willow, I'm amazed at her strength. Even in a moment like this, where all her walls are down and she's so vulnerable, it's her strength that shines through.

"I wish things could've been different, but wherever you are, I hope you've found peace."

With that, Willow stands and walks to the water, her feet half-submerged. Opening the container, she turns her back to the light breeze and empties the contents, letting it drift off with the wind. Some of it carries, but most of it sinks into the lake.

A small lump blooms in my throat and I'm not sure if it's for the girl standing in front of me or the finality of this moment—a life gone forever.

When Willow walks over and lowers herself back onto the blanket, I have an overwhelming urge to hug her. But I'm not sure if she wants that, so I wait, trying to be what she needs without overstepping her boundaries.

For a few minutes, we just sit in comfortable silence, listening to the ripple of the water. I can't stop thinking about what Willow must be going through and wishing I could take all the pain and heartache from her.

When she leans over and rests her head on my shoulder, I slip my arm around her and soak in the closeness while trying to give her all the warmth I can. But it doesn't keep her from shivering.

Reaching behind us, I pull up the edge of the blanket and wrap it around her shoulders. I also remember the thermos I'd brought with me and grab it, pour some hot coffee into the lid that doubles as a cup, and hand it to her.

Her eyes meet mine and in the dimness of twilight, they're almost black and staring straight into my soul. The pull I always feel toward her intensifies and I have to physically hold myself back because every cell in my body is telling me to hold her even closer.

After a few seconds, she clears her throat and breaks the trance. "Thanks for everything."

There's so much sincerity and appreciation wrapped up in those simple words. Coming from Willow, who was so closed off when we first met, it brings back the lump in my throat. I want to tell her so many things in return—*you're welcome, you're not alone... I think I'm falling for you.* But I swallow them down, saving them for another time.

"Any time."

CHAPTER 16

WILLOW

I'm sitting in the parking lot of Daisy's Nut House and wondering how my life took such a crazy turn. The past month has been a roller coaster of events and emotions.

From my audition at The Pink Pony to spreading my mother's ashes a couple nights ago, I never saw any of it coming.

I also couldn't have imagined crossing paths with Frankie Reeves again.

But here I am, getting ready to meet her and Maggie and Tempest for donuts and coffee.

I went from only having a couple people—Krista and Tony—who I communicated with on a regular basis, to having all of the Ericksons, plus their significant others.

For most of my life, I've wanted connections like this, but wouldn't allow myself to get close enough to people. On the outside, most people probably assumed I didn't want to be their friend. If you look up resting bitch face in the dictionary, I wouldn't be surprised if my photo was there. It's part of my armor. If I don't let people get close, then I won't be disappointed and heartbroken when they leave.

Because everyone in my life has left.

So, why am I here? Why am I letting myself get close? Why now?

I don't know the answer to those questions. All I can figure is I'm tired of being alone and I can't lie, it's been nice having someone to lean on over the past few weeks.

Quite literally, I think to myself as my mind drifts to Bandit Lake and Ozzi.

I think I might have almost kissed him.

There was this moment when it felt like the world stood still. He was so patient and sweet—two things I've never experienced with a man before—and I almost forgot myself... my fears, my reservations. All I saw was Ozzi.

A knock on my window startles me and I almost piss my pants.

Glancing over, Frankie is smirking at me through the glass. "Are you sleeping in there?"

"No," I say, opening the door and stepping out. "I was just waiting until you showed up."

"Come on," she says, motioning for me to follow. "Maggie and Tempest will be here in a few minutes. Let's get first dibs."

Standing at the counter, I'm not sure what to choose.

"The jelly-filled ones are the best," Frankie says.

About that time, the bell above the door chimes and I turn to see Maggie and Tempest walk in. "You better not take the last jelly-filled," Maggie calls out.

"I was actually thinking about getting the one with sprinkles," I tell the guy behind the counter. "And one black coffee."

"I did not take you for a sprinkles girl," Tempest says, coming to stand beside me. "I'll have a cinnamon roll and a coffee with cream and sugar."

Maggie and Frankie both order jelly-filled donuts and coffees and then we all take a seat.

"I'm so happy you could join us," Maggie says, sliding into the booth beside Frankie. "We say we're meeting to plan the wedding reception, but really, we just like to have donuts and coffee without the men around. They're great; don't get us wrong, but it's nice to just have some girl time, you know?"

No, I don't really know.

But I smile and nod. "Sure."

"Oh, and you're probably thinking we're crazy for meeting up so early, but if you don't, all the good donuts get picked over."

"Apparently," I say, rubbing my sweaty palms down my thighs.

I don't know why I'm nervous. It's not like they're strangers, especially not Frankie. But I really like them, which scares me, and I'm not used to being included like this. Most people assume I don't want to be invited to anything, thanks to my cold disposition.

And I tell myself I don't.

But deep down, everyone likes to be invited.

Even me.

"I thought Freya was going to wake up and insist on being included this morning," Tempest says, shaking her head. "She's usually still asleep at this time, but not today. I tiptoed into her room to check on her and she started fussing. It took a good five minutes of patting her back for her to go back to sleep."

"Will Cage get up with her if she wakes up?" I ask, thinking back about all the foster dads I've known and how none of them were very good with babies.

Ozzi and Vali, on the other hand, were so attentive and caring. But I haven't seen Cage with Freya, so I don't know what he's like.

"Oh yeah," Tempest says, waving me off. "He's the best. If she makes the tiniest whimper, he'll be jumping up and running in to save the day."

"He's one of the best dads I've ever seen," Frankie comments and I see a wistfulness in her eyes. I wonder if she and Gunnar have thought about having kids.

"And don't even get us started on her uncles," Maggie says, practically swooning out of her seat with her hands clutched to her chest. "I swear, every time I see Vali with that baby."

She pauses, biting her bottom lip.

"It's a good thing we're already married, I'm just saying."

Everyone laughs, including me, and it feels good.

When our donuts and coffee show up, Maggie holds her jelly-filled donut in the air. "To us," she says, waiting for us all to join her.

"To us," we say in unison.

If I was watching this scene play out on television, I'd probably roll my eyes and say something snarky about it being cheesy. But being here, at the moment, it doesn't feel that way. It feels genuine and real.

For a while, I just enjoy my donut and coffee and listen to them all talk. But I don't close myself off like normal. I make eye contact. I laugh when someone says something funny. I also find out Maggie's family owns the feed store, and she works there, while also writing for the local paper. But the part that really got my attention is she's an author.

Like an honest-to-goodness author.

And I love books.

But I try to just listen and keep my cool.

For now. But I one hundred percent plan on going to the library and Googling her the next chance I get.

Tempest talks about a new muffin recipe she's been working on at the bakery.

And Frankie mentioned that she's going to be leaving her job at the hospital in Merryville and starting a new job at a local doctor's office in two weeks.

All of these women are such Jacks of all trades. Or Jills rather.

And strangely, in a matter of half an hour, I feel like I'm part of their group.

"I've noticed you haven't been at the gym for a couple days," Tempest says, before taking a sip of her second cup of coffee. "Everything going okay?"

Natural instinct has me wanting to clam up and give her a vague response, but after sitting here and listening about their lives, I want to share a little of mine.

"I took Friday off and drove to Mountain City," I start, taking a deep breath. "It's where my mom lived, but she recently died and I had to go take care of some things."

I don't want to tell them about picking up her ashes, or the box that's still sitting on the small table in my trailer waiting for me to go through its contents. I told myself I'd do it yesterday, but after being so emotionally drained from Friday, I just couldn't do it.

Yesterday morning, I got up early and was at the Piggly Wiggly an hour before my normal shift. Then, I worked two hours late, came home, took a shower, and went to bed.

Maybe I'll open the box today.

"I'm so sorry to hear about your mom," Maggie says, slipping an arm around my shoulder.

"Me too," Tempest says, reaching her hand across and placing it on top of mine.

When I look up and see Frankie's expression, there's so much understanding there. She knows more about me than anyone at this table.

"Thank you," I say. "We weren't close."

Tempest squeezes my hand before letting go. "That doesn't mean it's easy."

No, she's right. It's been anything but easy.

"If you need anything," Maggie says, giving me a sideways hug. "Just let us know. My mama loves to make casseroles for people in mourning."

The way she says it makes me laugh and before I know it, the whole table is laughing.

"Speaking of." Tempest holds up a finger, like she just remembered something. "I'm supposed to invite everyone over for an Easter lunch. Peggy and my mom have decided to join forces and have a big lunch at the gym. We'll set it up kind of like the reception, with long, family-style tables. My mom should be calling your mom, Maggie, so you might want to give her a heads up. Unless y'all already have plans."

Maggie shakes her head. She has her hair up in a bun that's intentionally messy and it looks so good on her. When I try to do that, mine just looks like I crawled out of bed and didn't brush my hair.

"No, no big plans, just the usual," Maggie says. "A big lunch sounds fun."

"You should come too," Tempest says, glancing over at me.

Feeling my cheeks heat up, I wave her off. "Oh, no. I wouldn't want to impose."

"You're not," she says matter-of-factly. "I'm inviting you."

"You're invited to the wedding reception too," Maggie adds.

Glancing across the table, I see a sly grin on Frankie's face and I kind of want to kick her under the table. It's like this was her master plan, to coax me with a casual donut and coffee and then get me invited to all the things, knowing I hate being social.

Big family dinners and holidays and wedding receptions.

Those aren't things I do.

Even though my one impromptu dinner with the Ericksons *was* pretty great.

It doesn't mean I want to subject myself to the entire family, parents and all.

"Thank you for the invite," I force out. "I'll see if I can make it."

"Now, so we're not total liars," Maggie says, pulling out a small binder, "I did want to ask your opinions on some appetizers."

CHAPTER 17

OZZI

"*A*re you picking Willow up?" Tempest asks as she takes inventory of Freya's backpack.

A few days ago, when Willow finally came back to the gym for a training session, I asked her about going to the fight tonight. At first, she was hesitant, which I expected. But after thinking about it for a few minutes, she agreed.

We've discussed the need for her to see a fight in person and how it will help her be ready, if and when she decides to take the plunge and compete.

"She's meeting me here," I tell Tempest, while making silly faces at my niece. "I told her I would pick her up, but she insisted on driving herself to the gym."

About that time, Cage comes downstairs and walks over to Tempest, giving her an inappropriate kiss, before turning to me and taking Freya. "Are you ready to hang out with Nan and Pops?" he asks, nuzzling Freya's chubby cheek.

"She could just come with us," I say, in a singsong voice. But I know that's not an option. Mom and Dad would never let Cage and Tempest renege on a chance to spend the night with Freya.

Who knew we'd all become such baby hogs once she was born?

And start talking like cartoon characters.

"We'll be out way past her bedtime," Tempest says, reaching over and smoothing her daughter's strawberry blonde hair. "Besides, Peggy's been begging for her to stay the night and she'll have way more fun over there anyway."

"I don't know about the more fun part," I hedge, finally getting a big toothy grin from Freya.

None of us ever seem to get enough of this chunky little baby. Now that I've been around her every day for the past month, I'm not sure how I'll survive when I'm no longer in Green Valley.

That thought tightens my chest.

For the first time since I moved here, the idea of it not being a permanent location doesn't sit right with me.

I could blame that heaviness on Freya alone, but I'd be lying.

There's another girl who's had me thinking all kinds of crazy things lately.

"We're going to get a head start, since we're dropping Freya at Nan and Pops and then picking up Vali and Maggie," Tempest says, grabbing the backpack and a pink fuzzy blanket off the front desk. "So, we'll see y'all there?"

Gunnar left a little early and stopped in Merryville to pick up Frankie from the hospital. With most of us driving separately, we agreed to just meet at the entrance to the arena.

"Yeah," I say, checking my watch. "Willow should be here in a few minutes and then we'll head out."

"Great, drive safe!"

"Y'all too."

After they're gone, I make sure all the doors to the gym are locked and I'm just getting ready to punch in the code on the alarm system when Willow pulls her truck up to the curb. I can't help the smile on my face at the sight of her.

I'm not going to lie, a part of me was worried she'd back out tonight, but the fact she's here makes me happy. Not just for me, and the fact I get to see her, but for her too. It's a huge step and after her emotional week last week, she needs this.

She needs something positive in her life—something to look forward to.

"Hey," I call out as I turn the lock on the front door. "Perfect timing."

When I turn to look at her, I'm immediately struck with the desire to pull her to me. It's been building for a while, probably longer than I'd like to admit, but after our night at the lake, it's been worse. The little taste I got of her closeness—when she allowed me to console her—was bittersweet.

It let me know how good it feels to have her in my arms.

And now I want more.

Her long, dark hair is loose around her shoulders, framing her gorgeous face and somehow making her full lips and seductive eyes stand out even more than normal.

She's wearing a flannel shirt over a cropped top that shows a sliver of her toned stomach and it makes my mouth water. I've seen her in less, but there's something about that little peek of olive-colored skin that does me in.

And don't even get me started on the way her jeans hug the curve of her hips.

"Want me to drive?" she asks, pointing her thumb over her shoulder.

"No, I'll drive," I tell her, walking backwards down the sidewalk. "I want to make it to Knoxville before the fights start and you drive that old truck like a grandma."

Her eyes go wide before an amused smile lightens her face. "Jerk."

Shrugging, I open the passenger door on my Jeep for her. "I just call 'em like I see 'em."

"Me too," she deadpans as she effortlessly climbs in.

Chuckling, I jog around the front and get in the driver's side.

As I start the engine, I realize this is the first time we've been in a closed space like this and her usual scent is multiplied. While I ease out onto the street, I inhale, letting it permeate my senses. It's not floral or sugary sweet, like a lot of women.

It's airy.

With a hint of spice.

But also feminine.

Essentially, I just described the girl sitting next to me.

When I glance over at her, I notice she's turned slightly toward the window. "Everything okay?"

"Yeah, fine."

"Want to listen to some music?" I ask, turning it up a little. "I've got satellite radio, so feel free to scroll through until you find something you want to listen to."

For a second, she doesn't move, but then she tentatively reaches out and begins to scan the stations. "What do you like to listen to?"

"Anything," I say, adjusting in my seat a little as we make our way outside of town. "Country, rock, rap... shit, I'll even listen to classical if I'm in the mood."

Willow laughs.

"What's so funny?"

"I can't picture you listening to classical music."

I watch her out of the corner of my eye, keeping my focus on the road, but not being able to pass up a quick glance at her. "Why not?"

"Oh, I don't know," she says and I hear the sarcasm in her tone. "A six-foot, two-hundred-pound guy who looks like he walked off the set of Vikings doesn't really scream classical music fanatic."

Now, I'm the one laughing. "I'm six-one, actually, and not quite two-hundred pounds. My brothers remind me of that every time I get in the ring with them. Surprisingly enough, I'm not only one of the youngest Ericksons, but I'm also one of the smallest. I barely beat Vali's one-ninety by three pounds."

Willow laughs again. "You'll never hear women complain about being smaller than another woman. Or brag about weighing more than someone."

"Gender expectations are so fucked."

"So fucked," Willow agrees. "I think that's why I like this sport so much. It allows women to live outside the box... encourages it."

She pauses and then quietly begins to talk again, opening up and showing me another piece of herself.

"When I was in the fifth grade, my foster parents bought me a new outfit for Christmas. It was the first new clothes I'd had in years, maybe ever. I was living in a home that was more like a group home. They had eight foster kids, ranging in age from two to seventeen. It was kind of nice, because I felt like I could just blend in, instead of being the focus of anyone's attention."

I know what it was like growing up in a house full of kids, but they were all my brothers. I can't imagine what it was like being in a house full of strangers.

"Anyway, I wore my new outfit to school the first day back from Christmas break and this kid named Blake Wellston made fun of me from the moment I walked into class. He asked if I got it from Goodwill and had all the other kids calling me *Thrift Store* by recess."

I make a mental note to look up Blake Wellston and find out where he lives.

"I always sat on the swings at lunch… didn't really swing, just sat there and read a book. That day, he came up behind me and pushed me, making the swing go really high. The next thing I knew, my skirt was up over my head and he was laughing… Everyone was laughing. When I jumped off, he was standing there with this smug look on his face and the next thing I know, I punched him so hard he was lying flat on his back."

That's my girl.

"The principal told me that girls don't hit and that was a very unladylike thing to do. She wanted me to apologize to Blake."

"Fuck that!" I say, shaking my head in disbelief. "That little fucker had it coming, plus some. I'd kind of like to go find him right now and kick his ass. Please tell me you didn't apologize."

"Nope," Willow says solemnly. "Got me kicked out of that school and sent to a new foster home."

A huge weight settles in my stomach, not just from her confession, but from the sadness that creeped into her tone. "Sorry."

She lets out a long breath, like she's trying to expel the memory. "It's okay. It was a long time ago."

"Just because it was a long time ago doesn't mean it still doesn't suck."

Going back to the radio, she scrolls until she finds a sixties station and *Brown Eyed Girl* by Van Morrison is playing. I'm a little surprised when she stops and even more surprised when she starts quietly singing along.

For a good twenty minutes, I drive and listen to Willow sing. Eventually, a song comes on that she either doesn't like or doesn't know and she stops.

"Where did you live before you moved to Green Valley?" I ask, dying to know more about her.

She sighs, like she has to think about it, but then answers, "I'm originally from Mountain City, where I went Friday. From there, I moved to an even smaller town about fifteen minutes away. Stayed with those people for about six months, then moved back to Mountain City. Every time I switched foster homes, I'd usually move to another small town. Then, when I turned eighteen, I aged out of the system and moved to Merryville."

I knew the Merryville part was coming. I'd put that piece of her puzzle together due to her knowing Frankie.

"Lived there for a while, then found my way to Green Valley."

I'd like to know all the in-betweens of her moves—the where, why, and how—but I don't press for more, thankful for the bits of herself she's willing to give.

"Have you ever lived anywhere besides here and Dallas?" she asks.

"Nope."

She hums and I love the way it sounds, like she's contemplating my answer. "Have you traveled much?"

"Yeah, I've traveled quite a bit," I tell her—flashes of my adventures playing through my mind. Some of them seem worlds away, as I drive down an old mountain road with Willow by my side. And I can't decide if that's a good thing or a bad thing. "Guess you could say I've got a bit of wanderlust."

"Where's your favorite place?"

Here.

With you.

138

That's my knee-jerk reaction and it surprises the shit out of me.

Where the hell did that come from?

"I took a trip to Aruba once," I say, clearing my throat and trying to dispel the rogue thoughts invading my mind. "Whitest sand I've ever seen and the water was so blue... a shade I didn't know existed."

"Sounds amazing," Willow says dreamily.

"What about you?" I ask, feeling like I know the answer but wanting to hear it from her.

"Never been out of the great state of Tennessee. But I'd love to see the ocean. Oh, and Alaska. I'd really love to go to Alaska."

Smiling, I nod. "Yeah, that one is on my bucket list too."

Over the next fifteen minutes, we talk about random things and I learn that Willow goes to the library at least once a week and checks out books. Her favorite thing to read is suspense, but she recently got a copy of Maggie's debut novel, which is a historical romance.

I sometimes forget that my newest sister-in-law is a best-selling romance author.

Also, I love that they've started including Willow in their girl gang. It makes me love them all more than I already did.

When we get to the arena, I get lucky and find a parking spot close to the entrance.

"I'm nervous," Willow says as I open her door.

Offering her my hand, I'm pleased when she takes it.

It's kind of hard to believe that something that feels so soft and delicate packs such a punch. Pulling her closer, I guide her hand through the crook of my elbow as we begin to walk.

"There's nothing to be nervous about. We're just going to go in here, watch a few fights, hang out with my family, and maybe have a beer."

"Okay, but no beer for me. I don't like it."

Chuckling, I bring the back of her hand up and kiss her knuckles without thinking. "Duly noted."

Willow doesn't get a chance to react to my gesture because Gunnar calls out from where he's standing with Frankie near the front doors. "Hey guys!"

A minute later, Cage, Tempest, Vali, and Maggie come up behind us.

"Let's get ready to rumble," Gunnar sings out, rubbing his hands together like an idiot.

I don't miss Frankie's eye roll and the way she tries to hide a smile. Sometimes I wonder how she puts up with my brother. Where Gunnar is such an extrovert and so outspoken, Frankie is reserved and quiet.

"Simmer down," Frankie says with a smirk. "It's not your night, Gunnar *The Show* Erickson."

But then she says things like that and keeps him grounded.

Maggie laughs, giving Frankie an inconspicuous low five for her timely response. "What's it like to be at a fight and not be a participant?" she asks, unable to put her reporter hat away.

"Just gets me pumped for the next fight," Gunnar says, leaning in and kissing Frankie's neck as he whispers something that makes her blush.

"What about you, Cage?" Maggie asks, as we make our way toward the entrance.

"My time in the ring sometimes seems like a distant memory," Cage admits, but unlike a couple years ago, there's no regret or resentment in his tone. "I feel more comfortable on the outside these days."

It might seem like a distant memory to Cage, but that doesn't keep people from recognizing him.

And Gunnar too, for that matter.

From the moment we walk through the security line, until we finally make it to our seats that are just a few rows back from the ring, people stop them for everything from pictures to high-fives.

"They're like freaking celebrities," Willow murmurs once we're in our seats.

"Don't let them hear you say that," I mumble. "It'll just go to their heads."

She laughs and shakes her head as her gaze takes everything in.

Vali and Maggie offer to go get everyone drinks and snacks and while they're gone, the first prelim fight is announced.

"I want you to watch the girl from Kentucky," I whisper to Willow. "She's going to be at the fight Cage mentioned signing you up for and there's a chance you would end up on the same ticket as her."

There's not as much fanfare for the prelims, but they still play each competitor's hype song before they get in the ring. I watch Willow out of the corner of my eye and notice the way she sits up straighter in her seat. Fully locked in, she cranes her neck to get a better look and I try not to stare at her beautiful profile.

The announcer rattles off each of their stats while a referee checks their gloves and verifies each of them are wearing a mouthpiece. After he gives them a briefing of the rules, they go to their corners and then the fight is on.

At first, they dance around the perimeters, but as the seconds tick down, the one I mentioned to Willow makes her move, going in with a straight right punch.

The other girl dodges it, hands up like she's been trained, and bounces around on her toes.

Movement out of the corner of my eye turns my attention back to Willow and I watch as she reacts to what's happening in the ring.

Someone punches, she weaves.

Someone kicks, she ducks.

Then, I notice her hands are clenched into fists and I can see the laser focus as she predicts their next move.

My God, she's amazing.

Like a freak of nature, in the best way.

Fuck the fight happening in the ring, I'd pay all my money to watch her.

When the crowd begins to cheer, I glance back up and notice the girl from Kentucky has landed a knockout.

Her opponent is slowly getting up, but the referee has already called the winner.

"Damn," Willow murmurs. "She's good."

She's right, that girl is good, but my gut tells me Willow's better.

Maggie and Vali make it back just before the next fight and the girls insist on sitting next to each other. So, after a game of musical chairs, Willow ends up sandwiched between Tempest and Frankie, and I'm booted to the end of the row on the other side of Cage.

"What's wrong with you?" Cage asks, trying to adjust his large frame in the small seat. "Is your beer flat?"

Staring down into the foam, I frown. "No, it's fine."

"Good fights so far," he says, nodding to the ring. "That girl from Kentucky is impressive."

"Yeah, she's good."

He grunts, which is a common response from Cage. It can stand for many things —*cool, thank you, no thank you, shut the fuck up*—but I had a feeling there was something else on his mind tonight.

"You like her," he mutters, catching me off guard.

Thankfully, I hadn't taken a sip of my beer yet. "Who?"

"Willow."

Oh, her.

Yeah.

I do.

"She's great," I say noncommittally.

I could come out and just tell him how I'm feeling. It's not like I'm under a contract to not fraternize with the clients.

Besides, this is my brother. And even though he's my boss, he's not as much of a hard-ass as people think.

But I'm still figuring out exactly how I feel about Willow, so I'm not sure how to explain it to someone else. "We get along and she's finally starting to open up a little."

He grunts again, but follows it up with, "Be careful with her."

Always the protector, Cage's response doesn't surprise me, but it does kind of piss me off, because the last thing I want to do is hurt Willow.

"I wouldn't hurt her," I say, gritting my teeth to keep from saying more.

"Not intentionally," he replies, eyes facing forward as he leans over and rubs his bottom lip with his thumb and forefinger thoughtfully. "But I know you don't have any plans to stick around permanently, and you've never been one for relationships."

He's right, on both accounts, but it pisses me off even more that he's putting me on blast like this.

Just when I'm getting ready to ask him what his problem is, he continues. "It's obvious she has trust issues, which means people have probably walked out on her before. Don't add to that body count."

Swallowing, I try to calm my racing heart.

He's right.

Willow has had a lot of people walk out on her.

But that doesn't make me want her any less.

CHAPTER 18

WILLOW

"This is it," the spunky older lady says as she opens the door to the garage apartment. "It's not much, but it's clean and secure. I had an electrician and plumber go through it to make sure everything is sound."

Her *not much* is my everything.

Sure, it's not big, but there are two bedrooms and a bathroom that's three times the size of my current bathroom. It has a bathtub.

I could take a bath. It's been way too long since I've had a proper bath.

And the kitchen is small, but perfect. It has a stove *and* an oven. So, I could bake something—a cake, casserole...cookies.

Anything you want, Willow.

There's not much of a living area, but I could at least put a sofa and television in it... maybe a small table with a couple chairs.

"I love it," I gush. "How much would I need to put down to move in?"

"Just the first month's rent," Miss Faye says.

"And the utilities? Would I need to put down deposits or have them moved into my name?"

She waves me off. "No need. Your rent will cover those."

No deposits.

Just the rent.

"So, just five hundred dollars a month?" I ask, feeling like this is too good to be true. At that price, with the utilities included, I could afford to rent this place on what I make at the Piggly Wiggly. Which means, I could continue training with Ozzi and not have to worry about squeezing in a second job.

And still have money left over for insurance, my phone bill, and groceries.

Getting me one step closer to being ready for Hazel.

"Yes," Miss Faye says, glancing around the space. "But if you need a little time to pay the first month's rent, I can work with you."

"No," I say, shaking my head, still in a bit of disbelief. "No, I think I can actually do this."

When I turn back to her, she's smiling so wide her eyes are crinkled at the edges. "Wonderful," she says, reaching out to take my hand in hers. "I think you're going to like it here. And I know I'll enjoy having you as a tenant."

"Oh, one more thing," I say, as we step out onto the porch. "I probably should've mentioned this first, but I'm trying not to get my hopes up." Suddenly, my palms are slick with sweat, and I rub them down the front of my jeans.

"Do you have a dog or something?" Miss Faye asks, locking the door behind us. "As long as they're well behaved—"

"It's not a dog," I say, cutting her off. "I just found out I have a sister and I'm trying to gain guardianship of her…"

I trail off, not wanting to say anything more for fear of jinxing everything.

"A sister?" Miss Faye asks, her eyes lighting up. "How old?"

"Nine."

This time, her smile is soft and understanding. "I think that's wonderful, really wonderful," she says, reaching out and patting my cheek in a grandmotherly gesture.

I nod, unable to speak thanks to a lump of emotion clogging my throat.

After we make arrangements for me to drop my first month's rent off and pick up my keys, I hop in my truck and head to work. A few days ago, I spoke with the owner of the RV park where I've been living and he agreed to let me leave my trailer there for a month or so while I try to sell it.

Now, all I have to do is pack up my belongings and find some furniture.

For once in my life, things feel like they're working in my favor.

When I walk in the backdoor of the Piggly Wiggly, I'm greeted by Krista who's smiling at me like she just won the lottery.

"What's got you all worked up?" I ask, opening my locker and putting my bag inside, while I pull out my work vest. "Is there a sale on Ben & Jerry's?"

She laughs like I just told an insanely funny joke. "No, but your hot trainer was in here for his weekly ice cream run, but I think secretly he was looking for you. But you weren't here. Where were you?"

"Checking out an apartment," I mutter.

"Oh, cool," she says thoughtfully. "Well, that's not the best news. Wanna guess?"

I shake my head. "Not really."

"Okay, I'll tell you. I got hired on at the Pink Pony," she says with a screech that rivals a pterodactyl. "I hope you're not mad… you're not, right?"

Glancing up, I see that she's genuinely concerned. "What? No, I'm not mad. Good for you."

"Do you mean it?"

"Of course. If that's what you want, then I'm happy for you."

Exhaling, she wraps her arms around my shoulders and hugs me. "Okay, great, because I'm so excited! But," she says, pausing as she pulls back. "That means we won't see each other every day. Promise you'll come visit me, okay?"

"Sure, I'll come visit you."

I want to tell her that's a lie, but I don't want to kill her buzz.

For one, I never go out.

For two, I'm hoping I'll be the guardian of my sister soon, which means I'll have to rearrange my life to be a little girl's sole provider and caretaker.

My life doesn't include time for trips to places like The Pink Pony.

Thankfully, Krista lets it go for now and continues talking about how she gave Tony her two-week notice. Now, that interests me because maybe I'll be able to pick up a few of her hours. Not that I have a lot of time to spare. I'm already working fifty hours a week. But a few extra won't hurt and it will make me feel better if I can replace what savings I'll be spending to get the apartment set up.

Being without a safety net makes me anxious.

Later that evening, just before I walk into Viking MMA for my training session, my phone rings.

"Hello?"

"Willow Bernard?"

"Yes, this is Willow."

There's a slight pause, but when I pull the phone back and check the number, seeing it's a Mountain City number, my heart begins to race.

"This is Nancy Goodman, I'm the social worker who's been assigned to Hazel Monroe's case."

Hazel Monroe.

It's the first time I've heard someone say my sister's full name. I've seen it on documents and forms, but no one has said it. The fact she has my mother's last name brings up so many emotions and feelings I'd rather keep buried, but I can't now.

"I'm calling to set up a time for the two of you to meet."

Wanting to get this initial meeting over with, I tell her I'm off work tomorrow and she agrees to meet at the park in Mountain City at four. Since Hazel is at school during the day, it has to be later in the afternoon. But that still gives me time to make it back to Green Valley before my late-night training session with Ozzi.

"Sounds good," I tell her, trying to quiet the nerves twisting in my belly. "I'll see you then."

Part of me wants to turn around and get back in my truck and drive back to my trailer.

I still have so much left to do.

I need to go through that stupid box that's been staring me in the face for the past week and a half.

I need to pack.

I need to get my head on straight before I meet my sister.

But I know I also need this. I need the release I get from training. I need the exhaustion to fall asleep. And I need to see Ozzi.

He has no clue about Hazel and I still don't plan on sharing that with him.

Not yet, anyway.

The idea of meeting her and the possibility of me being her guardian is still too raw and new. I'm still processing it myself. So, sharing it with someone, even the man who I've come to trust in a short amount of time, feels risky. I'm well accustomed to life blowing up in my face and I'm better equipped to handle it on my own.

And there's also that feeling of not wanting to jinx myself that I can't seem to get past.

* * *

EVEN THOUGH THE sun is out today, the air is still crisp and there's a cool breeze blowing as I sit on a bench at the Mountain City Park. My hands are shaking, but it's not just from the cold.

I don't think I've been this nervous since my less than stellar audition at The Pink Pony.

Although, it wasn't all bad. It led me to Viking MMA... and Ozzi, as well as what is quickly becoming my passion.

I'd never thought of training and fighting as a passion until Ozzi took me to Knoxville.

And to think, I almost called and backed out at the last minute. But my desire to be with Ozzi, and spend time with the rest of the Ericksons, outweighed my fears.

Talk about lighting a fire in me I didn't know I had. Ever since I watched that first fight, I've felt a spark—something intangible, but real. If I'm not at work, I'm at the gym. And if I'm not at the gym, I'm at the library reading and researching everything I can about the sport.

And, when my mind isn't on that, it's on Hazel.

When a white SUV with the official Tennessee state seal on the driver's side door pulls into the nearby parking lot, my stomach begins churning with appre-hension.

For over a month this is the moment I've been waiting for. But now that it's here, I feel like throwing up. It's not that I don't want to meet Hazel, I do. But I have no idea what to expect and the unknown has always brought me fear.

With trembling hands and unsteady legs, I stand and walk toward the vehicle.

"Willow?" a woman, who's probably in her mid-thirties, asks as she steps out of the SUV.

"Yes," I say, shielding my eyes from the sun. "Are you Nancy?"

She smiles and it's kind, which makes my anxiety ease a little.

At least Hazel has a nice caseworker, I think.

That's something.

Because I didn't always have that luxury.

I catch a glimpse of what I know is my sister, but I can't make out any features, until Nancy opens the door to the backseat and Hazel steps out.

There's a moment, where it feels like the world both stands still and spins faster. Our eyes meet and even though we've never met and are complete strangers, there's a recognition—a knowing. But then I feel and see her guard go up, slam-ming closed like the door of a prison cell.

"Hi, Hazel," I say, trying to keep my voice from trembling like the rest of my body. "I'm Willow."

Your sister.

You're my sister.

I'm your sister.

We're sisters.

I want to say it every way I can, write it on walls, and tattoo it on my skin.

For someone like me, who's spent her entire life being alone and wanting a family more than anything else in the world, this moment means everything.

"Hazel," Nancy prods when she doesn't respond. "This is your sister, Willow. Can you say hello?"

"Hey," she finally says, but then turns her attention toward the playground.

I follow her gaze to a set of swings and think that maybe an activity will help break the ice. "Do you want to go swing?"

"That's for babies," she scoffs and turns her back to the SUV before leaning against it with her arms folded protectively across her chest.

I know that stance, I feel it in my bones.

Shit, I probably would've reacted the exact same way when I was nine. Especially when I was nine. Mom had left me at that age too. She was in prison.

On my tenth birthday, the only thing I wanted was a phone call from her. The social worker I had at the time tried to arrange it. But I waited all day and she never called.

"How about we sit at the table?" I suggest, motioning over my shoulder.

Reluctantly, Hazel pushes off the SUV and walks over to the table.

I see Nancy give me a solemn nod before she walks in the opposite direction. Unlike Hazel, she's probably going to go enjoy a nice swing. Because it's not just for babies. It's for everyone, but I don't want to argue with my little sister on our first visit, so I let it go.

Instead of sitting on the bench seat, Hazel chooses to climb up and sit on the table, so I follow suit.

For a few moments, we stare out at the tree line and neither of us speak. Finally, I exhale, gathering my nerve and realizing I have to be the adult in this situation... in every situation when it comes to the two of us, because I'm it. I'm all she has.

"Tell me about yourself," I start, deciding to treat her as an equal. I know that's what I would've wanted when I was her age.

When she doesn't reply, I prompt, "What do you like to do? What's your favorite subject in school? Anything."

"How about we talk about our dead mom," she says dryly, turning to look at me with empty eyes that look exactly like our mother's.

They're not almond shaped like mine, instead, they're big and round and the same hazel-green I remember hers being.

I swallow past the lump in my throat and ask, "What do you want to talk about?" It sounds weak and I realize my mistake the second the question is out of my mouth.

She can smell my fear and now she's going to pounce.

"Maybe about how shitty a mom she was? Maybe about how glad I am she's dead? You pick."

I feel my face drop and the blood drain before I can school my features.

"Don't say that," I whisper, trying to quickly regain my composure and failing.

"Why?" she asks, jumping off the table. "She gave you up. Why do you care?"

Slowly, I stand to face her. With my heart racing and my palms sweating profusely, I scramble for the right answer. "Because she's your mom... the only one you'll ever have."

That's what I've been telling myself my whole life. Any time I wanted to hate her, I reminded myself of that fact. And now that she's gone, I see it even clearer. She was shitty, I'll give Hazel that, but she had bad stuff happen to her too. It was a series of events that started with my father's death.

"None of us choose what happens to us, but we do get to choose how we respond," I tell her, giving her a piece of wisdom that was passed down to me. "She didn't respond well to the bad stuff in her life. I'll agree with you on that. But she did give us both life, and for that, I'm grateful."

Hazel scoffs and crosses her arms, and again, I recognize the protective stance.

"I'm also really glad I have a sister," I tell her, hoping to soften her hard outer shell with a little bit of my own vulnerability.

I know when I was nine, I was a hard-ass too, but I think she has me beat. If a long-lost sister had come to claim me, I'm pretty sure I would've jumped at the chance to be out of foster care. But Hazel doesn't seem to be budging.

"I don't need anyone to rescue me," she mutters. "I'll be fine on my own."

"You're nine," I say, unable to bite back my response. "You don't know what you need."

She whips around and the second she does, I see our mother in more than just her eyes. I see her in the harsh expression, and I know that Hazel got it from the source. "I don't need you."

Letting out a long, frustrated breath, I pinch the bridge of my nose and try to calm myself. It's not my nerves that are getting the best of me now, instead, it's my temper.

"Look, I get it," I say after a few awkward moments of silence. "You're hurt and scared. I've been there. I went to my first foster family when I was seven, so I know what you're going through—"

"You don't know anything about me!" Hazel screams as tears start to fall.

That's when Nancy reappears. She walks over to Hazel and places a comforting arm around her shoulder, giving me a sympathetic glance before whispering, "Maybe we should go."

I don't want to leave. I'm not ready to give up, but I also don't like to see my sister upset. My hands itch to reach out and comfort her, but I know that's not what she wants. It would only make things worse. And I'm not trying to ruin this relationship before it even truly gets started.

Sighing, I nod in agreement. "Okay."

"I'll call you," Nancy says before she guides Hazel back to the SUV.

As they drive away, Hazel doesn't even look back.

She hates me.

It's obvious she associates me with our mother.

And she's scared.

But I didn't even get to hug her.

Nothing in the past twenty minutes went the way I imagined, and I have no idea where to go from here. This is so far out of my wheelhouse I don't even know where to start.

Feeling completely and utterly dejected, I do the only thing I know to do; climb back into my truck and head back to Green Valley... to the gym... to Ozzi.

CHAPTER 19

OZZI

*T*he second Willow walked into the gym tonight, I knew something was wrong.

But she didn't seem to want to talk about it.

Shit, I couldn't even get her to say two words. All she would give me were shrugs and grunts. For a second, I wondered if she was the victim of body snatchers and some alien had swapped her with Cage. But at least he gives me one-word answers, even when he doesn't feel like entertaining my random conversations.

"Good," I tell Willow when she lands an impressive right hook as we spar in the ring.

She's dripping in sweat. We've been at this for almost an hour. The gym has been closed for two and we're the only two people left. Cage and Tempest went upstairs hours ago and are probably already in bed.

When I throw a combo, she ducks and dodges, her gloved hands up around her face, but I can still see the laser focus.

Ever since we went to the fight night in Knoxville, she's been a different person. On top of her God-given talent and that special something she's had since day one, there's also an added spark. The very thing I had been afraid might scare her off did just the opposite.

"Left then right," I instruct, my voice coming out in short pants.

Even though Willow is smaller than me, it doesn't mean she doesn't put me through my paces.

Sparring with her isn't easy. She gives as good as she gets and if I'm being completely honest, it's the hottest thing I've ever seen. But I don't have time to think about that. I can't let my guard down at all or she'll wipe the floor with me.

After a few more minutes, I call it. "Done."

"No," Willow says, hands back up in front of her. "Keep going."

"No, you're spent. I'm spent. That's enough for tonight."

"No," she says, her voice harder, more persistent.

I'm used to her changes in mood, and I'm actually getting good at predicting them, but this catches me off guard.

"Willow." Biting the Velcro on my sparring gloves, I rip one off and drop it to the floor, my eyes on her. "What's going on?"

She braces her still-gloved hands on her knees, breathing heavy. "I just want to keep going."

"Willow." This time her name comes out a little more demanding.

When her head falls between her shoulders and her breaths come faster, my heart rate spikes. Pulling off the other glove, I drop it and go to her.

"What's wrong?" I ask, kneeling in front of her. "Talk to me."

Unlike the other times, I don't hesitate to touch her and begin taking off her gloves.

As soon as her hands are free, she falls and I catch her, pulling her into me.

"She hates me," Willow says on a sob. "She's all I have and she hates me."

I tighten my arms, trying to give her a safe place to fall apart. "Who hates you?"

How could anyone hate this amazing creature? She's one of the strongest people I've ever met. And she's so smart and tenacious. Sure, she has some hard edges, but that just adds to what makes her Willow. She's unique and beautiful. I want to tell her all of those things. They've been on the tip of my tongue the last few times we've been together, but I haven't said them because I'm afraid of scaring her off.

"Who hates you?" I ask again when she doesn't respond.

After a few more shuddering breaths, she pushes away from me. "I'm sorry," she says, shaking her head as she tries to stand. "I—I don't know why I do that... something about this place and you and losing myself in the fight is..."

"Cathartic," I offer. "Do you feel drained? Like you've exhausted not just your body, but your mind too?"

"Yeah," she says, wiping the remaining tears from her face and standing. As she walks around the ring, she raises her arms and laces her fingers behind her head. "God, this is so embarrassing. I'm sorry."

"Don't apologize," I tell her, grabbing both sets of gloves and standing. "This isn't unusual. A lot of people feel like this sport exercises the demons, so to speak."

She barks out a laugh and it allows me to breathe a little easier.

At least we've moved on from panic attacks.

Even though I hate to see her cry, I'll gladly take tears over a complete break-down any day. In my book, that's progress.

"So, who hates you?" I ask, a little quieter.

She stops, leaning against the ring and lets out a long sigh. "My sister."

When her face falls, I want to kick myself for pushing. But her reply confuses me.

"I thought you were an only child."

Dropping her eyes to the floor, she crosses her arms over her chest. "I thought I was until a month ago."

A month ago? That would've been when she found out her mom died.

Holy shit.

"She's nine. Her name is Hazel. I met her for the first time today and…it didn't go well."

Running a hand through my hair, I once again try to put myself in Willow's shoes. "Shit, I'm sorry. So, what happened?"

"We met today at a park in Mountain City," Willow begins. "Her social worker organized a supervised meeting between the two of us, but…" She drifts off, shaking her head and when our eyes meet, I see pain in her gaze. "She's so scared and, God, Ozzi… I could see so much of myself in her. It was…"

Painful.

Heartbreaking.

Traumatizing.

I can fill in the blanks Willow leaves behind.

"After our mother's death, she was placed with a family. But I recently filed for guardianship."

"Wow." That's all I can manage because I don't have a clue what else to say. Guardianship means she'd have custody of her sister… basically be her parent. That's a huge responsibility.

For someone like me, who's always avoided relationships and anything that ties me down, I can't even imagine what must be going through her mind right now.

But I am sorry that she's hurting.

And I do think what she's doing is brave and admirable.

Even I can see that.

"She'll come around," I tell her. "You said it yourself that she was scared. Kids lash out when they're afraid. I'm sure you just need a little more time."

She nods, rubbing her hands down her arms, like she's cold. I want to go to her and make her warm. "That's what I keep telling myself."

When her chin starts to tremble again, I can't take it anymore.

In two long strides, I'm wrapping my arms around her and holding her to my chest. She fits perfectly, her head coming just under my chin. And when I feel her arms come around my waist, I hold her even tighter. Pressing my lips to the top of her head, I breathe her in.

"It's going to be okay."

If I could right all of the wrongs in Willow's world, I would.

At some point, we bypass what would be considered a friendly hug, but I can't force myself to let her go. Eventually, she lifts her head from my chest and our eyes lock.

It's one of those moments where the entire world could burst into flames and I wouldn't notice, because all I can see is Willow. I know she's hurting and vulnerable and I shouldn't want to kiss her, but I do.

Then, her tongue darts out and wets her bottom lip.

A surge of energy courses through my body as she leans closer.

The next thing I know, my lips are on hers and the entire world seems to tilt on its axis. But when she stiffens in my arms, I know this isn't right.

Pulling back, I shake my head. "I'm sorry," I say, running a hand down my face. "I shouldn't have done that. That was crossing a line and—"

"It's okay," Willow says, her eyes a bit dazed, but at least she doesn't look scared or repulsed. "I should go."

"I'll walk you out," I tell her, mentally berating myself for what just happened.

Why did I do that?

Holding her was one thing, she needed that. But kissing her was a dick move. I needed that and it was a selfish thing to take.

"Ozzi," Willow says, getting my attention.

She's pulled on her hoodie and standing by the front door.

Pieces of her long dark hair have fallen out of her ponytail and her face is a little puffy from crying. But she's the most beautiful thing I've ever laid eyes on.

"Thank you for always being a listening ear and for not pitying me," she says.

welcome."

second, I think she's going to leave and we won't be acknowledging what ened.

en she stops and slowly turns back, her eyes searching mine. "I wanted to kiss you too."

CHAPTER 20

WILLOW

*W*hen I wake up and there's sun filtering through my tiny bedroom window, I immediately panic.

What time is it?

Searching for my phone, I see it's after eight o'clock, but I also remember it's Easter Sunday, which means the Piggly Wiggly is closed and I have the day off.

I'm also going to Viking MMA to eat lunch with all the Ericksons, Cassidys, and O'Neals.

Thankfully, the awkwardness that settled around me and Ozzi after our kiss... or almost kiss, whatever we're calling it or not calling it, only lasted a couple days.

So, at least I don't have to worry about that.

After I left that night, he texted me to make sure I made it home okay, then apologized again. But there really was no need. I meant it when I told him I wanted that kiss. However, once his lips touched mine, I couldn't think, couldn't breathe. It wasn't enough and too much, all at the same time. So, when I panicked, he panicked, thinking it was because I didn't want it. But that's quite the opposite of how I was feeling.

I did want it.

And now that I've had a small taste, I want more, and that scares me. The last time I allowed myself to want someone like that, it didn't end so well. He'd betrayed what little trust I'd given him and he'd used me and I vowed to never let that happen again.

Exhaling, I try to push those thoughts out of my mind. Not like I had been over the past two years, where I was burying all of my hurts and fears, but in a healthy way. I'm choosing not to give things from my past a place in my present.

Lately, after each of my training sessions, I've felt like my mind is so clear and my soul feels unburdened. Ozzi's right, it is cathartic and healing, in such an unexpected way.

I also met with Hazel again this past week, and even though it wasn't a miraculous breakthrough or anything like that, we did make a small amount of progress.

She actually talked to me instead of yelling at me.

We discovered we share a love of reading, which made me so happy. Not only because we have a common interest, but because I know what reading did for me when I was her age—giving me an escape and comforting me in a way no one else could. I hope it does the same for her.

I'm not expecting her to want to move in with me tomorrow, but I can see the path to something resembling a relationship and that gives me hope.

Yesterday I got a call from Miss Faye, letting me know the apartment is ready and I can pick up the keys on Wednesday. Which means, I've got a few days to find some furniture, at least a bed, or I'll be sleeping on the floor.

Walking to the front of the trailer, I add some water to my one-cup coffee pot and turn it on. Then, fill a pot with eggs and water, before putting it on the stove to boil.

Maggie and Tempest both told me not to bring anything, but I can't go empty-handed.

So, deviled eggs it is.

That's an Easter-y food, right?

Honestly, I wouldn't really know. The few Easters I remember celebrating as a child weren't that great. I never got the big Easter baskets. The bunny didn't visit our house. And there were never big family dinners like what I've been invited to today, so I don't really know what to expect, which always brings me anxiety.

But after hanging out with all of them as a family and individually, I know it will be fine. They've all been more than welcoming and if I had to guess, the apples didn't fall far from their trees, and their parents will be just as nice.

Once I have my coffee and the eggs are on the stove, I sit down at the table and stare at the box of my mother's belongings.

Why has it taken me so long to open it? I don't know.

At first, I just wasn't mentally or emotionally ready for what I would or wouldn't find inside. Then, I felt like it was the last link to her and as long as I didn't open it, she wasn't really dead.

But after the past couple weeks, I've realized that opening the box won't define how I feel.

Like I told Hazel, we decide how we respond to the things that happen to us, and I'm trying really hard to practice what I preach.

Setting down my coffee, I inhale a breath for fortitude and stand to begin to peel the tap that's secured the lid to the box.

Once it's open, I just stare down at the meager contents. I knew there couldn't be much from the weight of the box, but what's staring back at me isn't what I expected.

But, then again, what did I expect?

Jewelry? No, because my mother could never hold onto anything worth a damn. If it was of value, she traded it or sold it for drugs.

Knickknacks?

Clothing?

Personal artifacts?

No, none of those.

But what was staring back at me had my eyes welling up with tears.

A photo of me, with my mother and father. We're standing in front of a white car, the one my dad was driving when he had his accident.

With shaking hands, I reach in and pick up the photo, bringing it closer.

At some point, my legs must give out, because the next thing I know, I'm sitting on the floor as tears spill down my cheeks. A few drip onto the picture and I quickly brush them away so they don't mar the one piece of evidence that proves I had a family.

Holding it to my chest, I close my eyes and try to remember the day. It's fuzzy, a memory I must've pushed so far back in the recesses of my mind that it's almost unattainable, but it's there.

Vague and faint.

But I remember.

When a sizzling sound comes from behind me, I jump up, remembering the eggs I'd put on to boil. Placing the photo back inside the box, I turn the stove off and pray I didn't ruin my contribution to Easter lunch.

Sagging against the table, I start to rummage through the remaining contents of the box.

There's an old purse that's empty, not even a wallet or driver's license inside, which doesn't surprise me. Whoever she was living with probably stole anything that was valuable, and I don't think she had a driver's license.

Under that are some random papers—a cutoff notice from the electric company and a phone bill from two years ago. Not even wasting my time with those, I immediately throw them in the trash.

The bulk of the box is taken up with a few pieces of clothing. Maybe I should feel sentimental about them, but I don't. They're nothing special and have definitely seen better days, so I leave them there.

At the bottom of the box is a beaded necklace, like one a child would make.

The pink and purple beads don't jog any memories for me, not like the photo. But it's definitely something a child made, maybe Hazel. I hesitate for a second, wondering if I should just leave it at the bottom of the box and donate it with the clothes.

With a heavy exhale, I decide to keep it.

If Hazel did make it for our mother, there might come a time that she'll want this memory, just like I want the photo.

*   *   *

A FEW HOURS LATER, I arrive downtown and end up parking in front of Donner Bakery. The whole street in front of Viking MMA is full of cars. For a second, I think about turning around and going back to my trailer.

I could make a meal out of the deviled eggs I brought... maybe a ham sandwich.

But I have a feeling Tempest would show up on my doorstep, drag me out, and haul me down here. She's very persistent.

You're a big girl, Willow.

You can do this.

I bark out a laugh at myself. To think, I was here less than ten hours ago, kicking the shit out of guys twice my size. And now, here I am, sitting in my truck, afraid to walk into a family dinner.

With that thought in mind, I square my shoulders, grab my dish of deviled eggs, and step out onto the sidewalk.

A minute later, I'm barely inside the front door when Ozzi greets me with his signature smile, the one that makes me forget my name.

It's the same one he gave me that first day we met.

I remember when I saw him checking me out and it made my walls go so far up I couldn't even see around them. But I also was attracted to him and hating myself for it.

We've come a long way since that first encounter.

"Happy Easter," he says, giving me a wink.

It's then I realize Ozzi isn't dressed in his usual athletic attire. He's not even in the jeans and Henley he wore that night we went to the fights in Knoxville. No, he's wearing a crisp white button-down with the sleeves rolled up to his elbows, exposing the tattoos on his forearms.

And don't even get me started on the black slacks that fit him like a glove.

Nervously, I run my free hand down the front of my dress. I didn't have a lot of options, since this is the only one I own. It's a simple blue A-line dress with short sleeves and a hemline that hits just below my knee.

"Happy Easter," I tell him, holding out the tray of eggs. "I brought these."

Taking the tray from me, he peeks under the foil. "My favorite."

"I didn't know what else to bring," I say awkwardly, still trying to force myself to relax.

"You didn't have to bring anything," Tempest says, coming up behind me and looking like she just walked off the pages of a fashion magazine in a deep-green dress that makes her red hair pop.

When she pulls me into a hug, I lean into it and hug her back.

What are these people doing to me?

Attending family lunches.

Doling out hugs.

The next thing you know, I'll be crocheting sweaters and baking for church bake sales.

"Everyone," Tempest calls out as we walk into the part of the gym that's been transformed into an Easter Wonderland. "This is Willow Bernard. Willow, this is everyone."

They all greet me in unison and the anxiety from earlier roars back.

"Not like I expect you to know everyone," Tempest says in a lower voice. "But I'll give you a quick rundown." Clearing her throat, she points to the head of the long table. "That's my dad, Butch, and the lady in the pale-pink dress and big hair is my mom, Shauna. Sitting beside my dad is Randy."

She doesn't even have to tell me who Randy is. If I passed him on the street, I'd probably stop and do a double take. He looks like an older version of Cage. Well, Gunnar and Ozzi, too. They all look so much alike, even Vali, although his hair is darker.

"Oh, and Peggy is upstairs with Freya," Tempest continues. "They'll be down shortly. At the other end is Maggie's mom and dad, Mr. and Mrs. O'Neal. Everyone else you've met, I think."

"Yeah," I breathe nervously, feeling completely out of my element.

She pats me on the back. "Don't worry. None of them bite. And they're all more worried about how moist my ham is than the newbie at the table," she barks out a laugh. "That sounded way dirtier than I intended, especially on Easter."

I can't help but laugh too and it helps ease the tension in my shoulders.

When Tempest leaves me to tend to her ham, I just stand there for a second, taking in the large spread of food and all the friendly banter happening around me.

So this is what it's like to be a part of a large family on a holiday.

My heart that's felt cold and partially dead for so long, beats a little stronger. I shouldn't let myself get so caught up in the moment, but I can't help it. It's all so picturesque and inviting. I decide to allow myself to have this day and let this memory override all the other Easters that weren't so great.

Frankie catches my attention and motions for me to sit beside her, which I gladly do.

When Ozzi comes and takes the seat on the other side of me, I sigh in relief. Not that everyone in this room isn't the epitome of friendly, but I feel more relaxed knowing I won't be immediately forced into small talk.

After Maggie's dad prays over the food, everyone begins to pass bowls and dishes around the table. All the men dole out their praise and approval, while all the women compliment each other on their contributions to the spread.

Mrs. O'Neal tells me my deviled eggs are better than Mrs. Murphy's, and that seems to be a compliment, so I smile and thank her.

The rest of the talk at the table rotates between the gym, Gunnar's upcoming fight, and of course, Freya, who always seems to be the center of attention. And rightly so. She's one of the cutest babies I've ever seen.

"You doing okay?" Ozzi whispers from my left.

I swallow a bite of banana pudding and smile. "Yeah."

"I'm glad you came today."

"Me too."

Looking up, I catch Ozzi looking at me, but I don't turn away. Since our kiss/almost-kiss, there's been a different vibe when we're around each other. Sure, awkwardness took over for a couple of days, but after that, we fell back into our normal routine. And since then, there's been a different level of comfort when I'm around him.

I feel closer to him than I have to anyone else in a really long time.

"Willow," Ozzie's dad says from the end of the table, getting my attention. "From what I hear, you're giving all these boys a run for their money in the ring."

"I don't know about that," I manage, feeling a blush work its way up my chest and onto my cheeks.

Ozzi nudges me playfully with his elbow. "She's amazing."

That one simple, yet powerful compliment has me feeling warm all over.

"Have you decided if you're going to compete next month?" Randy asks.

I look up at Ozzi, who merely smiles. We've talked about it a lot over the past week and even though I want to, I'm still nervous about it.

It's not so much fear. I'm not scared of the fight. But I am worried about disappointing Ozzi and Cage. I'm also worried about not winning and having to pay back money I don't have.

What if I'm not as good as they think I am?

"I'm still thinking about it," I admit.

He nods thoughtfully, then says, "Like I always told the boys, you'll never know if you don't try."

Is that dad wisdom? I've never been on the receiving end, but that definitely felt like it. And, honestly, I soak it up. Something about the words and the way he says it resonates with me, giving me the little push I needed.

Later, after saying my goodbyes and thanking Tempest for the invite, Ozzi walks me to my truck.

"I'm really glad you came today," he says, his fingers brushing mine and sending a zip of electricity through my body as we make our way down the sidewalk.

Turning to look at him, I swallow hard, struck by how beautiful he is. I know beautiful isn't a word that's often used to describe men, especially men like Ozzi —tall, muscled, and tattooed. But he is, on the inside just as much as the outside.

CHAPTER 21

OZZI

"Damn, Oz," Gunnar says, dodging one of my jabs, but missing the next. "What's got you all wound up today?"

"Faster feet," Cage barks, not in the mood for our shit today.

I heard Freya crying last night from my apartment. Sound does carry a little with all of this brick and concrete, but I've never heard anything before last night. Tempest said she's still teething, which must suck. But it has put Cage in an even more surly mood.

"Faster feet, jackass," I taunt Gunnar, ignoring his question.

Truth is, I don't know what has me so worked up.

Scratch that, I do know what has me so worked up, or *who* rather.

I just don't want to talk about her.

Her name is Willow and she's kind of making me crazy.

And sexually frustrated.

This is the longest I've gone without sex since I lost my virginity when I was seventeen. Not that Willow and I are anywhere near having sex. Shit, I couldn't even kiss her without feeling like I'd done something wrong. Even though she told me she wanted it too, I still felt like I'd crossed a line.

But tasting her, even that little bit, kicked my desire for her into overdrive. She's all I can think about when I'm awake *and* asleep.

I woke up last night with half a hard-on and ended up in the shower, taking care of business, at three o'clock in the morning.

Which is probably how and why I heard Freya.

"I like it when you're worked up like this," Gunnar says, with a smug grin. "Gives me a challenge."

When I see an opening, I go in for a combination I've been working on with Willow. A round kick off the front leg, followed by a back kick off the same leg, and then finally a sweep.

Gunnar hits the floor with a thud... and then a laugh.

"Shit," he moans, rolling over. "I think training with Willow has given you an advantage. I don't ever remember you being this hard on me when we used to spar back home."

Panting, I reach down and give him a hand up, patting his back a little harder than necessary. "Maybe you're just getting soft in your old age."

"Whatever, fucker. I'll always be younger than you. Don't forget that."

Vali hops up on the rings, gloves on and ready to go. "My turn."

Gunnar groans, but Cage's drill sergeant impersonation has his ass back in line faster than he can blink.

"Nice moves," Cage mutters when I come to stand beside him near the edge of the ring.

With sweat dripping down my forehead, I wipe it away and chug from my water bottle. "Thanks," I finally say. "Learned from the best."

He chuckles. "Willow's looking good too. Have you talked to her anymore about the fight coming up in Nashville?"

She is looking good, I think to myself, both in and out of the ring. "Yeah, we just talked about it last night. She's ready."

"Good, I'll submit the form and fees this week."

The pride I feel kind of takes me by surprise. Sure, I'm always proud of any of the fighters I work with, especially when they come so far in such a short amount of time. But it's different with Willow. My pride in her goes way beyond her work in the ring.

It's more than that.

She's also tackled some major personal issues. I've seen her transform from a guarded, jaded person who had a lot of natural talent, to a trained fighter who's poised and controlled.

It's not that she's a different person. She's the same Willow I met that first day, but she's a better version of herself. By working through her past and letting go of the emotional baggage, it's made her lighter on her feet and more confident in her skills.

Like a Phoenix rising from the ashes.

And even more beautiful.

"You're good with her," Cage says, pulling me from my thoughts.

Gunnar and Vali get a little close to where we're standing, so we take a step back.

"Hands up," Cage calls out, demonstrating what he wants Gunnar to do. "Anticipate his next move."

When Gunnar and Vali exchange a few more jabs and then start grappling, Cage turns back to me. "Not just with her," he adds. "You've got a knack for training. I know you're not planning on staying permanently, and you haven't decided what you're doing next. But I just want to throw it out there…you've got a place here. As long as you want it. The job and the apartment are yours."

Praise from my big brother has always meant more than I let on. He's someone I've always looked up to and admired. If I'm honest, I've always been envious of him. Not because he was a big, bad fighter who made loads of money and attracted worldwide fame.

It was because he was driven and knew what he wanted.

Even though I say I love wandering and living the nomadic lifestyle, deep down, I'd love to have purpose and just know where I'm supposed to be.

I'd like to say that's here, in Green Valley, accepting what Cage is offering. But I'm scared to say yes. What if there's something else I'm supposed to be doing? Something I haven't found yet?

When I think about settling down and staying in one place, my palms get sweaty and I start feeling antsy. But leaving this place doesn't feel right either.

"Don't overthink it," Cage mutters. "Shit. I didn't mean to spook the commitment-phobe."

I frown, my brows scrunching up. "I'm not a commitment-phobe," I scoff.

"Okay, cupcake."

Walking up to the edge of the ring, Cage yells out, "Let's do some drills!"

"Drillers make killers!" Vali adds, jumping down from the ring and running over to shoulder-check me.

He's always so amped after sparring.

"Save that energy for Maggie," I tease, wiping off his nasty-ass sweat from my arm.

He turns and waggles his eyebrows. "That's a fantastic idea. See you later, losers," he calls out, grabbing his sweatshirt.

"We're in on the Nashville fight," Cage calls back. "Call the organizers and get Willow on the ticket, preferably with that girl from Kentucky."

"I'll see what I can do," Vali says, saluting us as he walks out the door.

* * *

A FEW HOURS LATER, I hear the bell above the front door ring, signaling someone's arrival. I don't bother looking to see who it is because it's not time for Willow to be here and I've finished up with all my other training sessions today. But when I feel the atmosphere around me charge, making the hair on my arms stand up, I realize I'm wrong.

When I turn around, there she is, looking like a fucking vision, watching me intently.

Did she just lick her lips?

I don't know what's happening between us right now but the material of my shorts tightens across my crotch. When I grab at the hem of my shirt to pull it down over my dick, I realize I'm not wearing one. Typically, I wear a t-shirt, so this is the first time Willow has seen me like this and I'm pretty sure she likes it. I'm used to people checking me out, especially my tattoos, and there's not a shy bone in my body, but I feel like I'm on display for her. We're far apart yet, the room feels crowded and I have to do something to break this spell we're under.

Forcing myself to break eye contact with her, I search for my shirt and find it on the floor next to a mirrored wall. Quickly, I grab it and pull it on before walking over to where Willow is standing.

"Hey," I grunt out, not sure of what I should say.

Do I acknowledge the tension between us? Surely, she feels it too.

"Hey," she answers. I hate that her eyes are now everywhere but on me. I don't like seeing her unsure of herself but I also know I can't rush her.

In a strange way, she seems to be an active participant in her own life for the first time. I get the feeling she's been observing, more than living, and that's just sad. As much as I want her to experience all the things and as much as I want to be there when she does, she can only do it when she's ready.

I can be patient.

"I wasn't expecting you until later. Everything okay?"

Willow clears her throat. "Yeah, I'm fine. I was, um, wanting to ask a favor but if you're busy, that's okay. I can ask someone else."

Her rambling is adorable, but fuck her asking anyone else for anything.

"No worries. What can I help you with?" I ask, trying my damnedest to stay casual.

"Well, I'm moving into an apartment and I need a bed, so I just bought a futon. The guy at the furniture store down the street wanted fifty bucks to deliver it, but I don't want to pay that. So, I thought I'd ask my big, strong Viking friends to help instead."

Laughing, I nod my head. "Of course, I'll help. Let me grab Gunnar and we'll meet you at your new place. What's the address?"

She texts me what I need and says she'll meet me there. The futon is in the bed of her truck and she understandably doesn't want to leave it unattended for very long.

When she leaves, I go find Gunnar. "Put your shoes on, man. We have an assignment."

"What the hell?" he groans. "I need to head home and shower. Y'all nearly kicked my ass today."

"Nearly? That's some bullshit right there. We kicked it good and proper but enough whining. Willow needs our help carrying her futon into her new apartment. It won't take long."

Gunnar blows out a breath before reaching for his shoes. "Fine, but only because it's for Willow."

Ten minutes later, I pull my Jeep up to the driveway of the address Willow gave me, but I'm confused. This isn't an apartment complex, like I was expecting, it's a house. Willow's truck and the futon are here, though, so I must be at the right place.

I hear a door shut and my attention is caught by Willow jogging down a set of stairs by the garage.

Do not look at her boobs.

"Thank you so much for helping me with this," she says in greeting.

"No problem," Gunnar answers. "I was worried we'd have to carry the futon up some winding staircase or something, but this will be easy."

"Yeah, I was already mentally practicing my best Ross impression," I add. "Pivot! Pi-vot!"

Gunnar and I both crack up, but Willow is looking at us like we've lost our minds.

"Don't tell me you've never seen that episode of *Friends*."

Shrugging, her face falls a little. "I've never watched any of them. I actually don't even have a television."

Shit, I've made her feel bad, which is the exact opposite reaction I was hoping for.

"Looks like we have another item to add to our workout schedule," I tell her.

"What do you mean?"

"There are ten seasons of *Friends*, so we have a lot of catching up to do." I imagine the two of us starting off slowly, one or two episodes after Willow's workouts, and then building up to marathons... just the two of us.

Snacks, drinks, and maybe even some snuggling on her new futon.

Maybe I'll buy her a television for a housewarming gift.

And introduce her to Netflix... then, we can Netflix and chill.

Willow's smile is hindered by her teeth biting down on her lip, but I can tell she likes my idea. And not only do my shorts feel tight again, but so does my chest for some reason.

Choosing to ignore both areas, I change the subject. "Where do you want this?"

It doesn't take us long to haul the futon upstairs to Willow's apartment and get it set up. The metal frame wasn't very heavy, but the mattress was more difficult than I thought it would be. I'm glad, though, because my past experiences with futons involved thin, crappy mattresses that were about as comfortable as sleeping on nails. Knowing Willow will be getting a good night's sleep in a safe new place makes me feel relieved.

I'd like to offer to stay over and keep her *extra safe*, but I can't. Gunnar needs to get home and I'm still trying to be on my best behavior when it comes to Willow.

Besides, if anyone was dumb enough to break in, she'd have them pinned to the floor within seconds. That thought turns into me imagining Willow pinning me to the floor and I can't go there. Not unless I want to make this moment awkward AF, so I decide to pack that away and save it for when I'm alone tonight.

"Congrats on the new place," Gunnar says, making his way to the door.

"I'll meet you at the Jeep," I tell him, giving him a silent nod we've perfected over the years that lets him know I need a minute.

Willow lets out a satisfied sigh as she scans the small apartment. "Thanks again for helping me today. I really appreciate it."

I can see the pride radiating off her and it makes me proud of her... happy for her. It's not a huge space, but from what she's told me, it's a lot bigger than the trailer she's been living in since she moved to Green Valley.

"You don't have to keep thanking me. It was fun."

She rolls her eyes and lets out a laugh. "Moving furniture is not my idea of fun but no judgment, I promise. I'll be sure to call you up when I find a couch that's in my budget"

"You do that," I tell her with a laugh. "While we're on the subject, what *is* your idea of fun?"

Her face turns serious, and I wish I would've kept my stupid mouth shut.

She's beautiful when she's serious but she's stunning when she's smiling.

A few seconds pass before Willow brushes a loose strand of hair behind her ear and clears her throat. The small gesture has my fingers itching to reach out and do it for her, craving the smallest touch.

"I, honestly, don't know," she says, avoiding my gaze. "I really enjoy training..." Drifting off, I swear I hear her mumble something that sounds a lot like "with you", but I don't press.

"And I love to read," she adds, crossing her arms over her chest in a move I've come to recognize as Willow protecting herself from the unknown or something she's unsure about.

I wait, giving her all the time she needs, but eventually she shrugs, turning her eyes back to me. "I guess that's it. Kind of boring, I know."

I can see the honesty and vulnerability in her expression. The way her brown eyes go soft lets me know she's opening up. Every time she gives me a new piece of herself, I feel the connection between us grow stronger and my desire for her grows.

"Not boring at all," I assure her. "I love books too, actually."

Her face lights up a little at my confession. "Really?" she asks, her brows furrowed. "I didn't really peg you for a book nerd. But then again, I also didn't peg you for someone who likes classical music either."

There's a tinge of pink on her cheeks and I feel that spark that's been building between us grow to more of an ember.

"Just proof that you shouldn't judge a book by its cover," I tell her, cocking an eyebrow.

Her face breaks into one of those smiles that practically knocks me off my feet.

"You're right," she says with a nod.

"Well, challenge accepted," I say with a smirk, going for playfulness, instead of the intensity that's brewing inside me.

There's a honk and I roll my eyes, wanting to punch my brother. "I need to go," I tell her reluctantly. "Gunnar just finished up his last session for the day right before you showed up, so he's being a baby and wanting to shower."

"I thought I smelled something funky," she teases.

God, I love that.

I love that she's opening up to me, sharing stuff about herself, and letting me see a side of her I get a feeling not many people have seen.

"You up for a new challenge?" I ask as I walk to the door.

"What do you mean?" she asks.

"Cage always says a good fighter is one who's balanced, meaning they train hard and play hard. So, we're gonna spend a little more time on the fun part, but we have a lot of ground to cover. You up for that?"

Willow thinks for a moment and I start to worry she'll say no. Instead, she smiles, shrugging her shoulders. "I'm always up for a challenge."

"Good," I say, bracing my arms on either side of the door frame. "I know the perfect way to get started."

"What's that?"

"You being my date to Vali and Maggie's wedding reception."

CHAPTER 22

WILLOW

ou being my date to Vali and Maggie's wedding reception.

God, I want that.

I'd love nothing more than to go with him, but I can't.

"I have to work that night," I say, grasping for the first solid excuse I can think of. And that's not a lie. I do have to work that night. I work every Saturday night because I'm the only employee who doesn't have a social life.

Ozzi rolls his eyes, not accepting it. "I'm sure you can get off work this one time. I know you, Willow Bernard, and you're the model employee. Surely, your boss will grant you this one Saturday off."

My heart beats faster as I try to think of what to say next. The truth is, showing up to that reception is nerve-wracking on its own, but add on to that being Ozzi's date and I'm practically in a full-blown panic attack.

A date.

His date.

That makes all of the emotions and feelings I've been experiencing real and I don't know if I'm ready for that.

Plus, I don't have anything to wear. I wore the only dress I own for Easter, and a fancy new one isn't in my budget. I still have a lot to do before my home visit with Nancy, as well. She's going to need to see that I have a safe place for Hazel, fully equipped with a bed and all the other necessary things needed to care for a nine-year-old.

"I really need the hours," I say weakly, hating the way his face falls. I've mentioned that I'm trying to gain guardianship of Hazel, so I know he knows how much I need to work.

Finally, he nods his head. "I get it. That's cool. But if you change your mind, I'd love for you to come. I know Maggie already invited you and she'd love for you to be there too."

Exhaling in relief that he's letting this go, I give him a tight smile. "I know. It was sweet of her to invite me and it's even sweeter of you to ask me to go with you."

His eyes narrow, like he's trying to see beneath my bullshit. Ozzi is good at that. He's maybe the first person ever who's truly seen me. And he doesn't run away, even when what he sees is a mess and riddled with scars from the past.

And that scares me.

Because it makes me want him that much more.

But with someone like me, who's been abandoned and discarded, it's hard to let myself desire anyone or anything. In my world, that only ever equates to heartache, and I've had enough of that to last two lifetimes.

"I'll see you at the gym later," I tell him, trying to soften the blow of my rejection.

If he only knew, it's not him I'm rejecting. It's myself.

"See you tonight."

* * *

A COUPLE DAYS LATER, on my drive to Mountain City to see Hazel, I'm still thinking about Ozzi inviting me to Maggie and Vali's reception. That fact, in and of itself, should be enough evidence I'm in trouble and this crush, or whatever you want to call it, isn't going away.

Today, I had an early training session at the gym and the building tension between us was still there. It was all I could do to stay focused and not let my eyes linger on his tattooed forearms when we were sparring or his full bottom lip when he was instructing me.

Then, to make matters worse, I overheard a couple of women talking about him when I went to the bathroom. They were standing beside a water cooler in the hallway and talking about how sexy he is and how they'd like to experience their own *Viking Invasion*.

Apparently, Maggie coined that term in her advice column back when Vali first came to town and it's stuck with the locals.

But hearing them talk about Ozzi like that is what stuck with me.

I've been envious of a lot of people in my life—people with a mom, people with a dad, people with a mom and a dad—but until today, I don't think I've ever felt true jealousy.

Just imagining Ozzi with another woman made me irrationally jealous.

Thinking about someone else touching him or kissing him makes my stomach hurt.

When I arrive at the park, which has become our meeting place, I see the now familiar white SUV by the picnic tables. Pulling up beside it, I wave at Nancy.

Since Hazel and I have seen each other a few times, Nancy hardly even gets out of the car now.

Next week, we're going to get to have our first unsupervised visit.

Oddly, that doesn't scare me anymore. It did at first, especially after the epic fail of our first meeting. But now that Hazel and I are getting along better and starting to connect, I think I'm ready.

"Hey," I say, walking up to where Hazel is sitting at the table.

She squints up at me, blocking the sun with her hand, and I think I actually get a smile. "Hey."

Taking a seat across from her, I place the bag I brought with me on the table.

"What's that?" she asks, eyeing the bag.

"I didn't have a chance to eat much today and I had a training session, so I brought some PB&Js. I thought we could have a picnic."

Hazel doesn't say anything, so eventually, I look back up to see if I've upset her somehow or maybe she's gone back to hating me, but there's a softness to her eyes. It makes her look every bit the nine-year-old she should be, instead of the near-adult she comes across as sometimes.

"Do you like PB&Js?" I ask, when she still doesn't say anything.

God, I hope so. I hate to break it to her, but if I obtain guardianship of her, these will become a staple in her diet. But now that I'm in the apartment, I do have the space to cook more and I'm really looking forward to it.

"I love PB&Js," she says, almost shyly. "Strawberry jelly is my favorite but they never have it."

I cock my head as I unwrap the sandwich I made for her. It's already cut into triangles, like I like to eat them. "They?"

"The Wilsons," she says, her eyes meeting mine and an understanding passes between us.

I know how that feels—to never have anything you want.

"Tell me some of your other favorites," I prompt, wanting to know what makes her happy.

"Root beer," she admits quietly. "And sour cream and onion chips."

Giving her a small smile, I take a bite of my sandwich and she follows suit. "Do you like pizza?"

She nods fervently. "Pepperoni," she says around another bite.

"Me too," I tell her, a vision of the two of us making pizza together in the small kitchen of the apartment. My heart aches for the simplicity of it—to have her under my roof and the two of us being a family.

I also think about Ozzi and how much he loves pizza. And that thought leads me to wondering if Hazel would like him. I think she would. There's not much to *not* like about Ozzi Erickson. He's funny and caring and has this way about him that puts people at ease.

What would he think of Hazel?

She'll obviously have to come with me to the gym for my sessions because I wouldn't leave her at home alone. But I get the feeling that wouldn't be a problem, at least not with the Ericksons. They all seem very family-oriented, even Ozzi. I've seen the way he is with Freya and it's enough to make even my twenty-two-year-old ovaries ache. And I'm years away from wanting or needing a baby in my life.

"What about you?" Hazel asks, pulling me out of my thoughts. "What's your favorite food?"

"I love pepperoni pizza too," I admit. "And PB&Js, obviously."

Hazel lets out a small chuckle and I realize that might be the first time I've heard her laugh. I want more of it. I want her to get a chance to be a kid and feel safe and loved.

All the things I never had.

"And ice cream, macaroni and cheese, grilled chicken," I say, counting off on my fingers. "But I've been training lately, so I've tried to eat a lot of vegetables and I realized I don't hate them."

"Training for what?" Hazel asks, her brows furrowing.

I haven't really told her much about me, not because I'm trying to keep her at arm's length, like I do with most people. I've just tried to soak up as much of her as I possibly can during our few visits.

"Have you ever heard of Mixed Martial Arts?" I ask, trying to think of a good place to start. If she's anything like me, she's never taken any kind of class or participated in any sport. Outside of the required physical education classes I took through school, I never had the chance to play sports. I've always loved to run and physically exert myself. I just didn't realize how much until I started training with Ozzi.

Hazel scrunches up her nose. "I think it's like karate or something like that."

"Yeah, but it also incorporates other forms of martial arts, like kickboxing and judo."

Ozzi has been working with me on that last one quite a bit lately. Talk about a workout.

And the body-to-body contact.

I've decided grappling is my new favorite thing, as long as it's with Ozzi.

"So, you're training to fight?" Hazel asks. I can see the wheels in her head turning as her eyes grow wide.

Letting out a short laugh, I nod. "Yeah, I am. Kind of crazy, but I love it."

"You do not look like a fighter," she says, her head shaking from side to side in disbelief.

"What do I look like?"

She eyes me thoughtfully, her pointer finger coming up to rest at the side of her mouth.

It's so freaking cute I want to reach across the table and hug her, but we're not quite there yet.

"Like a librarian," she finally says with a shrug. "Without the glasses. Or the bun. But you did wear your hair in a bun that one time. I like it like you're wearing it today. Can you teach me how to braid my hair?"

For a second, I just stare at her, soaking in this moment. This is the first time since we started our visits that I feel like she's being herself, not holding back or putting up a front. And, holy crap, I love her so much.

"I'd love to teach you how to braid your hair." I have to cover up the crack in my voice with a cough.

"So what are you training for?"

"You mean, like what's my goal?" I ask, still processing that myself.

She nods, popping the last bite of her sandwich into her mouth and dusting the crumbs off her hands.

"Well," I draw out with a sigh. "I just signed up for a competition that's coming up in a month or so. Other than that, I'm just doing it because I really love it. It makes me feel good and I like the physicality and mental clarity that comes along with it."

"Like yoga," she says matter-of-factly.

"What do you know about yoga?"

Shrugging, she balls up the plastic wrap from her sandwich and tosses it back into the bag on the table. "We do it at school and I really like it, so I do it in my room sometimes. I don't have a mat or anything, but it makes me feel calmer."

"I agree," I tell her, making a mental note to buy a yoga mat… or two. "Ozzi and I do yoga sometimes during our sessions."

"Who's Ozzi?"

God, what a loaded question.

"My trainer," I begin, but for some reason, I don't leave it there. "He's also my friend." Clearing my throat again, I give her a forced smile as I try not to think about all the things I *wish* Ozzi was—more than a friend? A boyfriend? Someone I know on an even more intimate level?

Hazel snickers, drawing my attention back to her.

"What?"

She cocks an eyebrow at me, making her look more like a teenager than a nine-year-old. "You like him."

The second her accusation is out, I feel my cheeks warm. "Yeah, I do. As a friend."

"Bullshit."

My eyes grow wide and I look around, even though there's no one else by us at the table. All the other people at the park are over on the slides and swings. And Nancy is still in the car.

"You can't say that," I hiss, not sure how much of a disciplinarian I should be at this moment. On one hand, I feel like giving her props for calling me out like that. But on the other hand, I'm potentially going to be the person raising her

187

into the best human being she can be. And I feel like I'm not supposed to let her say things like that.

Hazel rolls her eyes.

"If you think I don't hear worse things every day at home and at school, you're crazy. Of course I'm going to repeat them," she says, throwing her hands in the air and inhaling deeply. Nailing me with those hazel eyes, she drops her voice. "I might be nine, but I've been taking care of myself for a long time. Just because I'm a kid doesn't mean I can't say what I think or have an opinion about things. Sorry to break it to you, but if you want a perfect little sister, I'm not it. So you might as well leave while the gettin's good."

I'm shocked, but I don't know why. Hazel has been a straight shooter from day one. And she's really no different than I was when at her age. By the time I was six, I was waking myself up in the mornings, making myself breakfast, and walking to the bus stop. When I got home from school, it was no different.

"I'm not looking for perfection," I tell her. "I actually hate that word. Nobody is perfect. I'm sure as hell not. So, how about we both give each other a little grace."

"What's that mean?"

I laugh wryly, realizing there will still be a lot of things I can teach her. And she'll teach me even more.

"It means I'll try not to get upset about things you say that are inappropriate for a nine-year-old, and you'll try not to get upset about me being the annoying big sister."

Hazel gives me a conspiratorial smile and then reaches across the table, with her pinky held up. "Pinky promise."

"Pinky promise," I agree.

"So, about Ozzi," she says, hopping straight back on that topic. "Why isn't he your boyfriend? Does he already have a girlfriend?"

Chuckling, I shake my head.

What happened to nine-year-olds thinking boys were gross?

"No, he doesn't."

"Do you know this for sure?"

"Yes, he actually asked me out on a… date?" I say it as more of a question than a statement.

Her eyes grow wide as she leans closer over the table. "Did you say yes?"

"No," I say, cringing, maybe at my response or maybe at my fear of hers.

"What? Why?" She's now standing, hovering over me with an appalled expression. "If you like him, why would you say no?"

"It's complicated."

She sits back down and rolls her eyes. I realize this is something I'm going to have to get used to because she's done it at least half a dozen times since we've been sitting here today.

"Adults are so stupid," she mutters.

I can't help but laugh again and realize I needed this so damn much.

Not just the laugh, but Hazel—today, this moment, our connection.

How crazy is it that I've only known about her for a couple months, actually less than a month, but feel more connected to her than anyone else in my entire life.

I've never believed in love at first sight, but I do now. When it comes to little sisters, I think it's possible.

"I have to work," I tell her, giving her the same lame excuse I gave Ozzi. "Plus, I don't have anything to wear. He invited me to a wedding reception."

There go the big, wide eyes again as her mouth falls open. "Oh, my gosh, Willow," she practically cries. "You have to go. Please, I've always wanted to go to a wedding, but I never got to. So, please go for me. Please."

Her begging hits me right in the chest, a direct hit to my heart.

How will I ever say no to her?

God, help me.

The day she actually sheds tears, I'll be a goner.

CHAPTER 23

OZZI

*M*aggie and Vali's wedding reception started out more like a wedding.

Under a large white tent set up behind O'Neal Feed and Fodder, Maggie walked down a makeshift aisle to where Vali waited with one of the local preachers. He said a quick word and they repeated their vows in front of their families, God, and everyone.

I've never seen my brother so happy.

And I've never seen Maggie so beautiful.

After their vow renewal, they were officially introduced as Mr. and Mrs. Vali Erickson and then the party got started—delicious food, amazing cake, and good booze.

Now, everyone is dancing and I'm missing Willow like crazy.

Not only did she turn down my invite, but we were so busy setting up this monstrosity of a tent, I had to cancel our training session yesterday. Well, she still went to the gym and worked out, but I wasn't here. Which means, I haven't seen her in over two days.

But it feels like an eternity.

"You gonna mope around in this corner all night?" my dad asks, coming up behind me and wrapping a beefy arm around my shoulder.

For an old dude, he's still ripped.

And he's also a bit too intuitive for my liking.

"Not moping," I say, keeping my gaze on the dance floor as I take a casual sip of my beer. "Just people watching."

He scoffs. "I've never known you to be a wallflower."

He's right. I'm never one to stand on the sidelines. I like to be in the action, wherever that may be. Any other time, if I didn't have a date, I'd be twirling my mom around the dance floor. But Willow's rejection stung a little more than I'd like to admit.

"I'll get out there in a minute," I tell him. "Just gonna finish this beer."

"This wouldn't be about some knockout fighter, would it?"

My shoulders stiffen and I know he feels it.

"That's what I thought," he continues, giving my back a hard pat. "Saw the way the two of you were looking at each other on Easter. She seems like a good one."

"She is."

I meant what I told him at Easter, Willow is amazing, in every sense of the word. She's not perfect, but I've never been interested in that. She's complicated and jaded. She's both a mystery and as familiar as one of my favorite hoodies.

Beautiful.

Talented.

Smart.

Tenacious.

A fighter.

I could go on, but my dad interrupts my thoughts.

"How much longer are you planning on staying in Green Valley?" he asks. "Cage mentioned he offered you a permanent position at the gym. Think that'd be a good fit for you, but I know how you are and I'm sure you're already getting the itch to go somewhere."

He chuckles good-naturedly and slaps my shoulder again. It's such a fatherly gesture, I can't help but smile, even though he does know me a little too well and I don't really like him calling me out on it. My plans, or lack thereof, have become quite the hot topic and I don't like it.

"Yeah," I say with a sigh. "He did, and yes, I am."

For the past week or so I've been doing a lot of Google searches—hiking trips, cheap plane tickets, a bungalow on a beach. But I'm not going anywhere until after Willow's fight. And even then, I'm still not sure.

I like to leave my options open.

It's when I start to feel boxed in that I get the itch my dad referred to. For now, I still feel untethered—free to roam when and if I want—so I'm happy to just continue to coast and go where life takes me.

"Well, well, well..." my dad croons, straightening his tie. "I think that one is looking for you. Guess I'll go find your mom and see if she saved me a dance."

When he steps away, I see who he's referring to.

Standing at the opening of the tent is Willow. Her dark hair is hanging in loose waves around her shoulders and she's wearing a black dress that makes my mouth water.

For a moment, I just watch her, my head reeling from the fact she's here. I mean, I had hoped she'd change her mind, but I figured she would've told me she was coming. So, seeing her is definitely a surprise, one of the best kinds.

When she spots me over in the corner, I give her a nod of approval before discarding my drink and making my way over to her. As I walk across the tent, a slow smile grows on her gorgeous face and it literally sets my soul on fire, along with the rest of my body.

Every part of me responds to her.

"I thought you had to work," I say, shoving my hands in the pockets of my slacks to keep myself in check.

Willow bites on her bottom lip to keep from smiling and sighs. "I was supposed to, but…"

"But…" I encourage when she doesn't continue.

"A certain nine-year-old asked me to come for her and apparently I can't tell her no."

For a second, I feel my chest deflate a little at the realization she might not be here for me, but then I see the same heat I feel inside reflecting back from her eyes.

"I think I might like this kid."

She huffs out a laugh. "She's pretty great, actually. And very persuasive."

Maggie spots us still standing by the entrance and comes over to hug Willow. Then, Frankie and Tempest join in, and for a minute, I think they're going to steal her away before I even get a chance to tell her how beautiful she looks. Thankfully, after some congratulatory hugs and gushing over dresses, a song they all like to dance to at Genie's comes on and they break off to find my brothers, leaving just the two of us.

"You look beautiful," I tell Willow, wanting to get that out before we're interrupted again.

She looks over at me and for a second, I get lost in her eyes. They're a little more noticeable tonight. Her lashes are darker. She doesn't have a lot of makeup on, but more than normal, and just enough to highlight her gorgeous features.

"Thank you," she says quietly, not looking away. "So do you."

The idea that Willow thinks I look beautiful makes me chuckle. I've been called a lot of things, but never that.

"What?" she asks, a smile pulling at her delicious lips.

Shaking my head, I look back to the dance floor as the music changes temp. "No one has ever called me that."

"Well, you are," she says nonchalantly, like it's common knowledge.

"Dance with me?" I invite, holding my hand out for her to take.

When she does, the feel of her skin on mine sends a jolt of electricity through my body. I'd love to know what the rest of her feels like. I'd love to kiss her, for real this time, and not feel like I'm committing a crime.

"I'm really glad you came," I whisper, as I pull her close and begin to sway to the music.

She smells amazing. Her normal spicy scent is mixed with something else, like perfume. And like her makeup, it's not too much, just enough to make her even more mouth-watering than normal.

"Me too," she says after a few beats, leaning in a little closer. "I have a confession."

"What's that?" I ask, loving the feel of her in my arms.

"I've never been to a wedding either…or a reception."

I can't help the smile on my face. Every time she shares these bits and pieces of her life, it draws me in a little more.

"Well," I say, wrapping my arm tighter around her waist. "The reception is really the best part. So, you're in luck. I mean, I guess if it's your own wedding the ceremony is important. But as a guest, I've always enjoyed the food, booze, and dancing."

I can feel Willow laugh against my chest. "That's such an Ozzi thing to say."

My lips graze her temple as I lean in closer for what I'm about to say. "And for future reference, it's frowned upon to upstage the bride."

CHAPTER 24

WILLOW

*O*zzi's warm breath on my cheek and his sweet words in my ear force my eyes closed.

God, he feels amazing.

And he smells amazing.

And he looks amazing.

The way his strong arm is wrapped around my waist as we sway to the music makes me weak. It's enough to make me forget about having walls of protection around my heart. All I can think about is him—dancing with him, being close to him, feeling his body pressed against mine.

I'm so engrossed in the moment I don't even realize when the song changes.

"Let's get some fresh air," Ozzi mutters.

"Okay," I say, as I leave my hand in his and allow him to lead me off the dance floor.

Once we're out of the tent, I welcome the cool breeze on my warm skin. My entire body feels flushed and when Ozzi pulls me back into his arms, the ember that's been smoldering inside me turns into a blaze.

"I want to kiss you." His voice is smooth and rough all at the same time, and it causes a jolt of need to course through me. "I promised myself I wouldn't though… not until you asked me to."

For a moment, it's just us and the Tennessee night.

No wedding guests or music playing in the background.

No crickets chirping.

No walls or perimeters of friendship.

Just Willow and Ozzi.

And I want nothing more than to feel his mouth on mine.

Grabbing the lapels of his jacket, I pull him closer. "Please kiss me."

The desperation in my voice is apparent. Ozzi hears it too.

His eyes grow hooded as they drop to my mouth. And I watch with rapt fascination as he darts his tongue out and licks his full bottom lip. The anticipation I feel, waiting for him to close the distance between us, is something I've never experienced before—like a current of electricity flowing through my body.

Then he does it.

He lowers his head and brushes his lips over mine, tentatively at first, causing my knees to grow weak with each pass. Then his teeth nip and I open, giving him access, and he begins to kiss me like I've never been kissed before.

It's possessive and demanding, while also giving me so much in return.

With one hand wrapped around my body, the other comes up to cup my face, his fingers lacing through my hair as he brings me impossibly closer.

I let out a moan and he swallows it down.

Every sweep of his tongue gives me breath and life, igniting something deep within me I haven't felt in a long time, if ever.

Need.

Want.

Desire.

Everything.

A throat clearing is the only thing that breaks us out of the lust-filled haze and the most amazing kiss of my life. I don't even register that someone saw us or that I should be embarrassed, because I can't pull myself from Ozzi.

"Hey, man," Gunnar says from somewhere behind me. "Uh, they want you inside for the toasts."

"Be there in a minute," Ozzi says, his eyes still on me. After a few seconds, he kisses me tenderly once more before pulling back and running the pad of his thumb over my cheek. "You okay?"

"Better than okay," I admit.

The smile that splits Ozzi's face is contagious. Biting down on his lower lip, he nods. "Good, because I definitely want to do that again, but first I have to go give a toast."

"Let's go," I say, motioning toward the tent.

Hand-in-hand, we walk back inside and Ozzi leads us over to the table where his family is seated, finding me a spot beside Frankie.

"I wondered where you went," she muses. "But I see you were in good hands."

That's when my cheeks decide to heat up and the reality of what just happened comes crashing down. As I sit and listen to Vali's brothers give him shit and proclaim their love for Maggie, I play back the last half hour like an old movie in my mind—the look he gave me when he saw me walk into the tent, the feel of his body against mine, the way his kiss completely rocked my world.

It's enough to distract me from everything and everyone around me.

But when it's Ozzi's turn to speak, I'm like a moth to a flame and I can't take my eyes off him.

"I'm surprised they're letting me have the microphone," he begins with a salacious smirk. "And I'm not sure what I can say that hasn't already been said, but I did want to congratulate my brother on finding the perfect person to put up with his ass." Everyone laughs and Ozzi shoots an apologetic grin to his mother who's sitting down the table from me. "Sorry, Mom."

When his eyes drift over to me, I feel the lingering heat from our kiss.

"They say when you find the person you're meant to be with, you'll just know. Before my brothers started falling in love, I honestly thought that was a load of crap. I mean, my parents have been married since the beginning of time. But I just figured they were an anomaly. However, now that I've been blessed with two new sisters-in-law in Maggie and Tempest, and Frankie, who already feels like my sister." He points in her direction and she chuckles, shaking her head. He continues, "I guess all that fate and destiny stuff might not be so far-fetched."

His eyes find mine again and I swallow. I'm not typically a crier, even though I've had more breakdowns than I'd like to count since I met Ozzi. Usually, I'm good at controlling my emotions and I have no reason to get choked up at this minute, but regardless, my eyes start to burn.

"And when I look at my niece," he says, finding Freya who's sitting with Tempest's mom and dad. "I know there must be a power bigger than all of us, leading us to the people we're meant to be with."

I glance down the table to see Randy wrap his arm around Peggy's shoulders as she dabs the corner of her eyes.

At least I'm not the only one getting a little choked up.

"To Vali and Maggie," Ozzi says, holding up his glass. "Congrats on your second wedding. Thanks for inviting all of us this time."

That gets a laugh from everyone and I see Vali rolling his eyes while he holds Maggie close.

"I wish you many happy years ahead... and lots of babies, because I'm an awesome uncle and this greatness shouldn't be wasted."

Frankie passes me a glass of champagne and we all toast the bride and groom.

When Ozzi walks back over to the table, he stretches out his hand. "Dance with me."

Of course, I can't turn down that request, not for all the champagne in the world. So, I sit my half-empty glass on the table, smile at Frankie who gives me an approving nod of her head, and I place my hand in Ozzi's to follow him back out to the dance floor.

For the next hour, we alternate between dancing and visiting with other guests, not only his family, but other familiar faces from the gym and people I've met while working at the Piggly Wiggly.

As the evening draws to a close, I find myself not wanting it to end.

I'm not ready to let go of Ozzi and I'm worried about what happens after tonight.

There's no way we can go back to just being friends, or student and trainer. In reality, we've been more than that for a while now, but neither of us wanted to admit it, or maybe that was just me.

"I wish I could drive you home," Ozzi murmurs in my ear as we walk out of the tent and through the field where everyone is parked.

I wish that too, but I also feel like I need a minute to process what we're doing.

"Mr. and Mrs. O'Neal would probably frown on me leaving my truck parked in the middle of their field for the night," I muse.

"Mmmm," Ozzi hums in my ear as he turns me, pressing my back into the cool metal of my truck. "I wouldn't mind spending the night with you in this field."

As our eyes lock, a rush of desire heats my entire body. "That… sounds fun," I say, swallowing hard when I see the same hooded expression from earlier.

The night air sizzles around us as he leans closer, brushing his nose against mine.

He wraps his arms around my waist and pulls me closer and then our lips meet.

If I thought our earlier embrace was a fluke, I'm proven wrong when this second kiss rivals the first. This time, there isn't anyone to interrupt us, as most of the guests have left and everyone who's still here is cleaning up.

Ozzi presses against me and his hard length is like a brand on my body.

When I moan into his mouth, he nips my bottom lip again, making it hurt so good.

Letting my hands roam his chest, I lean further into the kiss—into him.

"Fuck, Willow," he hisses as my touch gets closer to the waist of his slacks. "I want you so bad."

"I want you too," I say, my words coming out in breathless pants.

He leans back, the warm glow of the lights from the tent illuminating his gorgeous face, and for a moment he just looks at me and I suddenly feel exposed, like he can see through my walls and façade, straight down to the core of who I am.

It makes me feel more vulnerable than if I were standing in this field naked.

When I try to avert my gaze, he reaches up and holds my chin, forcing me to maintain contact. "Don't look away from me," he says, rubbing his thumb along my jaw. "And don't hide from me, okay?"

"Okay," I say with a small nod. Strangely enough, I don't want to hide anything from him, not anymore. He's the first person I've fully trusted in a long time, and he's taken every truth I've given him in stride, never making me feel bad about my past or my present.

He pushes his hands through my hair and I'm enthralled by his touch and words. Like earlier when he was giving his speech, I'm his captive audience.

"I just want you to know that I love every part of you I've been fortunate to see and I can't wait to see more, but I'm also not interested in rushing things and fucking this up," he says, sincerity dripping off every word. "I don't want to come between you and your training, because fuck, Willow, I believe in you. I think you're amazing and have so much potential. So, if you think this isn't a good idea… if we need to hold off or if you want me to talk to Cage about—"

"No," I say, cutting him off. As much as I love listening to him talk—especially his words of praise—I'm not interested in hearing him find an excuse why this can't happen. "I'm good. We're good. I think we're both mature adults and we can handle exploring a relationship outside of the gym and still make a good team inside the gym."

His smile is blinding and the next thing I know he's swooped me up and is spinning me around.

"God, I'm so happy you said that, because I was kicking my own ass for the bullshit I was spewing," he says with a laugh.

When I wrap my arms around his neck, he holds me tighter, and his playful mood shifts as we just hug each other. It's sweet and tender and perfect, and it makes tears spring to my eyes.

"Before I met you, I can't remember the last time someone hugged me," I admit into his shoulder, inhaling deeply and letting his warm, rich scent wash over me. "I didn't realize how much I missed it."

Ozzi stills and his arms grow even tighter around me. After a moment, he whispers, "I'm going to hug you so much you're going to get fucking sick of it."

CHAPTER 25

OZZI

*A*ll I've been able to think about the last few days is Willow, which isn't unusual. She's been invading my thoughts since the first day I met her, but after kissing her—for real this time—I can't get her off my mind.

Not only am I thinking about her when she's not around, but I had a dream about her last night, which led to a very uncomfortable situation with my dick this morning.

I handled that shit in the shower, but by the time I'd made it downstairs to meet my brothers for a run, I felt edgy, like I needed a release, even though I'd just had one.

"Giving you a little of your own advice," Gunnar says, checking me with his shoulder. "You need to get laid."

I'd like to trip him, but then Cage would beat my ass for messing with his prized fighter, so instead, I deflect. "You need to mind your own business."

"You can try to deny it but it's written all over your face."

Deny. Deny. Deny.

"I don't know what you're talking about. Besides, shouldn't you be more worried about your upcoming fight than my sex life?"

"What the hell ever, Oz. We all know you're pining over Willow, so just nut up and get your girl."

My girl. Why do I like the sound of that so much?

"I'm not pining. I don't *pine* for anyone, that's not my style," I remind him. Pining isn't the same as how I'm feeling. I'm not a lovesick puppy chasing after someone who doesn't return the same feelings. Willow wants me just as much as I want her.

At least I think she does.

Fuck.

I don't typically think too deeply when it comes to my relationship with a woman. If there's a mutual attraction and the woman in question is down for some fun then, fun shall be had. Hopefully, a lot of it.

Something tells me, though, that Willow is different and I should approach things going forward between us carefully. I'd never want to hurt her but I also can't assume she'd want anything serious either. Maybe it's enough for both of us to just have fun and enjoy each other for a while.

My gut twists at the thought I'm dead fucking wrong.

Regardless, I can't stop thinking about her and how it felt to have her in my arms and kissing her the other night. I want a repeat as soon as possible.

My phone vibrates through the pocket of my shorts, so I slow my pace and pull it out, smiling when I see I've received a text from Willow.

I wonder if she can't stop thinking about me, too.

Willow: Hey. Have any plans for today? I could use your help.

Me: I'm yours all day. Where are you?

Way to play it cool, Oz.

Willow: The gym

Hell yeah.

Me: Be there in ten.

"I know that look," Gunnar says with a disappointed groan.

"What?" I ask with a smirk, trying to play off the intense feelings surging inside me.

"It usually means you're meeting up with someone for a booty call." He stops, shrugging. "Like I said, I've seen the way you two look at each other and I don't know, I guess I just thought there was more there than a quick fuck."

"For your information, oh judgmental one, she needs my help with something, and not what you're thinking, so get your head out of the gutter." Giving his shoulder a hard slap, I turn in the opposite direction. "I'm heading back to meet with her. Feel free to shove your assumptions right up your ass."

As I pick up the pace, I try to shake off the pissed off energy brought on by my brother's meddling. Any other time, I'd have laughed and taken it in stride, knowing I've earned his lack of faith in me when it comes to relationships, but not today. He can say that shit about me but not Willow. No fucking way.

Once I make it back to the gym, I detour to the bathroom to wash up and then go look for Willow. I find her chatting with Tempest, and like iron shavings to a magnet, I'm drawn to her.

As I approach, Tempest glances up and gives me a smirk, like she knows a secret. Maybe she does. Maybe she knows how much I want Willow. Or maybe Willow has confided in her, telling her that she wants me. Regardless, I can't help but place my hand on Willow's lower back, my fingers itching to grab her hip and stake my claim, letting everyone in on the secret.

"Hey, beautiful," I murmur in her ear. Seeing goosebumps break out on her typically smooth skin makes me smile. I wish I could lick each and every one.

Willow turns, giving me a bright smile. "Hi, yourself."

The way her eyes light up when she looks at me makes my chest puff up a little.

I expect her to pull away and put a little distance between us, but when she leans into my side, allowing me to wrap my arm around her waist, that pull I felt when I walked up strengthens. If she's okay with being like this in public, so am I.

Having her this close—touching her, inhaling her sweet scent—makes it a struggle to not close the distance between us and kiss her. But I manage to hold back, allowing her to set our pace.

Tempest has the widest smile on her face as she excuses herself to help a client. I give her a silent nod, but I'm sure she'll demand full disclosure sometime soon. I'm just glad she's more discreet than my brothers.

"Thank you for coming over here so quickly. You don't even know what you've agreed to help me with," she says.

Shrugging, I smile down at her. "Doesn't matter. I'd help you with anything. I hope you know that."

"I'm starting to…" The blush that covers her cheeks is intriguing. Willow isn't really a blushing kind of girl, but I definitely want to see more of it—more of this side of her… more of the vulnerable, open, exposed Willow.

"So, what horrible thing are you making me do today?"

"We're going furniture shopping!" Willow bounces on her toes and claps and it's so out of character but adorable at the same time, I can't help but laugh.

"I don't think I've ever seen you this excited before and it's all because of furniture?"

"Well, the sooner I can get furniture, the sooner Hazel can move in," she explains, a little shyness creeping in.

This time, I don't give a shit about who sees, I pull her close to me, tucking her face into the crook of my neck so I can whisper, "You're amazing, you know that?"

"You're pretty amazing yourself," she says, pulling back to look me in the eyes and for a moment, I get lost. I forget we're in the middle of a busy gym. I forget that I don't do relationships. I forget that I'm supposed to stay unattached so I can go where the wind takes me.

For this brief moment, I'm so wrapped up in Willow Bernard that she's all I can see.

When a loud ruckus comes from the ring, it jars me out of my Willow-induced haze and I clear my throat. "Let's go get some furniture," I tell her, kissing the top of her head.

She grabs my hand and pulls me out the door and I'm still chuckling when we get to the parking lot. I turn toward my jeep but Willow tries to pull me in a different direction.

"Where are you going? My Jeep is right here."

"Dude, I have a truck. I don't need your Jeep, I need your muscles."

"That's fair," I agree and start following her to her truck. "But, did you just *dude* me?"

"Sure did. You got a problem with that?" she asks, unlocking the truck and opening her door.

"No problem at all, ma'am." I open the passenger-side door and slip inside, loving this new, playful side of her.

We sit in silence for a few minutes as Willow drives us out of Green Valley and it's kinda nice, relaxing even… until my vision zeroes in on the way her shorts ride up her toned legs, exposing more skin than I'm used to seeing from her.

Yeah, the raging hard-on I'm now sporting isn't relaxing at all.

I clear my throat while shifting in my seat, hoping I'm being discreet while I adjust my dick. "So, what kind of furniture are we looking for?"

"A bed."

How can one simple word change the atmosphere so drastically? I swear, the tension just went from ten to a hundred in a split second.

Willow feels it, too, because she quickly adds, "For Hazel."

The tension lessens but only a bit and I can't help but chuckle at our situation. I feel like we're in one of Maggie's romance novels or something and if we were, I'm sure the readers would be screaming for us to just bone already. Believe me, I want that, too, but I don't think this would be a one and done. Not for me, anyway. So, until it happens, I'll have to be patient. I already know she's worth the wait.

"I need to make sure she has her own room." Willow's voice is small, but there's a strength there that's unmistakable. She's a force to be reckoned with in and out of the ring, and if that's not the hottest thing ever, I don't know what is.

"When do you think she'll be able to move in?"

"Not sure yet. I still have the home visit to pass. Then she'll stay a weekend with me unsupervised as a trial run. After that, we just have to wait for the judge to declare me her guardian. It's great timing, too, with the school year ending soon. We'll have the summer to adjust to each other and, hopefully, bond like we should have years ago." There's an edge to her voice now but I get it. This whole situation sucks for both of them, but I admire the shit out of her for how she's stepped up and handled things.

"It's all gonna work out, Willow. I can feel it." This earns me a smile, so I grab her hand and pull it to my mouth for a kiss because I simply can't keep my hands to myself right now.

Eventually, Willow pulls into the parking lot of a second-hand furniture store and parks her truck.

"Frankie told me about this place. She said they have good stuff for pretty cheap, so I wanted to stop here first." Willow says as we get out of the truck and walk toward the entrance.

"Sounds good to me," I say, opening the store's entry door for her.

Once we're inside, we find the bedroom furniture and begin looking around. There's a decent amount of bed frames to choose from but I let Willow lead the hunt and wait for her to choose.

It doesn't take long before she's found something she likes. She's standing next to a white twin-sized bed that looks to be in really good shape. Flowers are carved into the headboard, making the piece especially pretty.

"I think she'll like this," Willow says, biting the cuticle on her thumb. "What do you think?"

I shrug. "I don't know her, except for what you've told me, but I can't imagine any nine-year-old girl not liking this bed. It's pretty."

Willow nods, like she's trying to convince herself. "When I was her age, I'd never had my own room. I would've killed for any bed."

My gut aches at her truth, but I try not to react like I want to, which is raging against the shitty reality she lived through. Instead, I nod. "It's a great bed."

"Yeah, it is. Okay," she says, exhaling. "Now all I need is some new bedding and we'll be good to go."

"What are her favorite colors?"

"She's more of a blue-green kind of girl than a red or pink one. And she loves sloths."

"Your sister sounds like a cool kid," I tell her.

"She really is. Maybe you can meet her one of these days."

"I'd like that" is what I say and it's not a lie, but it's a struggle to keep my facial expression neutral because until this very moment, I hadn't given any thought to how Hazel could affect my relationship with Willow.

I've never dated anyone with a kid before. Not that it's a hard limit for me. And I know Willow and I aren't really dating but I'd like to see where this goes, and I think she feels the same. I have no idea what that would be like with Hazel in the picture.

Fuck.

I need to get my head on straight before my thoughts get out of hand and I ruin this before it even starts.

Willow lucks out by finding some sheets and a comforter that fits the bed, and seems like something Hazel will like. Then, she goes to pay for them, as well as the bed and mattress set she found earlier.

While she does that, I peruse the shelves at the front of the store, which are filled with random items, when my eyes land on what looks to be a very soft and fluffy sloth stuffed animal.

How weird for something like that to be here, especially after Willow just told me it's Hazel's favorite animal? It's like the Universe put it there for me to find.

I don't know why, but I quickly grab it and take it to another cash register and pay for it before Willow can see. She eyes me warily when I meet her at the front door with my plastic bag in hand but doesn't say anything.

"We have to drive around the back so the bed and mattress can be loaded into the truck. You ready?"

"Absolutely."

Being the great team we are, Willow and I tote the bed into the apartment and put it together in no time. While she makes the bed with the new sheets and comforter, I run back to the truck and grab my bag from the store. When I return, Willow is standing in the doorway of Hazel's room, quiet and contemplative.

"Everything okay?" I ask.

She doesn't look at me but I can see that her eyes are glassy when she replies, "I really hope she likes it and is happy here."

It hits me all at once.

All the stress and worry and heartache Willow has dealt with… doing everything she can to keep her sister from going through what Willow already has while also taking care of herself… She truly is the strongest, most amazing person I know.

And I want her.

God, do I want her.

The voice inside my head screams at me to turn and run. Get the hell out of here so I don't mess this up more than I already have. But I don't listen. My feet stay put and my heart pounds as I slide my arm around her waist and pull her to me.

Willow seems to shiver when our bodies touch but I ignore it. It's just a hug. I'm only trying to comfort her, I tell myself, knowing good and well I'm full of shit.

"It's perfect, Willow. Of course she'll love it… and you." I pray I sound reassuring and that Willow doesn't notice the lust in my voice.

Again, I know I should leave but then I remember Willow drove today and my jeep isn't here. I can walk back to the gym, though. It'd give me time and fresh air to clear my head.

Before I can pull away and tell Willow goodbye, she turns and looks down at my hand. "What's in the bag?"

Clearing my throat, I open the bag and pull out the sloth I bought for Hazel and hand it to her.

"You found this at the furniture store?"

"Yeah, it was just sitting on a shelf, begging me to take it home," I say, trying to make it sound like a joke and lighten the mood.

"And you bought it? For my sister?" Willow asks, her voice sounding thick with emotion.

"Well, yeah. If you don't think she'll like it, I can take it—"

My words are halted by Willow's lips crashing into mine. I'm stunned for a second but quickly regain my senses, kissing her back with equal intensity. I try to pull her closer to me but can't because I'm still holding onto the damn sloth, so I toss it onto Hazel's bed before grabbing Willow under her ass and lifting her up. Her long, muscular legs close around my waist, holding our bodies as close as they can be while still wearing clothes.

I move to carry her into the bedroom but stop when I remember it's Hazel's room, not Willow's and I am not about to christen her new bed with all the dirty things I want to do right now.

"Where's your room?" I grunt out in between kisses.

Willow's mouth travels down the column of my throat as she answers, "Next door over but there's no furniture."

"You don't have a bed?"

She shakes her head while moving her mouth to my ear, clearly not wanting to be distracted.

Of course, she'd buy Hazel a bed before she bought herself one.

"We have to go to the couch over there." She points toward the living room area with her thumb over her shoulder, so I walk us to the couch that is not a couch, it's a fucking futon.

I'm gonna buy her a bed and a real couch tomorrow because there's no way this damn futon will survive.

I lay Willow down on the thin mattress while kneeling beside her and gaze down at her. Brushing a strand of her dark hair away from her forehead, I whisper, "You're so fucking beautiful."

"Oz..."

213

"Let me touch you."

Of course, I want so much more than that but I'm trying to pace myself. Instant gratification is my jam but with Willow, at this moment, I just want to make her feel good. And I want to savor our time together as much as possible because who knows how long it'll last.

There's also a part of me that thinks if this is to end sooner rather than later, Willow should be the one to do it. She's the one in control and I don't want to be responsible for breaking her heart.

You can still keep this casual, Oz. Once we've both given in to the lust, we can go about our business, no big deal.

Yeah, right.

Willow lifts her arms, allowing me to pull her tank top over her head, exposing her white cotton bra. Her chest heaves as I trace my fingertip over the outline of the cups holding her full breasts. She's so fucking sweet and the vulnerability in her eyes causes my chest to constrict.

You can stop and leave right now. She'd be pissed but it'd be better than you hurting her later.

I mentally give myself the middle finger, knowing I'm much too selfish to turn away now.

Groaning as I realize her bra clasps in the front, I make quick work of undoing it and pulling it away from her body, freeing the most beautiful set of tits I've ever seen. They're heavy but fit perfectly in my hand and my mouth waters as I lean down to pull a hard nipple between my lips.

Willow gasps as her fingers dig into my hair and pull, driving me wild while I feast on her. My tongue flicks one nipple then the other, over and over, as if I'm trying to decide which one I like better. Of course, there's no contest. They're both fucking perfect.

"You're driving me crazy," Willow breathes out. Her voice is raspy and pleading at the same time and I can't wait to hear her come.

While keeping my mouth on her breasts, I slowly drag my hand up the inside of her thigh, rubbing circles on her smooth skin. Willow's pelvis thrusts up, greedy and impatient, and I can feel her heat as I move closer to her pussy.

Just as I reach the lace on her panties, a phone rings.

I'm not even sure whose phone it is at this moment, and I don't really care. When it stops, I continue my movements... until it rings again not five seconds later.

"I think I need to get that," Willow breathes out. She reluctantly sits up and grabs the phone that must've fallen out of her back pocket when we moved to the futon. The lust haze is cleared, though, when it registers whose call she missed.

"It's Nancy, Hazel's caseworker. I have to call her back."

CHAPTER 26

WILLOW

*W*alking up onto the quaint front porch, I switch the pan of fresh banana bread from one hand to another and wipe my sweaty palm down the front of my jeans. I'm not sure why I'm nervous, but ever since I got the call from Nancy yesterday evening, informing me that the home visit is scheduled for this afternoon, I can't shake the nerves.

I couldn't even finish my make out session with Ozzi, which really sucks because I so badly want to be with him, but my head just wasn't in it.

As I knock on the wooden frame of the screened door, I take a deep breath to calm myself.

A few seconds later, I'm greeted by Miss Faye's kind smile. "Good morning, Willow," she says, swinging the screened-door open. "Come on in."

"Oh, it's okay," I tell her, holding the foil-covered pan out in front of me. "I just wanted to bring you this banana bread and tell you thank you for everything. I know it's not much and there's a chance you don't even like banana bread, but I didn't—"

"Willow," Miss Faye says firmly, cutting me off and getting my attention. "Why don't you come inside and you can tell me all about how you baked me my favorite treat. Hmm?"

She gives me another warm smile and motions over her shoulder.

"Okay," I acquiesce.

"Now, would you prefer coffee, tea, milk…"

"I really didn't bring this over to invite myself into your home," I tell her, eyeing the sitting area we pass on our way to the kitchen and feeling immediately at peace. Just like the apartment she's renting to me, this place feels so homey.

"Nonsense," she huffs, placing the banana bread on the table before going to the cabinet and taking out two small plates. "I've been meaning to come over and check on you, but every time I think about it you're either gone or you have company."

The sly smile she gives me makes my cheeks grow hot.

"Those Erickson boys are finer than a frog hair split four ways… or five, I guess. I haven't seen that oldest one much, but from what I did see, he's made from the same cloth as the others. And that one I've seen you with." She looks up at me, raising her brows. "He's about as cute as they come."

I clear my throat while fighting back a smile. "Ozzi is really nice. They all are, actually. I don't know what I would've done without them over the past couple of months."

"My Ralph is nice too, if you know what I mean," she says, waggling her eyebrows.

Oh, my God.

Placing my hand over my mouth, I shake my head and laugh. I can't help it.

Miss Faye is an audacious flirt and I love it.

"Now, coffee or tea? And don't tell me you're not having any. You're going to sit there and tell me all about how Ozzi Erickson has been helping you and keep me company for at least a few minutes. That's the least you can do for an old woman who's letting you rent her garage apartment."

When she gives me a wink, I laugh again, but quickly answer. "Coffee, please."

She pours us both a cup and then slices into the banana bread.

For a few minutes, I tell her a little bit about how I got to know the Ericksons, a brief synopsis of mine and Ozzi's relationship—which is fairly PG, even though I'd like it to be rated R—and lastly about setting up a room for Hazel.

"Which brings me to my other reason for stopping by this morning," I tell her, nervously picking at the crumbs that are left on my plate.

I have to admit that was the best banana bread I've ever made. Apparently, nervous baking is my jam.

"I got a call from Hazel's social worker yesterday evening and she told me I'll be having a home visit this afternoon. So, I didn't want you to get worried when you see a strange vehicle pull into the drive. It shouldn't take long. I mean, there's not much to see. But I did finish up her room last night and everything else is in order."

Miss Faye reaches across the table and places her wrinkled hand on top of mine. Outside of the hugs I've received from Ozzi, this is the most comforting gesture I've ever experienced in my entire life.

I stare at her hand on top of mine for a minute, soaking in the compassion and comfort. It brings tears to my eyes, but I quickly blink them away.

"Everything is going to be fine," she murmurs softly. "I have all the faith in the world that they'll walk in there and see the love you have for your sister. There's no way they'll be able to deny you this guardianship. You'll see."

"I hope you're right."

She draws her hand back, but the warmth from her touch lingers.

"This old bird is always right," she says with another wink as she gets up and refills both of our coffee cups. "Now, what are your plans for Hazel once she's here? I know you put in a lot of hours at the Piggly Wiggly and training at the gym."

Taking a deep breath, I sigh. "Well, I'm still working all of that out. It really depends on when the judge finalizes everything. If it's sooner rather than later, I might have to take a little time off work. When it comes to the gym, she'll just come with me. That shouldn't be a problem. And once she's in school, there's a before and after school program I can enroll her in. But my plan is to tailor my work schedule around her school day. It probably means I won't get as many hours, but we'll make do."

Miss Faye is shaking her head, waving a hand in the air. "There's no need for that. If you have to work and it's too early to take her to school, then you can drop her off here with me and I'll make sure she gets on the bus. And if it's after school and you're not home yet, I'll make sure she gets a snack and does her homework until you get home."

She says it so matter-of-factly I'm taken aback.

"I—I could never ask you to do that," I stammer.

"You're not, dear," Miss Faye says smoothly. "I'm offering."

Our eyes meet for a second and I can see the years of life and experience pooled together in her pale-green orbs. For someone I've only known for only a short amount of time, she puts me at ease and also puts me in my place faster than anyone ever has before.

"Before you come at me with any excuses," she says, holding up a hand and using a tone that brooks no argument, "I wouldn't have offered unless I wanted to do it. One of these days, when you're old like me, you'll realize you only have to do the things you want to do in life. It's the beauty of being an old woman—I do what I want and say what I want. And if you're thinking it would be an inconvenience, you're wrong. As much as I love Ralph, I get bored of just talking to him. You would be doing me a favor."

I shake my head, but it's not in protest.

I'm just in awe of her.

I want to *be* her when I grow up.

"But you haven't even met Hazel," I warn. "She's quite the little spitfire. Keep in mind she was raised by a drug addict and then tossed into foster care when our mother died."

That's the ugly, harsh reality. But if I know anything about Miss Faye, it's that she doesn't make bones about anything. She tells it like it is and she expects you to do the same. Plus, if she really means what she's offering, then I want her to know the truth about our past.

"All the more reason she should come and spend some time with me."

I bet Miss Faye has seen a lot in her years. She didn't even blink or wince at what I just said, so I have no doubt she's well-equipped to handle my little sister. And the thought of Hazel being taken care of and influenced by someone like Miss Faye when I'm not around calms a storm that's been raging inside of me.

"I would love that," I finally say. "Thank you."

When I eventually leave Miss Faye to head back to my apartment, I do so with renewed confidence. Knowing I have everything in place and an answer for anything they'll ask of me sets me at peace.

I know, without a shadow of a doubt, I've done everything within my power to become Hazel's guardian. So, if all else fails, at least I know I tried my best.

A few hours later—after I scrubbed and cleaned every nook and cranny of the small apartment, even though it was already spotless—a knock hits my door and I freeze in the doorway of Hazel's bedroom.

Glancing over my shoulder, I take in the stuffed sloth laying on the bright green pillow that looks like it's just waiting for a nine-year-old girl to come home and claim it. The few books I've managed to collect for Hazel are stacked neatly on the shelf by the window. I've even bought her a few new t-shirts and hoodies. I know she'll need more, but I want to wait until she's here before I buy anything else. I remember what it was like never getting to pick out my own clothes or have a say over what went into my bedroom.

The second knock is louder than the first and it draws me out of my inner thoughts and sends me toward the door.

* * *

When I walk into Viking MMA an hour later, Ozzi meets me at the door.

"How did it go?" he asks, seeming almost as wound-up and nervous as I've been.

"Good," I say, swallowing around the word. I'm still trying to convince myself that the home visit went well. When I inhale and exhale deeply, Ozzi takes a step closer.

"You've done everything you could do," he assures, his eyes locking onto mine before he pulls me into a tight hug and kisses the top of my head. "How long until the judge makes a decision?"

"If no one contests my petition for guardianship, it could be a few weeks," I say, sinking into his embrace. "I talked to Nancy after the home visit was over and she seemed to think there won't be a contest, but I'll still have to attend a guardianship hearing and potentially have witnesses."

Ozzi pulls back enough so he can see my face. "I'll be a witness. And I'm sure Frankie would be too. So, don't worry about that. We'll cross that bridge when we get there."

We.

When did he and I become a we?

As if he can sense that little mental slip, he pulls me in for one more bone-crushing hug. "Feel like squeezing in a workout?"

"Don't get offended," I begin. "But as much as I wanted to see you, I actually came here for a good sparring session."

With his hand to his chest, he stumbles back. "Oh, how you wound me," he says dramatically.

Letting out a small laugh, I can't help staring at him, this man who seems to know exactly what I need and when I need it. Ever since our first session together, Ozzi has had the ability to ease my stress and fears. Not just by being his amazing, talented, attractive, goofy self, but by *giving* me the tools to work through my emotions and find my inner peace.

He stares back at me for a brief moment, before clapping his hands together loudly. "Let's go, Bernard."

CHAPTER 27

OZZI

"Hello?" I say, answering Willow's call on the second ring. She doesn't call me much, but when she does, it makes me smile like a damn loon.

"Hey, sorry to bother you."

She sounds a little out of breath and I check my watch to see what time it is. It's a little after two o'clock, which means she still has an hour or so left on her shift.

"You're not bothering me," I reply, tossing a mat onto a stack so I can finish cleaning the floors. "What's up?"

There's a long pause before she says anything else. "My truck didn't want to start this morning and I'm supposed to go visit Hazel after work."

"How did you get to work this morning?" I ask, hating that she didn't call me first thing. And she better not tell me she walked. I feel my blood boiling at the thought. Her apartment isn't *that* far from the grocery store, nothing is *that* far in this town, but the thought of Willow walking anywhere, or needing anything, makes me irrationally angry.

"Miss Faye," Willow answers. "She was on her way to an early morning hair appointment and saw me messing around under the hood."

Her deep sigh makes me want to reach through the phone and hug her. I can read Willow so well now and I know this probably feels like one more thing stacked against her. She's spent most of her savings to get the apartment ready for the home visit and when Hazel eventually moves in with her. So, fixing her truck is something she doesn't have the time or money to deal with.

"Me and the guys will run over and see if we can figure out what's wrong with your truck," I tell her. "If we can't get it running by the time you need to leave, I'll drive you to Mountain City."

She sighs again and I know she's refusing my offer before she says it. "Don't worry about my truck," she finally says. "I'll deal with that when I get back to town. I just don't have time to do that and make it to Mountain City on time without taking time off work, and I can't really afford to do that."

"Willow," I warn. "I'm going over to your apartment and taking a look at your truck. Now, where are your keys? Are they with you?"

"Yes," she acquiesces.

I smile at that, because a couple of months ago, she would've balked at the idea of me helping her. But she's come so far, not only with accepting assistance, but so much more.

"Okay," I say, keeping my approval of her compliance low-key. "I'll see you in a bit."

I've watched her work through past hurts and grief.

She's overcome insecurities and fears.

And this current fight she's in, trying to get guardianship of her sister, is the bravest thing I've witnessed. It's a lot for a twenty-two-year-old to give up their freedom to take in a sister they didn't even know existed until recently. Not to mention, Hazel is only nine, so Willow will be her caretaker for the next decade, at least.

It's a lot.

Or maybe it's just a lot for someone like me, who's never seen themselves or even wanted to be tied down.

"Hey, Gunnar," I call out, walking toward the ring where he's sparring with Kevin. "Have you seen Cage or Vali?"

"Cage is upstairs with Freya," he says, mid-punch, not even breaking stride. "Tempest had to go to Merryville today for something."

Kevin grunts as Gunnar lands a nice jab and then follows it with an uppercut.

"Vali is probably at O'Neal's," he says, bouncing on his toes as he gives Kevin a chance to readjust his gear. "He had a meeting with Mr. O'Neal this morning and said something about hanging around to help Maggie with inventory."

Quickly, I finish wiping down the mats and make sure they're ready to go for the next class coming in later this afternoon.

Then, I run upstairs to let Cage know I'm going to see if I can figure out what's wrong with Willow's truck.

"Hey," I whisper, seeing Freya is asleep on Cage's shoulder.

Dang, she's cute.

Honestly, I'd never really even held a baby until Freya. But she makes me think about things I've never given much attention to, like settling down and having a family of my own one of these days. I'm not going to lie, the idea still makes me break out in a small amount of hives, but it's not as scary or suffocating as it once felt.

"What's up?" Cage asks, tilting his chin up in my direction as he rises from the couch in a fluid motion. "Everything good downstairs?"

"Yeah, it's fine," I say quietly. "I just wanted to let you know I'm going to run to the Piggly Wiggly and get Willow's keys so I can take a look at her truck."

He nods. "Need some help?"

"I'm going to stop by O'Neal's and see if Vali has time to go with me."

Cage nods again. "Let me know if you can't get it running. We can always tow it to Winston Brothers' Auto Shop and have Cletus take a look at it."

"Yeah, we might have to, but I'm hoping it's something easy."

When Freya stirs, I tiptoe quietly back to the stairs, but Cage stops me. "You're different with her."

"What?" I ask, slowly turning around to look at him.

"Willow," he says. "The reason I warned you to be careful with her was because I'd seen the way you hit it and quit it with other women. I just didn't want that to be the case with Willow. But you're different with her."

When I don't respond, unable to form words, he continues. "I know relationships aren't your thing, but you're actually kind of good at it. You might not see it, but it's the little things, like taking time out of your day to go look at her truck, that make a difference."

Is that what this is?

Am I in a relationship with Willow?

Feeling that uneasy sensation in my gut starts to stir, I clear my throat. "I'm not sure if we're in a *relationship*," I say, giving a noncommittal shrug. "We're friends and I care about her, not just as a client, but as a person."

I care about Willow Bernard.

I care about her so much I'm not sure what I'm doing any longer.

Cage smirks. "You keep telling yourself that."

It's on the tip of my tongue to ask him how I'd know if this thing with Willow was serious. But that would mean admitting my feelings and that he's right, and I'm not sure I'm ready for that.

Fifteen minutes later, I'm pulling into the parking lot of O'Neal Feed and Fodder, spotting Vali's truck by the side of the building.

When I walk inside, I'm instantly greeted by a chipper, "Welcome to O'Neal Feed and Fodder," from a familiar voice. Maggie is ringing up a customer at the counter and when she looks up to see it's me who just walked in, she shoots me a wide smile and motions with her head. "Vali is in the back."

"Thanks," I say, walking toward the stockroom.

After we spent a weekend setting up and tearing down for Maggie and Vali's wedding reception, I feel like I know this place in and out. Mr. and Mrs. O'Neal are some of my favorite people.

"What's up?" Vali asks as he checks off inventory.

"Stopped by to see if you want to drive over to Willow's apartment with me. Her truck wouldn't start this morning and I was going to see if I could fix it for her."

He glances over, giving me a wry smile, but unlike Cage, keeps his opinions about what's going on between me and Willow to himself. For now, at least.

"Let me finish this up and then we can head out."

Vali rides with me to the Piggly Wiggly and Willow runs her keys out to us, insisting it isn't necessary for us to do this. Of course, Vali and I both wave her off and continue our business.

Once we peek under the hood, we confirm it's not anything simple like a corroded spark plug or detached battery cable. The battery isn't dead and the starter seems to be working.

"If Viggo was here, he'd probably already have this thing running," Vali says with a grunt as he crawls out from under the truck where he's been checking for any leaks. "Think we could call him?"

I sigh, wiping my hands down the front of my shorts. "I don't know man. Last week, when I called, he didn't even answer."

"Yeah, he told me wherever he's staying doesn't have great reception or some shit."

Vali and I give each other a look like we don't know whether to believe him or not.

"It's obvious he's going through something," I say, checking every hose and cable I can get my hands on. "I just wish he wouldn't cut us all off while he's doing it."

"You know Viggo," Vali says. "He needs more alone time than the average bear."

He's right. Even when we were living together, there'd be weeks where we'd come home from the gym and he'd hole up in his room until the next morning. After the accident we were in a year or so ago, he kind of seemed depressed. But I assumed he was just bummed about his injuries and once he was healed up, he'd be better.

Then our family decided to sell the gym.

And now, he's basically shutting us all out.

We might've fought a lot growing up, but we've always had each other's backs. So, I'm hoping that whatever is going on with him is temporary and he lets us back in soon.

"I say we tow it," Vali announces, kicking at one of the tires.

"Cage mentioned Winston Brothers' Auto," I say, pulling out my phone. "I'll give them a call."

Later, when I park in front of the Piggly Wiggly to wait on Willow, I replay the conversations with my brothers through my mind. Vali, although not as gruff as Cage, still found a chance to bring up Willow.

Like Cage, he also commented on how I'm *different* with her.

And it's not lost on me that even Gunnar seems amused with our relationship.

Are we in a relationship?

I mean, I know technically a friendship is a relationship, but are we in a romantic relationship?

That thought is still plaguing my mind when Willow walks out, looking like a vision, even in her plain t-shirt and jeans. When she sees me, a smile breaks through her serious expression as she brings a hand up to her brow to block the sun.

And a new thought crosses my mind at that moment: Willow feels like the sun.

Even on her dark days, radiance shines through.

CHAPTER 28

WILLOW

"Why are you looking at me like that?" I ask, feeling Ozzi's gaze like a weighted blanket. It's not uncomfortable, but it's heavy.

He laughs, almost nervously, and I notice him run the palm of his hand down his jeans-clad leg.

By the way, I love Ozzi in jeans.

I love him in anything—shorts, sweatpants—but Ozzi in jeans is next level.

The fact we haven't had a chance to be alone for the past few days doesn't help. All I can think about is him and getting him out of whatever pants he's wearing.

"Can't I look at you?" Ozzi asks, his tone dripping with insinuation, and possibly subdued lust.

Fighting back a smile, I turn to look out the window. "Thanks for driving me today," I say, changing the subject. "I'm sure you had better things to do."

"No, just you."

The way he delivers the line, so nonchalantly, makes it take a minute to register.

Now that it has, not only am I fighting back a smile, but my cheeks feel hot and I squirm slightly in my seat. When he reaches across and squeezes my knee, leaving his hand resting on my leg, I feel that heat in my cheeks travel to the rest of my body.

Clearing my throat, I reach up and turn his radio on. No surprise, it's dialed into the sixties station. Ever since the night he drove us to the fight, he always has it turned to this station. I wonder if he does it before I get in or if it's always on this station now.

It's just one of the small ways he shows me he's thinking about me, even when I'm not around.

After spending most of my life as an afterthought, the idea that someone thinks about me is a hard concept. It's also difficult for me to understand someone wanting to help me.

"I really do appreciate you driving me."

Ozzi doesn't reply with words, instead, he removes his hand from my leg, taking the warmth with it, and picks up my hand, bringing it to his lips.

And for the next hundred miles, he continues to hold my hand as we drive down the road with a sixties' playlist as a soundtrack. Every once in a while, I glance over at him, admiring his gorgeous profile. Occasionally, I let my gaze trace the tattoos exposed by his short-sleeve t-shirt, following them down his arm to where our hands are linked.

I'd love to see the rest of them, not only tracing them with my eyes, but with my fingertips.

"You'll have to give me some directions once we get to the city limits," Ozzi says, bringing me out of my stupor. "You meet at the park, right?"

"Yeah," I say, turning my focus back to the road and the passing scenery. "She's going to be really excited to meet you."

Ozzi stiffens slightly. I wouldn't have noticed if he wasn't still holding my hand. But I did, and I wonder what made him react like that. Hazel is a nine-year-old little girl, not a baby like Freya. Besides that, I've never known Ozzi to be scared of anyone. He's one of the most extroverted people I've ever met.

"If you don't want to meet her," I start, ready to retract my statement and feel the old walls creeping back up.

"No," Ozzi says, cutting off my train of thought. "I do. I just wasn't sure what the plan was."

I decide to let his initial reaction go for now. Ozzi is always so good at not pushing me, so I can return the favor.

Half an hour later, we're pulling into the park as the sun starts its descent into the western sky, painting the playground in the pale afternoon light. We've still got a good hour before it fully sets, not as much time as I'd like, but it has to be for now.

Just as Ozzi parks the Jeep next to the picnic table, I see Nancy's suburban pull in behind us.

I jump out, grabbing my bag with the PB&Js, chips, and drinks. I also brought one of the books I found for Hazel at the thrift store last week. It's an old favorite of mine, one that gave me hopes and dreams I couldn't afford at her age, but indulged in any way.

When Hazel sees Ozzi, her entire face lights up, and I realize everything else I brought her today will pale in comparison.

"You're Ozzi," she says matter-of-factly, walking over until she's toe-to-toe with the Viking look-alike, neck craned back to see him. "I'm Hazel."

She sticks her hand out for him to shake and I watch as Ozzi's mouth pulls into a grin.

Leaning down, he braces one hand on his knee and takes hers with the other.

"Nice to meet you, Hazel."

Nancy gives a wave from the vehicle and I wave back before following Ozzi and Hazel to our table.

"You've got a lot of tattoos," Hazel points out, as she sits across from Ozzi and inspects his arms.

He laughs. "Yeah, I guess I do," he replies, holding out his right arm. "I guess I don't really notice them much."

"Do you have more?"

That is the million-dollar question, Hazel.

I'd love to explore in more detail what I've only had brief glimpses of at the gym.

"A few," Ozzi says, and if I'm not mistaken, his cheeks turn a light shade of pink.

Well, that's a first.

"I'm going to get a tattoo when I'm eighteen," Hazel announces, which is news to me. "Do you have any tattoos?" Now, her focus is turned on me, catching me off guard.

"Uh, yeah," I say, glancing over to see Ozzi invested in this admission.

Hazel frowns. "Really? Where?"

"On my side," I reply.

"What is it?"

Okay, having this little inquisition turned on me doesn't feel so great. Admitting what I have tattooed on my side, something that only the artist and I have ever seen, makes me feel oddly vulnerable. "A tree."

"What kind of tree?"

This time, it's Ozzi who's asking and when our eyes meet, my stomach does a flip.

"A willow tree."

He nods, letting his gaze fall to my side as if he can see the ink beneath my clothes.

"That's cool," Hazel says. "Like your name. I'm going to get a horse because I really love horses. And I just read a book about one. Her name was Persephone, like the goddess. Do you like Greek mythology?"

This certainly isn't how Hazel responded to me at our first meeting, but I guess I'm different. I'm the sister she didn't know existed and a tangible link to our dead mother.

Ozzi is… well, he's Ozzi. He exudes goodness and gentleness, even though he's big and tall.

From the moment she laid eyes on him, it was obvious there was a certain level of trust, although it might be surface-level right now, it's already there.

As she and Ozzi talk about Greek mythology, I try not to read too far into this interaction. I try not to think about what it would be like for the three of us to hang out on a regular basis. That's too much.

Too much hope.

Too much trust.

Too much happiness.

I don't know if my heart can handle that, or the fallout if I did allow it and everything came crashing down around me.

"I brought sandwiches," I announce, needing to redirect my thoughts. Besides that, the sun will only allow us another half an hour before it completely sets, ending our time together. "PB&Js, sour cream and onion chips, and root beer."

Setting everything out on the table, I smile up at Ozzi. "Brought enough for you too."

He returns my smile with a wink. "How did you know root beer is my favorite?"

"No," Hazel says, snagging a can. "It's *my* favorite."

"Well," Ozzi says, grabbing his own can. "Seeing that I'm older than you, I kind of called it first."

Hazel's expression makes me laugh.

Completely offended by his audacity, she asks, "How old are you anyway?"

"Twenty-five, which makes me sixteen years older than you."

I fight back a grin as I watch the two of them spar.

"When's your birthday?" she asks before taking a large bite of her sandwich.

Ozzi pauses, with his sandwich in mid-air. "September fourth. How about you?"

"December sixteenth," Hazel responds, sounding a little dejected. "I was hoping my birthday was at least before yours. Do you know how much it sucks to have a birthday nine days before Christmas?"

"Try being born in July," I chime in. "I never got to have a birthday party and invite all my friends from school."

Actually, the sadder story is that I never had a birthday party because my mom was always drunk or high. And then, I went to foster homes where birthday parties seemed like a frivolous expense.

"There was this one foster home I was in," I say, getting lost in a memory. "They made me a big strawberry cake and homemade ice cream. It wasn't really a party, but the cake was delicious."

Feeling two sets of eyes on me, I glance up to catch Ozzi and Hazel both watching me. Hazel's expression is one of understanding, and Ozzi's is just sad. To be honest, I hate both. I don't want Hazel to understand where I'm coming from and I don't want Ozzi feeling sorry for me, so I change the subject.

"I brought you a new book," I say, dusting breadcrumbs off my hands before digging into my bag. "I hope it's not one you've already read."

Hazel takes the book, her eyes scanning the cover, and then she flips it over to read the back, like a true bibliophile. She probably doesn't want to hear it, but she reminds me so much of myself at this moment, so much so it makes my heart clench a little. For so many years, I just wanted to belong. I wanted a family.

She's giving me that.

But I wonder if I'm enough for her.

"I haven't read it," she says, turning her attention back to me. "Sharon has a bunch of books and she lets me pick one at a time. But she doesn't have this one. I like the horse on the front."

Smiling, I nod. "I thought you might."

"Maybe Sharon will want to read it after me," she says, flipping through the pages. "Sometimes we talk about the books I read."

When Hazel brings up Sharon, one of her foster parents, I always get a twinge of anxiety mixed with uncertainty. She seems to be nice. I've only spoken with her on the phone, but those interactions have been amicable, if not pleasant.

"Well, it's yours to do with as you wish."

"Thank you," Hazel says thoughtfully, her attention going back to Ozzi. "Do you like to read?"

Ozzi nods. "Yeah, probably not as much as you or your sister, but I enjoy a good book from time to time."

That spurs a new conversation between the two of them that lasts until the sun begins to set. They agree on mystery and disagree on scary books. Hazel says she doesn't like to read anything that gives her bad dreams, and I have to agree.

"Next week is our sleepover," I remind Hazel as she climbs back into Nancy's SUV. "So I'll see you in Green Valley."

Hazel gives me a wide smile. "See you in Green Valley."

Once they're gone, Ozzi opens the passenger door of the Jeep and I climb in.

"She's great," he says as we make our way out of Mountain City. "I'm not sure what I expected, maybe something along the lines of your first meeting with her. But she's a really great kid. I can see a lot of you in her, which I know sounds strange since you weren't raised together."

I nod, swallowing down a sudden lump in my throat. "I see some of myself in her too."

"That's gotta feel good, right?"

"Yeah," I say quietly, trying to avoid the emotions I feel bubbling up inside.

He reaches over and laces his fingers with mine. "What's wrong?"

As the first tear slides down my cheek, I quickly swipe it away and avert my eyes out the window. "Nothing. It's stupid."

"Tell me," he says, pulling gently on my hand to get my attention.

For a few moments, I collect my thoughts as I watch the streetlights fade into the background as we venture further out of town. Part of me wants to confide my fears and worries to Ozzi because I know I feel better when I do. But the other part of me is scared to lean on him that much. By entrusting him with those parts of me, I'm letting him see things no one else ever has, and no matter how trustworthy Ozzi has proven to be, I'm still scared to let go.

"Am I doing the right thing?" I finally ask, needing to at least let a little of this built-up tension out.

Ozzi's quiet for a moment, obviously thinking about his response before he gives it. Blowing out a hard breath, he squeezes my hand tighter. "Yeah, I think you are. The two of you were obviously meant to find each other. It's a lot of responsibility, but I think it's an admirable thing you're doing."

"She seems like she's adjusting well." My voice is barely above a whisper as my deepest secrets come to the surface. "I'm worried that I'm projecting my own past and fears onto her. The home she's been placed in doesn't seem anything like what I experienced. What if I'm being selfish?"

"You're not selfish," Ozzi exclaims. "You're the most unselfish person I've ever met. And Hazel is lucky to have you. I can't speak from experience on this, but I can only imagine that her being with you will beat any foster home, regardless of how many books they have."

I can't help but laugh at that, he always finds a way to turn a bad situation around.

"I'm obviously going to have to up my game."

Bringing my hand to his mouth, he kisses my knuckles and I try not to overthink things as we drive home.

A couple of hours later, when we're pulling up to my apartment, I realize something's missing.

"Ozzi?" I ask, scanning the path that leads to Miss Faye's and back.

"Yeah?"

"Where's my truck?"

He puts his Jeep into park and turns off the engine. "I had it towed to Winston Brothers' Auto. They're going to take a look at it and call me tomorrow."

"Why did you do that?"

Ozzi turns in his seat to face me. "Vali and I looked at it this afternoon like I told you we would, and we couldn't figure it out. It wasn't any of the usual culprits, so I called them and had them come get it. I'm sure it's just a fuel pump or something simple. But they're going to call before they do anything."

When tears prick my eyes for the second time in a matter of hours, I angrily scrub at my face to make them disappear.

"Are you mad?" Ozzi asks, trying to assess the situation. "I just thought—"

"Thank you," I say, abruptly cutting him off. Taking a deep breath, I try to rein in my emotions. "I'm just not used to… I don't know. But thank you. And I really appreciate you and Vali spending time out of your day to do that. I should've told you that earlier, but I—"

"Willow." This time it's Ozzi who cuts me off. "You're welcome. It's not a big deal. And if you can't afford to fix your truck, I'll help you."

"No," I say, shaking my head as I let out a chuckle and feel my nose start to tingle. "I have a small amount of money stashed away for that old beater. I knew one day it would break down on me. I'm fine."

I am fine.

Everything is fine.

Sure, I'm turning into a blubbering mess in the front of Ozzi's Jeep, but it's just because I'm feeling so overwhelmed. Between him helping me with my truck and driving me to Mountain City, it's just a lot. Add on top of that him and Hazel hitting it off and practically becoming BFFs before my eyes, and I have a lot to process.

"Come here," he says, taking my hand and pulling me to him.

In an instant, I'm across the center console and straddling his lap. With Ozzi's arms wrapped around me, I feel like everything truly *is* fine. He somehow rights all the wrongs in the world by just being him.

"Thank you." When I wrap my arms around Ozzi's neck, he holds me even closer, our bodies pressed against each other reminding me of how desperate I've been for him since our heavy make out session on my couch a few days ago.

For a few moments, we sit there in the quiet, breathing each other in, our hearts beating in tandem. Then, Ozzi brushes his lips along the side of my neck and every cell in my body stands to attention. I'm aware of every single inch of me that is touching him and I want more.

More touching.

More kissing.

More than just a heavy make out session.

I want everything.

"Do you want to come upstairs?" I ask, hoping he hears the need and desperation in my voice and that he's feeling the same.

"I thought you'd never ask," he says, a deep chuckle reverberating in his chest and then the Jeep goes silent again and we sit there, clinging to each other, our breaths coming out hot and heavy.

Then I feel him harden beneath me and I know if we don't get out of here now, we'll never make it upstairs.

Reluctantly, I climb off his lap and grab my bag from the floorboard. Before I can make it up the steps, Ozzi is behind me. At the top, he holds the screen door for me while I dig for my key.

When I finally get the door open and we walk through, Ozzi kicks it closed behind him and then spins me against it, his mouth devouring mine.

Our kiss is frantic, the built-up tension and desire ready to erupt like a volcano.

This has been building for longer than a few days.

This is the result of being attracted to each other from the beginning and trying to shut those feelings down.

"God, I want you so fucking bad," Ozzi murmurs against my mouth before nipping at my bottom lip. "If for any reason you don't want me to fuck you tonight, I need you to let me know now, before this goes too far."

His chest heaves as my body screams for him not to stop.

Don't ever stop.

"We'll go at your pace and we don't have to have sex for me to get you off, but I need to know."

"I want you inside me," I confess, feeling the last of my walls crumble at our feet. "I want everything."

Ozzi grips my ass with both hands, hoisting me up. "Hold onto me," he demands.

As he walks us the short distance to the futon, his mouth is back on mine and I start pulling at his shirt.

"Show me how to make this into a bed," he says, placing me on my feet.

Pulling forward on the back of the futon, I release it, letting it fold out.

"Ta-da," I say with a smirk, waving my hand in the air.

For a second, I feel the tension ease. The live wire that's linked us for the last ten minutes diffuses momentarily while we take each other in. His eyes search mine. What they're looking for, I don't know, but when a smile spreads across his face, I breathe a sigh of relief.

This is happening.

"You're such a little smart ass," he says, reaching for me and pulling me into his chest. "Get over here and let me kiss you."

When he picks me up and practically launches me onto the bed, I'm thankful it's a sturdy metal and hopefully strong enough for whatever is about to transpire.

In a split second, the intensity is back and rises above me, his hands are at the hem of his shirt. He's about to give me what I want—him, naked—when he pauses. "Fuck."

"What?"

"I've gotta run out to my Jeep and grab a condom."

"Okay," I say quickly, brushing some hair behind my ear. "Yeah."

Why hadn't I even thought of that? It's not like me. Not that I've been with that many men in my life, but I've never not considered protection before.

What does that say about me?

What does that say about Ozzi?

About my feelings for him?

I have an IUD and I know I'm clean, but I don't know if the same is true for Ozzi. I'd hope he is, but that's not a conversation we've had. I don't even know when his last hook-up or relationship was.

Closing my eyes, I force my brain to turn off. I don't want to think about any of that right now. All I want to think about is Ozzi and how good he makes me feel… and how much better it's going to be when he's finally inside me.

A few moments later, Ozzi is back. He must've sprinted all the way there and back because he's breathing heavily.

"You sure about this?" he asks, holding up two foil packets as he shuts the door.

I nod fervently. "So sure."

In two long strides, he's hovering over me as his arms cage me in. "You have entirely too many clothes on. Once you mentioned that fucking willow tree tattoo, it's all I've been able to think about, wondering how I could've missed it during all of our training sessions."

As Ozzi talks, he removes my shirt, then my sports bra, until I'm naked from the waist up.

"It's here," I say, lifting my right arm so he can have an unobstructed view of the black ink on my rib cage.

He swallows hard as his eyes travel from my boobs down my stomach and then finally landing on the tattoo. "That must've hurt," he murmurs, tracing the lines with his finger. "I know the pieces on my ribs hurt like a bitch."

"Yeah," I say, my breath hitching in my throat when his hand splays over my side. "But it reminded me I was alive."

"Tell me about it." His eyes lock on mine and coax out all my truths.

"Besides the obvious reason," I start, giving him a smirk as I run a hand through his hair, relishing in the closeness and intimacy of the moment. "It symbolizes new life and I was in desperate need of one of those… a new beginning, a place to call my own. I was searching and felt alone, but this was a permanent reminder I'm not, as long as I have myself."

Ozzi nods slowly, his teeth scraping against his full bottom lip. "You're one of the strongest people I've ever met. This is the perfect tattoo, even if it wasn't your name. I'd expect nothing less for you."

"Did you know a willow branch can be planted on its own and it will eventually grow into a tree?"

Leaning forward, he brushes his lips against my ribs causing me to shiver as heat spread through my body. "A survivor, just like you," he murmurs against my skin.

I can't help but moan as he travels down my stomach to the waist of my jeans, my fingers lacing through his hair.

"I'm going to make you feel good," he promises. "I'll remind you you're alive."

His words cause a tidal wave of emotions to flood through me—desire, lust, want, need, thankfulness. I've never thought someone like this would come into my life. It didn't seem to be in the cards for me. I'd been dealt a shitty hand from the beginning and I always figured God had a different path for me.

But Ozzi makes me believe in things I've only read about and hope for things that have always felt out of my grasp.

Once he unzips my jeans, I raise my hips so he can pull them off, along with my underwear.

Lying here, completely naked, should make me feel self-conscious. Only one other person has ever seen this much of me, but they didn't really see *all of me*. Not like Ozzi. With them, my inner walls were completely up, all they got was my body, not my heart or my soul.

Ozzi is slowly taking everything—I'm *giving* him everything.

The second he licks the inside of my thigh, following it up with a gentle nip, I feel desire pool between my legs.

Oh, God, it's been so long.

"Ozzi." His name falls off my lips like a prayer. "Oh, God. Please."

The sensation of his mouth on me is almost too much to handle, but I also want more.

Tilting my hips up, I thread my fingers into his hair and Ozzi groans.

"Damn, Willow. *Fuck*, you taste so good," he groans right before he sucks my clit into his mouth and presses two fingers deep inside.

As Ozzi fucks me with his fingers, curling them to hit the perfect spot, I feel my insides begin to tremor with an orgasm. I haven't experienced one in so long. Not even at my own hand, but I know what it feels like and this is unlike anything I've felt before.

When I look down and see him watching me, I lose it.

All conscious thoughts.

Any intelligible words.

Control of my own body.

It's all… gone.

All that exists is Ozzi and the way he's making me feel.

"I'm going to come," I moan as the white, hot intensity continues to build. My toes curl into the cushion beneath me and my fingers grip his hair.

"That's right, baby," Ozzi coaxes. "Come for me. Come all over my tongue."

When the wave of my release crests, it takes me with it—high above the surface and then thrusting me deep under—as euphoria takes over.

It's not until I feel a soft stroke on my cheek that I start to come back to my senses.

"Hey," Ozzi says, hovering above me with a sly grin. "You okay?"

CHAPTER 29

OZZI

The most brilliant smile spreads across Willow's face as her eyes lazily open.

"I feel alive."

A deep, somewhat dark chuckle erupts from my chest. "Oh, baby, we're just getting started."

Lowering my body, I give her amazing tits a little more attention before I kiss my way back up to her mouth. When I start to kiss her, she's tentative at first, but then, it's like a switch is flipped.

"Pants off," she commands between kisses, our teeth clashing. "I need to feel all of you."

Her hands move to my waist and begin unbuttoning and unzipping. Between the two of us, we manage to complete the task and Willow sighs into my mouth.

A moment later, her legs wrap around my waist and her wet pussy is rubbing against my swollen cock.

"Willow," I warn, blindly reaching beside me for one of the condoms I brought in, but she's not stopping and it feels so fucking good, I don't want her to. I'd love nothing more than to take Willow bare and feel every inch of her, but we haven't had that talk yet and there's no time for it right now.

I need to be inside her more than I need my next breath.

When my hand finally lands on the foil packet, I pull myself away from her and push up onto my knees. Tearing the packet with my teeth, I remove the condom and slide it over my cock, keeping my eyes locked with Willow's the entire time.

For a second, I let her drink me in, hoping she likes what she sees. But when she licks her lips, I can't wait any longer.

"I have to be inside you," I tell her, pushing her knee up to give me better access. "I need to feel your sweet pussy squeezing my cock."

Willow's eyes go wide for a second and I see a faint blush that starts on her cheeks and travels down to her chest.

"Do you want that?" I ask, needing to be completely sure this is what she wants. It would be pure torture to stop now, but I would, if she asked me to.

Her head slightly nods, but it's not enough.

"I need you to use your words, baby. Tell me what you want."

She swallows hard, her throat bobbing. "I want your cock inside me."

It's barely above a whisper, but it's exactly what I wanted to hear. She's not a dirty talker, I've figured that out, but I love that she's vulnerable for me, showing me and telling me what she wants.

Taking her mouth with another searing kiss, I place my cock at her entrance. The other thing I don't know about Willow is when her last relationship was or how long it's been since she had sex. But I know she's tight, so instead of thrusting into her like I want to, I take it nice and slow.

Willow wraps her legs around my hips, allowing me to bury myself deep inside her. For a second, I just breathe with her—in and out... in and out—basking in the complete perfection of being inside Willow Bernard.

"I want to feel you move," Willow says, still quiet, but full of need. "It—you feel so good. I want to feel what it's like when you move inside me."

Slowly, I pull out and then ease myself back in, partly for her, but mostly for me. There's already a tingle starting at the base of my spine and if I really wanted to, I could blow my load in just a few minutes. But I want this to last. I want it to be just as good for Willow as I know it's going to be for me.

Her pussy is so tight.

And she's so perfect.

When Willow digs her heels in a little, I pick up my speed until my balls are slapping against her bare ass.

Her quiet moans turn into louder cries of pleasure.

"Let me hear it, baby," I tell her, feeling the first bead of sweat trickle down my forehead. "I want to hear how good I make you feel. How good my cock makes you feel."

"So good," Willow cries.

Leaning down, I kiss her lips, pushing my tongue inside. As I wrap my arms under her shoulders, I use them as leverage to push her down even harder onto my cock, angling her hips just right.

"You're so deep," Willow says, her eyes fluttering closed as her mouth hangs open on a silent cry. "Oh, God... so deep."

"I want you to come for me," I tell her. "I need to feel you come around my cock."

Reaching between us with one hand, while holding her to me with the other, I make small circles around her clit until I feel the walls of her pussy start to clench around me.

"That's it, Willow."

"Ozzi." She cries out as she lets go and I've never loved the sound of my name more than at this very moment.

In the next breath, I thrust quickly inside her—once, twice, three times—and then I'm following her orgasm with my own.

Flashes of light erupt behind my eyes as my body spasms, my release emptying into the condom. It's long and hard, probably the best orgasm I've ever had, and I'd love for it to go on and on, but eventually I drift back down.

Carefully, I pull out of Willow, immediately missing her warmth, but she doesn't let go.

For a minute or two, we just breathe in tandem.

"I'll be right back," I finally say, needing to toss the condom and get my head on straight. Being with her like this has me thinking all sorts of crazy things, things I know I shouldn't say because I don't know if I can follow through.

I'd never want to promise Willow anything I can't deliver on.

I never want to hurt her, but I know there are things we should discuss, things we probably should've talked about before tonight happened. But we didn't.

After I take care of business, I splash some water on my face and dry it with a hand towel.

When I walk back into the living room, Willow is sitting in the middle of the futon, still naked and looking so fucking beautiful it makes my heart ache.

"You okay?" I ask, crawling up beside her and pulling her down next to me.

"Better than okay," she says, reaching up to run her fingers through my hair. Not like when I was between her legs, that was intense. This time, it's gentle and soothing, and if she doesn't stop, I'll be falling asleep on this shitty-ass futon.

Drawing her even closer, I nuzzle my face into her neck and breathe her in. She still smells like her—spicy and sweet—but she also smells like me and it's intoxicating.

As she continues to run her hands through my hair, I feel my cock begin to stir.

It's not surprising. I'm always hard for her, I've just spent the past few months hiding that fact. There have been so many mornings of me rubbing one out in the shower, I've lost count. And don't even get me started on the cold showers I've taken after our workout sessions and sparring.

Honestly, I need some sort of contraption to keep my dick under wraps.

After a moment, Willow must feel it, because she stops her wandering hands and pulls her head back to look at me. With a sly grin, she cocks her head. "Round 2?"

"I thought you'd never ask."

She laughs, tossing her head back and giving me access to her neck. When I roll on top of her, trapping her beneath me, I feel that ache in my chest again. Her hair is fanned out around her, wild and untamed, and the look on her face takes my breath away. She looks so happy and sated, yet hungry for more.

And all of this is for me.

How the fuck did I get so lucky?

When I lower my body to hers, she sighs, wrapping her arms around my shoulders to force me down even more.

"I'll crush you," I say, not wanting to give her all my weight.

"You won't."

Willow is the strongest person I've ever known, and that's saying a lot. I come from a family of fierce fighters, men and women with a Viking spirit—courageous and strong. But this woman—so much like her name—is stronger than any of them.

Since I can't tell her everything I'm feeling—at least not yet—I show her.

After a few minutes of slow, passionate kisses, I roll onto my back, taking her with me.

"Grab that condom," I tell her, giving her ass a good slap. "I want you to ride me."

A few minutes later, I'm once again deep inside Willow as she rides my cock.

I could die right here and I'd die a happy man, zero regrets.

CHAPTER 30

WILLOW

"*D*o you want me to leave?" Ozzi asks groggily.

After four orgasms, two of those being back-to-back, which I've never experienced before, I'm completely drained. I know Ozzi is too. He's lingered on the brink of sleep for the past half hour.

"I can go if you want me to."

Do I want him to stay?

Yes.

Is it a good idea?

I don't know.

Even after all this time, I don't really know what Ozzi's intentions are. I've tried not to think about his nomadic ways and the fact he could pack up and move on any time, but I'd be lying if I said I haven't. It's actually what's been on my mind while he's been in and out of consciousness.

I realize we just fucked, twice, but somehow, sleeping beside him feels even more intimate.

I want that.

I've never felt as safe as I feel right now, tucked into his side with his arms wrapped around me.

But I also feel exposed and vulnerable. Normally, my walls would've gone up the moment he made me feel something deeper than a carnal need, but they didn't.

"Stay," I whisper, lightly stroking his arm, our legs tangled beneath a blanket.

Ozzi gently kisses my jaw. "Thank you."

Chuckling, I bring my hand up to cup his face. "I know you're not thanking me for letting you sleep on this futon."

His eyes meet mine and I expect to see humor there, but instead, I'm met with a seriousness I don't see very often from Ozzi.

"Not for that. You're right, this futon is horrible," he says, mirroring me by cupping my jaw and holding my gaze. "Thank you for trusting me. I know what happened tonight was something special. I know you don't let just anyone sleep in your bed, both figuratively and literally. I just want you to know I don't take it for granted and I'm honored you chose me to share this with."

I swallow down a lump in my throat.

I will not cry.

I will not be *that* girl.

"You're welcome," I say, my voice sounding a lot stronger than I feel. He's right, I don't let just anyone in my bed and tonight was special. Not just because it was the best sex of my life, but because it was more than just sex.

Ozzi brushes his thumb across my cheek. "Can I ask you something?"

"Sure," I say, feeling surprisingly open as we lie in the dark, feeling like I could, and would, tell him anything he asks.

"Have you ever been in a serious relationship?"

I nod. "Once."

"Will you tell me about it?"

As I let my mind go there, I want to warn Ozzi to not judge me for what I'm about to tell him, but I know that's unnecessary. He wouldn't. He doesn't have a judgmental bone in his body. With that assurance, I begin.

"It was right after I left my last foster home when I was eighteen. I moved to Merryville to start a new life," I say, letting out a sigh as I think back about how optimistic I was. "My social worker had helped me apply to college and I'd been accepted. I also got approved for some grants. They didn't cover everything, but it was enough to get me started. So, I packed up my small bag of personal belongings and headed off."

Ozzi drops his hand from my face and finds my own, linking our fingers together. "I knew the second I graduated college I'd never step foot back in a classroom," he says with a chuckle. "But I bet you rocked it."

"I was an okay student," I tell him. "If I applied myself, I could make the grades. And I liked college. But after a few months, I started feeling pressure to find a job. I realized the grants were only going to last for so long. So, I applied for a few jobs and ended up getting hired at this restaurant, waiting tables at night. The tips were good, but the nights were long, and it started messing with my grades."

I pause for a moment, realizing how long it's been since I let myself go back to this part of my life. Even when Frankie and I reconnected, I didn't let myself think too far into it.

"But while I was at the restaurant, I met this guy, Riley. He was the owner's son. To make a long story short, we dated for a month or so and he asked me to move in with him. It was almost summer and I was already feeling burnt out from working too many hours and trying to keep up with my school work, so I took him up on it." Pausing, I let out a sigh. "I realize now that makes me sound desperate, but I didn't have anyone to turn to or ask for help. So when he offered, I said yes. And I did like him, but under normal circumstances, I wouldn't have agreed to it."

Ozzi's thumb strokes the backside of my hand. "How long did you live with him?"

"About four months, I think," I say, trying to remember.

"What made you leave?"

This was the part I hated to talk about. I've vowed my entire life to not be like my mother. For eighteen years, I felt like I had accomplished that… Until Riley.

"I just want to get this out first," I start, needing to rip the band-aid off. "He wasn't nice to me. From the second I moved in, what little bit of romance there had been between us was gone. He still wanted to have sex with me, but that was it. There wasn't a relationship, but more like ownership. He started ordering me around like I was his maid or built-in servant. Even though he was the one that said I didn't need to pay him anything because his dad paid for his apartment, he still made me feel like I was indebted to him. I should've gotten out sooner, but I didn't have anywhere else to go."

Ozzi's body tenses beside me, and I hate it.

"One night, after a late-night shift, I came home to an empty apartment, which wasn't unusual. So, I went to bed and fell asleep. Sometime around two o'clock in the morning, I woke up to go to the bathroom and I heard voices in the living room. I don't know why, but instead of going to the bathroom, I tiptoed down the hall instead. When I got in earshot, I heard a man's voice I didn't recognize and he was talking about making a drop," I say, feeling the same cold chill I'd felt that night. "You have to believe me when I tell you I had no idea Riley was into drugs. If I had, I would've never gotten involved with him, regardless of how desperate I was."

"I believe you," Ozzi says, pulling me closer.

That faith in me is something I haven't experienced often in my life. I can list on one hand the people who have actually believed me. Believed *in* me.

Leaning into him, I take a cleansing breath before continuing. "The next thing I remember was the man asking Riley if *the girl* was going to do it. At first, I didn't realize who they were talking about, but then Riley told him "She'll do what I tell her to do", and I knew he was talking about me."

"Willow," Ozzi whispers, almost pleading, and I know what he's thinking.

"I didn't do it," I tell him, shaking my head. "All I could think was that I couldn't be my mom. She wasted her life away on drugs and being used by men who sold them, and I refused to follow in her footsteps."

Ozzi sits up, facing me, so I do the same and pull the sheet with me. Even though he's seen every inch of my body and the room is dark, I feel extremely exposed.

"I went back to the bedroom and shoved everything I could into my backpack—some clothes and what little money I had—then climbed out the window and ran."

His eyes meet mine and it's like the pieces to the puzzle start falling into place. "That's how you met Frankie."

"Yeah, I didn't know where to go, but I ended up at this gas station and the older man working behind the counter asked me where I was headed. I told him I didn't know. When he asked if I was in trouble, I told him yes. He happened to be friends with Helen, the lady who runs the women's shelter, so he made a call and half an hour later a car pulled up in front of the station. She gave me a ride, a place to sleep... and I ended up staying there until I could get back on my feet."

Ozzi swears under his breath, running a hand down his face. "What about Riley? Did he ever come looking for you?"

"No," I say, biting the inside of my cheek. "He was arrested a week later at an industrial park in Knoxville. There was a sting operation and the guy he made the drop with was an undercover cop."

"Fuck," Ozzi mutters. "That could've been you. I mean, not that you would've done it... not willingly... fuck. I can't even think about that."

I nod, swallowing down the hint of bile. I know exactly what Ozzi means; I've thought about it a lot over the years.

"My first somewhat-serious relationship and that's how it went down," I say with a chuckle. "To say I lost a little faith in myself would be an understatement."

At that, Ozzi pulls me into his lap and wraps his arms around me, holding me close.

"That bullshit is not on you," he says, kissing my temple. "You got out before it was too late... you saved yourself. I hate even thinking about you being with the bastard, but no one gets to judge you for the decisions you make, not even you."

Wrapping my arms around his waist, I close my eyes and soak in his words and the honesty behind them. I know he's right. But I'm not sure I fully believed that until right this second.

CHAPTER 31

OZZI

"We should all go to Genie's tonight," Vali says as he helps me put away the extra mats. We just finished helping with Tempest's self-defense class and it's Friday night. Any other time, I'd jump at the chance to drink a few beers and be entertained by the locals, but not tonight.

"Can't," I say, tossing the last mat onto the stack.

Vali chuckles. "Hot date?"

"Hazel is coming for the weekend."

"Oh, shit. Is that this weekend?" Vali asks.

All of my family is informed and invested in Willow's journey of gaining guardianship of her little sister. Sometimes they talk about her like they already know her, which I guess, in a way, they do. I love how they're rallying around Willow because she needs all the support she can get.

It makes me really fucking sad when I think about how alone she's been all these years. I'd like to think having my big, crazy family around makes up for some of it.

"Yep, it's this weekend and I'm going over tonight to make pizzas and watch a movie."

"Maybe we can all meet up at the park tomorrow?" Vali suggests. "I know Maggie really wants to meet her. We all do. It's supposed to be nice this weekend and Freya had a blast on the swings the last time we took her."

I nod. "I'll mention it to Willow and let her make the call. Not that she won't want everyone to meet Hazel, but I don't know if it will be too overwhelming to meet everyone at once."

"The park would kind of be a chill way to do it."

He's right, and since the park in Mountain City is kind of Willow and Hazel's thing already, maybe that would help her feel comfortable.

"I'll text you and let you know."

Heading upstairs, I rush through my shower and shave. I'm dressed and ready to walk out the door in less than fifteen minutes.

Willow said she'd buy all the ingredients for the pizza before she left work, but I don't want to go over empty-handed, so I asked Tempest to bring home some muffins. I didn't make any special requests, figuring she'd just bring home what was left over, but her being the awesome sister-in-law she is, of course she went above and beyond.

The box I grab on my way downstairs has a special new concoction—*This One's For The Girls*. But she said I could have one too, even though I'm not a girl, because I'm her favorite. That statement was followed up by a warning to not tell Vali or Gunnar because they'd get their feelings hurt.

Pussies.

As I slide into the driver's seat of the Jeep, I lift the box to my nose and inhale, letting out a groan. God, they smell amazing. She said it's her own personal take on Funfetti with a white chocolate drizzle and a Fruity Pebbles crumble on top.

The thought crosses my mind that I could eat the whole box on my way to Willow's and no one would be the wiser. As I'm contemplating that possibility, my cell phone rings and makes me practically jump out of my seat, like I've been caught with my hand in the cookie jar... or the muffin box.

Do both of those euphemisms sound extremely sexual or is it just me?

"Hey," I say, putting the phone on speaker as I place the box of muffins safely in the passenger seat and start the Jeep. "Headed your way."

"Okay," Willow says, sounding off.

"You alright?"

She sighs into the phone and I'm afraid she's getting ready to tell me something happened and Hazel isn't coming or some other bad news.

"I'm good, just feeling really anxious… and I needed to hear your voice."

Damn, this woman is getting so far under my skin I'll never get her out, not that I want to. What does that mean? I honestly have no clue. I just know I love being around her. She makes me feel good—about myself, about the world around me. She's restored some lost love for the sport I've lived my entire life around. And when she's vulnerable and lets me see her softer side, I want to wrap her in my arms and never let go.

"Everything is going to be fine," I assure her, turning right onto the main road. "Tempest made some amazing muffins that I was seconds away from devouring when you called, but now that you rescued them, I promise they'll make every-thing better."

She laughs and it's music to my ears. "Her muffins do work miracles," she says, already sounding better. "I just got a call from Sharon and they'll be in Green Valley in about twenty minutes."

"Are you home from work yet?"

"Just got here."

"Why don't you take a quick shower and by the time you get out, I'll be there. Unless you think it'd be better if I'm not around when they get there."

"No," Willow says. "I want you here and Hazel will be really happy to see you."

"Then I'll be there."

"Okay, I'll see you in a few."

"See you in a few, beautiful."

No sooner do I end the call than my phone rings again.

"Did you forget something?" I ask.

There's a grunt that comes from the other end of the line and I realize it's not Willow. At least, I hope it's not Willow.

"No, I didn't forget anything," Viggo's gruff voice answers. "Did I catch you at a bad time?"

"Where the fuck have you been and why have you been ignoring us?" I ask, unable to keep the bite out of my tone. I don't mean to be a little bitch, but he basically ghosted us and it's not cool.

Viggo groans and I know he's probably regretting calling me already, but I don't care. Now that I have him on the phone, he's going to give me some answers.

"At least tell me you're okay."

"I'm okay."

Rolling my eyes, I take a calming breath to keep me from saying something that will piss him off and send him back into hiding. "Did you make it back to Texas?"

"Yeah... I did," he says. I can hear some noise in the background, like he's working on something. "My reception has been shit, so I haven't been getting all of your texts and phone calls right away."

There's a pause and I'm getting ready to drill him for more answers, but then he says, "Sorry I haven't been in touch."

Viggo rarely apologizes, so I accept this rare peace offering and decide to move on.

"Everything going okay? Where've you been staying?"

"Found a spot for the time being," he says vaguely, obviously not wanting to give more information. "And I've been working some odd jobs, just trying to fill the time and figure my shit out."

With my eyes on the road, I nod like he can see me. "I'm glad you're doing okay. And thanks for finally calling me back," I tell him as I turn down the road that leads to Willow's apartment.

"Everything going okay there?"

"Yeah," I say, putting my Jeep into park. I think about mentioning what's happening between me and Willow, but it would take more time than I have to talk. "Everything is good."

"Your new fighter, is she ready for the ring?"

A smile breaks across my face. "She's more than ready."

"Keep me posted on that," he says. There's some static on the line and I think the call is getting ready to drop. Then I hear him break through. "Listen, I've gotta go. I'm going to try to give Cage a call, but if I don't get a chance, let him know we talked and that everything is going okay."

"Will do," I tell him. "Take care of yourself."

The line goes dead after that and I'm not sure if he hung up or the call dropped. Regardless, I'm glad he called. There's a sense of relief knowing he's past giving us all the silent treatment. Hopefully, he finds some peace and happiness in whatever he's doing.

Grabbing the box of muffins, I hop out of the Jeep and head up to Willow's apartment. Before I can knock, the door opens, and Willow's gorgeous face is smiling at me.

"Hey," I say, stepping in and kissing her soundly.

It's been a few days since the night we spent together. I've seen her at the gym for our training sessions and we all did a sort-of round robin exhibition type of sparring last night. But we haven't had a chance to be alone. Willow's really put in some solid hours at the gym and then she has to get in bed for work the next day. I want to be selfish and demand all of her time, but I'm so fucking proud of everything she's accomplishing, I also don't want to stand in her way.

"That's the best hello I've had in a while," she muses when I finally pull away.

"I've missed you," I tell her, closing the door behind me.

She chuckles. "I just saw you last night."

"Yeah, in a ring full of sweaty dudes who are all related to me," I murmur.

Her smile is literally lighting up the room. Even with wet hair and no makeup, she's the most beautiful woman I've ever laid eyes on, and probably ever will.

"Well, tonight won't be spent with a bunch of sweaty dudes, but a nine-year-old will be here any minute," she says with a deep inhale as she rubs her palms down the legs of her jeans.

Taking her hands, I shake them out, like I would if she was getting ready to go fight in a ring.

"Hazel is going to love it here," I assure her. "She's going to love her room and more than anything, she's going to love being with you."

Willow nods, swallowing down her anxieties. "And I'm doing the right thing?"

"You're one hundred percent doing the right thing. Trust me when I say she will thank you for everything you're doing for her one day. When she's your age, she's going to look back and see where her life could've gone and where it went because of you. Because of your big heart and warrior spirit."

She turns her head and pulls one of her hands away to swipe under her eyes. "Don't make me cry. I don't want to be a blubbering mess when they show up, that won't look good. Nancy will think I'm unstable or something."

We both laugh as I pull her to me. "You're the most stable person I know."

"I'm not sure that's saying much coming from the company you keep."

I kiss the top of her head, wanting to do so much more, but knowing we don't have time for what I want. "The girl has jokes."

Her arms tighten around me and we stand like that for a while, until we hear a vehicle drive up.

When Willow pulls away, there's a new resolve in her eyes, something I've seen from her in training sessions. Times when I've pushed her to what she thought was her limit, but then she surpassed it and realized she's built for more.

There's a knock and Willow gives me a smile before opening the door.

"Hey," she says, sounding more casual than I know she's feeling.

Nancy is standing behind Hazel with a reassuring smile. "Hello," she says cheerfully. "Are you ready for a fun weekend?"

"So ready," Willow says, reaching out to pull Hazel into a hug. "How about you?"

"So ready," Hazel repeats.

I'm standing back, trying to give them some space, but when Hazel sees me her eyes light up even bigger and she shoots me one of her blinding smiles. "Ozzi!"

"I'll be back tomorrow at five," Nancy says, giving us a wave before retreating down the steps and back to her SUV.

When the door is closed, the three of us stand there for a second, sort of frozen in time.

If I had to guess, Willow is committing all of this to memory—the first time she's had a family member, someone she's related to, under the same roof as her in over fifteen years.

Hazel seems to be taking the place in, her eyes scanning every nook and cranny.

And I'm just feeling honored to be a part of the moment.

Willow takes Hazel's backpack from her shoulder. "Wanna see your room?"

"I have my own room?" Hazel asks, eyes wide with disbelief.

"You sure do." Willow spins Hazel toward the room before giving her a little nudge. "Go check it out."

As Hazel rushes to the room, I call out. "See if you can guess which surprise is from me while you're in there!"

Willow laughs then lets out a deep breath as I wrap my arm around her waist. "I told you it'd be great."

"Yeah," she relents. "I just don't want to screw this up, you know?"

"Which is why you won't," I assure her.

Hearing Hazel squeal and laugh as she explores her new room, I take advantage of our brief alone time by turning Willow's face toward mine and kissing her. I manage to keep the kiss at a PG-thirteen rating, even though I'm dying for more. But when she hums against my lips, the vibrations go straight to my dick causing me to pull away with a groan.

"Baby, you can't be doing shit like that when Hazel's here. Sporting a woody in front of your little sister would not be cool."

"Shh, lower your voice," Willow fusses at me while trying not to laugh.

The current situation might be funny, but the reality of how we're going to be able to have private time once Hazel moves in is concerning. It's been in the back of my mind ever since our first night together but I'll feel like an asshole if I bring it up.

Obviously, there's more to our relationship than sex but we just started getting physical and I want her all the time. It'll be hard—pun very much intended—to keep my hands off her.

"We're going to have to get creative once she's here permanently," Willow says.

It's as though she can read my mind and I'm so fucking relieved we're on the same page.

"We'll think of something. I have no doubt my family would babysit for us if we asked."

"Miss Faye has already volunteered to watch her whenever I need her to," she adds.

"See? It's all gonna work out fine. Otherwise, you'll have to learn to be more quiet when I'm inside you." I nip her neck, teasing her with my words and my mouth.

Willow elbows me in the side just as a knock lands on the door.

"Yoo-hoo! It's Faye!"

"Perfect timing. I'll let her in so you and I can go *look for something* in my jeep," I murmur in her ear.

Catching onto my innuendo, she swats at me, laughing. "You're trouble, Ozzi Erickson."

"Not the first time I've been told that."

Willow opens the door to a beaming Miss Faye holding a platter covered in foil.

"I wanted to drop off some cookies for y'all to enjoy once Hazel gets here. She likes chocolate chip, doesn't she?"

"I'm sure she does but you can ask her yourself because she's already here," Willow gushes.

"She is? Oh, I'd love to meet her if it's not too much for her."

"She's been in her new room for a few minutes now. Let's go see what she's up to."

The ladies start to head for the bedroom when I step in front of Miss Faye to take the tray of cookies. "Let me put these on the counter for you."

"Oh, thank you! My goodness, I do love a man with good manners." She smiles at me before turning to Willow and stating, "Helpful *and* handsome... you can't beat that!"

The three of us are quiet as we stand in the doorway watching Hazel like she's an art exhibit. She's stretched out on her new bed, snuggling the sloth, and reading a book and it's so heartwarming I think we all get a little misty-eyed.

"She looks so comfortable... and natural. Like, she's always been here," Willow whispers with a sniffle.

"She really does," I agree, kissing the top of Willow's head.

"Why are y'all watching me?" Hazel asks, sounding more like a teenager than the nine-year-old she is.

"We were trying not to disturb you but there's someone here we'd like you to meet."

Hazel closes her book and lays it aside before sitting up. Willow takes Miss Faye's hand and leads her to the bed. "Hazel, this is Miss Faye. She owns the apartment we live in, and you'll be staying with her on days I work late."

"Hello, dear," Miss Faye says warmly as she sits gingerly on the edge of Hazel's bed. "What a beautiful young lady you are. I think you and I are going to be great friends and have lots of fun together."

"Do you have any animals?"

"I used to have a rat terrier named Booger, but he passed away last year."

Hazel starts to laugh but stops. "Sorry, I was laughing at his name, not that he died."

"Oh, I know." Miss Faye pats Hazel's hand in understanding. "It's a funny name for a dog and to this day, I don't know why my husband, Ralph, named him that. It just stuck, I guess," she chuckles.

"How do you like your room?" Willow asks. I can tell she's been dying to ask and couldn't keep quiet any longer. She's so damn cute.

"Are you kidding me? It's the best room ever!" Hazel exclaims.

Relief covers Willow's face and the smile she produces is breathtaking.

"Thank you for my sloth, Ozzi."

"How did you know that was from me?" I ask.

Hazel shrugs. "I just saw it and knew."

"Well, I'm glad you like it. Miss Faye brought you something, too."

"Really? You didn't have to do that but thank you." Hazel smiles brightly at Miss Faye and I know it won't be long before these two are thick as thieves.

"I made you some chocolate chip cookies and if you'd like to learn, I can teach you how to make them one day."

"Those are my favorite kind of cookies! Can I have one now?"

"Of course you can. I mean, as long as your sister says it's okay."

Hazel, Miss Faye, and I all turn to look at Willow who is wiping tears from her cheeks. They look concerned and in Hazel's case, a little confused as to why Willow would be crying, but I know how special this moment is for her. I swear, my own heart has grown like the Grinch's just witnessing Willow's journey to get here.

Seeing that Willow is struggling to control her emotions, I lift the cookie I snagged a moment ago to my mouth and take a loud, crunching bite out of it. "Mmmmm, this cookie is amazing. If Hazel doesn't want the rest, I'll take care of them."

"What? No way!" Hazel yells, jumping onto her knees with her hands on her hips. Willow laughs and wipes at her face again before giving me a smile that secretly thanks me for the distraction.

I wink at her before suggesting we all get a cookie in the kitchen so that crumbs don't get in Hazel's new bedding. Hazel agrees and patiently waits for Miss Faye to stand and walk out of the room before she runs the remaining steps to the kitchen.

This afternoon couldn't have gone better and I'm thrilled for Willow and Hazel, but I can't help but wonder what the future holds for us and how I'm going to fit into this new life they're creating.

CHAPTER 32

WILLOW

"Willow. Paging: Willow. You have a phone call on line one in the breakroom."

Seriously?

There have to be approximately two customers in the store right now and James, Piggly Wiggly's latest hire, thought it was necessary to page me over the loudspeaker rather than walking to the aisle I'm in?

Using a carrier pigeon to deliver the message would've been better than hearing my name screeched throughout the entire store.

Only two people have this number for me—Nancy and Ozzi—so it's safe to assume this call is important. I leave my inventory sheet on the shelf I was working on to hold my spot for when I return and then briskly walk to the breakroom. Thankfully, the "hold" light is still flashing, so I grab the receiver and push the button for line one before saying hello.

"Willow! I have great news."

Hearing this from Nancy can only mean one thing but I refuse to get my hopes up and jump to conclusions.

Swallowing down the rush of anxiety, I squeak out, "You do?"

"The judge has officially granted you guardianship of Hazel. You did it!" Nancy's voice is genuinely happy and excited, which makes this news even more special. She was the first person to believe I could accomplish this goal and I wouldn't have been able to do it without her.

I brace myself against the counter, closing my eyes and letting her words sink in. *I did it.*

"Really? She's really mine? No take-backs?"

Nancy laughs. "No take-backs. You and Hazel are officially a family now. I mean, not that you weren't already, but she's legally yours and the two of you will always have each other."

Tears flood my eyes as I allow this new reality to wash over me and settle in my bones. I finally have a family. I'll be able to take care of my sister and make sure she never has to be in foster care again. Hazel will never go to bed hungry or scared and she will always know she's loved. Neither of us will ever be lonely again.

As God is my witness, I'll make sure of it.

"Thank you so much, Nancy," I manage to say through my quiet sobs. "I know those words don't even come close to expressing the gratitude I have for all you've done for us, but I don't know what else to say."

I don't even try to hide the fact I'm crying. I've earned these tears and they aren't sad at all. They're full of relief, happiness, and pride because that's exactly how I'm feeling right now.

On top of the fucking world.

"The best way you can thank me is to continue doing what you're doing—being the best sister and support system Hazel could ask for. You have no idea how delighted I am. My job often doesn't end this happy, so seeing the two of you together is more than thanks enough."

"What's the next step?" I ask.

I hear some papers shuffling in the background before she finally answers.

"I've already been in touch with Hazel's foster family and because the school year ends this Friday, they're willing to let her stay for the remainder of the week. That means, she can move in Friday night or Saturday morning, which-ever works better for your schedule."

"Can I pick her up from school on Friday?" I ask.

"Well, as her guardian, I'd say you can do whatever you want," Nancy says with a soft chuckle.

"Oh, yeah. That's gonna take some getting used to, I suppose."

Nancy laughs. "Well, I can go ahead and let the school know she won't be returning in the fall and have them send her school records to Green Valley for you."

Leaning my head against the wall beside the counter, I see the flyer on the bulletin board I'd read over last week from the school. When I first saw it, I immediately thought of Hazel, but didn't allow myself to hope or make plans. But now, I can.

"That would be great," I say, taking the flyer down and sticking it in my locker for later. "I was thinking about enrolling her in a summer program so she can meet some friends before the school year starts back."

"See, you're already planning ahead," Nancy says confidently. "You're a natural, Willow, and Hazel is very lucky to have you."

"She's also been lucky to have you," I tell her, thinking back to some of the case workers I've experienced throughout my life. Some of them were okay, but others couldn't have cared less what happened to me.

We chat for a few more minutes about some minor details, before she lets me go, promising to talk again soon.

After I hang up the phone, I take a few deep breaths before exiting the break-room and heading back out into the store. Somehow, I manage to get my work done, but my mind is moving a mile a minute, thinking about all the last-minute things I need to do before I pick Hazel up on Friday. I hate admitting I've had to recount a few different products on my list because I'm having so much trouble focusing.

Once I'm finished, I check in with Tim to make sure he doesn't need anything else from me before I clock out. He says everything is good and thanks me for doing all the restock and inventory.

I'm happy to do it, honestly, because it means job security for me, something I need more than ever now that I'm solely responsible for another human being.

Grabbing my bag from my locker, I walk out and make it to the parking lot just in time to see Ozzi step out of his Jeep.

"Hey, beautiful," he greets me as he opens the car door for me.

Always such a gentleman.

"Hey, yourself. Thanks for picking me up. Have you been waiting long?"

"Nah, just a few minutes but you know I'll wait as long as you need me to." He kisses me gently and I can't help but swoon. I know we won't have a lot of alone time once Hazel gets here, so I'm going to soak up as much of Ozzi Erickson as I can.

"How was your day?" he asks.

"It was amazing actually." I'm not even trying to hide the goofy smile I know I'm wearing right now.

"Oh, yeah? Big day at the Wiggly Pig?"

Gah, every time he makes me laugh, I fall even harder for him.

"Well, I don't know about the Pig, but it was a big day for Willow," I hedge.

When I glance over at him, he's looking at me like a kid on Christmas morning —so anxious and happy. His entire demeanor is exuding excitement and I haven't even told him the news. But that's Ozzi, just the idea of me having a good day is enough to make him happy.

"Dammit, woman, would you spill it already? I'm dying here."

Letting out a laugh, I shake my head, euphoria rushing through my veins. "I'm Hazel's guardian!" I exclaim, still trying to let it sink in. "The judge approved my petition and Nancy called to tell me the news!"

Suddenly, Ozzi jumps out of his seat and runs around the Jeep to my side, throwing my door open. "There's no way I could've hugged you properly from my side of the car," he explains before pulling me out of my seat and into his arms. Instinctively, I wrap my legs around his waist and he twirls me around, the sounds of my laughter filling the parking lot.

"You fucking did it! God, I'm so proud of you, Willow."

Ozzi stops spinning us and pins me against his Jeep, causing my exuberance to quickly morph into lust. I sink my fingers into his thick hair and pull him to me for a kiss, moaning as his tongue fills my mouth.

I have no idea how long we stay here making out, but we don't pull away until a truck full of teenagers yell at us to get a room as they drive by.

"That's an excellent idea," Ozzi murmurs into my neck. "Is there anywhere you need to be right now?"

I just need to be where you are is what I want to say but that's way too scary to admit, so I just shake my head.

"Good." He smiles before kissing me again then carefully sets me back in my seat. Once he's behind the steering wheel and buckled in, Ozzi grabs my hand and brushes his lips across my skin before holding it on top of his thigh.

Who knew a big, bad Viking could be so affectionate?

As soon as we're inside my apartment and the door is locked, we start pulling each other's clothes off. We were pretty quiet on the ride over here and I think we were both soaking up the sexual tension between us because we're absolutely ravenous for each other.

"God, I can't wait to be inside you," Ozzi tells me as he slides a finger between my folds, finding me wet and swollen. Slipping two fingers inside, he pumps them in and out, making me even more wet.

"Now, Oz," is all I can manage to say because I'm so freaking desperate for him.

He quickly slips a condom on and sits down on the futon. When he notices my hesitation, he says, "Come here, I want you to ride me."

Memories of our first night together come flooding back and a smile spreads across my face as I straddle his lap and position myself over his enormous erection. Anticipation builds low in my belly as I watch him stroke himself.

Ozzi fists the base of his cock, rubbing his tip through my wetness before gently guiding my hips into position. Slowly, I sink onto him, allowing my pussy to stretch and accommodate the size of his cock, but once our hips are flush, my instinct to move kicks in.

"Fuck, that's it, baby. Move any way you need to. I want you to feel as good as I do," Ozzi says with a grunt.

His hands grip my hips as I move over him, letting me control the pace. Never have I felt so full and complete with every nerve ending in my body on fire. It doesn't take me long to realize every time he's fully seated, my clit hits his pelvic bone perfectly, eliciting moans from deep in my belly and making me lose my mind.

"Oh, God," I cry out, letting my head fall back as I brace myself on his shoulders. "You're so deep... I—I've never felt anything like this...nothing."

Ozzi cups my breasts and brings them to his greedy mouth and I swear my clit pulses every time he sucks on my nipples.

When I bring my gaze back to his, those blue eyes are blazing with lust and desire and so many more things I can't label. Things I'm scared to acknowledge. I had no idea fucking him like this would make me feel so sexy and powerful but it does. Being in control of his pleasure and mine is a heady feeling.

Our bodies become slick with sweat as I increase my pace, making sure to squeeze around Ozzi's dick as I ride him hard and fast.

"Just like that, Willow. That's it, baby." He grips my hips tighter, quickening the pace. "Fuck, I love the way you feel. I'm so close, baby."

"Me, too," I gasp out. "So close."

Reaching between us, Ozzi presses his thumb against my clit, and it's exactly what I need to soar over the edge. My orgasm erupts throughout my body as stars light up behind my eyes.

Ozzi begins muttering a string of unintelligible words before crying out my name, over and over in an erotic chant, as he finds his own release.

Eventually, our movements slow and Ozzi collapses against the back of the futon with me on top of him. His arms wrap protectively around me, holding my bare chest to his. This skin-to-skin contact feels so good, almost as intimate as the sex.

After a moment of just breathing, he cradles my face in his hands and kisses me lazily, our tongues joined in a slow dance, and I swear, I've never felt so sated.

Later, as we snuggle on the futon, we're still wrapped up in each other, we're just wearing clothes again. It's a shame, really, but we knew if we didn't cover up the goods, we'd never make it to the gym tonight.

"What's going to happen between us once Hazel is here?" The question leaves my mouth before I can stop it, but if Ozzi is caught off guard, he doesn't show it.

"What do you mean?" Ozzi asks as he strokes my arm in soothing circles.

Scooting up to a sitting position, I cross my legs and look down at him. "I mean, she'll be here and we won't be able to just barge into my apartment and have sex in the middle of the afternoon. I realize we just started having sex and had a friendship before then. So, I guess what I'm wondering is what are we...friends? More than friends? Friends with benefits? I've already told you I don't have a lot of experience with relationships, and I suck at trusting my instincts. So, I guess I'm asking you to spell it out for me."

Ozzi chuckles and runs his fingers through his hair as he sits up across from me, bracing his elbows on his knees.

"I think it's safe to say we're more than friends. Calling you my girlfriend sounds a bit juvenile, but if you need a label, that one works."

He eyes me with something that looks a little like caution. I'm the queen of walls and if I didn't know better, Ozzi might be in the process of putting one up. The way he shifted from completely relaxed and in the moment to the Ozzi who jokes about things and makes light of every situation is a little disconcerting. But I don't call him out on it because he's riding this roller coaster with me, so I give him the benefit of the doubt that this is just his way of handling the situation.

"I'm sure things will change," he continues. "I've never, uh, dated anyone with a kid before. But I've watched Cage and Tempest since they had Freya and they seem to make it work."

He takes a deep breath, his focus landing on the floor, and I watch as he searches for the right thing to say, holding my breath for what's next.

"We probably won't see each other a lot at first," he says, his eyes shifting back up to me as he puts on one of his famous, reassuring smiles. "But once things settle, I'm sure we can get creative with how we spend our alone time. I'm all for being adventurous, so you'll hear no complaints from me."

273

In a split second, my Ozzi is back and I can't help but roll my eyes and laugh.

"Does it bother you to be dating someone with a kid?" This is the question that's been keeping me up at night, so I'm glad he brought it up. "Please be honest with me. I can take it."

There's a long pause and just when I think he's going to blow it off and respond with a joke or something typically-Ozzi, he levels blue eyes at me.

"Shit, Willow, what do you want me to say?" he asks, running a hand through his hair again.

His voice isn't angry, but it's more abrasive than usual—stressed almost, which is out of character for him.

"I've just never been with anyone who has a kid, but it's not because I'm against it. It's just never happened. My family would say it's because I struggle with commitment, but I disagree. I'm not a commitment-phobe, I just really love my freedom and being able to go where the wind takes me. How that part of me will react to our twosome becoming a threesome, I honestly don't know. But I do know I'd never intentionally hurt you or Hazel."

"I believe that," I assure him, appreciating his honesty. "All I ask is if you ever feel overwhelmed or need a break, please talk to me before you run off or shut me out."

"I promise."

CHAPTER 33

OZZI

illow's eyes grow wide when she walks out of the Pig the next day, expecting to see me in my Jeep, but instead, I'm leaning against the hood of her truck.

"Is it fixed?" she asks. "I thought they said it would be a few more days until the part came in?"

As I walk toward her, I hold the keys out. "Came in early and they called to say it was ready, so I picked it up this afternoon."

"How much do I owe you?" she asks, taking the keys and shielding her eyes from the sun.

I shake my head. "Nothing."

Her happy expression falls. "You're not paying for my truck repairs," she insists, dropping a hand to her hip and exhaling loudly. "I just got the money from selling my trailer and I intentionally put it back to cover the cost."

"Good," I tell her, snaking an arm around her waist and pulling her to me. "You can use that money for a new mattress because the futon sucks balls. Plus, Hazel will be here in a few more days and if I ever want to have you in a bed again, this is my best chance. Call me selfish."

"Fine, I'll go buy a mattress," she says reluctantly, returning my hug with a sigh.

I know she hates accepting help of any kind, but I want to do this for her. She's been through so much and brought herself out on the other side. I'm so fucking proud of her.

"This isn't charity. It's a gift," I tell her, needing her to know the difference. "I want to do something nice for you because I care about you. See how that works?" I ask, leaning back to look down at her.

She twists her lips into a smile and rolls her eyes.

Pulling her back to me, I growl into her ear. "Keep rolling your eyes at me and we'll be christening your truck on the way home."

"Don't tease me."

Exhaling my frustrations, I huff.

"God, I want to be bad with you," I tell her, hoping she knows how much she drives me crazy, in the best way possible. "But you really do need a bed. You have that whole room with nothing in it and Hazel isn't the only one who deserves a bedroom. Besides wanting to get in your pants, I also need to make sure my prizefighter is well-rested. We only have two weeks until Nashville and I need you in prime condition."

She eases away from me and nods. "Fine, let's go buy a bed."

Instead of having a couple hours of downtime between working and the gym, Willow and I head to a small furniture store not far from Viking MMA. There aren't a lot of options, but she finds something she likes that's in her price range, and we load it into her truck.

After a quick call to Vali, the two of us haul it up the stairs and have it put together in no time.

"I'm going to owe you a steak dinner," Willow says, wiping her forehead with the back of her hand.

While we'd assembled the bed, she'd driven to a second-hand store and found some sheets and bedding.

"Nah," Vali says, waving her off. "You just keep being a badass in the ring and we'll call it good."

Willow rolls her eyes, hating the compliment, but she smiles anyway.

What's she going to do when everyone sees just how good she is, because Vali's statement of her being a badass in the ring wasn't blowing smoke. She really is *that* good. Where it came from and how it got missed all these years, I'll never know. But she's a beast and only getting better with time and practice.

Getting this first fight under her belt is going to be a game-changer, I can feel it. She's primed and ready and all that's missing is some real ring time.

"How about we head back to the gym and spar a few rounds with Gunnar, then we'll all go out to Genie's for a beer?"

"You better be glad Cage isn't training you," Vali teases. "All you'd be getting is water and rabbit food."

We all laugh, but he's not wrong. Cage is a hard-ass and he makes his fighters walk a tight line. I'm a little more lenient, believing that balance is what makes a great fighter. It can't always be all work and no fun.

"It's a good thing I don't really like beer, then, huh?" Willow says, tossing her long, dark hair over her shoulder. "I will go to Genie's with you, though. It sounds fun."

Together, the three of us leave Willow's, feeling accomplished. Her truck is back up and running. She's no longer sleeping on a fucking futon, which also means we won't be fucking on a fucking futon. Hazel moves here in three days. And Willow is ready to kick some ass in Nashville.

I'm not sure things could get any better.

Life feels good.

CHAPTER 34

WILLOW

I've had five days for this to sink in, but I'm still pinching myself as I drive up to Hazel's school and get in the pick-up line. Nancy made the arrangements for me to be able to pick her up today, letting the school know about the approval for guardianship and that she was now legally mine.

All of her paperwork has been transferred to Green Valley for the next school year, and Nancy went earlier today to her foster family's house and collected her belongings. We're meeting up at the park before we leave town.

I can't say I'll never come back to Mountain City, but I can say it will be a long time before I do.

There's so much history here. Not all of it is bad. I do have a few happy memories of our mother and, of course, this is where I met Hazel for the first time. I'll always be thankful for this time we've had, but I'm ready to move on.

When I hear the bell ring, my heart beats a little faster.

Hazel knows I'm coming to get her from school today, but it doesn't mean I'm not nervous. It's more than just this monumental moment, it's all the moments that will follow. As much as I've struggled with whether I'm making the right decision, I'm still worried I'm going to screw up.

Actually, I'm confident I will at some point, because I'm human. But I know, no matter what, I'm going to love Hazel and give her the best life I'm capable of giving her.

The second the doors open, I see her.

She's in line, a few kids back, but I can see her scanning the line of cars looking for me. The moment she spots me, her hand flies up in the air and she begins to wave.

I can't help the smile that splits my face—it's so big it makes my cheeks hurt—and I lean over to roll down the window and wave back.

"Happy last day of school," I tell her when she climbs into the cab of the truck, handing her a box from Donner Bakery with a special cupcake from Tempest.

"Is this another one of those Fruity Pebbles muffins like we had last weekend?" she asks, her eyes growing wide as she cracks open the box.

I shake my head, soaking up this moment and the fact she's sitting here, in the truck with me, while also trying to play it cool.

"Nope, it's one-of-a-kind, just for today," I tell her. "Tempest made it especially for you."

She looks up at me, those wide eyes growing even wider. "Just for me?"

"Yep," I tell her, nodding as I put the truck in drive. "Put on your seatbelt. You can eat it while we're at the park. We're meeting Nancy there to pick up your things."

Quickly, she buckles herself in and I slowly pull away from the school. I want to ask if she's sad about this being her last day, not only at this school, but with her foster family and in Mountain City, but I don't want to bring up anything that's going to upset her.

"I'm not going to miss this place," she says with a sigh. "Is that bad?"

With a chuckle, I shake my head. "No, it's not bad."

"I think you're supposed to be sad when you leave somewhere, but I'm not sad. I'm just happy I get to be with you and everyone else in Green Valley. And I'm not even scared about starting a new school."

Letting out a sigh of relief, I lean back in my seat and roll down the window, letting in the warm breeze. "That's the best news ever, Hazel, because I'm happy too."

I turn to look at her and she smiles over at me, and in that moment, I know we're going to be okay. As long as we have each other, we'll make it through whatever the world wants to throw our way.

"Look who it is," Nancy says when we arrive at the park. "The big fourth grader! How was the last day of school?"

She's already sitting at our usual table, looking the most relaxed I've ever seen her. Not that she's ever been uptight, but there's a lightness to her demeanor today that I haven't seen before.

"Great!" Hazel says, sliding into the seat across from her as she opens the box from the bakery. "Tempest made me my very own special cupcake."

Nancy looks up at me with a smile. "Well, isn't that nice?"

"I brought a box for you too," I tell her, pulling the other box from the truck and bringing it over.

"Oooh, thank you," she says, cracking the box open and pinching off a bite.

When she pops it into her mouth, her eyes roll back. "Oh, my God. This is the best thing I've ever tasted."

"Donner Bakery is world-famous," Hazel announces as she takes a large bite of her own muffin. "Have you ever heard of the Banana Cake Queen? She's the owner. That's Tempest's boss. And Tempest is known as the Duchess of Muffins."

I raise my eyebrows at her retained knowledge of all the comings and goings of Green Valley.

She's going to fit right in.

"Well, I can't wait to visit more," Nancy says, dusting crumbs off her hands and placing her half-eaten muffin back in the box. "I hope we'll be able to meet up from time to time."

"Definitely," I tell her, my throat clogging with emotion. Nancy is the one part of all this I don't want to say goodbye to. She's been a godsend and I'm grateful to have her on our side.

Standing, she walks over to her SUV and opens the back hatch. "How about we get this stuff moved over so you two can make it home before dinnertime."

"Yeah, we better get going soon."

Sadly, Hazel doesn't really have that much. There are two duffle bags and a box of some odds-and-ends, and that's it.

"I also had the school make copies of her records. They've sent everything over to Green Valley, but I wanted you to have a copy. Her immunization records are in there too."

Shot records, right. "I'll find her a pediatrician next week."

Nancy nods. "It's not a rush, but she'll need a checkup before school starts."

Blowing out a breath, I take the file from her and tuck it into my bag.

"You've got this," Nancy says quietly, taking my hands in hers. "Just one step at a time and if you have questions about anything, I'm only a phone call away."

"Thank you, again," I tell her, squeezing her hands. "I know I've said it a million times, but I mean it. You've been so great through all of this and I'm so glad you were assigned to Hazel's case. Knowing you were looking out for her gave me peace of mind."

"It's been my pleasure."

On the drive back to Green Valley, we mostly ride in comfortable silence. Occasionally, I hear Hazel humming and I smile. Glancing over at her, I see the most content look on her face and it fills me with so much warmth I feel like my heart might explode all over the cab of the truck.

It's crazy how much she reminds me of myself at her age—loves to read, inquisitive, a dreamer... even her humming. Genetics are weirdly amazing. Take two people, like me and Hazel, who had the same mother but never knew each other until a few months ago yet have such similarities.

I have an overwhelming feeling of rightness as I pull the truck up in front of our apartment—*our* apartment. Hers and mine.

"How about we get inside and get you settled, then we can fix some dinner," I say, pulling the keys out of the ignition and turning to face her.

The look on Hazel's face is like looking in a mirror. She looks so happy. "Then can we go visit Miss Faye?" she asks, opening her door and grabbing her backpack. "Wait, do you have to go to work?"

"No, I worked this morning, the early shift, and my boss gave me tomorrow off so I can be with you."

"Is that okay?" she asks, biting on her thumbnail, again reminding me so much of myself.

That edge of worry in her tone makes my stomach twist.

"It's fine," I tell her, realizing I'm probably going to have to be a little more transparent with her than I'd like. But I remember what it felt like when I wasn't in foster care for the first time. I was always worried about my next meal and how I was going to take care of myself. I was eighteen when I experienced that for the first time. She's only nine and way too young to worry about stuff like that.

"Hazel," I say, getting her attention. When she turns her greenish-brown eyes to me, I hold her gaze, so she knows what I'm telling her is the truth. "I can't promise it's always going to be easy, but you don't have to worry, okay?"

Reaching across the seat, I take her small hand in mine and thankfully, she lets me.

"We don't have a lot, but we have enough," I assure her. "And I have money saved up for emergencies. We won't ever go without food and I'll always make sure we have a roof over our heads. Your clothes won't always be the best, but they'll always be clean. And if there's something you really want, we'll work hard to try to get it, okay?"

I see her swallow and I pray she doesn't start crying, because if she does, I know I won't be able to hold it together. Her happiness and sadness are directly linked to my own.

When she cries, I'll cry.

When she smiles, I'll smile.

"Okay," she says meekly, much more somber than the sassy nine-year-old I'm used to, but I understand the emotions and what she's feeling.

"And Hazel," I add, realizing I've never said these three words to anyone before. Maybe I've always been saving them for her. "I love you."

Her chin trembles and the next thing I know, she bursts across the seat and wraps her arms around my neck. She doesn't say the words back, but that's okay. It took me twenty-two years to get here, and it wasn't until I felt unconditional love myself, that I felt free enough to say those words.

She'll get there.

And in the meantime, I'll take her hugs.

"How about after dinner and a visit with Miss Faye, we go to the gym and see Tempest? You can thank her for the muffins and meet Baby Freya."

Hazel's eyes grow wide, like they always do when she's excited. "And see Ozzi?"

"Yep, I need to get a training session in. Would that be okay?"

Bouncing in her seat, she claps her hands together. "I can't wait. Can we just eat a PB&J?"

"Sure," I tell her with a laugh. "Let's get the truck unloaded."

A few hours later, we're back in the truck headed to Viking MMA.

All of Hazel's belongings are either in the dirty clothes hamper, waiting for laundry day, or put away in her room. Some of her clothes looked questionable, so I didn't want to take any chances with them not being laundered properly.

I'm so grateful to Nancy for collecting her things for us. I was dreading that task. Not that I have any ill will toward the family Hazel was staying with, but I didn't want to have to go there. Maybe it's past trauma from my own time in foster care creeping up, but regardless, I'm glad I didn't have to go.

We'd stopped by Miss Faye's for a few minutes. I think she's as excited about Hazel being a permanent resident of Green Valley as I am. They'd already made plans to *hang out*. Their budding friendship makes me smile and I can't decide who will benefit from it more. Me, because I won't ever have to worry about Hazel when I'm at work. Hazel, because she'll have a role model like Miss Faye in her life, or Miss Faye, because I know she'll be thoroughly entertained by Hazel's presence.

"So, who do you fight?" Hazel asks, her eyes trained on the road ahead of us. "I mean, do you hit people?"

I chuckle. "Well, for now, I just spar with Ozzi and his brothers—Gunnar and Vali. Gunnar is a fighter too. He'll be competing in Nashville with me in a couple weeks."

Now that she's here and getting ready to meet everyone, I wish there had been time last weekend for us to get together with the Ericksons like Vali had suggested.

I know she feels like she already knows Tempest because of her amazing muffins.

And she's heard me talk about the rest of them quite a bit, so hopefully, she'll feel right at home, just like I did when I first met all of them.

Pulling up at the curb, I put the truck in park. "Do you have your book and sketch pad?" I ask, wanting to make sure she's not bored while she waits.

She nods, holding up her small bag. "I also brought Sid," she says, showing me the sloth Ozzi bought her.

"Sid, huh?" I ask with a smirk.

"Yeah, like from *Ice Age*."

"Great name."

When we walk in, I have to do a double take. The entire front desk is full of green balloons and Ozzi is standing there with a huge grin on his face.

"Welcome home, Hazel!"

Vali, Maggie, Gunnar, Frankie, Cage, Tempest, and Freya are there too, all waiting in the background tentatively, like they're afraid they're going to spook Hazel.

But in true Hazel fashion, she looks around the room and lets out a laugh. "Are all of these for me?"

"All for you, kiddo," Ozzi confirms, his eyes going to the sloth in her hands.

When he glances up at me, I have to blink away the tears that are threatening to spill.

They're happy tears, but nonetheless, I'm tired of crying.

"*Thank you*," I mouth to Ozzi before wrapping an arm around Hazel's shoulders. Kneeling, I tell her, "This is everyone I've been telling you about."

Tempest is the first to step forward, bringing Freya with her. The chubby baby is all smiles as she approaches. When Hazel reaches a hand forward, Freya grips it firmly, making Hazel laugh.

"She's so cute."

"This is Freya," Tempest says. "And I'm her mama. My name is Tempest."

Hazel nods. "I know, Willow told me all about you. Thank you for the yummy muffins."

Tempest smiles widely. "You're more than welcome. I'm glad you liked them."

Eventually, everyone takes a turn introducing themselves to Hazel. I watch, checking for signs that this big family is too much for her, but all I see is happiness and pure joy as she puts faces to the names I've already told her about.

"We should get to it," Ozzi says, nudging me with his shoulder. "I think Hazel will be fine."

"I think you're right," I say, watching her play with Freya on one of the mats Tempest has set up with a blanket and toys.

As Ozzi and I begin our warm-up, I don't forget about Hazel, but I do start to focus on the task at hand. I also can't take my eyes off Ozzi. I know he's responsible for all the green balloons. No one else knows that's Hazel's favorite color.

He's constantly doing things like that.

Quietly showing he's listening and that he cares.

"Give me ten on the treadmill," Ozzi demands, making my insides react.

When I raise an eyebrow, he quirks one back.

"So bossy," I tell him, walking over to one of the treadmills and setting it on the right speed and incline.

"I'd like to boss you around later," he whispers. "Think we can get creative tonight?"

My face flushes, and not from exertion. "We might be able to figure something out."

CHAPTER 35

OZZI

"*A*re you sure she's going to be okay?" Willow asks for the second time since we pulled away from the gym.

I see Cage glance back in the rearview. Vali is up front with him and Frankie and Gunnar are in the backseat. Since we're driving back after the fight, we thought it'd be better for us to all be together. I offered to drive my Jeep, giving the rest of them the flexibility to stay overnight, but Cage wants to get back to Tempest and Freya, and Frankie has to be at the clinic tomorrow.

Reaching across the seat, I take Willow's hand. "She's going to be great. Between Tempest, Freya, and Maggie, she won't even have a second to miss you."

Willow brings her thumb to her mouth and starts chewing on her nail.

"We can call them in a couple hours and check in," Cage adds.

She finally gives a half smile and nods. "Yeah, okay."

"Try to relax," I whisper, wishing we were alone so I could properly distract her and take her mind off everything. Not only is she leaving Hazel for the first time, but she's headed to her first competition. If I was her, I'd be stressed too, but I need her to focus.

The remainder of the trip to Nashville is uneventful. Since it's so early, we stop once for coffee refills and then hop straight back into the car.

Frankie and Willow start talking vaguely about when they met at the women's shelter. I'm not sure how much Vali and Cage know about how the two of them met, but from the look on Gunnar's face, he does. But we just listen to them talk because it seems to be taking Willow's mind off of her concerns about leaving Hazel and the upcoming fight.

Thankfully, when we arrive at the event center, we're super early and there aren't a lot of people here yet. Cage goes ahead and gets Willow and Gunnar checked in, securing the rest of us all-access passes.

By the time we make it to the weigh-in, Willow is zoned in.

I'm not sure what changed in the last four hours, but I'm grateful, except now I'm the one freaking out. It's not that I've never trained a fighter, but I've never been this invested. And even though I trust Willow's skills and ability, I'm still worried about her.

I don't want to see her get hurt, but I realize that's a solid possibility, especially with this being her first fight. There's always a learning curve when you're in the ring for the first time. It takes some people a fight or two to get the hang of it, and others never truly conquer the mental game that comes along with competing.

"You okay?" Cage mutters under his breath as Willow and Gunnar put their shoes back on and we make our way down the hall to the warm-up facility.

"Fine," I tell him, trying to play off the nerves.

He huffs. "You look like you're about to throw Willow over your shoulder and make a run for it."

I didn't realize I was being that obvious, but I clear my throat and run a hand through my hair.

"I'm just... fuck, I don't know. I'm good, really. I know she's ready, but it doesn't keep me from being worried about her."

"I get it," he says. "If I was you and she was Tempest, I can't say I'd be any better off. But she's a force to be reckoned with, and you've trained her well. Trust in that."

Taking a deep breath, I hold it and then let it out, nodding my head.

"She needs you," he adds, and that hits me right in the chest.

There's no way I'm letting her down.

Gunnar and Willow warm-up together, putting each other through the paces and sticking to themselves. I notice how Willow watches him and follows his lead, but she also seems sure of herself and holds her own.

We break periodically for water and some last-minute coaching—Cage, Vali, and I all chiming in and giving the two of them every ounce of ammo we can. Frankie stands back, watching from the sidelines, ready to rub out muscle cramps and anything else we need her to do.

I wish everyone was here, including my parents, but the six of us make a damn good team.

"Bernard," one of the organizers calls out, making Willow's head snap around.

Walking over to her, I take the roll of tape and start prepping her hands. "You've got this, baby. You hear me?" I bend down a little until I'm eye level, wanting to drill in what I'm about to say. "When you get in that ring, I want you to remember one thing, I believe in you. I know you can win this fight. Keep your head in it, and whatever you do, don't quit until she's knocked out or that final bell rings. Got it?"

With a fire in her eyes that I've never seen before, Willow nods once, taking the mouth guard and slipping it in.

Cage walks up beside us, his eyes straight ahead. "I truly believe you can do anything you set your mind to," he says. "I've seen you do it. So from the second you step into that ring, you need to make up your mind that you're walking out a winner."

When he looks over at Willow, she holds his gaze and gives him another nod.

"Attack hard, change angles, and use that killer high kick."

There's a glimmer of a smile on Willow's lips, but she doesn't break, keeping her expression as neutral as possible. I've seen a little of this warrior that's coming out, but nothing like this.

When they call her name and the music she picked begins playing, adrenaline has replaced every ounce of blood in my body and I feel like I'm the one getting ready to battle it out.

I guess, in a way, I am.

Willow feels like an extension of me.

From the moment she steps into the ring, everything else fades away.

There are no people, no buzzers, no bright lights.

Just Willow.

I watch as she rolls her shoulders and bounces on her toes, staying loose as the referee checks their gloves and goes over the rules.

Willow's opponent, Heidi McCutchen, is known for her mean right hook. She only has a few bouts under her belt and is working her way up to a title fight. When it comes to height, she has Willow beat by a couple inches, but Willow makes up for that in muscle. Over the past few months, she's toned up what she already had. Just looking at her, she doesn't seem all that menacing, but she packs a punch, and what Cage told her is right, her high kick is lethal.

Once the referee has said all he needs to say, he has them step forward and touch gloves, then instructs them to get back to their corners.

"You've got this," I say simply, feeling Cage at my back, but he stays quiet. "I believe in you. Now, get out there and kick some ass."

When I reach up to rub Willow's shoulders, she leans into me just a little. It's subtle, but enough to let me know she hears me.

The next thing I know, the buzzer sounds and she confidently moves out to the middle of the ring, just like we practiced. As she dances around, waiting for her perfect opportunity, gloves up, I can't take my eyes off her.

Her moves are orchestrated and smooth.

Heidi takes the first strike, but Willow ducks and weaves, then counters with a left hook that makes contact.

For the rest of the round, they continue to trade punches. A few of Heidi's hits make contact, but Willow takes them in stride, not stopping or letting them knock her off course.

When the buzzer sounds, the ref sends each fighter back to their corners. Willow's forehead is covered in sweat and her right eye is already red and starting to swell, but none of the skin is broken or bleeding.

"You look great out there," I tell her, squeezing water from a bottle into her mouth and then taking a towel and wiping her face. "Keep an eye on her right hook, hands up, and I want you to use that kick in this next round. How do you feel?"

"Good," she says, not sounding out of breath, which is a great sign. Endurance is half the battle. "She's fast and that hook is nasty."

I chuckle, nodding. "You're faster and she hasn't seen your high kick yet." Raising my eyebrows, I lock my gaze with hers. "Let's show her what Willow Bernard is packing."

Willow nods in agreement, popping her mouthpiece back in.

It's ridiculous, and I know I can't, but all I want to do at this moment is kiss the shit out of her. Instead, I pound my knuckles against her gloves. "Let's go, Bernard. Make it hurt."

During the second round, Willow starts out a lot like the first, dancing her way around the ring, waiting for an opportunity to strike. But unlike the first round, this time she doesn't go easy with a left or right hook, she unleashes the kick on Heidi and has her scrambling to stay on her feet.

At the end of the round, Heidi has already hit the mat twice, but made it back to her feet before the final count.

"More of that," I tell Willow, pulling her mouthpiece out and giving her some water. "That's exactly what I'm fucking talking about."

I hear Cage shouting some encouragement and instructions out to Willow, she nods to let him know she hears him, then turns back to the ring, ready for round three.

This time, instead of starting out slow, Willow is like a shark scenting blood in the water and she goes in for the kill.

Her right hook lands on target and then she follows it up with a roundhouse kick.

Heidi goes down and the referee lays flat out, slamming his palm to the mat.

"Ten, nine, eight, seven, six, five, four, three, two..."

The ref jumps to his feet, waving his arms, signaling that the bout is over, and Willow just won by a fucking knockout!

When she turns to me, it's obvious she's still trying to register what happened. I see a moment of concern for her opponent, but when she sees Heidi slowly get up off the mat, relief washes over her face, and then she looks at me with a smile that stretches from ear to ear.

"Yeah, baby!" I exclaim, picking her up and spinning her around. "That's my girl!"

Cage comes up behind us, getting in on the celebration.

The referee comes over to Willow, raising her arm to declare her the winner.

When she turns back to look at me, there are tears in her eyes and the weight of the moment crashes down. This is more than a first win or a knockout. This is months of hard work paying off. This is a risk that ended up being worth all the hours, sweat, and tears.

She fucking did it.

I knew she could, but I'm confident there were days she wasn't convinced, but this moment—standing in this ring with her arm raised high—it's the validation Willow has needed her entire life.

"Thank you," she says, arms wrapped tightly around my neck as her voice breaks. "Thank you for believing in me."

Words get stuck in my throat. I can't speak, so I just hold her, my lips pressed to her forehead.

When I shift my mouth to her, I pour all my admiration into that kiss.

CHAPTER 36

WILLOW

J'm still in a daze when we all stumble into the gym, completely exhausted from the day.

After Gunnar won his fight, we piled back into Cage's SUV, grabbed a quick dinner to celebrate, and refueled, before heading back to Green Valley. As thrilled as we were to leave Nashville victorious, we were just as ready to get home and be with our families.

It took a while for my adrenaline to ease up after my bout and once it did, I mentally and physically crashed. I was able to pull myself together long enough to enjoy watching Gunnar kick ass in his bout, but I quickly learned I need a little solitude and silence after such an intense experience.

Maybe I should look into starting yoga.

Maybe Ozzi would do it with me.

That thought makes me smile.

As the guys unload all the equipment we brought with us, Frankie and I walk upstairs to check in with Tempest.

When we walk into the apartment, we catch her quietly closing the door to Freya's nursery. She holds a finger to her lips and waves us over to the large dining room table.

"So, how does it feel to win your first bout?" she asks, pulling me in for a hug. "Willow 'KO' Bernard."

"I think it's a bit too early for that," I say, leaning into her embrace.

Vali had started calling me that after my bout and it took off like wildfire. By the time we left the arena, everyone was referring to me as 'KO' or 'KO' Bernard.

She chuckles. "Well, Cage sent me a video and you were awesome. I can't wait to be there for your next one."

My next one.

God, I never even allowed myself to see anything past this one fight, but now that I've done it and won, I can't imagine stopping. It's more than an adrenaline rush. I felt alive out there, even more so than when I'm training.

"Is Hazel asleep?" I ask, my gaze going to the closed door.

Tempest nods. "She fell asleep right after Freya. She wanted to make a pallet beside the crib, so I brought a mat up from downstairs and piled blankets and pillows on it for her. It's so cute. Come see," she says, tiptoeing back to the door.

When she opens the door, the light shines in just enough for me to see Freya sound asleep in her crib and Hazel curled up with Sid on the floor beside her. They look so cute and peaceful it makes my heart ache.

"God, they're adorable," I whisper, clutching my chest.

"So cute," Frankie says, coming up beside me. "It makes my ovaries ache, but don't tell Gunnar. If it were up to him, we'd already be trying for baby one of six."

"Six?" I ask as we back away from the door.

She fights back a smile, shaking her head, but when she speaks her voice is almost wistful.

"Gunnar is so delusional."

"Keep that shit under wraps," Tempest says with a smirk. "If he's like Cage, he's got good swimmers."

The vision of a baby with Ozzi's blue eyes flashes into my mind and I quickly shake it off. I've never given a lot of thought to babies, but I have to agree with Frankie, being around Freya, and even Hazel, does something to me.

"Should I wake her up?" I ask, feeling a sudden rush of exhaustion.

Tempest shakes her head. "No, let her sleep. It's two in the morning. Just go crash at Ozzi's and we'll celebrate your big win at breakfast, when everyone wakes up."

Hesitantly, I glance back to Freya's nursery where Hazel is sleeping. "Are you sure? What if she wakes up and thinks I didn't come back for her?"

A warm hand squeezes my arm and I look up to see Frankie's knowing gaze.

"She's not going to think that. You just talked to her a few hours ago. Besides, if she wakes up, Tempest can call you," Frankie says, looking over at Tempest for backup.

"Definitely. I've got the baby monitor. I promise she'll be fine."

Letting out a sigh, I nod. "Okay, thank you again for watching her today. I know she had so much fun. I can't tell you how much I appreciate the way you've taken her under your wing."

Every day since Hazel arrived, we've been at the gym. She's spent her days with Miss Faye and her evenings watching me train and hanging out with Tempest and Freya, and sometimes Maggie and Frankie. They've all made her feel so welcome. The other night, Tempest was even letting her *work* at the front desk.

"She's a great kid," Tempest assures me. "It feels like she was always meant to be a part of this big, crazy family... just like you."

"Thank you." It's all I can manage because I'm physically and emotionally spent.

When I walk back downstairs with Frankie, the guys are standing around recounting the events of the day, talking animatedly about the fights. I don't know how they're still standing, let alone sparring at two in the morning.

"I think it's time to call it a night," Frankie says, taking Gunnar by the arm. "I have to be at the clinic in five hours."

Gunnar leans over and kisses her soundly, before turning to his brothers, saluting them as they walk toward the door. "See you fuckers tomorrow."

"Great win today," Cage calls out, before turning to me. "You too. I couldn't be prouder of what you accomplished tonight."

"Thank you," I say weakly, feeling myself practically wilt in the spot I'm standing.

Ozzi comes up beside me, wrapping an arm around my waist. "Is Hazel staying with Tempest and Cage?"

"Yeah, she's asleep in Freya's room."

"Good," he says quietly, pulling my body closer to his. "You can stay with me."

Vali slaps Cage on the shoulder, throwing a hand in the air. "I'm out. Maggie's already texted me twice, so I need to get home. I'll see y'all tomorrow."

"I'm taking a rain check on our morning run," Ozzi says.

"Let's have breakfast instead," Cage suggests.

Vali and Ozzi both cock their heads, as if in disbelief.

"Did you just propose breakfast in place of a run? Are you feeling okay?" Ozzi teases. "Should we call Mom?"

Cage's mouth turns up at one corner. "We all deserve one day off after wins like we had tonight."

"Y'all heard it," Vali announces, pointing at me and Ozzi. "You're my witnesses. Cage might be human after all."

"Get the fuck out of my gym," Cage mutters, heading for the stairs. "But lock up and turn the lights out before you go."

Ozzi laughs, dragging me closer. "Go," he says to Vali. "I've got the lights and the doors."

Once we're alone, Ozzi secures all the locks and turns out the lights, leaving us in the pale glow of the security lights and one over the ring they always leave on.

Leading me over to the stairs that go up to the apartment on the opposite side of the building, he turns, walking backwards. "Need me to carry you up?"

"No," I say with a tired chuckle. "I can make it."

"What if I want to?" he asks, pausing at the bottom of the stairs and caging me against the brick wall. For a long moment, our eyes meet and something in the atmosphere shifts. I watch as Ozzi swallows hard before licking his bottom lip. "I'm so fucking proud of you."

"You mentioned that," I tease, trying to lighten the somber mood that's seemed to settle.

Ozzi nods. "I know, but I mean it. You were amazing today, but it's not just about today. You're amazing *every* day. The way you've tackled hurdles and overcome adversity is *amazing*. I've never met anyone like you, Willow Bernard. You've got more heart and drive than a room full of fighters. But you're also compassionate and selfless. It's... I don't know... overwhelming. Inspiring. Sometimes I don't feel worthy of being with someone like you."

My brows furrow and I press my head back against the wall so I can see his face.

"That's the craziest thing anyone has ever said," I retort, ignoring the way my face flushes with his praise. "How in any universe are you not worthy of me? Because the way I see it, Ozzi Erickson, I'm the one that should be eternally grateful. You believed in me from day one, even when I had no clue what I was doing. And every day since then, you've given me the gift of your friendship and endless positivity. I've broken down on you more times than I can count, and you've never made me feel anything less than normal, validating my struggles and heartache. If anyone should feel unworthy, it's me."

He chuckles, but it's kind of dark and humorless. As he runs a hand through his hair, I wonder where all this is coming from. It's like he's having some sort of internal battle and I hate the tortured expression on his ruggedly handsome face.

"It's late," I tell him, reaching out to touch his cheek. "We should get some sleep."

On an exhale, he nods, but doesn't speak.

Taking his hand, I lead the way up the stairs, pushing down the twisted feeling in my gut. This has been an emotional day for everyone, not just me. Ozzi has put everything he has into training me. Even though I was the one who had to battle it out in the ring, he was there too—right beside me every step of the way.

Whatever this is, whatever he's feeling, I have to believe a good night's sleep will help.

When we reach the top of the stairs, he turns to me. "I'm going to get the shower started for you. I wish I had a tub for you to soak in, but a hot shower will have to do."

"Thank you," I tell him, feeling raw and vulnerable but also so thankful for this man. Even if he doesn't see it, I do. He's exactly what I need.

A few minutes later, I'm stripped out of my clothes and in the shower. For a second, I think Ozzi's just going to leave me to it, but he steps in behind me, leaving his boxer briefs on.

"What are you—"

"Turn around so I can wash your hair," he says solemnly, and I do as he says, allowing him to run his hands through my hair under the water.

Methodically, Ozzi squeezes shampoo into his hands and then works it into my scalp.

I feel the tension from the day and night roll down and out of my body. Closing my eyes, I give over to Ozzi and let him not only wash and condition my hair, but my body as well. He pays special attention to my shoulders and arms, kneading them and releasing even more tension.

It's not erotic or sexual.

It's the most tender and intimate moment I've ever experienced, and it brings hot tears to my eyes. Thankfully, they mix in with the water and I don't have to explain them away. I wouldn't be able to put it into words. It just feels good to be cared for. I feel... *loved*.

When he's finished washing my thighs and calves, he stands and places a chaste kiss on my back, reaching around me to rinse out the washcloth. Then, he turns the water off and steps out onto the bathmat, grabbing a towel and holding it up for me to step into.

Just like when he washed me, Ozzi takes his time drying my body and even my hair.

"There's an extra toothbrush in the drawer," he says, pointing beside the sink. "I'll go find you something to sleep in."

Taking a towel with him, he walks out of the bathroom and I'm left standing in awe.

Ozzi Erickson never ceases to amaze me.

After I crawl into his bed, loving the way his t-shirt feels against my skin, I immediately fall asleep in his arms.

Later, when the sun is barely coming up, I wake to the warmth of Ozzi's body pressed to mine—his fingers lightly stroking my stomach and the hardness of his erection pressed against me.

Heat quickly begins to pool in my belly. Aroused by his touch alone, and still feeling a bit raw from the past twenty-four hours, I need him. I need to feel him inside me and be reminded of how perfect we are together.

When I turn in his arms, I see the same desire reflected in his gaze.

Ozzi reaches behind him to the nightstand and grabs a condom, rolling it on quickly as I push my panties down my legs, kicking them to the foot of the bed.

He quietly pushes inside me, making me feel everything, and erasing all other thoughts.

After a shower and another mind-blowing orgasm, Ozzi and I make our way downstairs to find the gym quiet. But there are distant giggles coming from Tempest and Cage's apartment that I recognize immediately.

The second we ascend the stairs I'm greeted by Hazel who has a handmade sign that reads: Willow 'KO' Bernard is #1.

I can't help the laugh that erupts. It's all so surreal.

The fact Hazel is even here.

This patchwork family we're building.

My win from yesterday.

And even the part where I won by a knockout.

In all my wildest dreams, I never conjured up this exact moment or outcome.

I've always hoped for good things, wished and prayed for them even, but deep down I'm a realist who doesn't like to set herself up for failure. I'm always thinking about worst-case scenarios and trying to plan on how to get myself out of them.

So none of this lines up with what I've become accustomed to.

This is the polar opposite of a worst-case scenario.

This feels a lot like living my best life.

"We made you celebration muffins," she announces, bouncing on the tips of her toes. "Tempest let me measure alllll the ingredients by myself and I even got to use the oven mitts to put them in the oven!"

My eyes go wide as I look at Tempest, who has Freya on her hip and the warmest smile on her face. "She did such a good job. We might have a future award-winning baker on our hands."

"Smells amazing," Ozzi says, squeezing my waist before stepping away.

There's something different about him. Ever since last night and our interaction at the foot of the stairs, something about him feels desperate or guarded... maybe a little of both. It's like he's holding on tightly, but also letting go.

But instead of dwelling on it, I walk over to Hazel and wrap my arms around her slender shoulders, leaning over to bury my nose in her hair. She smells like sugar and spice mixed with baby powder. It's the most wholesome, heartwarming scent and I want to bottle it up and keep it forever.

"Thank you for the sign and the muffins," I tell Hazel, giving Tempest a grateful smile. "I'm starving. Let's eat."

CHAPTER 37

OZZI

"*A*gain," I coach, holding up the mitts for Willow to punch. "Left, right, roundhouse."

Willow does as instructed, her face set in the laser-focused expression I've become accustomed to. I wasn't sure how our training sessions would go after the fight. Shit, I was also concerned they'd be affected by Hazel's arrival, but Willow has been more determined than ever.

She's committed, driven, and even hungrier for success.

It's attractive and addictive. I find myself wanting her more and more every day. That shouldn't concern me or freak me out, but it does. The deeper I get with Willow Bernard, the more I question my own intentions, because there's a lot at stake here.

Not only Willow's heart, and mine, but Hazel's too.

And what happens if things between us don't work out? Will she continue to train at Viking MMA? I'd never forgive myself if I kept Willow from realizing her full potential. What I saw in the ring last week was pure greatness. I've never seen a fighter crush their debut bout like that. Some people might call it beginner's luck, but I beg to differ.

There was no luck involved.

"Again," I say, almost as out of breath as Willow is. I know I'm pushing her, but I think we both needed an intense workout. I've had a lot on my mind, and I can tell Willow has too.

"Switch it up," I demand. "Right, left, right, then a high kick."

Willow's breaths remain controlled, even though I know she's spent. It's this kind of conditioning that will let her continue to win bouts. Even if I'm not around. Even if she trains with someone else or at a different gym. This ground-work we're laying will be solid for the rest of her career.

"Do a roundhouse," I hear from the side of the ring. "That's my favorite."

From the corner of my eye, I see Hazel hanging on the ropes. She's become a permanent fixture around here. In the short time she's been coming to the gym with Willow, she's acquired a role as Freya's babysitter—I use that term loosely because Tempest or Cage are never far away, but Freya and Hazel are thick as thieves. The little shit has become my niece's new favorite person, which I firmly held the title to before she came around.

Hazel is also proficient at checking people in. She's a wiz at the computer and the girls have even trained her to answer the phone. It's the cutest fucking thing, and if I had to guess, we're getting more business because of her adorable little face peeping out just over the front desk.

"Roundhouse," I tell Willow, earning me a hint of a smile before she complies.

Not only does she do a roundhouse kick, but she unleashes on me, calling an audible and virtually kicking my ass. I can't keep up with the punches and combinations she's throwing my way.

As I scramble to deflect her advances, I hear hoots and hollers coming from onlookers, mainly my dumbass brothers. There's even an ear-splitting whistle I recognize as Maggie's and Tempest cheering her on.

When she finally relents, backing off and giving me a smirk that feels like it could burn this entire fucking place to the ground, I exhale.

Throwing the mitts to the ground, I brace my hands on my knees. "Were you trying to kill me?"

"Just giving you a taste of your own medicine," she counters.

The roar from the crowd makes her blush and she waves them off, but they don't stop.

A few seconds later, Gunnar is jumping into the ring, eyes mischievous. "Want to go for round two?" he asks Willow, pulling on his gloves and tightening them up with his teeth.

"You want some of this?" Willow asks, side-eyeing my brother with so much moxie it's oozing from her pores. "If you think you can handle it, let's go."

Pounding her gloves together, she incites the crowd and now every person in Viking MMA is glued to the side of the ring.

Fuck, we should pull up some chairs and sell popcorn. This is about to get good.

Gunnar meets Willow in the center of the ring and they bump fists, then break away and start dancing around the ring.

Unlike when the two of them are battling true opponents, there's a lot of laughing and good-natured shit talking.

"You fight like a girl," Gunnar says, bobbing just in time to miss Willow's right hook.

"You only wish you were as good as a girl," Willow retorts, earning some hearty cheers from Maggie and Tempest. "People always say you should grow some balls, but a vagina is tougher."

Gunnar throws his head back and laughs, and while he's distracted, Willow gets a nice high kick in with no resistance. He grunts and points a glove at her, like he's coming for her, but that only makes her faster and more agile.

"Come and get me, pretty boy," she taunts.

Everyone is eating it up and I have to say I love the way she gives it as good as she gets.

When Gunnar swipes her off her feet, I wince, but Willow barely misses a beat. Jumping back up and immediately getting her hands up, she's ready for whatever he has next.

They go back and forth like this until they're both panting.

"Truce?" Gunnar asks, hands on his knees.

"For now," she says, giving him a smile as she catches her breath.

The two of them clear the ring and instead of everyone going back to their regular programming, Vali and Cage grab some gear and climb in.

Before it's all said and done, we've all taken turns pounding on each other and it feels like old times, back in Dallas. The only thing missing is Viggo and our mom yelling at us to not hurt each other.

"Sure wish Viggo was here," Vali says, sweat pouring off him. "I miss that fucker."

"Me too," I admit. "Has he answered any of your calls recently?"

He shakes his head, tossing his gloves into a basket. "I haven't talked to him in a few weeks. Even then it was just a brief conversation."

"Same here," Cage adds. "I can't get him to answer his goddamn phone."

We're all toweling off when Tempest comes up and kisses Cage on his sweaty cheek. "I'm going upstairs to put Freya to bed. Don't be too long."

Her tone is suggestive, and I give my older brother a look, which earns me a shove to my shoulder.

"Mind your fucking business," he says gruffly, but I don't miss the slight smile under his grizzly beard.

Maggie latches onto Vali, pulling him to the door. "I'm tired and you promised me you'd make me dinner."

"You're right, baby," he says, looping an arm around her waist and kissing her. "Sorry."

She eyes him up and down. "Don't apologize."

"Good God," I mutter. "Y'all need to go home and make some fucking babies."

Maggie chuckles and Vali doesn't bark at me like Cage did, which tells me that's exactly what's on the menu at their house.

The few students left are standing around visiting, and I notice Willow talking to Hazel at the front desk. Tossing my towel in the basket, I walk over to them.

"Are you guys heading out?" I ask, noticing Hazel zipping her backpack up with Sid's head sticking out of the top.

Willow stands up, brushing her hair back into her ponytail. "Yeah, I need to get her home."

Hazel walks toward the door and I grab Willow's hand to get her attention. "Can I come over later?" I ask, glancing around the gym that's now practically cleared out. "It'll just take me a bit to get everything put away and locked up... maybe an hour or so?"

Willow hesitates, her gaze searching out Hazel and then coming back to me. "Okay," she finally says, nodding. "Text me when you're on your way."

Leaning forward, I kiss her quickly, loving just the small taste I get and the way she sucks in a breath. Things have been a little tense between us the past few days, but when we come together, there's still a freedom like I've never known.

The way I feel when I'm with Willow is unlike anything I've ever felt. It's not just the physical attraction, even though that's off the charts, it's more than that. She makes me feel honored just to be in her presence, let alone share a bed with her. And when I told her last weekend that I don't feel worthy, I meant it.

There are moments when I'm reminded of the life I left—the life I love—and I'm not sure I can be the person she deserves. The man who stands by her side and stays. Not only is it Willow who needs and deserves that kind of stability, but it's Hazel too.

After everyone is gone and all the equipment is put away, I run upstairs to shower and throw on some fresh clothes. Then, I'm slipping out the back door and jumping in my Jeep.

Me: On my way.

As I drive down the quiet streets of Green Valley, I try to picture myself here in the years to come—five, ten, fifteen. Could I be happy here for the long haul? Cage and Vali seemed to have settled in nicely, but I don't know if it's for me.

I've always been the one jetting off to one adventure after another. Since coming to Green Valley, this is the longest I've gone without flying off to another state, let alone another country.

Is that something Willow would be okay with?

Can the lifestyle I'm used to living and hers work together?

When I pull up to Willow's apartment, she's standing at the bottom of the stairs with a blanket draped over her arms.

"I thought we could throw this in the back of my truck and look at the stars," she says, walking over and dropping her tailgate down.

"Sounds good," I say as I help her with the blanket. "Is Hazel asleep?"

Willow nods. "She was dozing on our way home."

Once I've helped Willow up into the bed, I climb in beside her. "All that work makes her tired."

"She's obsessed with that place," Willow muses. "Miss Faye offered for her to stay with her this evening. She was even making homemade mac and cheese, but Hazel politely declined. She told her she was needed at the gym."

Leaning back on the bed of the truck, I make a spot for Willow to snuggle in beside me. "Cage is going to have to put her on the payroll before long."

"Don't get her started. She already asked me how old she has to be to work there."

We both laugh, completely enamored by the little wisp of a girl who's stormed in and stolen everyone's hearts.

From where she's laid her head on my chest, Willow looks up and holds my gaze for a moment. I'm just getting ready to ask her what's on her mind when she stretches up and takes my mouth with hers, running a hand into my hair and drawing me closer.

Moaning, I roll her on top of me to straddle my lap, putting her hot center over my hardening dick and we make out like a couple of horny teenagers in the back of Willow's truck.

After a few minutes, she stops and sits back, putting some space between us. Her sleek, dark hair is pulled up in a messy bun, fresh out of the shower. The only light shining on her is from the moon and it makes her look ethereal.

"What do you want?" Willow asks.

"What do you mean?" I ask in return, a little confused about where this is going.

Her tone isn't seductive, like she's wondering where the night will lead us, but it's not argumentative either. It's merely searching.

She shrugs, sliding off my lap and sitting to face me. "You've asked me what I want before, but I've never returned the question. What does Ozzi Erickson want... in life... in the future?"

I want to accuse her of being in my head and reading my thoughts, but I see the sincerity on her face and I wish I knew an honest answer to give her. "I don't know."

"What about us?" she asks.

The simple question makes my heart splinter.

What about us?

That's what I've been trying to figure out for the past week. I know how I feel about her, but those feelings scare the shit out of me and I don't know if I'm ready to voice them out loud.

I promised I would never hurt her or Hazel.

But if I told her how I'm truly feeling, it would only confuse her. Because the truth is I'm falling in love with her, and I'm scared I can't commit to those feelings.

Maybe my family is right and I am scared of commitment, or maybe I just don't trust myself enough to be the man Willow deserves.

What if I tell her how I feel and then end up disappointing her or breaking her heart?

"I care about you," I start. "I want you to be happy, and—"

"I know you don't like talking about the future and what comes next," she says, cutting me off. "But I feel like you've been pulling away from me the past few days and I really need to know where your head is at. I know how I feel about us... I know how I feel about you. But if you don't feel the same, then..."

Then, what?

She's quiet for too long and my stomach drops when I see the look on her face. I know that look. I've seen it when she's facing something hard, but she's already made her mind up that whatever it is won't beat her. It's her warrior face.

And it scares the shit out of me.

I want to take all the uncertainty back, swallow it down like a pill, and go back to her initial question. I want to tell her I love her and I see myself here, with her and Hazel. But that's a promise I can't guarantee.

This is going to make me sound like a pussy, but the thought of having an instant family… not only having Willow to care for and protect, but Hazel too, it feels like a huge responsibility.

One I'm not sure I'm ready for.

CHAPTER 38

WILLOW

*I*nternally, I'm screaming at myself to stop—*shut up, Willow, you're ruining everything*—but I can't. My sense of self-preservation is strong and it's what's driving me forward.

I'm not sure if it's the impending words on the tip of my tongue or my heart already breaking, but my eyes begin to sting with tears.

When I look back up at Ozzi, one slips down my cheek and he quickly reaches up to wipe it away.

"What's wrong?" he asks, sounding as torn up as I feel. "Please tell me so I can fix it."

Shaking my head, I press my lips together and try to put into words how I'm feeling without doing too much damage in the process.

"This is probably going to come out all wrong," I start, trying to steady my voice. Clearing my throat, I continue. "I'm falling for you... falling in love with you. I've known it for a while, but over the past couple of weeks, I've started to realize how deep my feelings are for you. I've never felt this way... and not just when we're together like this. It's when we're laughing or talking or training. When we're hanging out with Hazel. Any time I'm with you, I feel a sense of rightness."

Pressing a hand to my chest, I pause and watch Ozzi for a moment. Usually, he's easy for me to read, but I see a myriad of emotions pass across his face and I'm not sure which one I want to hang onto the most—love, fear, confusion, desperation. They're all there and prevalent and I don't know what to make of it.

"It's that rightness that forces me to say what I'm about to say," I tell him, exhaling deeply and closing my eyes. "If you're not planning on sticking around, I need to know now."

Ozzi starts to say something, but I stop him.

"Let me finish," I say, holding up a hand. "I realize that sounds an awful lot like an ultimatum, or like I'm putting our relationship on a timeline, but that's not it at all. I'm just trying to protect not only myself, but Hazel too. She's already looking to you for so much—advice, love, acceptance, friendship. With kids like her, like I was at her age, we see so many people walk in and out of our lives, we become calloused. But deep down, all we really want is for someone to stay."

I watch as Ozzi's face falls and he brushes a hand through his hair with a little more force than normal. Falling back against the truck, he exhales. "Fuck."

"This is killing me," I tell him, needing to say a little more before I'm done. This last part feels like it's being ripped from the depths of my soul. "If you can't promise you're going to stay, then I need to end what we're doing. Not the training and friendship, but everything else. I'm not going to be responsible for another person walking out on Hazel and I can't allow my heart to be broken like that. I—I mean, it's already breaking, but if we end this now, it won't be as bad as it will be a month or two down the road. Because the longer I'm with you, the more I want from you."

Forever.

The rest of your life and mine.

I want babies and a home.

I want a family.

I want everything I've never had and so much more.

Pure anguish washes over Ozzi's face and I brace myself for his response. "You're asking me to promise something I can't. And I refuse to lie to you, just to get what I want. I'd never do that to you. I'd never intentionally hurt you, or Hazel. I—I care about you both and I want you to be happy. That's all I want."

"Thank you for being honest with me," I say, trying not to break down. My throat feels like I'm trying to swallow a boulder. "I'm sorry, but I can't do this anymore. I can't continue to let myself fall in love with you when I know there's a chance you'll leave."

When Ozzi pulls me into his chest, it feels a lot like goodbye, and I physically can't hold back anymore. As the tears start to fall and my body quakes, he only holds me closer, staying true to his words and not making any promises he can't keep.

CHAPTER 39

OZZI

*A*s Vali, Gunnar, Cage, and I run our last mile back into town, I feel the dread increasing in my gut. When I met them downstairs before daylight this morning, they all made a point to comment on the fact I look like shit, which is fine because I feel like shit. Everything hurts—my mind, my body, my soul, my heart.

After my unexpected talk with Willow last night, I held her for what felt like hours. I didn't want to let her go, but I knew, after she left everything on the table, I had to. Reluctantly, I finally severed the connection and walked her to her front door, where I placed a kiss on her forehead and soaked in as much of her as I could, in hopes it would last me a long time.

But I knew, from the moment I walked away, that it would never be enough.

I'll always want more of Willow Bernard.

"Are we going for muffins?" Vali asks over his shoulder.

He and Gunnar are in the lead, with Cage and me right behind them. It's always Vali's idea to grab muffins. It's like Tempest slips a drug in them and we're all addicted.

"Stupid question," Cage says with a grunt, never breaking stride. "But Gunnar is juicing this morning."

"You're a fucking sadist," Gunnar mutters.

"We have another fight coming up in a couple months and I need you ready."

Willow will be on that ticket as well, and the idea of her doing it without me makes my stomach drop to my feet.

"I think I'm going to skip the muffins," I say, as the small downtown comes into view. "I, uh… I'm heading out today."

It's not how I planned on breaking the news, but no time is a good time to tell them I'm leaving.

"Going somewhere with Willow and Hazel?" Gunnar asks.

I can feel Cage's eyes cutting over to me as I hesitate. He's good at reading people, especially those he's related to, and I know if he could look into my eyes right now, they'd spill all my secrets.

"No," I finally say. "I'm going to find Viggo. It's bullshit he's not at least answering text messages, so I thought I'd drive around until I find him."

Collectively, we all come to a halt, right in the middle of the street. Thankfully, it's still early and there aren't any cars on the road.

Vali turns to me, his eyes narrowed. "That's like finding a needle in a haystack."

I shrug, turning my attention to the brick building to my left. "A road trip will do me some good. I'm itching to get away and go somewhere. It's been too long."

The words taste like ash on my tongue, even though only a day ago, I was wondering if that's what I needed. However, now that leaving feels like the only option, all I want to do is stay. But I can't do that, because to give her what she asked for—ending our relationship—it will require a clean break on my part.

"What about Willow's training?" Cage asks. "When will you be back?"

Not anytime soon.

Never.

I wish I was a better man, one who could respect Willow's wishes, stick around and just go back to being her trainer and friend, but I'm not. I also wish I could promise her what she wants, but I can't do that either.

My entire being feels like it's ripping down the middle and all I can do is walk away, leaving half of myself here, and hope I haven't done too much damage. In time, Willow will move on and find someone who's willing to plant roots in this small town.

That thought of some other man—holding Willow, celebrating her wins, waking up each morning with her—makes my gut knot.

The thought of someone else helping raise Hazel is also a hard pill to swallow.

So, why the fuck am I leaving?

"I'm not sure when I'll be back." *If ever*. Regardless of the cacophony going on inside my head, I continue to spew bullshit. "So, I thought you could take over Willow's training. The two of you have a good rapport and she works well with Gunnar."

Cage glares at me for what feels like a millennium. "What does Willow say about it?"

"She doesn't know," I say, unable to look at him, at any of them. "We had a talk last night and—"

"You're running away," Vali accuses with a humorless chuckle. "I can't fucking believe this. No, wait, actually I can."

His harsh words sting, worse than if he'd punched me in my face.

Gunnar gets a jab in next. "Frankie was just saying how she never thought Willow would ever allow herself to fall in love because she can't trust people. But then you came along and changed that. This is a low blow, man."

Kill me now.

"She basically asked me to leave," I manage to say as my insides feel like they're going to rupture and leave me lifeless on the sidewalk. "She asked me to promise her I wouldn't leave and I couldn't do it. I can't... I don't know. It's a huge commitment, okay? And you can all go to hell if you think you wouldn't be second guessing every move you make when someone like Willow's heart is on the line, and don't even get me started on Hazel. They deserve the best... of everything. And I don't know if I'm good enough to deliver that."

If Sheriff James or Tempest's cousin, Cole, were to drive by right now, they'd probably assume we're about to brawl, but I see the second my brothers' expressions shift. They don't like what I'm telling them, but they understand the magnitude of my fears.

"Go find Viggo," Cage orders gruffly, looking away like he can't stand the sight of me. Fair enough. I can't stand to look at myself either. "And while you're at it, figure your shit out," he adds. "And don't worry about Willow, I'll make sure she's ready to fight."

I know how to read between Cage's lines and he's not just promising to make sure Willow is ready for her next bout, he's promising to take care of her in my absence, being the man I can't be.

He always has been.

Unlike me, Cage has never struggled with knowing who he is or where his place is. Shit, look at how he picked up his life, came to this small-ass town, and started the fuck over. He's made a life for himself here and a safe place for everyone else to land. I owe him so much, because without him, I never would've had the privilege of meeting the most amazing woman in the world.

And that makes me the dumbest fucker in the world to do what I'm about to do.

"Thank you," I tell him. Feeling my emotions get the better of me and refusing to break down in the middle of the goddamn street, I abruptly turn and walk away.

If I don't leave now, I'm not sure I'll ever find the strength.

Even though I'm experiencing more pain than I have in my entire life, through all the fights and brawling, I can leave knowing Willow is in a good place. She's found her passion and knows what she wants. Hazel is safe and the two of them have each other. They're going to be okay, more than okay, they're going to thrive.

As long as I can hold onto that, I'll survive.

CHAPTER 40

WILLOW

"How are you doing?" Tempest asks as she slides a box of muffins my way.

Our attention is focused on Hazel pushing Freya in the baby swing.

I love the easy smile on Hazel's face. It reminds me how resilient she is, which I'm grateful for, and it makes my heavy heart feel a little lighter.

After Ozzi left, I worried about her.

I had worked up a story I was planning on delivering to her, built mostly around the truth, but something that would soften the blow of his abrupt departure.

But unbeknownst to me, he'd left a note for her at the gym. It was sweet and to the point. He didn't try to make excuses or shift the blame, just told her he had to go and he was sorry, but that he'd always be there for her. He even left her all the ways he can be contacted—telephone number, email address, and even a messenger app he uses.

Of course, she doesn't have her own phone, but when the day comes that she wants to call him, I'll be more than happy to let her use mine.

"I'm okay," I say, willing it to be true even as the words leave my mouth. "As long as Hazel's happy and we're together, everything else will be okay."

I inhale and exhale before turning back to face Tempest. Maggie is sitting beside her and Frankie beside me. The four of us have met for muffins at the park quite a bit in the last week and a half.

Those first few days after Ozzi left were a blur. I was on autopilot, refusing to allow the sadness to pull me under. Thank God for Hazel, because I know if I didn't have her to take care of, I would've curled up under a blanket and not come out until the ache in my chest was gone.

But now I realize that's probably never going away.

"I'm really proud of the way you've handled everything," Frankie says, adjusting her sunglasses as she turns around to lean against the picnic table. She's just on a short break from the clinic, so she likes to soak up as much sunshine as she can.

I shrug. "It's not like I had a choice."

"Yes, you did," Maggie says, reaching across to place her hand over mine. "We always have a choice. You could've drowned yourself in wine and ice cream or eaten your weight in pizza and tacos... not showered for days on end... turned one of Hazel's stuffed animals into a voodoo doll of Ozzi. The possibilities are endless."

That makes me laugh and I turn my palm up to hers, squeezing. "Thank you for that."

"Really," Tempest says. "Maggie is right. We've all had heartache and dealt with it in our own way. I mean, look at me, when Asher cheated on me with Mindy, I lost my damn mind."

That makes us all laugh again. Stories of Tempest's time in jail are honestly some of my favorites. Not because I like to think of my friend behind bars, but because it's so far from the person I know now. It's hard to picture her needing anger management. But here she is, on the other side of so much pain and turmoil, living her best life.

The three women surrounding me give me hope.

"I just want to set a good example for Hazel and show her we're not defined by our situation. We're responsible for our own happiness."

320

"Are you sure you're not forty-two instead of twenty-two?" Frankie asks, her head tilted up to the sun. "I swear you're more mature than most of the elderly patients I see come through the clinic on a daily basis."

I huff out a laugh, but the truth is I am who I am *because* of what I've been through. I can't say I'm thankful for it, because I'm not. If I could go back and change my past, I would. I'd have a dad who didn't die, a sober mom, and a family to call my own. But I can't change any of that. All I can do is live my life to the fullest and make the best decisions I can for me and Hazel.

When I'd told Ozzi I couldn't be with him anymore if he couldn't promise he was staying in Green Valley, it never occurred to me he'd leave. I should've guessed that would be his course of action. The look on his face when I asked him what he wanted told me everything I needed to know.

Ozzi had been thinking the same thing.

He'd been second-guessing our relationship and wondering if it was right for him.

As much as I was falling for him, and am still in love with him, I'd never ask him to do something that wouldn't make him happy.

He says all he wants is for Hazel and me to be happy. Well, I want the same for him. He deserves everything he gives to everyone else—love, acceptance, understanding.

The fact that Ozzi Erickson is one of the best people I've ever met makes it easier for me to accept this outcome. I don't regret anything about him. I don't regret building a friendship with him, confiding in him, falling for him. He helped me see so much good in the world and gave me a safe place to work through my grief.

I'll always be grateful, even for the Ozzi-shaped hole in my heart.

That place, where he dug himself into so deep, will never be filled by anyone else.

The thought of loving someone else the way I love Ozzi is unfathomable, and if I never love again, that's okay. At the ripe old age of twenty-two, I'm content in knowing I found true love once. I know what it's like to find the other half of your soul. I know what complete euphoria feels like. I know what it's like to wake up in the arms of the person you love. I know what it's like to cry with them and laugh with them, exchange past heartache and regrets.

Ozzi said he wasn't sure if he could be the man I needed, but he doesn't see himself the way I do. If he did, he would know, without a shadow of a doubt, he's more than enough.

"Are you training with Cage and Gunnar this afternoon, or do you work at the Pig?" Tempest asks, closing the box on the muffins. "I don't mind taking Hazel with me back to the gym."

Rising from the table, I wipe my hands on my jeans. "I promised Miss Faye she could have her all afternoon. They're making cinnamon rolls and apparently her recipe takes hours."

Tempest laughs. "Well, take it from me, they're worth every hour. She's been known for those cinnamon rolls since I was a kid."

I love that about Green Valley. It's one of those towns where generations of families live. There's so much history and familiarity. Everyone knows everyone and even though to some that might feel stifling, to me it feels like home. I want Hazel to one day be able to tell her kids, if she decides to stay here when she's grown, that Miss Faye taught her how to make cinnamon rolls and Tempest taught her how to make muffins.

She learned how to properly dress a wound from Frankie.

And Maggie taught her how to write an essay the summer before her fourth-grade year.

Sure, my life, once again, isn't turning out exactly as I'd hoped, but I'm still so grateful—for this place, the people in it, and the family we're choosing for ourselves.

"I'll make sure some of the cinnamon rolls make it to the gym tomorrow morning. Cage had me flip my schedule a few days a week to match up with Gunnar's. So, I'll be training earlier instead of later."

There's a twist in my stomach when I talk about training without Ozzi. I miss him so much, not just the romantic or physical aspect of our relationship, but everything—the training, the banter, the friendship. But I push on.

"Hazel," I call out. "We need to get going."

Tempest walks over and takes Freya, kissing her chubby cheeks. "Tell Auntie Willow and Hazel bye."

Auntie Willow.

That will never get old.

CHAPTER 41

OZZI

$\mathcal{W}$ ith my cell phone connected to the Jeep's Bluetooth, I dial my brother's number and listen to the rings as the call goes unanswered.

Again.

Viggo has never been the most talkative Erickson brother but he's never ghosted us like this before. Frankly, I've had enough of his shit so I'm going to keep calling him until either he answers or his battery dies.

This is day two of driving for me. I'd spent the night in a small town in Arkansas, and now I have no plans of stopping unless I find Viggo. I assume he's still in Texas but if he's not, I'll keep driving until I can look the bastard in the eye and demand answers.

I can acknowledge my anger is somewhat misguided. I mean, yeah, I'm pissed at him for not keeping in touch with the family but even more than that, I'm pissed at myself for leaving Green Valley the way I did... for leaving Willow and Hazel.

Being in that tiny town, knowing I could run into Willow at any moment, was too much for me. I had to get out and using Viggo as an excuse was the perfect plan... until I crossed the state line and realized there's no going back.

I left.

I did exactly what Willow was afraid I'd do, breaking both our hearts in the process. I'll always regret not fighting for her, not fighting for us, but I'm still unsure I can be the man she needs and deserves while staying true to myself.

Driving back to Tennessee right now won't change that, no matter how strong the urge is to do a U-turn and break some laws to get back there.

I try Viggo's number again and, miracles of miracles, he answers.

"Yeah" is the only greeting I get, and it takes all the energy I have left to control my temper.

"What the fuck, man? I've been calling you since yesterday and that's all you can say? I swear I'm gonna punch your face when I see you."

"Well, I guess it's a good thing you won't be seeing me for a while. You'll have cooled off by then."

I smirk, gazing out at the long stretch of road ahead of me. "Guess again, asshole. I'm on my way right now, so tell me where you are."

Viggo's laugh fills the inside of my Jeep and my chest twinges at the realization of how long it's been since I've heard it.

"You want me to give you my location so you can come kick my ass? Is that what I'm hearing?" he asks, still chuckling.

"No, I want you to tell me where you are so I can see your face, hug your neck, *then* kick your ass."

"Two out of three ain't bad, I suppose," he says with a reluctant sigh. "What are you really up to, Ozzi? You're running away from something, are you?" His voice is somber and I have to take a steadying breath before I can answer him honestly.

"I'm not running, I was asked to leave." That may have sounded more defensive than I planned.

"Uh-huh, okay," he says, disbelief heavy in his tone. "You just get here safe, and we'll sort out your bullshit."

"Are you going to tell me where or do I have to guess?"

Viggo waits a beat before he finally answers. "Fischer Falls, Texas."

KO

Hours later, I'm finally getting close to the town my brother is in. It was weird driving through Dallas and not stopping. It's also weird that none of us live there anymore. When I stopped by to tell my parents I was leaving Green Valley, their first question was if I was moving back to Dallas.

Of course, when I told them I'm going to find Viggo, they forgot all about my reasons for leaving, which was what I was hoping for. Having to tell one more person about why I was leaving was the last thing I wanted to do.

After a tearful goodbye from my mom and a hearty slap on the back—and a *take care of yourself*—from my dad, they sent me on my way with their best wishes.

And a container of cookies for Viggo.

I ate the cookies before I hit the Tennessee border, but that's what the asshole gets for going MIA.

A few minutes back up the road, Viggo shared his location with me, and I'm now pulling into a parking lot of what looks like a diner. I can't complain too much because I'm starving but I also can't help but wonder why he's in this speed trap of a town.

I put the Jeep in park and hop out, stretching my legs a bit before turning around and coming face to face with my big brother. Not sure what I was expecting, but I'm relieved to see he mostly looks the same. His dark hair is a bit longer and his beard is fuller, but I'd recognize him anywhere and I'm so fucking happy to see him.

"You gonna keep staring at me or are you gonna come kick my ass?"

"I said I was going to hug your neck first, remember?"

Viggo opens his arms wide. "Come on, little brother. Get in here."

I don't hesitate. I hug my brother and I hug him tight. This is the man I've looked up to my whole life. We've shared secrets, fought, and had great times growing up. We even recovered from a car wreck together last year. I've been so caught up in trying to find reasons to avoid creating a life in Green Valley, I hadn't realized how much I've missed him until this moment.

"It's good to see you, Oz. I missed you." His words surprise me but I don't react, I just let him tighten his grip on me.

A few more seconds pass before Viggo releases me, slapping me on my shoulder a few times. "I'd say the mountains are treating you well, but you look like shit."

"Thanks a lot. I could say the same about you, you know. Except you don't have mountains here, you have…" I take a second to look at our surroundings. "What the hell *do* you have here?"

"Booze. And quiet. That's all I need. A good burger helps, too, and you look like you could use one of those. Let's go inside."

Viggo wasn't lying about the burgers. I honestly don't know the last time I had a hamburger this good.

Texans just do beef better and I'll die on that hill.

As we eat in silence, apart from the moans I can't seem to keep to myself, I look around the diner and take in the local ambiance. It's a nice place—clean and tidy, kind of like a grandma's kitchen—and very busy. I wonder if it's the only eating establishment here and if so, I wonder how Viggo is surviving without his weekly sushi fix.

I also notice that most of the locals either stop to say hello to Viggo or give him a wave or nod in greeting. It reminds me a lot of Green Valley, how after I was in town for only a week or so, it was like I became one of them.

"You seem to be a popular guy around here. You running for mayor or something?"

"I work here."

Drinking from my water glass was a bad decision at this moment because Viggo's response has liquid spewing from my mouth, surprising us both.

"For fuck's sake," Viggo mutters, tossing his napkin at me.

"Sorry, I wasn't expecting you to say that." I take his napkin and mine and quickly dry my face before lowering my voice. "Are you okay? You know…

328

money wise? I assumed you still had some of your share from selling the gym, but if you need money, what's mine is yours."

"As much as I appreciate the offer, and as much as I'd like to take you up on it just so I can give you shit about it, I'll pass."

Did he just roll his eyes at me after I tried to help him? No wonder he doesn't have any friends.

"But, Vi–"

"Oz," Viggo says, cutting me off with a gruff tone that reminds me entirely too much of Cage.

Which makes me think of Willow, but when am I not thinking of her. From the second I drove away from her apartment, all I've been able to think about is her.

"I said I'm fine," he continues, pulling me out of my thoughts. "I still have the majority of my money in savings and stocks, I just work here because I got bored and Harry needed some help. Plus, I like it here."

We sit in silence for a minute, the hustle and bustle of the diner buzzing around us.

"I still don't understand why," I finally say, needing to get some shit off my chest. "Why did you leave? Why settle here, if that's what you're doing? Why ghost your family?"

My throat catches on that last question as my emotions get the better of me.

Viggo lets out a deep sigh and pushes up from the table. He takes out his wallet and tosses some cash on the table before looking back at me.

"Come on," he barks, motioning for me to follow, which I do because I obviously don't have any other choice. Then he mutters, "I'll show you why," and that piques my interest.

Fifteen minutes later, I'm parking next to Viggo's truck outside of a small cabin. I step out and look around, marveling at the scenery. Dark green trees surround us and stretch out as far as the eye can see. I almost feel I'm in another world. The sound of water splashing catches my attention and I turn to see a dog coming out of a nearby pond and running to Viggo, shaking the water out of its fur along the way.

"Hey, baby girl," my brother greets the dog. "Did you have fun today? Yeah, that's my good girl." She licks his face in response and Viggo lets her, rubbing behind her ears in return. The affection exchanged between him and this dog is staggering.

I can honestly say I've never seen this side of Viggo.

Our family was always too busy to have pets but that didn't stop all us boys from wanting them. It's funny to me that Viggo is the first to get a dog after all these years.

"Who's this?" I ask as they step closer.

"This is Dolly." Viggo rubs behind the dog's ears, smiling.

"As in Parton?"

"Is there any other?"

"Fair enough. How did you two find each other? When?" I feel like I'm meeting a new version of my brother and I'm pretty excited to be getting to know him better.

"I found her while on my travels, before I settled here. I like to think we found each other, rescued each other. We were both strays and bonded immediately."

That stings.

"Viggo, you're not a stray. You fucking ran off and left your family."

"Look who's talking. I can tell you're not here for a simple recon visit. Wanna 'fess up now or can I grab some beers first?"

Damn him.

"I could use a beer. Or six."

After I bring my bag inside and get the short tour of the cabin, Viggo lights a fire pit in the backyard. Tossing me a beer from the cooler by his feet, he nods his head at me. "Now talk."

Straight to the point as always.

I let out a humorless laugh. "I don't even know where to begin, man. Things were going well... I was helping out at Cage's gym, keeping everything casual, and then I met this girl." I pause, hating the way *this girl* just came out of my mouth. Willow was never *just some girl* to me.

Viggo continues for me. "Let me guess, things became *not* casual real fast."

"Not that quickly, but yeah." I take a pull from my beer and watch the water in the pond while Viggo watches me.

"Tell me about her."

A smile forms but I tamp it down. "Willow's a fighter and I was her trainer." Viggo's eyebrows shoot up and I chuckle. "Yeah, she's just getting started but she's a fucking natural."

"And you two hooked up, I'm assuming."

"No. We fell in love." This is the first time I've allowed myself to admit those words to myself, much less say them out loud, but I know it's true. There's no way it could be anything else.

"Well, shit, what's the problem?" Viggo asks while tossing his empty bottle into a nearby trash can.

"She recently got custody of her little sister, Hazel." I ignore Viggo's eyebrows this time. "But that's not the problem, it's me. I'm the problem."

"Lots of guys don't want to be with someone who already has a kid."

"But, that's not it. I'm crazy about Hazel, too. You know I've never been in a serious relationship before and this one comes with a little girl who looks up to me. I started feeling claustrophobic and like I wasn't good enough for either of them. I was also afraid of how I was changing, going from a single, adventure-loving guy to a family man in an instant." I let the words hang in the air for a couple of minutes before I continue. "The thing is, I could see myself with Willow and Hazel forever, but I worried that I wouldn't be able to satisfy the wandering part of my heart."

"So, you just left?"

"No. Well, yeah, but she told me to. I mean, not in exactly those words. She could tell I'd been pulling away some and she said she needed to not only protect her heart, but Hazel's too, so if I wasn't serious about a future with them, we should stop seeing each other."

"You're a dumbass."

"Thanks a lot." I give him a sarcastic look to make sure he knows I'm not serious.

"I mean it. You found this great woman who loves you and she has a sister who also loves you and you threw them away because you want to do what... go bungee jumping?"

"I was doing what she asked! I couldn't stand the thought of only being her friend or trainer again or running into her at the Piggly Wiggly. I also didn't want to make things hard on her."

A few minutes pass before Viggo speaks up. "Sounds like you have some major soul-searching to do and I'm happy to report, you've come to the right place."

"Oh, yeah?" I ask, not believing him.

"Anytime you're feeling lost, you should go spend some time in the woods. It's worked for me," he admits with a shrug.

"Then why are you here?" I ask, turning his words back on him.

"This is my home now. I'm building a house from scratch just over there." He points to a nearby area that has already been marked and framed according to how the house will look once it's built. "Right now, that's my passion, so I'm staying."

I don't even try holding back the look of shock I know is covering my face.

"You'd rather live out in the boonies, working in a town with a total of one caution light, than be around your family? I don't get it. I love you, but I don't understand you."

"Sounds like we're both a work in progress."

Fucking understatement of the year.

CHAPTER 42

WILLOW

*I*t's been a month since I last saw Ozzi.

The Fourth of July has come and gone. Hazel and I went to a jam session at the Green Valley Community Center. They had a big fireworks display. Not to mention all the food you could ever want—cotton candy, barbeque, hot dogs, and of course, the world-famous Banana Cake made by Tempest's boss, Jennifer.

Hazel ate so much she almost made herself sick. But when I see her having fun and enjoying herself, I can't stop her. Sometimes, I feel like I'm living vicariously through her. It's as good for my soul as it is for hers. We're healing more and more every day. I even got us both enrolled in some group therapy sessions in Merryville. We go once a week and make it a sister date.

Therapy and ice cream. It doesn't get much better than that.

Today is Saturday and I recently swapped from opening to closing at work so I can spend my mornings with Hazel. I have to work this afternoon, but afterward, the girls are taking me out to Genie's to celebrate my birthday and the guys are going to entertain Hazel and Freya.

I don't consider it babysitting, because let's face it, Hazel isn't a baby and, in another year or so, she'll probably be babysitting Freya all on her own. You'd think, after having such a shitty example of a mom, Hazel wouldn't be that great at nurturing and caretaking, but she's a natural.

"Hey, sleepyhead," I say, knocking lightly on Hazel's bedroom door. Since she moved in, she's really made this room her own. From pictures she's drawn and painted, to a larger-than-life poster of Gunnar "The Show" Erickson, her walls are nearly covered.

Hazel groans, rolling over to cover her head with her blanket, with Sid tucked under her arm.

"Daisy's Nut House is already open and if you sleep too late, all of the good donuts will be gone."

At that, she pops up, her bedhead in full effect. "I want a jelly donut... and chocolate milk."

God, I love her.

"Well, then you've gotta get out of bed and brush that hair, because I'm not taking a rat's nest to breakfast. It's unsanitary."

She pats the top of her head, throwing me a dirty look. "It's *not* a rat's nest."

That look, paired with her tone, tells me we're going to be in for a wild ride when she's a teenager, but oddly enough, I'm looking forward to it. I wish I'd been around for everything from her newborn cries to her terrible twos and all of the phases and stages between then and now.

"Oh, I beg to differ. An entire family of rats could live up there."

With a huff, she tosses the blanket off and puts her feet on the floor.

"Frankie wants us to bring her a donut to the Farmer's Market, so rise and shine."

I can hear her muttering under her breath as I turn to walk out, and I can't help but smile.

We typically get up early and go for a donut at Daisy's Nut House, then we always head over to the Farmer's Market. Frankie has a booth there, where she sells her mom's soaps and honey. Hazel loves it. She's quite the little entrepreneur, already brainstorming ideas of things she can make and sell next summer.

"We should get a maple bar," Hazel says wistfully staring at the case of donuts.

I glance down at her and then back at the guy taking our order. "I thought you wanted jelly-filled."

"I changed my mind."

Smiling, I give the guy an apologetic look. "One maple, two jelly-filled, a chocolate milk, and two coffees to-go, please."

"What was that all about?" I ask her when we're back in the truck on our way to the Farmer's Market. She loves jelly-filled donuts. Frankie bought her one during her first week in Green Valley and she's been obsessed ever since.

From my peripheral vision, I catch her shrug. "I just felt like getting something different."

Keeping my eyes on the road, I nod. "It's always good to change things up."

We sit in silence as I drive us the rest of the way.

"Maybe you'll see some of the kids from the summer program," I say as we get out of the truck, Hazel carrying the donuts and me with the drinks.

"I need to go find my friend Molly's mom's booth," Hazel announces. "She sells flowers."

That makes me smile, not only the idea of fresh flowers, but Hazel having a friend. I had hoped when I signed her up for the program that she'd meet people, but she's exceeded all my expectations.

"How about you eat your donut and drink your chocolate milk and then you can go find Molly."

Hazel gives me an excited smile. "Yay."

"Yay," I repeat, throwing an arm around her shoulder.

The second we come into view of Frankie's booth, she practically takes off running. "Hi, Frankie! We brought you a donut and coffee!"

Frankie glances up at her, dressed in an apron and looking adorable. "Look who it is; my favorite nine-year-old."

"I'm almost ten," Hazel says, a little out of breath from all the running.

I give Frankie some raised eyebrows. Hazel has been *almost ten* for the past month since she officially turned nine-and-a-half. Since I missed her last birthday, and all the ones before that, I kind of went overboard and made her a chocolate cake and blew up some balloons and hung them around the apartment. Then, I invited the girls and Freya over for some cake and ice cream.

So, I guess it's partially my fault.

"Who got the maple bar?" Frankie asks, her nose crinkled as she peers down into the bag.

"I did," Hazel says matter-of-factly. "It reminds me of Ozzi. He likes maple bars."

It feels like the wind has been knocked out of me.

Sometimes, out of nowhere, it happens. I pick up something at the gym and the smell reminds me of him, or Hazel and I make pizza and I can picture him in our kitchen… riding down the road listening to oldies on the radio… laying in the back of my truck counting the stars.

Frankie must see the look on my face because she quickly covers. "Oh, well, I love those too. Good choice. I bet it'll go good with your chocolate milk."

Hazel smiles, unaffected by the onslaught of memories she just threw my way.

The three of us sit behind the booth and enjoy our donuts. Well, I pretend to listen in on Frankie and Hazel's conversation about this boy at the summer program who can burp his ABCs, but really, my mind is on Ozzi.

Where is he?

Is he okay?

Do simple things, like maple donuts, make him think of me?

"Willow," Hazel says, a little too loud, making my head snap up.

When she rolls her eyes at me, I realize she's probably been saying my name for a minute.

"Sorry, what?" I ask.

"Can I go see Molly? Her mom's booth is right over there," she says pointing about fifty feet away.

I nod, eyeing the booth. "You can only go there and back. That's it. Okay?"

"Okay," she agrees, already moving in that direction.

"Stay where I can see you," I call out.

Frankie reaches over and pats my back. "She'll be fine. But how are you?"

Taking a bite of my donut, I fight back the first urge to cry I've had in a week. I thought I was fine. I thought I'd come to terms with Ozzi's departure—grateful for our time together, sad that it didn't last, but resolved to move on and be happy. So, what the hell was that?

"I don't know," I say honestly. "I just hadn't heard his name in a while, you know? We've been busy and no one at the gym mentions him. He's like the elephant in the room no one talks about. So, I think when she mentioned that the donut reminded her of him... I don't know."

We're both quiet for a minute, watching as people pass by her booth. A couple stops, but they're just browsing. Then, Frankie says, "I'm sorry."

"For what?"

With a sigh, she shrugs. "Sorry you're going through this. I'm also sorry that Ozzi felt like he couldn't be the person for you, because I know deep down, he is."

I swallow a bite of donut, unable to speak.

"The two of you surprised me," she admits. "But I guess I shouldn't have been surprised. I've always felt like you're a lot like me and Gunnar is a lot like Ozzi. So, it didn't come as a shock the two of you ended up together."

"What would you do if you were me?" I ask, my voice barely above a whisper.

She's right, she and I are an awful lot alike. We have traumatic pasts, even though our trauma is different, it's there. Unlike me, Frankie was never in foster care, but she did have to be self-sufficient from a young age. We're independent and guarded. We've both built extremely tall walls around our hearts in an effort to protect what's left. And, somehow, we both fell in love with a couple of Vikings.

"I wouldn't give up," Frankie says, equally as quiet. "I can't believe I'm even saying this, because I'm not one to give second chances. But I think Ozzi is searching. I've seen it time and time again. And when people are trying to find themselves, unsure of what they have to offer, they often make really stupid decisions. Like leaving because they think they're doing what's right."

That wasn't what I thought she was going to say, so it throws me for a loop.

I expected a tough love speech about moving on and picking myself up by the bootstraps.

"Don't tell Gunnar I said that," she adds. "I think he'd like to kick Ozzi's ass for real."

A laugh erupts from my chest, but it's just to hide the pain, because the thought of anyone hurting Ozzi makes me physically ill.

"If anyone's going to kick his ass," I deadpan. "It'll be me."

* * *

LATER THAT EVENING, I'm sitting in a booth at Genie's with Frankie, Maggie, and Tempest. The table was covered with bar food, there's country western music playing in the background, and couples are spinning around the dance floor.

"These chicken wings are to-die-for," Tempest says with a moan.

From the amount of food we have, you'd think the guys were joining us, but they're back at the gym with Hazel and Freya. Cage made them dinner and they're watching a Disney movie on a large projector he bought for the gym. It's meant for when we have our own fight nights, but tonight, it will entertain two little girls. Although, I think the guys were just as excited.

Vali was in charge of popcorn and Gunnar brought over the ingredients for s'mores.

Cage normally won't let him splurge, but made an exception, since it's my birthday.

Gunnar told me the other day he thinks I'm making Cage nicer. He claims that ever since he started training the two of us together, he's not as much of a hard ass. His words, not mine.

"Can I get y'all a refill?" a waitress asks, stopping at our table. "Napkins? More wings?"

Maggie chuckles. "I'll take another root beer."

"I'll take some more water, please." Even though Cage gave us the night off, I don't want to fill my body with things that will weigh me down. Tomorrow's training session will be brutal enough.

"I'm good," Tempest tells her. "I already feel like I can't breathe."

"Me too," Frankie adds, leaning back against the booth.

The waitress smiles and nods. "I'll be right back."

"We should dance," Maggie says as she cranes her neck to see who's on the dance floor.

"The next line dance song, it's on," Tempest agrees, reaching across to give her a high five.

When "Boot Scootin' Boogie" comes on, the two of them force Frankie and me out onto the dance floor. I've never danced much, but the few times I came here with Ozzi, I did enjoy being held in his arms while we swayed to the music.

This, though, is way different.

After a minute or so, I start getting the hang of it and by the end of the song, I'm laughing at how ridiculous I probably look, but also how much fun I just had.

Even with memories of Ozzi filtering through my mind, I'm still able to smile and be present with my friends.

"A round of shots for the birthday girl," Tempest calls out over the music.

Once we've downed a lemon drop shot, which wasn't so bad, we're back out on the dance floor.

I'm on my way to working up a sweat when someone's hands wrap around my waist and spin me around. Caught off guard, I practically fall into the chest of a man who's at least a foot taller than me.

"Haven't seen you around here," he says, keeping up with the beat of the music and the people dancing around us. "How about after this dance, I buy you a drink?"

Glancing over, I see Frankie watching me hesitantly, like she's trying to decide if she needs to intervene or not. I turn back to the guy and politely try to put some distance between us, but he's not having it.

He's also not the least attractive man I've ever seen. His eyes are green and he has a bit of scruff on his jawline. The cowboy hat sitting on top of his head hides most of his dark hair, but it works for him.

However, I'm not interested, so I push a little harder. "No, thank you."

Instead of replying, he smiles, like he didn't hear me and continues to spin us around the dance floor. Just as I'm getting ready to speak up—or kick his ass, I haven't decided yet—Maggie squeezes between us.

"Sorry, cowboy. She's with us," she tells him with a wide smile on her face. "But that blonde over there sure does look like she'd like to take you for a ride."

My eyes grow wide at her boldness.

Typically, Maggie is sweet and wholesome. And then Romance Author Maggie O'Neal takes over and she's audacious and brass. I love that version of her.

"Thanks, Mags," I tell her, giving her waist a squeeze. "I could've handled him, but I appreciate the save."

"That's what we were afraid of," Tempest says, a laugh bubbling out of her. "The next thing you know, I'd be calling Cage to come bail us out of jail. Been there, done that. Have the t-shirt to prove it. And I don't look good in stripes."

We all laugh at that, making our way back over to our table where there are fresh waters and another round of shots.

"He was pretty good-looking though."

The three of us give Tempest a look of disbelief.

"Hey," she says, holding up her hands in defense as she slides back into the booth. "Just because I'm a married woman doesn't mean I can't do a little window shopping."

"Does Cage know about this little hobby?" Frankie asks with a mischievous smile.

That earns another laugh as Tempest passes around the shots. "Trust me, Cage would not be threatened by that. He knows he's it for me and he trusts me implicitly, just like I do him."

Knowing what I do now about Tempest's past and her cheating ex-husband, I appreciate the confidence she has in her and Cage's relationship. They are definite relationship goals.

"To Willow," Tempest says, holding up the shot glass. "Thank you for being born! Without you, we wouldn't be here tonight, having lemon drop shots and fending off sexy cowboys. I know things haven't been easy for you, but you're an inspiration to us all. Now, let's make twenty-three your bitch and kick some serious ass this year."

"To Willow," Frankie and Maggie say in unison.

We toss back the shots and I can't help but smile as I look around the table.

These women have become more like sisters, especially in the last month or so. I've leaned on them, cried with them, laughed with them. My entire life, I've wanted family. I always thought that ship had sailed. But here I am, with some of the best friends a girl could ask for.

And Hazel, who I never allowed myself to even dream of.

When I moved here, I thought I was coming to a quaint, small town to blend into the scenery and fly under the radar. Little did I know that fate had other plans.

"So, about that cowboy," Tempest hedges, pulling me out of my thoughts.

"No," I say with a chuckle, picking up my water and taking a healthy drink.

"Is he not your type?" she asks.

I know what she's getting at, but the answer is simple. "I'm not ready to move on," I tell her, my eyes going to Frankie as I think about our conversation from earlier today. "I'm not ready to give up."

That might be a pipe dream, but later, when Tempest pulls out a box of muffins and birthday candles, I'd be lying if I said my wishes didn't include Ozzi.

CHAPTER 43

OZZI

"Order up," I hear the cook call from the kitchen.

Viggo walks past my table to grab the food and slaps me on the back of the head in the process. On his way back to the customer's table, he leans over. "You could be doing something useful instead of taking up one of my tables."

"Last time I checked, all these tables belonged to Harry," I say, without looking up from the crossword I've been working on.

In my time here in Fischer Falls, I've become quite the crossword connoisseur.

Basically, I'm now a seventy-year-old man. I come to the diner practically every day. I drink coffee with the locals, shoot the shit with the old dudes, work a crossword, and annoy my brother.

All-in-all, it's a good time.

When I'm not occupying a table at the diner, I work at Viggo's house. And when I'm not working on Viggo's house, I find somewhere to hike or kayak. There's even this great rock not far from here we found to climb.

Viggo and I also spar in the front yard and go on runs.

Basically, I try to keep myself busy and my goal at the end of the day is to be so exhausted I pass out. The worst is on days when it rains and we don't get outside much. Those are the nights I can't sleep and all I do is lay in bed, stare at the ceiling, and think about Willow.

What's she doing?

How's she doing?

Does she still think of me?

Does she miss me?

I call Cage once a week, under the ruse of checking in and telling him about what's going on here. But we both know what I'm really calling for. He's my only lifeline to Willow and even though he gave me shit the first couple of times I called—about how if I was really concerned about how she's doing, I wouldn't have left in the first place—now he'll at least tell me how training sessions are going.

I do also have Hazel.

When I left the note for her at the gym, I wasn't sure if she'd actually call me, or if Willow would let her. But I should've known Hazel is much more streetwise than her nine years, which she now makes me refer to her as nine-and-a-half or almost-ten.

But I don't try to get information about Willow out of Hazel. That was never the intention of me leaving my contact information for her. We just talk about random things, what she had for dinner, or the ice cream dates she and Willow go on.

I've heard all about the summer program she's in and how Maggie's been teaching her how to write essays and one day she wants to be an author just like her.

She also fills me in on the town gossip.

According to Hazel, someone at the Farmer's Market started selling the same kind of soap Frankie's mom makes and that caused a stink, because Frankie's been selling her mom's soap there for years and it's against the rules to sell something someone else is already selling.

Also, Miss Faye let it slip that Bernice Williams was seen at the jam session last week with Clyde, who is *not* Bernice's husband.

"Coffee refill?" Harry asks.

Picking up my cup, I see it's empty. I'm not even sure when I drank it all.

"Sure. Thanks, Harry."

With confidence born from years of experience, he fills the cup without spilling a drop.

"Hey, Harry," I say, my eyes going to the picture of the Eiffel Tower hanging on the wall in front of me. "I've been meaning to ask, what's with all the photos in here?"

There are shots in front of the Taj Mahal and one with the Great Wall of China. Over by the front door is a framed photo of Big Ben and next to that is one from the London Bridge. If I had to guess, there are over fifty photos from all over the world hanging in here.

It's not quite what you expect to see in a small-town roadside diner.

"You like those, do you?"

He sets the carafe on the table and slides into the booth across from me.

"Love them," I admit. "Are they from a personal collection?"

Harry hums as he lets his eyes roam around the room, almost as if he's recollecting memories.

"Alice took all of them," he eventually says, bracing his elbows on the table. "She was my wife of fifty-three years. She passed two years ago, but before then, we traveled to every continent, visited seventeen countries, and marked off every wonder of the world from our bucket list. If you get close enough to the photos, you'll see me in all of them. She always insisted on getting me in front of whatever landmark or monument we were visiting. I always told her to get in the picture too, but she said she enjoyed being behind the camera more. She loved photography... these photos in here are just the tip of the iceberg."

"Wow," I tell him, looking at the photos in a different light. They're his life—his memories, his adventures, his wife.

"Now when I look at them, I don't see myself, I see her."

That's one of the sweetest things I've heard in a long time.

"Have you traveled much lately?" I ask, feeling a twinge in my chest I'm trying to ignore.

He shakes his head, once again focusing on the photos instead of me. "No, not since Alice passed. I told her almost sixty years ago that I never wanted to go on an adventure without her. She was my greatest one, after all, and besides, I've been everywhere I want to go. Nowadays, this place keeps me busy and it's all I need. It's where I feel closest to her."

Swallowing, I try to tamp down the rush of emotions—empathy for his loss, mixed with a recognition I feel deep in my soul.

Ever since I left Green Valley, all I've thought about is going back, which is crazy because it's a small town with none of the excitement I'm used to. But it's not the town I miss, it's the people in it, particularly two—Willow and Hazel.

If Harry and I would've had this conversation six months ago, I would've thought it was a great story. We could've swapped travel tales and I would've gone on my merry way, not thinking another thing about it.

But now, after falling in love with Willow, I feel every word he's said in my bones.

"I'm sorry for your loss," I tell him, clearing my throat and taking a sip of my coffee.

Harry gives me a grateful smile. "Thank you. I miss her every day. And thanks for giving me a reason to talk about her today."

"I'd love to hear more about your travels and see more of her beautiful photos."

"Is there someone special waiting for you out there?" he asks, eyeing me inquisitively. "You showed up here out of the blue, but I get the feeling you're not here to stay. Where's home?"

For a second, I feel like I'm unable to breathe as the truth comes crashing down on me. I'm pretty sure it's been there this entire time, but no one has asked me about it in this way or made me think about it like this. Looking at Harry is like looking at myself in fifty years.

"She's in Tennessee."

"What are you doing here?"

As if the question is rhetorical, he slips out of the booth, picks up the carafe, and pats my shoulder as he continues along, refilling customers' coffees.

Glancing up, I see Viggo staring at me knowingly, like he was eavesdropping on mine and Harry's conversation. When he ducks back into the kitchen, I pick up my phone off the table and walk outside.

I'm already dialing before the door shuts behind me and Cage answers on the second ring.

"What's up?" he asks, and I can hear the familiar sounds of the gym in the background.

The strongest feeling of homesickness hits me like a tidal wave. I have to lean against the side of the building because my legs feel weak.

"Oz?" Cage asks. "Did I lose you?"

"No," I say, my voice sounding gravelly, even to my own ears. Clearing my throat, I try again. "I'm here."

"Everything alright?"

"How's Willow?" I ask, wanting to know so much more but hoping any morsel he'll give me about her will be enough to ease the ache in my chest.

There's a long pause, but I know he's still there because I can still hear people in the background. But then the sounds grow fainter and Cage says, "What's this about, Ozzi?"

"I was just calling to check in," I say, trying to sound casual about it.

"It's Saturday. Your weekly update isn't for two more days."

I know he's been onto me from the get-go, so I might as well stop with the bull-shit. Staring out across the gravel parking lot, my eyes land on a tree growing on the other side of a wooden fence.

It's not just any tree.

It's a willow tree, standing strong as its long, slender branches sway in the warm breeze.

All this time and I've never noticed it, not once.

Lifting my face to the sky, I close my eyes. "I just need to know if she's okay."

"Are you asking as her former trainer or something else?"

"I'm asking as someone who's so fucking in love with her he doesn't know what to do with himself. And he's wondering if he's fucked up too bad to make it right, or if she even wants him to. Just… give me something," I beg.

The plea is met with silence, and I kick off the building and pace the sidewalk.

"She's good," Cage finally says, exhaling loudly. "As her trainer, I can tell you she's on track and kicking ass. I didn't think she could get in any better condition, but over the past month or so, she's become even more focused and driven. I have no doubt she'll dominate in this next fight."

My insides war over that information. It's great news, the best news. I'm so fucking happy she hasn't let my absence affect her training. Although, there was never a doubt in my mind that Willow would excel. That's just who she is, when things get tough, she gets tougher.

But my heart wishes she at least missed me half as much as I miss her. I hoped I wasn't a passing memory, but someone she still thought about, at least.

"As her friend," Cage continues. "I can tell you she has good days and bad days, but she doesn't let the bad days keep her down too long."

There's another pause, but not as long this time. "As your brother," he says matter-of-factly. "I'm telling you to pull your shit together. If you want to be with her, fucking be with her. She hasn't moved on, if that's what you're asking. She misses you and thinks about you every day. But if you're still confused or whatever, thinking you're not good enough for her, she doesn't need that bullshit."

A fire starts burning in my chest. It's not anger or resentment. It's also neither doubt nor fear.

It's resolution.

"I'm not confused."

For the first time in a while, I can honestly say I'm definitely not confused. I know what I want, who I want, and I'm not afraid to go get it.

Cage doesn't say anything again for a minute and I can picture his surly face as he runs a hand through his beard, contemplating whether I'm telling the truth or not. But if he could see my face right now, he'd know.

"I mean it," I add. "If I could just talk to her—"

"Listen," he says, cutting me off. "If you're going to call her or text her or whatever, don't do it tonight. She's at Genie's. We're watching Hazel. But don't wait until next week. I need her focused on the fight and not on your bullshit."

She's at Genie's?

Her birthday is coming up in a few days, so maybe she's out celebrating. I mean, I'm glad she's out, but who the fuck is she with?

Cage doesn't give me a chance to ask any more questions, he just abruptly tells me he's busy and needs to go. The next thing I know the call ends and I'm left staring at the screen, trying to read between the lines and feeling emotions tangle inside me—longing, jealousy, want, need.

And for the first time in a long time…hope.

CHAPTER 44

WILLOW

"*H*appy Birthday," Hazel yells, startling me awake.

She's standing at the foot of my bed with a plate that has two waffles and a candle. It's not lit, but it's the thought that counts.

"Happy birthday to you," she starts to sing, walking around to the side. "Happy birthday to you. Happy birthday to the best sister in the whole wide world. Happy birthday to you."

I can honestly say, this is the first time I've ever been woken up on my birthday with a serenade.

With tears stinging my eyes, I press my lips together, shaking my head. "Thank you," I finally manage without breaking down.

I will not cry today.

I know the old song about it being my party and I can cry if I want to, but I don't want to.

I want to spend the morning with Hazel eating these awesome waffles, go to work this afternoon, and then train this evening at the gym. Sure, it sounds like an average day, but it's exactly what I want.

The only other thing I want I can't have, and I'm trying to come to terms with that.

"I think we need more than two waffles," I tell Hazel as I get out of bed and pull her in for a hug. "And maybe some chocolate milk."

She smiles at me, nodding. "On my birthday, I want hot chocolate with marsh-mallows."

"Noted," I tell her, taking the plate and walking into the kitchen.

We play music from my phone and have a dance party in the kitchen while we wait on more waffles to toast. Then, I make two extra-large cups of chocolate milk and we sit in the middle of the kitchen floor and feast.

A couple hours later, I drop Hazel off at Miss Faye's, who meets us at the door with a lunch packed especially for me. "Chicken Fettuccine Alfredo," she announces with a satisfied grin. "And if that Cage gives you any crap about it, you have him come talk to me. No one should eat a peanut butter and jelly sand-wich on her birthday."

I laugh, feeling my cheeks blush. That is what I have packed in my bag, along with some carrots and the protein drink Cage has me drinking before workouts.

I guess those will have to wait until tomorrow.

"Thank you, Miss Faye," I tell her, already smelling the amazing food. I'll have to forgo eating dinner, for the sheer fact I'll be so stuffed by then I won't be able to consume another morsel of food. "I'll be back around six."

"Be good," I instruct Hazel.

The warning is a mere formality. Surprisingly, I haven't had any issues with her since she moved in. If you'd asked me at our first meeting if I thought things would go this smoothly, I would've laughed. But Hazel is a really good kid and we get along pretty well. Outside of typical kid stuff—a little attitude here and there, not wanting to go to bed from time to time, and being a little smarty pants —she's really good.

Knock on wood.

"Don't worry about her," Miss Faye says, shooing me out the door. "She keeps me in line most days."

I laugh, holding up the lunch as I walk to my truck. "Thanks again for the lunch."

"Happy birthday, dear."

At work, Tim has a large card in the breakroom for me that everyone has signed, along with some cupcakes from the store's bakery.

Seriously, why does everyone feel the need to celebrate with food?

I'm gracious, because I remember years when no one wished me a happy birthday, smile and go about my day as usual—stocking shelves, checking out customers, and bagging groceries.

"Big plans for tonight?" Krista asks as we straighten the end caps before our shift is over. Even though Krista got hired on at the Pink Pony, she still works part time here as well. Since her shifts there don't start until the evenings, she works mostly days. Our schedules are closer to the same again and it's good to have her to chat with during the day.

"No. But I did go to Genie's Saturday night with Tempest, Frankie, and Maggie."

"Um, how about an invite next time?" she asks. "That sounds like a fun time."

Sorting through the magazines everyone reads while they're waiting to check out, I give her an apologetic smile over my shoulder. "Sorry, I should've invited you."

"I'm kidding, but seriously," she says, coming to stand next to me. "So, what about tonight?"

"I'm training," I tell her. "We're going to Memphis on Thursday."

She snaps her fingers. "That's right! One of these days, I'm going to come see you fight."

"Cage is talking about having another exhibition at the gym soon."

"That would be awesome," she says. "Think there's another Erickson brother lurking around somewhere?"

My stomach does its typical free fall and if I had to guess, my face did too.

"Shit, sorry," she says, taking the magazines from my hand and finishing my job for me. "I wasn't even thinking about it, it just slipped out."

"It's fine, really," I tell her, dusting my hands on my jeans. "I should be over it by now anyway."

She turns to face me. "Says who? Because as far as I can tell you're in love with him. Those kinds of feelings don't go away overnight."

In love.

Am I still in love?

Yes. Yes, I am.

"There is another brother," I tell her, trying to redirect the conversation. I've already been down this road with the girls. They're supportive of me not giving up, but they're realistic when it comes to Ozzi's track record. He's never been in a long-term, serious relationship. But none of them want to give up on him making a return to Green Valley either.

Maybe, deep down, we're all just a bunch of hopeless romantics.

Just that thought makes me want to laugh, not at them, but myself. I've never, ever considered myself a romantic, not in the slightest. A realist, yes. The only explanation for this glimmer of hope I've held onto is love. That's the only variable that's changed.

I've never been *in love* before Ozzi Erickson.

And Krista is right, I'm *still* in love with him.

"That's right," she says. "What's his name?"

"Viggo," I reply, taking my rag and dusting the edges of the shelves.

"Is he as good looking as Ozzi and the rest of them?" Krista asks with a dreamy lilt to her voice.

I laugh. "I don't think your last name can be Erickson without being good-looking. It's a prerequisite."

"Yeah, I've seen their dad in here a few times. He's a DILF."

My cheeks heat up as she talks about Mr. Erickson. I want to plug my ears like a child and sing to the top of my lungs so I can't hear her, but I don't.

She's right though; his sons definitely inherited their good looks from him, and Peggy too.

"Well, time to clock out," I say, looking at the large clock on the wall. "I'd love to finish this awkward conversation but I've got to go pick up Hazel and get to the gym and pray Mr. Erickson doesn't decide to drop by tonight."

Krista laughs. "Tell him I said hello."

"Absolutely not."

Half an hour later, when I walk into the gym with Hazel in tow, I'm pleasantly surprised to find it blessedly quiet and the only Erickson's around are Cage and Gunnar.

"It's the birthday girl," Gunnar announces, hopping out of the ring, running over, and wrapping me in a bear hug.

"Happy birthday," Cage adds, a lot more subdued than his brother. "You had a delivery earlier."

He points over to the desk and it's then I notice a large arrangement of flowers.

I look back at Cage. "Those are for me?"

There's a slight smile that's hidden by his facial hair, but I see the twitch.

"Who are they from?" I ask, going to them and pulling the envelope from the holder in the flowers. "I've never—"

I'm getting ready to say *I've never had flowers delivered to me*, but I stop when I see the card.

These blue irises remind me of you—unique and beautiful. Happy Birthday. -O

He says they remind him of me, but there's something about the blue hue of the petals that remind me of him, of his eyes. I've never seen anything more beautiful.

"They're so pretty," Hazel says, sitting on her knees in the chair and leaning over to smell the flowers. "But they don't smell like much."

Leave it to her to keep it real.

"Some flowers are so pretty they don't need to smell good to get your attention."

She gives me a thoughtful look and then nods her head. "Are they from Ozzi?"

I look over at her, kind of surprised she'd put two-and-two together. "Yeah."

"That's nice," she says, hopping down from the chair.

Watching her for a second, I collect myself before turning back to Cage.

"Can I have just a second?" I ask, reaching for my phone in my bag.

Cage nods. "We'll start in fifteen."

"Yeah, okay," I agree, already opening my text app.

Me: Thank you for the flowers. They're beautiful.

I don't expect to see the three little dots pop up so quickly, but they do, and my heart practically jumps out of my chest. Ozzi and I have had zero contact since the night I told him I couldn't be with him anymore. The night he walked away, cutting himself completely out of my life.

He did what he thought was best for all of us, but it doesn't mean I'm not hurt and angry.

When the dots stop, I inhale and close my eyes, willing myself to calm down. There are so many things I want to say to him right now, but none of them seem right or good. He sent me flowers, the first flowers I've ever been sent, and it was a sweet gesture. But why—

Ozzi: I couldn't let the day go by without wishing you a happy birthday and letting you know I'm thinking of you.

Fuck.

My traitorous heart wants to teleport through the phone and wrap my arms around him so tight, but my brain is telling me to keep myself in check. I said I'm not giving up hope on Ozzi, but that doesn't mean I can free-fall back into him. If, and that's a big if—possibly even a never—he were to come back to Green Valley, there would be a lot to figure out.

So, I can't do that.

Me: I appreciate the thought.

I want to add on that it means a lot—it means everything—but he's going to have to be the one that bridges the gap, not me. I didn't walk away, he did.

CHAPTER 45

WILLOW

*W*hen we pull up outside the hotel that's attached to the convention center where the fights will take place, Hazel lets out a sound of pure amazement.

"Wow," she says, pressing her nose to the window of the van. "This place is huge."

It's her first time staying at a hotel and it's all she's been able to talk about. Well that, and finally seeing me in a *big fight*.

A month or so ago, when Cage was finalizing the travel plans for this event, we all decided it would be fun for everyone to go. So, he rented a sixteen-passenger van and this morning, a little before six o'clock, we all piled in and headed for Memphis.

Randy and Peggy followed behind us in their vehicle, with Maggie's parents, which left plenty of room in the van for the rest of us—me, Hazel, Cage, Gunnar, Frankie, Maggie, Vali, Tempest, Willow, and Freya.

Unlike our first trip, which we made in record time, we ended up making three stops. Once for drinks, once for food, and once just to change Freya's diaper.

"Valet will unload all of this," Cage instructs as we all exit the van. "I'll go in and get us checked in."

"What's valet?" Hazel asks, grabbing her backpack and Sid.

"It's a person who unloads your luggage and parks your vehicle for you," I tell her, checking to see if Tempest needs any help with Freya, but she's a pro and already has her unbuckled.

As we walk into the lobby, the brothers get the typical stares. I get it. they're big dudes, with big muscles, and impressive beards. If I wasn't with them, I'd stare too.

It's hard to miss one of them, let alone three.

"What do you think?" Maggie asks Hazel as we all congregate in the lobby and wait for Cage to get our room keys.

"I love it," Hazel says, her eyes roaming the impressive space.

Maggie smiles. "You know, it wasn't long ago I went on my first Erickson Family Road Trip."

"Where did you go?"

I'm not sure who's more inquisitive, my little sister or Maggie—they're two peas in a pod.

"New Orleans," Maggie tells her with wide eyes and even wider smile. "It was the first time I'd ever been out of Tennessee."

"Ooooooh." Hazel's giddiness is infectious. "I want to go to New Orleans."

About that time, Cage, Gunnar, and Vali walk up with keys for everyone's rooms.

"Let's get the bags to the rooms and be back down here in thirty minutes," Cage instructs to me and Gunnar. "We'll go over and get checked in and then we can decide what to do for dinner."

"If you don't mind," Randy says, walking up beside Cage. "Us old folks are going to get some barbeque and then turn in early, but we'll be more than happy to babysit later if you need us to."

Tempest smiles over at him, bouncing Freya. "I might take you up on that. She's a little fussy after being cooped up in the van all day. We'll just have to see how she does through the afternoon."

"Don't hesitate to call," Peggy chimes in. "And we'd love to have Hazel too."

"Thank you," I say, giving her an appreciative smile. They're always so inclusive with Hazel. They're like that with everyone, but I can't thank them enough for the way they've taken us both under their wings.

Once our luggage is unloaded, we all go our separate ways. The parents head to Beale Street. Tempest puts Freya down for a nap. Maggie finds a quiet place to write. And the rest of us walk over to the convention center.

Not two minutes after we arrive, I hear a female voice call out.

"Bernard," she barks, getting not only our attention but everyone else in the vicinity and I feel my cheeks warm under the scrutiny. "Heard you've got a mean right hook and a roundhouse to back it up."

Her combative tone immediately puts me on edge and I try to figure out her angle. Unsure of what to say, I simply nod.

Now that I've gotten a good look at her—a little shorter than me, with broader shoulders and a nasty scowl—I recognize her as my opponent for tomorrow's bout. Kristy McCreedy. She's newer to the sport, but she's still had a lot more experience than me.

My blood starts to boil as she grins like the Cheshire Cat, feeling like she's bested me somehow.

Mental game is half the battle.

Ozzi taught me that.

"Cat got your tongue?" McCreedy goads. "I'm thinking that beginner's luck might be wearing off. You seem pretty docile to me."

She must feel Cage's gaze because her attention shifts to him and some of her cockiness fades. But I don't need Cage to fight my battles for me, I'm equipped to do that on my own.

"I like to let my ability speak for itself," I say calmly.

McCreedy's eyes slide back to me and she smirks, trying to regain some of her footing, but I hold strong—chin high, shoulders back.

"I guess we'll see what it has to say tomorrow."

"Looking forward to it." I want to bite out my response and bare my teeth, but I rein in the fury and save it for tomorrow in the ring.

As Kristy walks off, Hazel scrunches her nose. "Who was that?"

"My opponent for tomorrow," I say, gently urging her to keep walking.

Hazel looks up at me with disgust. "Well, I don't like her. She's not a nice person."

That makes us all laugh.

"From the mouth of babes," Vali says.

"Fucking Kristy McCreedy," I hear Cage mutter behind me.

Gunnar saddles up beside me, as we continue to walk—Hazel already forgetting the interaction and leading the pack like she knows where she's going.

He speaks quietly, like he's laying out a strategy for war. "Don't let her get to you. That's what they all do when they smell fresh meat—try to get in your head and ruin your mental game. But you're stronger than her and she lets her emotions get the best of her. So, as long as you keep your cool, you don't have anything to worry about."

* * *

THE NEXT AFTERNOON, after a morning of breakfast with Hazel and the girls, I decide to go over to the convention center to do an early warm-up and get my head in the game.

I also spend the entire time, trying not to think about Ozzi—what he's doing, what he would say to me today. More than once, I have my phone in hand and almost ready to dial his number when I stop myself.

"There you are," Cage says, coming up beside the treadmill I have set on a low and steady pace.

"Hey."

"Tempest said you left a while ago. Everything okay?"

His tone is even, but I can tell he's low-key worried something is wrong.

"Everything is fine," I tell him. "I just needed some time to get my head on straight.

His piercing blue eyes, ones a shade lighter than his brother's, stare me down. With his thick arms crossed over his broad chest, he looks menacing. But I know Cage and he's just concerned about my mental well-being as much as my physical.

"You're my first female fighter," he says. The statement kind of comes out of left field, but I can tell he has more to say so I just keep my pace on the treadmill and let him talk. "We had some female fighters back in Dallas, at our old gym. But I never trained them."

He's quiet for a minute, obviously lost in thought.

"On my way over here this morning, I overheard a couple guys talking about us." He smirks, scratching a hand through his blonde beard. "They were saying they think we'll be a force to be reckoned with in the years to come. Named you as one of those reasons." His eyebrows raise and he nods. "I have to agree. Gunnar is a legacy; everyone expects him to be as good as he is. He was born into a family that breed fighters. But you... you're different. You're a diamond in the rough, owners and trainers around the world just wait for someone like you to walk into their gym."

I've never been good with compliments, but this is so much more than that. My throat is tight with the magnitude of what he's saying.

"I know the past weeks have been hard on you," he continues. "But I just want you to know, no matter what happens today, I'm proud of you. And I'm glad you took the chance on us."

God, he's not the one who should be saying all of this. I should.

"I'm thankful you took a chance on me," I manage to croak out, the tremor in my voice masked by the fact I'm still jogging on the treadmill.

"I guess you could say I recognized a piece of myself in you the day you walked into the gym. When I arrived in Tennessee, I was lost, searching for what was next in my life. I never could've dreamed this is where we'd all end up. I've found everything I needed in Green Valley—the love of my life, a new career path, and a place to call home."

He smooths a hand over his beard, exhaling.

"I hope you find all of that too."

"I'm working on it."

A couple hours later, Cage, Vali and Frankie are ringside, while I get a pat down from the ref. My focus is on my opponent across the ring and the task at hand, but I feel their support.

The ref went over the rules and regulations in the back, but he gives us the high-lights again.

"Let's have a clean fight. Touch hands. Back to your corners."

It's hard to explain what happens when I'm inside the ring. The only way I know how to describe it is the world falls away. The roar of the crowd hushes to a quiet murmur and all I hear are Ozzi's words.

I believe in you.

You can win this fight.

Keep your head in it.

Don't quit.

I glance briefly over to Cage, our eyes lock, he gives me a nod, and then the buzzer sounds.

CHAPTER 46

OZZI

*M*y phone rings and I answer through my Jeep's Bluetooth without looking at the caller ID.

"Hello?"

There's some commotion in the background and for a second, I think it's Viggo. He must be at the diner. It is All-You-Can-Eat Fish today, after all.

"Viggo?" I ask when there's still no response.

He must've butt-dialed me, which means I'm talking to his ass.

"Oz?" It's my brother, just not the one I expected.

My adrenaline spikes, making my heart pound in my chest. "Yeah, I'm here."

"Can you hear me?" Cage asks.

"Yeah, I can hear you fine. Are you at the fight?" I ask, glancing down at the time on the dashboard. If I hadn't been stuck in traffic on I-40 for over three hours due to a wreck earlier, I would've already been there. I knew the second I saw the cars start piling up that I wasn't going to make it in time to watch Willow fight.

But the only person who knows I'm coming is Hazel. I made her promise to keep it a secret. Since she's *almost-ten,* she loves secrets, so I doubt she ratted me out.

365

"Cage?"

Just when I think I've lost him, he starts talking. "Sorry, I had to go somewhere so I could hear better... Willow's on her way to the hospital. Frankie and Vali are with her. I had to stay back with Gunnar since he's not fighting for another hour. Shit, man, I wish you were here. But I just wanted to call and let you know... I know if I were you, I'd be pissed if no one called me."

If I wasn't sitting, my stomach would be on the floor. "What the fuck happened?" I ask, increasing my speed and passing a couple cars. In the process of turning this stretch of highway into a speedway, I pass a sign for Memphis that says I'm only fifty-four miles away, and that's fifty-four miles too many.

"Did she get knocked out? Concussion?" That's the most common injury in MMA.

"No, Willow won the fight, fair and square. She took some hits, but she's got one of the toughest chins I've ever seen. By the end of it, McCreedy didn't even have any gas left in the tank. I thought Willow was going to get another KO under her belt, but it came down to the judges."

He sighs and I'm about to go off when he continues.

"That bitch McCreedy," he growls. "I knew she was a dirty fighter, but I didn't think she was so vindictive. She waited for the judges to call the winner and when the ref turned around to announce Willow as the winner, she swiped Willow's legs out from under her. Tried to make it look like an accident, but I saw the whole thing. Willow tried to catch herself and fell just right, snapping her arm," he sighs again as my stomach rolls. "Fuck, man. It's bad, and we won't know the extent of it until she gets some x-rays, but I think it'll need surgery."

"I'll be there in less than an hour," I grit out.

"What? I thought you were in Bumfuck, Texas? How the hell—"

Slamming my fist on the steering wheel, I let out some of my frustration, probably looking like a maniac, but I don't care. My girl is hurt and I'm not there.

Fuck.

"I was already on my way, tried to make it for her fight, but got stuck in Arkansas on I-40. I'm fifty miles out from Memphis."

This time when Cage sighs, it's one of relief. "About fucking time."

"Where's Hazel?"

"At the hotel with Mom and Dad."

Trying to rein in my worry and frustration, I nod like he can see me. "Okay, keep me posted on Willow. I'll let you know when I'm there."

When the call ends, I bang my fist on the steering wheel again, willing my Jeep to magically appear in Memphis.

The next half hour seems to crawl and I constantly glance over at my phone, like I'm not going to hear it if it rings. But what if my service is bad? How long had Willow been at the hospital when Cage called? Shit, I should've asked more questions.

Just as I'm getting ready to call him back and ask for an update, it rings.

"Yeah," I say, forgoing any formalities.

"Okay," Cage says, sounding calmer than the first time he called which makes me feel a little better. "Frankie just called and they did some x-rays. Forearm fracture, but she just broke the ulna. They've given her something for the pain and are getting ready to set it now. She'll be there for a while, but Frankie is going to stay with her. Vali came back for Gunnar's fight and Maggie and Tempest took an Uber over to the hospital. Mom and Dad have Hazel and Freya and Mr. and Mrs. O'Neal stayed here. We're dividing and conquering, and I didn't want you killing yourself to get here." He pauses. "But I'm really fucking glad you're coming."

The sense of relief I feel is huge.

She's going to be okay.

We can handle a broken bone.

A small voice in the back of my head tells me we can handle anything, as long as we're together. And that's where I fucked up.

"I'll be there as soon as I can."

367

I know I was a coward to leave. It was bullshit. I should've stayed and fought through my fears. Willow is worth all the sacrifices. She's worth me re-arranging my life for her. I've always lived life, waiting on my next adventure.

Well, Willow is it.

If she'll have me.

Instead of going to the hospital, where Willow is being well taken care of, I go to the one person who was expecting me today. I know Hazel and she's probably inwardly freaking out, but she won't tell Mom and Dad she's scared, because she's a tough kid. Life has made her that way. But I need to see her.

When I pull up to the hotel, I hop out and hand my keys and a twenty to valet. Then, I text Cage. It has to be getting close to Gunnar's fight, but I'm hoping he sees it.

Me: What room are mom and dad in?

Cage: 1024

A few minutes later, I'm knocking on the door. When my dad opens it and sees me, he cocks his head in confusion. "Hey, Oz. What—"

He doesn't get a chance to finish the question because a ball of fire streaks past him and right into me. Hazel's arms wrap around my waist and I squeeze her to me, leaning down and pressing my nose into the top of her head. She smells like Willow.

"Hey, kiddo."

My heart begins to mend for a split second, until I hear her crying.

Hazel doesn't cry.

She's just not that kind of kid, so I squat down to see her better. Holding her by the shoulders, I urge her to look at me. "Hey, what's wrong?"

"You said you would be here!" When her eyes meet mine, I see fire in them. So much like her sister. And when she shoves me, I have to catch myself before I fall onto my ass. "You said you were coming and you weren't here and then Willow got hurt!"

Oh, God.

I can take a lot of things, but I can't stand the look of fear in her eyes right now. When I try to hug her again, she slaps my arms away, but I hold her gaze, not backing down or running away.

I'm here.

I'm never leaving again.

"I'm sorry," I say with as much sincerity as I can pack into two words. "I'm so sorry. I wanted to call and tell you I was running late, but I couldn't. You don't have a phone, remember? And I didn't know Willow was going to get hurt. None of us did. If we had, we all would've prevented it from happening. Okay?"

Her expression starts to soften, morphing from anger back to sadness.

"And she's okay. I just talked to Cage and her arm is broken, so she'll have a cool cast, but she'll be fine," I continue. "Remember me telling you about how I broke my arm?"

She nods, brushing her hair behind her ear and wrapping her small arms around her body.

"Look at it now," I say, holding it in the air so she can inspect it. "Good as new."

"Where were you?" she asks, changing the subject and still sounding a little pissed at me for not being here.

"There was a bad wreck on the highway, and I had to wait for the emergency vehicles to clear it."

When she closes the distance and hugs my neck, I feel my nose start to burn and a large lump clogs my throat.

I hug her back and hope that her sister will forgive me too.

"Don't leave again," she warns.

"I wouldn't be back here if I was planning on it."

CHAPTER 47

WILLOW

I feel like I've been in a deep sleep that wasn't long enough, leaving me groggy and confused.

Why is my mouth so dry?

And what's with the beeping?

I try to lift my arm so I can rub my eyes, hoping it clears the fog from my brain, but I quickly realize my arm is in a cast and everything comes flooding back—the fight, the win…the fall.

Who knew you could break your arm *after* a fight?

When I feel someone squeeze my hand, I almost think I'm dreaming because I could swear I recognize that hand. It's a weird thing to recognize, but I spent a lot of time memorizing it.

Since I'm a glutton for punishment, I open my eyes to find I'm right.

Ozzi Erickson is here.

And he's holding my hand and watching me, no doubt bracing himself for my reaction by the expression on his face. His infuriatingly beautiful face that I've missed so much and can't bear to see so upset.

"What's wrong?" I have to whisper because I'm so thirsty my throat feels like I swallowed sandpaper.

Ozzi laughs without any humor in his voice, looking up to the ceiling. "You just got out of surgery and you're asking me what's wrong?"

"Can I get some water?" I wince.

"Shit. Of course. Let me tell the nurse you're awake." He kisses the hand he was holding before rushing out of the room, leaving me with my head spinning.

I'm not sure if it's from the anesthesia or the fact Ozzi is here. In Memphis. In my hospital room.

My medical knowledge is limited to the little I've seen on television, so I can only assume the IV in my arm is giving me some much-needed pain meds.

Maybe I'm on the good drugs and this is all a hallucination?

When the door swings open, I blink my eyes a few times, just to see what happens. But when they focus, I see a nurse walk in, followed closely by Ozzi, which means he's really here.

"Hello, Willow. My name is Carrie and I'll be taking care of you tonight. Can you rate your pain for me from one to ten?"

"A three, maybe?" I ask, not really sure how I'm feeling at the moment. "But my throat is so dry. Is that normal?"

She nods as she walks over and checks the bag attached to the IV. "It's standard procedure to intubate during a surgery, so it's perfectly normal for your throat to feel sore and scratchy right now. Thankfully, it shouldn't last too long. Do you need anything else?"

"Just some water," I tell her.

"Absolutely. I'll get you a pitcher of water and some ice. I've notified the doctor that you're awake so he'll be here within the hour to check on you and answer any questions you have. In the meantime, press this button here if you need anything." She hands me something that looks like a small remote control and points to a button labeled *Nurse*.

Ozzi stands by the door when she walks out, like he's afraid to sit back down.

We just stare at each other after Carrie is gone, neither of us breaking the silence. I know I've thought about seeing him again and all the things I'd say, but here, now, after breaking my arm and having surgery to fix it, my mind is a muddled mess.

A few minutes later, Carrie brings me a pitcher of water and fills my small cup. "Here you go," she says, watching as I take a drink and try not to show how really fucking bad it hurts to swallow.

To appease her, I give a thumbs up and she smiles before giving Ozzi and me some privacy.

Once I'm finished with the water, Ozzi takes my cup and sets it down on a nearby table before sitting back in the chair, arms resting on his knees.

"What are you doing here?"

Ozzi flinches at my question, but I refuse to feel guilty about it. I might be laid up in a hospital bed, but I'm not going to brush over the fact he left and now he's back. After the flowers earlier this week, I wanted to ask him what he was doing, but I didn't. Now, he's sitting in front of me, and I want to know. Is he in or is he out? Here or gone? With me or without me?

He blows out a breath, obviously struggling with whatever it is he needs to say.

"I came for you," he finally says, eyes lifting to meet mine. "I was already on my way here when Cage called to tell me you were injured." Pausing, he inhales deeply, closing his eyes. "I should've been here." His voice is barely above a whisper and I hear the pain in his words. It's like he's the one with the broken arm. "I would've been on time for the match if not for a major wreck that held me back for three hours."

What?

"You were coming to see the fight?"

"No, I was coming to fight for you."

Those words leave me speechless.

"Willow, I'm so fucking sorry I left. It was stupid and weak. I thought it'd be easier if I left so you and Hazel could move on without me being in the background of your new lives together."

When he looks at me this time, there are tears in those blue eyes I love so much. I want to reach out and wipe them away, but they feel necessary and part of the moment.

"I'm the one who broke up with you," I remind him. "I understand why you did what you did. I mean, it hurt and I'm not saying it wasn't stupid, but I'm actually grateful because it allowed me to see I could do this without you."

Once again, my words cut deep and Ozzi winces.

"But," I continue, not wanting to prolong his pain, "I don't want to."

The furrow between his brow begins to soften and I watch as his expression shifts.

"I love you, Willow."

Those three words paired with my name coming from Ozzi's lips makes my heart pound. I actually think the monitor is beeping a little faster, too.

I'm too stunned to say anything so Ozzi continues. "I knew I loved you before I left but was too scared to admit it. When I thought about what a huge responsibility it is to truly love someone, it freaked me out. I still stand beside my claim that I'm not afraid of commitment. I was scared of failing you, not being the man you need me to be. And I didn't think I could live the adventurous life I'd always been accustomed to and be in a serious relationship at the same time but that was so fucking stupid."

He reaches out for my hand and runs his thumb across the back of it. "Willow Bernard, you are my greatest adventure."

My eyes close as I allow his words to cover me and seep deeply into my bones. I should probably still be angry with him or at the very least, mildly upset, but how can I be when he has shown up, not knowing how I'd react, to confess his sins and his love.

"Does this mean you're coming back to Green Valley? For good?"

"I want to be wherever you want to be. If you still want me, that is. The location doesn't matter; you're home to me. I'm never leaving again unless you're with me... or you explicitly tell me to."

He laughs and I feel the heaviness in my chest ease.

"Promise?"

Ozzi leans over and places his lips gently on mine. "I promise."

Those two words have never sounded sweeter because I know they mean something coming from him. He might've taken a while to figure things out, but I know Ozzi wouldn't lie to me. His honesty is one of the things I love most about him, along with the way he makes the world feel better by just existing.

I feel the Ozzi-shaped hole in my heart begin to fill.

"I love you," I confess, the words falling from my lips without permission or hesitation. "I've never told anyone that, except Hazel. So, I hate to break it to you, but you're stuck with me."

Ozzi chuckles, but I can hear the emotion behind it. Standing, he faces the wall and I can hear him sniffle as he wipes at his eyes before turning back to me. "I love you so much... so fucking much. Loving you and Hazel is what I want to do for the rest of my life if you'll have me."

"Oh, my God, where's Hazel?"

I suddenly feel a rush of panic at the thought of my baby sister worried for me and fresh tears spring to my eyes.

"She's fine," Ozzi says, coming back to sit beside me. "She's worried, but I told her she can see you in the morning."

I pull my brows together in confusion. "Wait? Was she up here?"

He shakes his head. "I went to see her first."

Why does that make my heart ache in the best way? The fact Ozzi checked on Hazel before me makes me feel better somehow.

"I knew you were being taken care of and there wasn't a lot I could do," Ozzi says, like he needs to explain why he went to her and not me. "Frankie, Tempest, and Maggie were up here, so—"

"I'm glad you checked on her first," I tell him, cutting off his rambling excuse. "If I hadn't already told you I love you, I would've said it now, just so you know. It means more than you'll ever know that you care so much about my sister. Thank you for making sure she was okay when you left. That letter you left her is one of her most prized possessions."

375

Ozzi gives me a crooked smile, melting my heart a little more.

"Did she tell you we talk on the phone?" he asks.

"What? When?"

He smirks, crossing his arms over his chest. "Sometimes when she's at the gym or Miss Faye's. I also talked to Miss Faye and I called Cage once a week to get an update on how my fighter is doing."

His fighter.

I'm more his than he realizes.

Even after he left, I was still his.

"I made the mistake of telling her I was coming today. I thought it'd be fun to surprise everyone and let her in on the secret. I had no clue I'd get stuck behind that damn wreck. So, when I showed up at the hotel, she was excited the first few seconds but then she got pissed."

My eyes go wide. "What did she say?"

"She was mad that I wasn't here... here to surprise you, protect you. She almost pushed me onto my ass." Ozzi smiles as he says this but my jaw is practically on the floor.

"She pushed you?"

"Yeah, but I don't blame her. She loves you and she was scared... I was pretty pissed at myself. I can't tell you how many times I've wanted to kick my own ass over the past month and a half."

"Forty-seven days," I mutter absentmindedly before I realize what I've said. "But who was counting?"

I feel my cheeks blush as Ozzi walks over and braces his arms on either side of me.

"I was," he says, before covering my mouth with his.

This kiss is different. It's still gentle, but it's more passionate and desperate, reflecting how I feel inside. When I reach up to cup his cheek, he covers my hand with his, holding it to him.

"I've missed you so fucking much," he breathes against my lips.

* * *

IT'S BEEN a month since Ozzi came back.

What a day that was. I won my fight, broke my arm, and woke up from surgery to find him sitting beside my bed.

Thankfully, the weeks since have been less eventful. Outside of me getting my cast off and starting physical therapy, it's been fairly uneventful. Hazel starts school next week, and she's really excited. With her being enrolled in the summer program, she's made good friends. All she's really worried about is who her teacher will be.

Oh, to be almost-ten again.

Ozzi is back in his apartment and comes over a few times a week to eat dinner with me and Hazel. We've also started having Erickson Family dinners once a week at Peggy and Randy's house. It's basically like a holiday every Friday night.

Tonight, when we were getting ready to head home, Peggy cornered me at the kitchen sink where I was drying the dishes Tempest was washing, asking if she could have Hazel for the night. Freya was also spending the night and she thought it would be fun for them to have a sleepover at Nana and Pop's.

The fact that they treat me and Hazel like part of the family makes me emotional every time I think about it. But it also makes me so happy I feel like my heart is going to explode.

"Think I should call and check on her before bed?" I ask Ozzi when I come back to the futon with a bowl of ice cream and two spoons.

He pulls me between his legs. "No, I think she's fine."

I nod, knowing he's right and slip onto his lap.

When we get settled, he takes one of the spoons and we share the ice cream.

There are times when I still want to guard my heart and Hazel's too. Sometimes, my instinct is to pull back, pull Hazel back, from this big, crazy, loving family. That urge comes from years of abandonment and fear that it will happen again.

Thanks to the group therapy I started going to a couple months ago, I can recognize that now. Not that I couldn't before, but I didn't have the reassurance that it's okay to trust again.

Even though Ozzi left, I know now that he did it for me and Hazel. He thought by leaving it would make it easier on us and until he was one hundred percent sure he could commit to being here and see himself with us for the long haul, he removed himself from the equation.

I would take the heartache and this outcome over him staying and being unhappy —or always second guessing—a million times over.

In the grand scheme of things, we're just getting started, but in the short time I've known Ozzi, we've also come so far. He's helped me in ways I can't express. Even in his absence, I learned valuable lessons about myself and other people.

One, not everyone walks out of your life for selfish reasons.

Two, it wasn't Ozzi who made me great at fighting.

Three, I'm in charge of my own happiness.

Last but not least, I get to make the choice of who I love and who I want in my life.

And every day, I choose him.

"What's going on in that brain of yours?" Ozzi asks. "If you're worried about Hazel, we can—"

"I'm not. I know she's in good hands and she's probably having way more fun over there than she does when she hangs out with us."

Ozzi chuckles. "Speak for yourself. I'm *super* fun."

"You're pretty fun," I say with a smirk.

"Nuh-uh, no way." He takes the mostly empty bowl from my hands and places it on the floor beside the futon. "Admit that I'm the funnest."

"I don't think that's a real word," I tease.

"It absolutely is a real word."

The next thing I know, he's flipped me on my back and he has me pinned to the futon.

"Admit it. I'm the funnest. Funner than anyone you've ever met."

I can't help but laugh, and he's not wrong. From the moment Ozzi Erickson entered my life... or maybe I entered his—even though I tried really hard not to like him—I knew he was someone I'd remember forever.

I'm just glad he no longer has to be a memory.

I get to play around with him, tease him, confide in him, laugh with him... love him, hopefully, for a long time... maybe forever.

And even though I could get out of this hold, if I wanted to, I don't

Because I love the way Ozzi's body feels pressed against mine. I love the way his eyes dance with mischief. And I especially love the way his jaw tenses when I grind against him.

Another thing Ozzi has helped me discover is my sexuality.

I'd been sexually active before him, but I'd never experienced the passion I feel when I'm with him. Maybe the difference is love. I knew what we shared was different from the first time we had sex, even though the words hadn't been spoken, all the emotions were there.

I could feel it.

He's always been good at showing me how he feels.

When he pushes up and kneels between my legs, I swallow hard.

He's a work of art—bare chest, beautiful tattoos, and a look he reserves just for me.

His fingers loop into the waist of my shorts and I tilt my hips to help him remove them, taking my panties along with them.

"I'm going to show you just how fun I can be."

Those blue eyes never leave mine as he lowers himself to my pussy and slowly drives me to the brink of an orgasm. Just before I explode, he pulls back.

I hear the familiar tear of a package and when I open my eyes, I catch a glimpse of Ozzi sheathing himself before guiding his cock to my entrance.

"I want you to come with me inside you," he says, thrusting deep and then pulling back. "I love the way your pussy feels when it clenches around my cock."

His husky voice paired with his explicit words makes my insides begin to quiver.

But it's the way he looks at me that sends me over the edge—like I'm every-thing... his entire world and his sole focus... the beginning, middle, and end.

The rush of my orgasm causes me to cry out and Ozzi starts moving faster, lifting one of my legs to give him deeper access.

"Fuck, that's it, baby."

I ride it out, one wave crashing into the next.

When Ozzi finally comes, my body tenses again and he reaches between us, pressing a thumb to my clit and making small circles. The next orgasm is what takes me under, causing me to forget my name, the day, the meaning of life.

It takes a few minutes, maybe longer for my soul to rejoin my body.

I'm briefly aware of Ozzi disposing of the condom and then crawling back onto the futon, manipulating my body where he wants it and pulling me tightly against his chest.

"I love you," he mutters into my hair. "I love you so fucking much... even if you don't think I'm the funnest."

Laughing, I turn my head to look up at him. His expression is lazy and sated, just like his gorgeous blue eyes.

"You're the most fun," I admit, lifting my good arm to brush my hands through his unruly hair. "You're my best friend, my confidant, the person I want to tell all my good and bad news to."

Ozzi stays quiet, closing his eyes as I continue to stroke his hair.

"Earlier, when you asked me what I was thinking, I was thinking about you and me, and how I wouldn't change anything about us. I'll take the mistakes with the wins, the lessons and the triumphs. I want it all and I want it with you."

He opens his eyes and I see a sheen of emotion, making them even more blue than usual.

"Thank you," Ozzi says, leaning forward to kiss the tip of my nose.

"Thank you for loving me."

He kisses my cheek.

"Thank you for trusting me."

He presses his lips to my forehead.

"Thank you for trusting me with your heart and with Hazel."

When he leans back, locking his gaze with mine, I feel every word like it's being written on my heart… in permanent ink.

Ozzi Erickson is here to stay and he's mine forever.

EPILOGUE

WILLOW

Two Years Later

"You ready to go back to the real world?" Ozzi asks as I buckle myself into my seat.

"Yes and no," I reply. "Yes, because I miss Hazel and our family but no, because I'd love to stay in Europe with you forever."

"Mmmm, same," he murmurs before kissing me. When he pulls back, I recognize the playful look in his eyes and brace myself for the question I know is coming. "You sure you don't want to join the Mile High Club?"

He asked the same thing when we first took off for our honeymoon two weeks ago and I can't help but laugh just like I did then. The idea of someone as huge as Ozzi having sex in an airplane bathroom is ridiculously funny to me. He can barely fit when he's alone. Besides, my lady bits need a break from all the newlywed sex we had all over Europe.

Sex in an Airbnb with a view of the Eiffel Tower.

Sex in a tiny cottage outside of Dublin.

Sex in a pub bathroom in London.

We christened every bed and room of every place we stayed.

"Quite sure, husband. Thanks for asking, though."

"The offer always stands, wife."

Wife.

I still can't believe I'm Ozzi Erickson's wife.

Our wedding was perfect and I still feel as though I'm floating on a cloud. Having an outdoor ceremony on Miss Faye's property, surrounded by the people we loved the most, was everything I'd ever imagined. Even now as I think back on the details of our special day, with Hazel as my maid of honor and Freya as the flower girl, being walked down the aisle by both Miss Faye and Cage, I can't help but get emotional.

It was the most perfect day.

BONUS ERICKSON FAMILY UPDATE

Five Years Later
Setting: An Erickson Family Dinner

Tempest and Cage recently bought a piece of property on the outskirts of town and built a house for their growing brood. Freya started first grade this year and is already a kickboxing prodigy. Leif is in preschool and looks exactly like his daddy—blond hair, blue eyes, and a scowl that will stop you in your tracks. Astrid is the newest baby on the block and she's stealing the show with her red hair and stunning blue eyes. With a booming business at Viking MMA, Cage and Tempest are constantly busy, but they wouldn't want it any other way.

Frankie and Gunnar got married two years ago. Gunnar was the most recent Erickson to tie the knot. Last year, they bought a building down from Viking MMA and turned the upstairs into living quarters and Frankie moved the clinic into the lower level. Since their one-year-old, Eric, was born, it's been nice to have work and home so close together. Gunnar currently holds the UFC middleweight title. He's still fighting but is considering making an early retirement to spend more time with his family.

Vali and Maggie built a house not far from her parents and have a three-year-old boy named Davynn and a two-year-old girl named Valentine. Maggie became a

USA Today Bestselling Author with her third novel. On top of being a wife, mom, and bestselling romance author, she also recently became full owner of O'Neal Feed & Fodder. Her parents come in when needed, but she's enjoyed the freedom to make the changes as she sees fit. Vali's advertising business has expanded to Nashville and Memphis, with clients all over the great state of Tennessee.

Willow, Ozzi, and Hazel are now the only ones living in the apartments at Viking MMA. Hazel started high school and teaches kid's boxing classes at the gym. Ozzi is still training fighters and recently became an official co-owner of Viking MMA. Last year, Willow won the women's flyweight championship. With her winnings, she went back to college and is studying medical billing. But there are even more big changes coming. Tonight, they're announcing that they're pregnant with twins.

For now, all we can say about Viggo is he's happy, healthy, and settled in his new life and career. To find out more, we hope you'll join us in our new Fischer Falls series coming soon!

A THANK YOU FROM JIFFY KATE

As we come to the end of Willow and Ozzi's story, we're finding it so hard to type those two magic words authors dream about. *The End* seems so final and we hate saying goodbye.

We're so grateful to Penny Reid for giving us the opportunity to write in this wonderful world. We were Green Valley lovers before we ever wrote the first word of Stud Muffin. But spending the last few years exploring the ins and outs of the town and creating our own characters to live there, we've fallen even deeper in love.

Thank you to all of the amazing and loyal readers (Sharks, we're looking at you), for embracing our characters and giving us a chance.

We hope this isn't a goodbye, but a *see you later*.

Much Love,

Jiffy Kate

ABOUT THE AUTHOR

Jiffy Kate is the joint pen name for Jiff Simpson and Jenny Kate Altman. They're co-writing besties who share a brain. They also share a love of cute boys, stiff drinks, and fun times.

Together, they've written over twenty stories. Their first published book, Finding Focus, was released in November 2015. Since then, they've continued to write what they know--southern settings full of swoony heroes and strong heroines.

* * *

Website: http://www.jiffykate.com
Facebook: https://www.facebook.com/jiffykate
Goodreads: https://www.goodreads.com/author/show/7352135.Jiffy_Kate
Twitter: @jiffykatewrites
Instagram: @jiffykatewrites

Find Smartypants Romance online:
Website: www.smartypantsromance.com
Facebook: www.facebook.com/smartypantsromance/
Goodreads: www.goodreads.com/smartypantsromance
Twitter: @smartypantsrom
Instagram: @smartypantsromance

OTHER BOOKS BY JIFFY KATE

Finding Focus Series:

Finding Focus

Chasing Castles

Fighting Fire

Taming Trouble

French Quarter Collection:

Turn of Fate

Blue Bayou

Come Again

Neutral Grounds

Good Times

Table 10 Novella Series:

Table 10 part 1

Table 10 part 2

Table 10 part 3

New Orleans Revelers:

The Rookie and The Rockstar

The Ace and The Assistant

The Setup and The Substitute

Smartypants Romance:

Stud Muffin (Fighting For Love, Book 1)

Beef Cake (Fighting For Love, Book 2)

Eye Candy (Fighting For Love, Book 3)

Standalones:

Watch and See

No Strings Attached

To keep up-to-date on all Jiffy Kate news and releases, signup for their newsletter and receive Holiday, a novella by Jiffy Kate, for free -- click here

ALSO BY SMARTYPANTS ROMANCE

Green Valley Chronicles

The Love at First Sight Series

Baking Me Crazy by Karla Sorensen (#1)

Batter of Wits by Karla Sorensen (#2)

Steal My Magnolia by Karla Sorensen (#3)

Worth the Wait by Karla Sorensen (#4)

Fighting For Love Series

Stud Muffin by Jiffy Kate (#1)

Beef Cake by Jiffy Kate (#2)

Eye Candy by Jiffy Kate (#3)

Knock Out by Jiffy Kate (#4)

The Donner Bakery Series

No Whisk, No Reward by Ellie Kay (#1)

The Green Valley Library Series

Love in Due Time by L.B. Dunbar (#1)

Crime and Periodicals by Nora Everly (#2)

Prose Before Bros by Cathy Yardley (#3)

Shelf Awareness by Katie Ashley (#4)

Carpentry and Cocktails by Nora Everly (#5)

Love in Deed by L.B. Dunbar (#6)

Dewey Belong Together by Ann Whynot (#7)

Hotshot and Hospitality by Nora Everly (#8)

Love in a Pickle by L.B. Dunbar (#9)

Checking You Out by Ann Whynot (#10)

Architecture and Artistry by Nora Everly (#11)

Scorned Women's Society Series

My Bare Lady by Piper Sheldon (#1)

The Treble with Men by Piper Sheldon (#2)

The One That I Want by Piper Sheldon (#3)

Hopelessly Devoted by Piper Sheldon (#3.5)

It Takes a Woman by Piper Sheldon (#4)

Park Ranger Series

Happy Trail by Daisy Prescott (#1)

Stranger Ranger by Daisy Prescott (#2)

The Leffersbee Series

Been There Done That by Hope Ellis (#1)

Before and After You by Hope Ellis (#2)

The Higher Learning Series

Upsy Daisy by Chelsie Edwards (#1)

Green Valley Heroes Series

Forrest for the Trees by Kilby Blades (#1)

Parks and Provocation by Juliette Cross (#2)

Story of Us Collection

My Story of Us: Zach by Chris Brinkley (#1)

My Story of Us: Thomas by Chris Brinkley (#2)

Seduction in the City

Cipher Security Series

Code of Conduct by April White (#1)

Code of Honor by April White (#2)

Code of Matrimony by April White (#2.5)

Code of Ethics by April White (#3)

Cipher Office Series

Weight Expectations by M.E. Carter (#1)

Sticking to the Script by Stella Weaver (#2)

Cutie and the Beast by M.E. Carter (#3)

Weights of Wrath by M.E. Carter (#4)

Common Threads Series

Mad About Ewe by Susannah Nix (#1)

Give Love a Chai by Nanxi Wen (#2)

Key Change by Heidi Hutchinson (#3)

Not Since Ewe by Susannah Nix (#4)

Lost Track by Heidi Hutchinson (#5)

Educated Romance

Work For It Series

Street Smart by Aly Stiles (#1)

Heart Smart by Emma Lee Jayne (#2)

Book Smart by Amanda Pennington (#3)

Smart Mouth by Emma Lee Jayne (#4)

Play Smart by Aly Stiles (#5)

Lessons Learned Series

Under Pressure by Allie Winters (#1)

Not Fooling Anyone by Allie Winters (#2)

Out of this World

London Ladies Embroidery Series

Neanderthal Seeks Duchess by Laney Hatcher (#1)

Well Acquainted by Laney Hatcher (#2)

CPSIA information can be obtained
at www.ICGtesting.com
Printed in the USA
BVHW072244091022
649053BV00001B/73